A TIME IN THE SUN

Books by Jane Barry

THE LONG MARCH
THE CAROLINIANS
A TIME IN THE SUN

Jane Barry

A TIME
IN THE SUN

DOUBLEDAY & COMPANY, INC.

GARDEN CITY, NEW YORK

1962

For Ray Clement

who knows why

WITH THE EXCEPTION OF ACTUAL HISTORICAL
PERSONAGES, THE CHARACTERS ARE ENTIRELY
THE PRODUCT OF THE AUTHOR'S IMAGINATION
AND HAVE NO RELATION TO ANY PERSON IN REAL
LIFE.

FOREWORD

AN ACCOUNTING AND AN ACKNOWLEDGMENT

For those who do not like to be left with loose ends or abandoned on the narrow bridge between fact and fiction, it would seem well to set down the following truths.

The major American characters in this book existed only within its pages, but they are projected on a screen of events which occurred essentially as they are here related. Victorio, his chiefs and warriors, Lieutenant Royal Whitman, William Oury, Jesús Elias, Marijildo Grijalba were historic personages, as were the Apache, military, and administrative figures whose roles herein are minor, but who, in the determining of our Indian policy, were pre-eminent.

It might also be well to cite here several facts which bear either directly or indirectly upon this narrative. The Apache, for largely superstitious reasons, did not refer to himself or to other men by name, particularly after his adult name had been assumed. He was generally given a childhood name based upon some particular personal characteristic, perhaps from a toy he clung to, or a manner of speaking, dressing, or carrying out a specific duty. The adult name, bestowed at puberty, was chosen in like manner and was permanent unless replaced by a more fitting name acquired on the raid or in battle. He was often named for some physical feature of locality, but never for an animal. Over the years, through the white man's peculiar Anglicized Spanish argot, the names became bastardized. Cochise was possibly not Cochise, but a word phonetically similar. It is easier this way for the white man.

The Apache's method of communicating identification under these somewhat trying circumstances made for extensiveness but was fairly uncomplicated. He would say, "The man I speak of is the nephew of the man who is best among us at the making of bows, and the brother of the man who stole the three sacks of pinole from the garrison at Janos."

This is obviously impractical for the purposes of fictional dialogue.

The conferring, or blood acquisition of a Spanish-Mexican *nombre segundo* was a matter of pride, and once gained was probably literally used to the exclusion of all others, as in the case of Mangas (sleeves) Colorado (red), a name which has been variously misspelled in nearly every account of his affairs.

Formidable foe that he was, the Apache was never eager to engage in open warfare, although a lone Apache, knowing he had been mortally wounded, was quite willing to make a suicide run on an entire cavalry company. He was a master at guerrilla tactics, the ambuscade, the hit-and-run strike, the sneak attack, employing not only his own innate talent for it but the natural advantages of the country which bred him. He was a superb horseman, and there is general agreement that he was an expert marksman, a point in strong contrast to the slipshod handling of the white man's weapons evinced by other tribes. He had a thrifty habit of saving his ammunition for the human quarry. He did not like to hunt with a gun anyway; with bow or lance he could get into a herd of animals before they knew he was there; the first gunshot scared them off. Once he acquired the shotgun, he perceived immediately the merit of double sights. John C. Cremony reported he seldom saw such a weapon that had not been knife-sawed near the breech, and the sliver of metal raised and notched to form a rear sight. But he never forgot the value of his own weapons. The lance was fifteen feet long, and he used it with both hands, over his head, guiding his mount with his knees. His arrows were effective at five hundred feet and were often constructed to leave the point in the victim. Here were some dismal facts for a man under attack to take into consideration. Little wonder that Mexican troops on pursuit detail, with heartening cries of *"Marchamos, valientes,"* were known to rush off in the opposite direction to that taken by the object of the pursuit.

Logistically, one warrior told Cremony that whenever an Apache heard a gun fired he disappeared to lie low until he knew for a certainty what was happening. The American, on the other hand, hurried instantly to the scene, and that was how he managed to get himself killed with such regularity. It seems a more than adequate summation of the Apache's totally reasonable attitude toward and effective waging of a type of warfare initiated and, in the main, conducted on his own terms.

Probably the most popular misconception concerning the Apache is that of the blood rite: the slashed vein, the commingling of the stuff of life, which was supposed to make men brothers. There is little doubt that this is purely a ceremonial invention of the white man and that it was never practiced by the Chiricahua, much less by any tribe of Apachería.

For the purposes of this narrative I have deemed it necessary to make a distinction between Chiricahua and Mimbreño. Actually the Mimbreños were one of three Chiricahua bands, the northeastern, the southern, and the central or so-called Cochise Apaches. These Apaches are now a fully constituted tribe operating under a corporate charter and have unfortunately largely lost their identity as separate bands. The last Indians to surrender their way of life, and as recently as forty years ago existing under shameful conditions, they are now moving slowly upward. If pinto beans are the staple of their diet, if they sometimes still prefer the wickiup, if they remain reluctant to accept many of the innovations of the white man's way or facets of his civilization, that is a matter of choice.

Cattle made the big change. Jeaned, booted, Stetsoned, the Apache is a cowboy, riding herd on some of the finest Herefords in the world. He is a farmer and a factory worker. He has won distinction in a dangerous field as a professional forest fire fighter, perhaps as psychologically attracted to it as the Mohawk is to the hazards of high steel construction.

For the reader with a resentment toward what he may consider an inconclusive leave-taking, Victorio won his lands at Ojo Caliente, after a short, unsatisfactory stay at Tulerosa. Once the Mimbreños were settled on their ancestral promised lands, they were abruptly removed to the San Carlos reservation in what General Willcox, commanding the Department of Arizona, called a "harsh and cruel measure" springing out of "unjust dealing." Victorio broke away from San Carlos at the head of sixty Mimbreños and a hundred Comanche. He held out for his lands, but they were now public domain and he never regained them. In 1880 he made an incredibly valiant last stand in the Tres Castillos Mountains of Sonora, where he was shot by a Mexican officer. Following his death, Nané, nearly eighty and crippled with rheumatism, led the remnants of the Mimbreños, with some Mescaleros and Comanche, on a war chase which over a thousand U.S. troops, the armies of Upper Mexico, civilian posses, and Texas Rangers were powerless to quell, and which makes Geronimo's better-publicized exploits pale by comparison.

Cochise made his peace with General Oliver Otis Howard. He died, probably of cancer, in June 1874 and was secretly buried in the Stronghold. Young Tahzay kept his father's pledge, but died of pneumonia two years later on a visit to Washington, D.C.

When John P. Clum, the New York State farmboy who had some progressive ideas on how a reservation should be run (i.e., dispensing entirely with the military) and was therefore considered notional, went west in 1874 to assume the agency at San Carlos, he stopped at Camp Grant and found Eskiminzin in chains, making adobe brick. Clum removed the Arivaipa to San Carlos, where Eskiminzin repaid him by establishing the first Apache police force, an organization so fanatically loyal it gunned down erring family members.

I have taken several minor liberties in the course of this book. The first message from Tucson to Camp Grant was carried by a Corporal Clark, who was beset by the misfortune I have described. The second message was carried by Sergeant Jared King, P Company, 21st Infantry. The Camp Grant trial was held in December, and Peter Kitchen's son killed in the summer of 1871. Wherever possible, I have used intact or paraphrased actual conversations.

Over the fifteen-year period I have been collecting data on the Southwest, many persons have been generous with their time, knowledge, and material. It is not possible to name them all here, any more than it is possible to make any acknowledgment without mention of those men and women, the intrepid Spanish, the American soldiers and civilians, who first went to live with the Apache: Casteñada, Oñate, Benavides, Garcés, Captain John C. Cremony of the Bartlett Commission, John R. Bartlett himself, who bequeathed us his personal narrative; Captain John G. Bourke, Lieutenant Britton Davis, James O. Pattie, John P. Clum, Martha Summerhayes, Frederick Remington, Frank C. Lockwood, and the hundreds who left us their invaluable records.

I wish to express my gratitude and indebtedness to the National Archives and Records Services, in particular to F. Hardee Allen of the Justice and Executive Branch, and to Jane F. Smith; to Ethel B. Fast of the United States Department of the Interior, Bureau of Indian Affairs; Charles J. Rives, Superintendent of the San Carlos Indian Agency; Albert M. Hawley, Superintendent of the Fort Apache Agency; Dr. Morris E. Opler, whose *An Apache Life-Way* is the cornerstone of the field, but who had no part in the design of this novel and no advisory or veto function in respect to execution and detail; Robert Carlson of *Arizona Highways;* Yndia L. Moore of the Arizona Pioneers' Historical Society; the Bureau of American Ethnology; the Association on American Indian Affairs; the late William T. Haswell, who served in Arizona with the Sixth Cavalry; and to my John, whose encouragement sustained me and whose patience and fortitude while this book was being written were almost . . . but not quite . . . worthy of Victorio's.

The post outside Tucson is old Fort Lowell. It has been left nameless in deference to the memory of Colonel J. G. C. Lee, Tucson, commanding, and the officers and men of the 21st United States Infantry who garrisoned it in 1870–71.

J.B.

ARIZONA TERRITORY – 1870

One

The four men paused in accord at the summit of the hill. They walked the horses, but the need for haste was in them. Below this place, where they loomed against a sky which contained no other largeness or shape than the largeness and shape of itself, the stage road sliced empty, a narrow scar on a shifting flesh of sand. The wild spring desert flowed away and beyond this shallow cicatrix, running straight as an arrow shaft, then curving into the vacuum of distance, along the miles of massed mauve and blue bloom born of the rains.

The big man named Shafter said, "We split here, Linus."

It was half question, half statement, but he, all of them, looked upon it as statement purely. He did not wish to sound presumptuous. Shafter was overloose in the worn McClellan saddle, and yet he might have been portion of it, sprung out of it, suddenly, into the air, so easy you could wonder how awkward he might look without the horse. His lip was framed in a slim down-drooping blond mustache which tapered at the ends, and his eyes, under a beaten and shapeless Kossuth hat, looked out of a face creased with sun and wind, made bluer than any born-blue by the complement of weathered skin. They looked at the running stripe of the road and the spring land blurring away, aware, withdrawn, discerning, abstract, the eyes of a man who keeps his own counsel.

Beside him Linus nodded. It was a fagged, used-up gesture. He thought he learned the way of these men with irritating slowness. They thought he learned with speed and thoroughness; they trusted and accepted him. His voice was muffled through the dust-grimed handkerchief which covered his mouth and nose. "If we haven't found anything by noon, Shafter. . . ."

Shafter shifted in the saddle, restless. "If we ain't hit it by noon we never gone to," he said.

Over the rim of the gritty handkerchief the boy's eyes were direct on him, stricken and gone almost blank, as eyes bearing too much to be borne will go dead and without color. A lock of light hair was plastered to his forehead, under the sweat-stained trooper's cap. Unlike Shafter, his young body, lacking in flesh, very slender and straight in the dusty blue and gray army garb, was erect and conscious. He rode by rote, knowing horseflesh as he had been taught to know it, considerate of and dependent upon his mount, any mount, but without sentimentality for it.

It was, perhaps, the only sentimentality Shafter knew.

"All right," Shafter said. His mouth barely moved under the blond mustache. He looked away from the empty road and at Linus' burned-out eyes, and at the two men at his left, both of them dark men turned darker by this country: Willson, steady and so grave you wondered always if some ponderous thing was in his mind; Obre, a quarter Comanche and three-quarters Irish, so black of brow and skin and hair you thought first of Comanche and then of Irish. "Obre," he said.

"I'll go with Linus," Obre said.

They separated. The hoofs sank in the soft sand and sank when they reached the bottom of the hill, crushing the mat of mariposa and lupine. Having drunk deep, the ocotillo stood tall and spiny, bearing at its tip ends scarlet shreds of blossom. Quail skittered through the sand verbena. Linus and Obre were on the road, still walking the horses. Shafter and Willson still edged along the high ground. But there should be more of us, Linus thought wildly: there should be the whole garrison, filing out with precision, under the clear bugle.

Obre said quietly, "Your pa's gone to be all right, Linus. He's gone to say, 'Just what I would of did myself, Lieutenant.'" Obre thought Linus was worried about his father.

He said nothing, because he wanted to say, my father should be here. He could not say that to Obre. He looked up and saw Shafter's big bulk growing out of his horse, just below the skyline. Not even to Shafter, who had not questioned. Not for these men the rage and terror he fought to guard inside himself, saved whole for his father. He was badly nerved up, physically ill.

On the hillside, approaching the snaking flower-strewn arroyo, Shafter was narrowing his eyes against the reflective glare of sunlight on the land. He was deeply depressed although nothing showed on his hard bland weathered face. He was forty years old and he felt older than God. He had felt that way since the South went down and he had taken off the familiar Confederate gray in which he had slept and eaten and fought for four years. He had grown out of any illusions in about the same way you grow out of your boots, but he could remember the nice youthful feel of them and he was not embittered enough yet to deride them in another man. Once or twice he looked down the long slope of the hill and watched Linus. He had thought Linus would be straining at the leash by now; he saw as tangible the length and breadth of the control the boy practiced.

Shafter thought he knew army men. Since the war there had been army men, a long line of them pulled taut along the forts from Missouri westward. There were the still hot to go left-over majors and colonels with whom the government did not know what to do. Some of them studied with good intention and operated from a base of erroneous and pointless conclusion. Some came on the assumption they had only to bark once, push a little wind through a bugle, and all the Indians from New Mexico to Sonora were going to throw up their arms and walk meekly into captivity. Some were the spit and polish young Academy officers who came like hounds on the quarter, eager to flush out adventure and rank. They grew morose and irascible with boredom before their transfers came through. Linus should be one of these. Yet Linus was not the young lieutenants Shafter had known. For one thing, the most important thing, he did not think he knew it all and that all was decided by his decisions. It was something Shafter had to get used to.

For Linus Degnan, walking his horse on a scar of road a man named Butterfield had traced across the desert, there were no illusions either in this moment. His smoldering resentment against his father was tempered somewhat by the knowledge that it was totally unreasonable. But the fact remained: Colonel Walter Degnan had managed to be somewhere else with over half the garrison at the most crucial moment of his son's life. And the girl his son was going to marry was, had been, on a coach which had never reached Tucson.

He could have taken out the men who remained to garrison the post during his father's ill-timed foray. He chose instead Shafter, who hung around Tucson and whom he liked without knowing exactly why.

When it got so late he knew there was no sense waiting any longer, he knocked on every door, swung into every saloon, hunting Shafter. In town there was talk, but a missing coach was the army's trouble. Specifically, it was Linus' trouble. Over the quick tilted bottle he told Shafter. The girl was on the coach. And a Mexican girl, going to Sonora. Because of the Mexican girl there were ten *rurales* come up for escort. They were to have picked up their charge at Santa Fe.

Shafter drank his whiskey thoughtfully. "Ten, eh?" he said.

"Damn it, Mexicans won't fight," Linus said.

"Sure they will," Shafter said in his easy southern voice. "Sure they will. Jesus, Linus, you can't just lose a coach and ten greasers." He already knew you could.

"I'll trail with you," Willson said. He always trailed with Shafter anyway. Obre had only looked at them out of his handsome eyes, one blue and one black. He did not drink because he was very accurate with guns and liked to keep his hands steady. When they saddled up, he went with them.

Obre did not care much about talking, except as a necessity, but he thought a lot and, in the main, he liked folks and occasionally regretted he had killed some of them. What he liked best about any man was that the man listened to other men who knew more than he did. It was why he liked the colonel's son: one, because he felt the colonel's son didn't know his head from a hole in the ground, and two, because the colonel's son had guts enough to admit it and ask a man who did.

Shafter did. Obre raised his strange Irish-Indian eyes and saw that, while Willson still rode the skyline, Shafter had disappeared down the arroyo. He hung around Shafter, when he could, in case Shafter wanted anything done. They had been together a long time now. He did things for free for Shafter; he expected even if he had to use his guns for Shafter some day he'd do that for free, too. Like this. There was no money in this. But he was curious because Linus' woman was on that coach. He wondered what Linus' woman was like. A namby-pamby, eastern-grown daisy who got scared when night came and branches scratched on her windows.

He liked to think about that kind, but when it came down to brass
tacks he didn't want one; that kind ended up doing all the taking
and he liked the kind that gave back. He tried to think what Linus
would do if they cut sign of what they were looking for. He was
stoic but he half hoped they wouldn't. He tried to think what Colonel Degnan would say when he found his son had gone off with
Shafter and left fat old Sergeant Stern to run things. He could see it
might not be all cherries to throw father and son together at the
same post, but likely the two fools had wanted it that way and
twitched all kinds of strings to have it that way.

Maybe I will get to shoot me an Apache today, Obre thought.

Linus kept watching the road almost fiercely, as if it could tell
him how long since wheels had run here, or if they had run at all.
Willson, from his vantage point, was casting the whole country under him. Obre was just kind of along for Shafter. Shafter, squint-
eyed and up out of the arroyo now, looked for two things: smoke
and buzzards.

When he saw he could not soften it for Linus he told him
straight out. Sure, they would kill the Mexicans. Yes, wasn't any
doubt they'd take the women (but inside he was saying, maybe).
The boy nodded, white-faced. Shafter hesitated. "Listen, Linus. I
don't care what palaver you heard, Apaches don't rape. It just don't
ever seem to occur to 'em." Linus kept nodding, as if his head had
got going and he couldn't stop it. "The worst can happen is the
squaws'll torment her a little and they'll work hell out of her. All
right?" "All right," Linus said.

They were traveling rough-east. In the pitiless morning glare the
Dragoons thrust into the white sky, gray and gilded, without any
of the blue softness which folded itself into them in the afternoon.
Now they were harsh and oppressive. Everything was harsh, even
the endless stretch of brief flowering which comes upon the spring
desert. The colors were too rich and vivid and hurried, red and
magenta and white silken cups of flower released from things which
normally bore only spines, yellow and blue and lavender spires and
spikes and bowls and trumpets sprung from seed lying dry a year's
length in the unremitting sand. Austere gray-green rosettes of spears
suddenly birthing the shivering, creamy towers of Spanish bayonet,
staghorn covered with fuzzy new whiteness, palo verde veining its
gold along the slopes. There was something bitter in it, as there is
in any single hour of ultimate beauty: the interminable leagues of

desert exploding almost with violence under the outflung arms of
the saguaro.

From the crest of the ridge, which had begun to drop away and
level itself, Willson called, "Shafter."

Shafter swung back up the sandy slope. There were the dark
circling birds he looked for, up ahead, hanging under the polished
cup of sky. He was watching Linus, pacing a quarter mile or so
ahead on the road.

"You see 'em?" Willson said.

"Sure." He inclined his head toward the road. "He ain't, though."

"Where you figure?" Willson said.

"Looks like Dragoon Springs. Maybe the old Butterfield station."

When Linus looked back and saw them coming down fast off the
slope, he pulled up and waited. His eyes had been too busy on
the road, but Obre knew.

"What is it, Shafter?" The skin, under the eyes, was drawn tight
across the young planes of the boy's face.

"Buzzards," Shafter said.

"Buzzards." He tore the handkerchief away. The shouted quality
of his own voice startled him, ringing like metal against the hot
metallic morning.

Shafter knew he was going to say more, so he said blandly, "Let's
get moving."

The Butterfield relay post at Dragoon Springs had fallen into dis-
use, except as a bivouac for troops deploying, parties from the mining companies following the old trails, prospectors questing over the
silent reaches, Indians lying in where water was accessible, men on
the quick move from law or women or any of the myriad misfortunes
which beset them. The war had killed the Butterfield Overland, the
war and the short-lived Pony Express, and the adobe stations threading the distances of New Mexico and Arizona were fading into
gaunt hollow skeletons, hosting lizard and sidewinder, destined to
crumble, dedicated early to the merciless onslaught of wind, sand,
desolation.

It used to be, before the San Pedro and Cienega Springs stations,
the next stop to Tucson, before they shifted you over from the
celerity wagon to the fancy Concord coach they used coming into
town and at the end of the runs. On either of the two wagons you
could rock back and forth like a moored dinghy on the leather

thorough braces from which the body was sprung, and on the Concord you could fold the seats down and sleep in relays on the russet leather if you were of a mind. But you got inured to anything; you got so you could sleep sitting bolt upright and smashing into the ceiling and sides of the stage, especially if you were making the twenty-five-day run from St. Louis to Frisco. You got so you could sleep on a bed of nails after a half-hour break three times a day to eat and change horses and sometimes drivers and occasionally passengers. You got so you could sleep on a mess of cholla to quiet your belly after the rancid bacon and half-raw pork and leadweight sourdough bread of the relay stations. You were waiting, if you were a traveler, for the iron miracle, the railroad, but track had not been laid this far west.

There were still stage lines running, but they were the end result of imagination and enterprise far inferior to that of John Butterfield. They still ran through the Puerta del Dado, hell's gate, a six-mile-long saddle separating the Chiricahuas and the Dos Cabezas. It was called Apache Pass now, but in any jargon it meant the same. At the eastern end of the pass, sprawling, ugly Fort Bowie, on the site of the Butterfield relay station, provided you a military escort in the event you didn't feel like trying to make the run on your own. There were plenty of graves along the stretch. There were plenty of men didn't make it. It was a grim and forbidding malpais, the kind of country that was going to look the same a hundred, maybe even a thousand years from now.

The coach had got through all right. It was a very fine one, painted glistening yellow, with fancy brasswork around the doors and bright canvas curtains at the windows. It lay just off the trail on its side, in the shadow of the walls of the old Dragoon Springs station, showing the black leather straps which laced its belly. An attempt to burn it had failed, although the man strapped face up on the right rear wheel had apparently ignited without any trouble, and one red curtain, caught outside the door, was charred half through. Flung against the dobe walls of the station were small blue heaps which Linus identified as bundles of old clothes. The black birds went up heavily, enraged.

He sprang clear of the charred black wheel and onto the crazily tilted thing and hung on the door, with his head through the window and his hands clenched on the sun-hot brass bars which bordered it.

Shafter dismounted and bent to examine the severed traces. Four horses, he made it. That meant they'd have had four or eight more for relief, plus probably some mules. He stood up. "See if any of 'em alive."

"What's that, a joke?" Obre said. He turned over with the toe of his boot a shapeless thing at the doorway of the station. Then he hunkered and retrieved something from it.

Shafter couldn't see what it was. He felt a little unsettled in his belly when he looked around. They were badly mutilated. Ten of them. Ten greasers. "Linus," he said.

Willson was walking, leading his horse. "This one's alive, Shafter."

"How much alive?" Shafter said.

"Not so's you'd notice. He ain't got any. . . ."

"Finish him," Shafter said.

Obre came down from the doorway with a big, heavily carved pistol in his hand. He had picked it off the dead Mexican. "I'll do it," he said.

"Linus," Shafter said again, but it wasn't until the pistol went off in Obre's hand that Linus staggered back off the door. For a moment he looked down into the fire-blackened face of the man on the wheel; when he hit the ground he vomited.

Shafter was studying the blurred imprints in the sand. After a long time he looked up into Linus' face and saw a sickness and terror on it he thought he had done seeing on the faces of men five years ago. "Here," he said.

Linus came. He was so straight Shafter thought he was going to fall over backward. "You see this? Steel shod. Horses and mules. This is deerskin shoeing, run clear up to the fetlock. So they won't cut their feet. Apache ponies." He rose. His voice was quiet. "We might's well go back to the post. I ain't tellin' you your business, Linus, but you'd ought to get a burial detail out. Maybe Willson or Ob can ride into Bowie."

Linus said dumbly, "What are you going to do, John?"

Shafter couldn't remember Linus calling him that before. "Stick here awhile yet," he said. Then he saw Linus' whole body had begun to twist, rather than shake, like something trapped that flexed and contorted itself to throw off a living coil. "If you mean are we gone anywhere but back to the post, no. There's nothing we can do here." He looked up and around, seeing the sharp sea of mountain which nearly ringed them in, chain merging into chain, beginning to go blue in the folds now, pledging darknesses and enigmas and secret things for some men, and for some men, no thing at all. He knew that one man's mysteries were not often those of another.

Obre came down, stepping over the place Linus had been sick, and stood watching Linus. "Me and Willson'll stay," he said. He kneaded the fist of one gloved hand into the palm of the other.

Linus kept looking stupefied at the indistinct clues the sand still held. "You think we ought to go back?" he said, agonized, trying not to pit his judgment openly with Shafter's.

"Mount up," Shafter said. "Don't unsaddle, whatever you do, Ob. You got plenty of ammo? Water?"

Obre grinned and nodded, teeth a savage white slash in the dark face. He was caressing the long pistol, shining the lock with his glove.

They rode out of the place, with the buzzards still hanging over them, waiting, foul, necessary. Linus was for haste now, any kind of headlong, impotent haste, but he matched the long lope to which Shafter held his dun gelding. He was empty as dried gourd, not from the sickness, but from the shock which galvanizes and freezes and prevents the stiff reality from forming into anything recognizable. He saw suddenly that he was actually clutching the saddle and that the reins were dragging loose. Twice he fumbled awkwardly at them and then gave it up.

After a time Shafter said, "Pick up your reins, Linus." This time he made it. Shafter said, "Before you get a fit of the talks, I want to ask you something and you got to answer straight."

"Yes," Linus said. He could feel his legs shaking where they hung to the stirrups, and cold, although the kersey breeches were wet and the yellow stripe dark with his sweat.

"Don't leave out anything," Shafter said, "even if you don't figure it's important. I want to know everything she said in that letter. So it makes sense."

Linus licked his lips, but his tongue was dry and swollen. "This Mexican girl . . . they met in the hotel, in St. Louis, and came out together. Then the girl . . . the Mexican girl . . . was going to visit some relatives, a sister I think, in Santa Fe." He reached for his canteen and got the cap off and raised it. "Two days, she said, and wanted Anna to go with her. I guess it was one of those friendships girls form . . . you know." His voice was apologetic, but whether for his own analysis or the girl's idiocy Shafter couldn't tell. He waited. "The girl's father had sent up a coach, and the *rurales*. From Sonora. They were coming into Tucson; then the girl was going on home."

Shafter said, "So she couldn't be just any Mex filly." He ran his hand over the pale stubble of beard. "Landed gentry. Private coach, hired *soldados*. Know anything about her?"

"I can't remember the name." Linus was disgusted with himself. "Isabel, I think . . . Isabel something. Been East for schooling and going home to be married." Again he was apologetic; his face, under the layered dust and sweat and fatigue and shock, was almost hesitant. "Like Anna. I guess that's why they made friends like that, so fast."

"That's all?" Shafter said.

"God, I can't remember. Yes, that's all. Shafter, do you think . . . ?"

"One more thing," Shafter said. "This girl of yours. What's she like?"

"You mean look like?"

"I mean like. You know her well enough to know how she'd handle herself in an emergency?"

He fought to control the trembling of his legs, which was making his horse nervous; the physical effort made him feel sick again, and the water he had drunk made a threatening, thunderous sound in him. He knew his voice shook now, too, but he could do nothing to stop it. "I've known Anna all my life. Her father and mine were in the army together. He's dead now, and her mother, too. . . . She lived with an aunt in Washington, but she's my father's ward. I don't think she ever *had* any emergency."

"Well, did she sit and stitch all day, or could she sashay around," Shafter said impatiently.

"She rides. She walks a lot. She's used to army posts." He wanted to yell at Shafter now, as if Shafter was somehow deliberately tormenting him. "Don't ask me what she'd do . . . she's unpredictable, like all women are, I suppose." He saw Shafter shoot him a curious, almost mocking glance, but he stumbled on. "Sometimes she's pretty serious, but mostly she isn't. . . . My God, John, I don't know, she's only nineteen."

Shafter looked dead ahead and toed the dun lightly in the ribs. He did not ask any more questions nor did he appear to ruminate on the answers to those he had already asked.

The fort was not stockaded and was made up of twelve or thirteen buildings of varying sizes, barracks, officers' quarters, commandant's office, quartermaster storehouse, commissary, laundry, bakery, guardhouse, all strung around the parade ground, with the corral and stables some distance off. The adjutant's office and officers' quarters were wood, a material hard come by in this area, the remainder of the buildings adobe. The regimental flag hung limp, pinioned against a massive cloud, but there was movement of men, of horses, and of wagons. Shafter surveyed the stark, dingy scene somewhat grimly. What he was thinking was, there's going to be hell to pay in Washington, even the President's going to say a few words about this, and there is going to be wailing in Sonora when the word gets there about the little *señorita* and the ten dead greasers, but what he said was, "Your pa's back, Linus."

"Yes," Linus said. There was a hard white line along his upper lip.

"I reckon I'll push off," Shafter said.

"Will you wait?" The resentment he had felt a few hours ago was subdued, beginning to flatten out and taper off; he already knew that there was nothing to be gained by accusation or argument. The weariness began to flow out of him when he thought that perhaps now, between them, Shafter, his father, himself, some order, some clear course of action would rise from the day's wreckage.

Shafter said, "I'll wait."

Two

Linus' gooseneck spurs complained when he walked across the planking of the commandant's outer office. The nearly middle-aged orderly had allowed himself the privilege of sitting down outside the colonel's door, which was closed; his shirt was open at the neck and his web suspenders had been conveniently dropped off his sloping shoulders for comfort. He sprang up when he saw Linus.

Linus said, "Tell the colonel Lieutenant Degnan's compliments and it's urgent."

"Yes, sir," the orderly said, flipping up his suspenders and fumbling at his topmost shirt button. The door opened, swung a quarter closed, opened again, letting the orderly out and Linus in.

He had seen, when the door opened, that the New York newspaper correspondent was closeted with his father. He was pretty much all right, the correspondent, capable as all hell and a fine artist to boot. He took a lot of ribbing from the troops because of the number of horses he could exhaust in a short time because of his heft, but he had a heart like a lion and he never intruded. He would have been a good soldier. Instead he recorded with reverent fidelity, with sketchbook and brush and word the life he saw around him—army, Indian, prospector, the hunt, in all the far reaches of the frontier. The garrison was proud to have him there, but now Linus had to decide quickly whether or not he wanted Tony Bleeker to hear what he had to say. Yet anyway.

Bleeker sat in a corner, one heavy leg in tweed knickers and a high boot crossed over the other. Linus nodded at him, saluted his father formally. In the privacy of the room his father seemed surprised at this, looking up from behind his desk with a half smile slitting under his thick gray mustache.

"*Buenos,* shavetail," Bleeker said.

"Linus, you look like you'd been out rolling around in the sand," his father said. "Sit down. Draw up a chair." His face stiffened a little. "I can't say, by the way, I was exactly delighted to ride in this morning and find Sergeant Stern in sole command here."

"I can't say I was delighted to go off and leave him in sole command here," Linus said.

Colonel Degnan laughed. A stranger looking at father and son, as Tony Bleeker did now, could see in the older man precisely how the younger man would look at the same age. The flesh of years was on Degnan now, heavily through the shoulders, but he was neat, trim, active, alert, in fine physical condition. The face, which was Linus' face also, had broadened, but those were the same clear-white eyes. The sensitivity of the mouth, still open and a little sensual in the son, was tempered by maturity and discipline in the older man. Bleeker could have picked them out of a crowd and paired them. While he thought this he noted for the first time the strain on Linus' face, saw the colonel's face grow rigid and questioning in response.

"Is anything wrong, Linus?" Colonel Degnan said.

Linus turned to Bleeker. "Look, Tony, this is something I want you to know about, but not right now. If you don't mind. . . ."

Bleeker rose. He had picked up the scent, but he knew his own reputation as a good sport. "I'll wait outside," he said.

When the door had closed behind him, Linus leaned over his father's desk, bracing himself on his hands. "I'm glad you're back, Father. I went out yesterday because I had to, and it made my heart sick you weren't here."

"Now look, Linus, you know damned well when a report comes in here that Amarillo's been raiding stock within five miles of this post I am damn well not going to sit on my tail and let him get away with it."

Linus said wearily, "You listen too hard to Jesús Elias. Every time that man rides two feet out of Tucson he's seen Amarillo somewhere. But maybe I better listen, too. Maybe Amarillo is around. If he is, he's got Anna."

The colonel stared up at him. His hands, lying on the open pages of a report book, shot out of his cuffs and made a convulsive jerking motion. He said, "Anna? Anna? Linus, it was today you expected she'd be in. . . ."

Linus was shaking his head. "Yesterday. I thought you knew it was yesterday. We found the coach at Dragoon Springs."

"No sign of . . . of anyone?"

"The women are gone. The *rurales* all dead."

Colonel Degnan was on his feet. Everything about him, stance, mein, attitude, mirrored Linus, except that there was a queer, un-fulfilled wet glistening in his eyes. "It can't be true. It's impossible."

Linus was shaking his head again. "It's happened before. It never happens to you, does it?" He raised his hand and struck himself hard across the breast. "Christ, I'm numb. I just want to *do* something."

"Goddamit," Degnan said, "I thought it was foolish for her to get off that overland coach in the first place. . . . She could have sat tight and been safely on an army buckboard by now." His eyes were on a level with Linus'. "You didn't go out there alone."

"Obre and Willson are keeping the birds off. Shafter went with me."

"Shafter." Degnan's head turned, slow. "Shafter. Obre. Willson. My God, Linus, you pick the dregs, don't you?"

"I pick the men who know what they're doing," Linus said. "The war's over, Father. Shafter knows that, if you don't."

That glistening liquidity in Degnan's eyes had sheeted hard, as if it had frozen over. "And what has Shafter decided we're to do?"

"Shafter hasn't decided anything. I think he'll help us."

Degnan leaned against his desk, arms folded. "I regret I must ask favors of him."

Linus said drily, "I've drunk with Shafter in every saloon in Tucson. I asked."

Degnan reached over and closed the book on his desk. Linus was right, of course. But he didn't like it. He didn't like any of the Texicans, Shafter and Willson, who had worn gray as long as they could and then drifted west, and Obre. Good God, Obre, protecting his hands in those black ugly gloves, with his black ugly face and his black ugly guns. And all the filthy knowledgeable desert men. "Where is he?" he said resignedly.

Linus went to the door and opened it. Shafter was leaning against the far wall, holding his shattered hat. His hair was too long, the greasy buckskins open nearly to the waist. He came into the office.

"Sit down, Shafter," the colonel said. "You, too, Linus." He went around and seated himself behind his desk again. His mouth was partially open and his teeth clamped together. "Linus might have told you, Shafter, I had a report Amarillo was in the area. Our Apache scouts didn't find a trace of him. West of here. Could he have cut east and hit Dragoon Wells in such a short time?"

Shafter examined the old imprint on his hat, where the insignia

had lain. "He could of. But I don't think it was **Amarillo**. He hasn't
got more'n eight or ten fighting bucks and mostly he's yellow as his
name. I don't reckon he'd take ten armed men. Let's say Apaches
who belong right here."

The colonel said, "You think the Chiricahua?"

"Maybe. Cochise's gettin' old, though, he'd ought to start loosin'
his taste for it. What I was thinkin' was Victorio's up at the Stronghold with a bunch of his Mimbreños. For the *noshti,* the big smoke.
He's got the taste, got it plenty hot."

Linus was looking at him without doubt, with complete acceptance. "Could we get them to come down and talk?"

"That's something you never know till you try," Shafter said. "Offhand, I'd say no." Then he said, "I could try gone up, I reckon."

"No," the colonel said. "I won't have that." He opened a brass
box on the desk, selected a cigar, and pushed the box across to
Shafter. "What will happen if I attempt to take troops in there?"

"You'll be the first man who ever did it," Shafter said quietly.
"And if you try it, you'll have two dead women to think about."

After a time the colonel said in a terrible voice, "Isn't there a
possibility we'll have that anyway?"

"Yes," Shafter said. "But they took the women, so I reckon they're
still alive. And you ain't gone to find out by tryin' to get up there."

Degnan bent his head. "I know that. I know it as well as you do,
Shafter." He looked up and his eyes were determined. "I'll tell you
frankly that I don't know the things you know. That I don't think
I could ever learn them. But I've been out here since the war ended,
Shafter. I'm not a greenhorn. I know what we've done right with
these damned Apaches and I know what we've done wrong, and
I know that any talk we make now of appeasement or policy or
handling of them is down the goddamn drain pipe." He ran a hand
almost nervously over his clipped gray hair. "This is my ward." He
heard Linus' long indrawn breath. "This is a Mexican woman from
a family of wealth and position. They simply cannot do these things.
To begin with, I don't know what you recommend, other than your
suggestion that you make an attempt personally . . . I appreciate
that . . . but I want telegrams off immediately to the War Department and to the President. I want Bleeker to get this into every
paper in the East. I want a runner into Sonora to that girl's family."

"For the love of Christ," Linus burst out. "What about Anna?"

There was silence. Shafter drew from his belt a small thin-bladed knife and carefully sliced the tip from one of the colonel's cigars. Linus watched the end of it disappear under the slim mustache. Shafter said, "You're right. Linus is right, too. You do your end and I'll do mine. Time ain't gone to make much difference now. You send your telegrams." He lit the cigar almost voluptuously. "You forget I ain't under orders to you, Colonel."

"You are under the military jurisdiction of this territory. If I must take the expedient of contacting Division HQ. . . ."

Shafter grinned around the cigar. "You got any better ideas?"

"I will not under any circumstances be responsible for. . . ."

Shafter interrupted him again. "Hell, I could be clear into Mexico City on shank's mare before you'll get a howdy out of Division HQ." He swung an ankle up on the other thigh and placed his hat over his knee, holding it by the high battered crown. "In one breath you tell me you're no greenhorn and in the next you tell me you want to try and take troops into the Chiricahua Stronghold. You disappoint me, Colonel."

Degnan rose. "Say we sent one of the Apache scouts up there with a demand, say we cut off both ends of Apache Pass."

"Say you do," Shafter said mildly.

"You object?"

"Colonel, you can't starve 'em down. They got plenty of water. They're in a natural hunting ground. No matter what precautions you take, they'll come down at night and kill your sentries and run off your horse and steal your supplies. There ain't any way to box 'em in up there." His fingers moved in the air, making a rocking motion. "They're touchy. A little too much pressure, even from the big nantan in Washington, and, like I said . . . dead." He picked up his hat by the crown and let it fall on his knee again. "I reckon Obre and I can maybe do it. Obre palavers better than I do."

"I'm going with you," Linus said.

"No, you're not, Linus," Shafter said.

"If you think I'm going to stay here and sweat blood while you go out there, you're crazy."

"I did what you asked," Shafter said. Now you do what I tell you."

The colonel went to the door and called Bleeker. Bleeker came and sat down with his sketchbook on his knees. "You tell him," Degnan said to Shafter.

Shafter told him.

Bleeker was astonished and horrified and in a sense elated. He made notes on his sketch pad, which was already covered with pencil lines. Shafter leaned over the arm of his chair and looked. There was Degnan's orderly, with his suspenders slipped down and his chair tilted back against the wall, asleep with his mouth open. Bleeker was a good reporter, but he was human. He asked questions but he did not ask what Degnan was going to do, or mention troop movements, or ask Linus for a personal statement. "This will arouse the populace," he said.

Shafter gave a rare laugh. "So you're the one does all that populace arousing in print, Bleek? I should of known." He slid down in his chair. "I remember a few of those populace-arousing headlines. My ma even saved the first one. Back from '35 it was. Terrible massacre by the Mimbreños. Whoever wrote it forgot to say what caused the terrible massacre. It wasn't you, was it? That wrote it, I mean."

"Of course not," Bleeker said somewhat indignantly. "That was the Santa Rita affair, wasn't it? When the whites loaded cannon with metal scraps and blew all those women and kids to hell while they were down getting their free bags of corn. I wasn't even born yet. They killed Juan José, and then Mangas Colorado came to power."

"Old Red Sleeves is dead now," Shafter said. "Now it's Victorio."

"You think it's the Mimbreños then." Bleeker scribbled some more. "Juan José and Mangas Colorado and Cochise, and now Victorio." He surveyed his notes and said, "The last of a great breed. That's rather good. The last of a great breed."

Shafter was on his feet. "How the hell do you know it's the last? I could name you twenty chiefs are gone to make you wish you'd stayed home before they're flushed out." He straightened. "Colonel, I'm gone to ask something of you."

Degnan's face was wary.

"I want a fresh horse. I want my gelding taken care of. Whatever it costs, I'll pay you."

Degnan's eyes went dark with anger. What was it with this man? No true animosity stood between them, nothing Shafter had said had been mean or petty, and yet somehow Degnan was aware of those things in the atmosphere. He wondered if they were in himself. For that small time the desk which kept them apart might have been a bloody ditch and he, the Union officer, across it, breasting the Confederate bayonet. Then he knew what he hated: Shafter did not feel whipped. Shafter had never been whipped.

In the softening late afternoon the shafting saguaro, darkening in the waning sunlight, bisected mile after mile of the encircling mountains. Shafter saw how the light would go over them, and how the hanging clouds would begin to flush and burn, lying on the peaks. There was a quietness, which came even to the men moving about the post, and to horses standing in their stalls. The desert quiet was like no other quiet in the world, stretching forever, trapped and contained within the ring of hill, light and cool and drifting, yet of a substance to be held in the hand. Infinitesimal things were in motion in it, not the least of which was man, but the immense thing, the vastness, was still and silent. A petal turning outward, a grain of sand shifting, might have made sound. There was something up there, out there. Shafter knew it. He did not know what it was. Nobody knew what it was. But it was there, arcane, imponderable. It pulled Shafter in a thousand directions, like currents swirling and sucking at a piling. It was never discussed, it was often contemplated, it was. There were times when a yearning which was half tenderness, half passion, but greater than any other form of love, rose in him. When that moment came it was the sort of moment a man walks out with gladness to meet his own death. It was intangible and it ran in his blood and formed bone and muscle. It was a nothing and it was a sword in his heart. It was a woman and whiskey and God. It was a red flag of old desires still shaking out the shredded remnants of promise. The form of it stood always on the brink of discovery, but it had no form.

He picked up a fresh horse and the post's number-one Apache scout, rolled a black Sonora cigarette, and rode into Tucson.

Three

Through the rounded opening she could see a single vedette, down the trail. He rose out of rock on an emerald sky which was full of late stars. Outside fire still burned low: it, and the night shine, fattened everything here with light and fell off into lean shadow.

She had slept. Sleep is quick to conquer. Now she was awake, lying motionless on her side. She could see Ysabel, sitting against the wall of the wickiup, face drugged and swollen from crying, breathing through her mouth, with the thin ragged line of blood crusted on forehead and temple.

The place smelled of smoke and dried brush and old hides and flesh, but it was the spring moon and the air was fresh, chill, sweet. The People had washed clothing and blankets. They had caked their heads with mud and dried in the sun and plunged into the stream, so the lice were gone. The men had sat in the sweat houses with the hot steaming stones and emerged with a weakness of body and a strength of spirit: *Ysen* had sent the good green time. Now the wagons with men and supplies would move again, and cattle and sheep and mules and horses would be turned out into the grassland for the taking.

She was cramped and changed her position as quietly as she could. Beside her the old woman made blowing sounds in her sleep, sucking in her withered cheeks and popping them out again. Once Ysabel moaned and shifted, against the wall. The immobility of the vedette was hypnotic. She did not think once that she dreamed and would waken in a moment to find herself jolting on the carriage seat, with the sunlit expanse of incongruously flowering sand flowing past the window.

She knew where she was.

In the earlier evening, while she lay here, she had tried to remember every scrap of knowledge Linus had passed on to her. She strove to recall what the newspapers had told her and her kindred sheltered race of the people who inhabited this world beyond civilization. There would be, must be, a clue to conduct somewhere in those fragments. She was very afraid. And yet a certain craftiness, a succession of small tactical plans, the will for survival, were tremendous in her.

Her simple, even frugal, masculine-dominated, early-orphaned, and sinless life had led thus far only to what she and her guardian aunt had taken pleasure in referring to as the great adventure: the long journey across the entire country to the wilderness of the Southwest. Experienced travelers had warned her of the varied discomforts, the aunt had warned her where to conceal her money, and Linus had warned her about whiskey drummers. She had the confidence of youth strengthened by a pure and wholesome joy in the knowledge that after a lifetime of acquaintance and a year of anguished separation she was going to marry Linus.

It was, of course, as even Linus in his naïveté had guessed, the parallel situations of their immediate presents and futures which drew her and Ysabel together. Yet it was strange, after a month shared, how little she had really known Ysabel and how unpredictable the complicated fellow being may prove. Ysabel was very high spirited and could make her eyes flash devastatingly, even though she had a great sadness. Nothing, not even the sadness, could daunt Ysabel; yet when the time came it was Ysabel who cracked and broke.

It was Ysabel who had been the consummate actress and she the fascinated audience. It was Ysabel's dark eyes and pink mouth which sent constantly, deliberately, half promises and muted signals all the way from St. Louis to Santa Fe; it was Ysabel's slim shoulder and haughty nose which lifted in disdain when some intemperate male response arose to annoy her. But that was only when she knew she was safe. Over the station tables, to the heavy breathing men who sometimes shared the overland coach which took them on the main leg of the journey she might have emerged from a convent.

There was enough of the child in Anna Stillman for her to be delighted and amused by the performance. To begin with, the girl was more beautiful than any girl Anna had ever seen: the charming procrastination of the Indian and the dark grandeur of the *castellano* fought to command her. A year of eastern schooling had not much influenced her and she emerged unscathed; she said she had braved the most part of Shakespeare and preferred Cervantes.

...fter the ordeal of the runaway. Ysabel was uncon...
...d on the door panel.

...ld climb to the locked valise. She pushed the doo...
...her head, jumped, caught herself on the bottom o...
...e, hard across the belly, hoisted up, went down o...
...st headfirst. She had only gained her feet when some-
...d close and she felt her hair come free of its pins and
...short. The rawhide loop went about her throat and
...against the heaving pony.

...d not regain consciousness. They tied her on a horse,
...fall over face down. All the frantic words were left to
...on a foaming Mexican horse, all the knowledge of the
...s, though she did not see what work they did, all the
...peals to his Virgin of the man burning on the wheel, until
...bed his mouth with sand.

...rridor went up and up. None of her senses responded and
...t was bruised and sore. A blur of red, gray, brown, moved
...r eyes; no face turned to her. There were rocks and trees
...narrow trail threading, and then more people, and dogs,
...men. Ysabel was on the ground, conscious, hysterical. Hands
...Anna and she fell off the Mexican horse. A fat woman came
...spat in her face. Another woman put her hands on Ysabel's
...rs and shook her violently, as though to silence her, and
...Ysabel shrank and screamed the woman shattered a clay *tus*
...her forehead.

...ng into the brush- and hide-covered wickiup, they lay listen-
...paralyzed. There was much talk outside, and dogs barked.
...n Anna finally crawled to Ysabel, she thought her heart would
...t in her. Blood was congealing on the girl's forehead; her skirts
...e torn to the waist. She was in a state of deep shock. Trying
...wipe away the blood with her own skirt, Anna made hideous
...estions.

"Ysabel, are they going to torture us?"

The girl's eyes were fixed, not focusing on anything.

"Please . . . are they going to kill us, Ysabel?"

Then she said dully, "We are *mozas* now. Servants. Slaves."

No one came near them. Anna fell into and struggled out of one
...black abyss of fear after another. At sundown Ysabel began to
...scream again, and to pray. Anna could not make her stop. When

There was not much opportunity for pleasure in the cold barren canyons of the East: her grandmother had been with her.

Grandmother had died of influenza. This was why she was returning home alone. Ysabel crossed herself rather offhandedly when she imparted this information. A padre who had a mission in a place called Brooklyn had offered to accompany her, she said, but he was much too young and virile-looking, and also he was Italian. Anna could not help laughing, which was of course what Ysabel expected and required.

Then there was Ysabel's great sadness, which was that since she was thirteen . . . she was now nineteen, just Anna's age . . . she had been promised to a certain man. *Con mucho dinero,* Ysabel said. *Muy rico. Pero—gordo.* Her slender hands made an enormous fat-bellied gesture. *Y viejo.* Her lashes fell, lying like smudges on her white cheeks.

Anna was sympathetic and appalled. This was a true, genuine matter, however Ysabel dramatized it. Imagine, her practical western nature whispered in revolt: to be promised at thirteen to a fat rich old man. His name was Don Ignacio, and Anna's indignation was not appeased when Ysabel let slip that he was all of thirty. What made it unbearably sad was that Ysabel also had a Great Love. He was very young and handsome, a magnificent horseman. He worked in her father's stables; therefore it could Never Be. Anna fancied night-softened guitar song, tense, impassioned, under the window where the girl dreamed. The reply with the tossed white rose. Sorrowful stolen trysts in the shadow of some thick moonless wall. It developed that the extent of this courtship had been a daily *buenos días* when he brought Ysabel's mare to the *casa* in the mornings.

The girl's witchery of contradictions worked their spell on Anna, who had previously assumed herself quite sophisticated, having been shunted about various army posts, as Linus had been, and educated in that most cosmopolitan metropolis, Washington, where she studied, secure, all through the war. While she was without boldness, she nevertheless believed that nothing could really shock her, a theory often untested which sometimes occurs in those under the stresses of extreme ennui or in possession of abounding animal good health.

Then there was Ysabel's family, in Santa Fe. The sister was married to a well-to-do landholder, considerably older than she and built to the proportions Anna summoned as characteristic of Don Ignacio. She had three wonderful children, and the cool house was full of laughter and music and good food and *vino* and religion. Doloresita, Ysabel called her older sister . . . Little Sorrow . . . and yet she had seemed plump and happy to Anna.

Ysabel explained. It would be the same with her. After the first child, or perhaps the second, Don Ignacio would find a mistress and then all would be harmony in the household. She shrugged; it was their way. She was fascinated, a touch envious, when Anna disclosed that although she and Linus had in no way been promised since childhood they had always enjoyed a tacit understanding, as had their families. They had even agreed that he must finish at the Point and see a year of service before they married. This was far too logical a thing to fail to make its impression upon Ysabel's shallow, surface-passionate nature: how fortunate Anna was, how free.

Anna was in a turmoil of impatience when they left Santa Fe in the pretty yellow coach of Don Arturo Calibrán y Vasquez, with the reassuring mounted guard. She was so near the end of the journey now. She talked of Linus constantly. They made plans, as young women will: Ysabel would visit the post, Anna and Linus would come to Mexico on their own wedding journey, to see Ysabel married. (And Ysabel's face could never quite muster the proper despair.) At the entrance to Apache Pass they stopped at Fort Bowie. They did not need escort; they had ten armed *rurales*. The sight of the familiar uniform, like an old friend, made Anna burn with eagerness to be off again; without knowing why, she did not mention that she was Colonel Walter Degnan's ward and, virtually, daughter-in-law. A patrol went through the pass with them anyway. The troopers did not want to offend the Mexicans, who were far from offended. They were, in point of fact, overtly nervous.

They cleared the pass without seeing anything more than a lizard. The troopers returned to Bowie. The coach went on its way.

"Perhaps we will come to Dragoon Springs by noon," Ysabel said. "There is water there. They say your army scouts found it years ago." She leaned from the red-curtained window. "Luis."

He came up, the *rurale* captain, stocky, squat, blue-clad, with a wide sweaty smile.

"*Qué hora es, Luis?*"

He drew out a big silver watch. "*Diez y media, Señorita.*"

"*El sitio del agua?*"

"*Sí, Señorita.*" He rai
aquí." There was a quick
he stiffened and fell out
quick flat sounds. It was A

Upon Ysabel's face was
behavior; she looked half as
his clumsiness and half as i
surprising and ungraceful d
made one loud cry and fell on

But Anna hung out the win
ing; then she saw horses: sv
clamped tight around them; he
wildly, kicking up a smothering
face. She dropped to the floor b
with the calm gravity of a disbeliev

The coach was rushing, rocking
the horses now because the driver
dashboard.

Twice Anna looked out the windo
dust rolling. She thought angrily, why
horses. Then the wild swaying flung h
terror sucked away her strength and sh
ing.

In a casual feminine gesture she had pa
rim-fire .41 derringer with which old Ma
her, amid much careless laughter, at the
had given for her. The valise was lashed te
She made a sound of utter anguish and clu
slid back and forth on the floor for an endless
then Ysabel began to scream, with her eyes
face rigid and expressionless.

It seemed to her hours, trying to calm Ysabe
good hardheaded army words Major Shaw and
little derringer she could not get to. Sand spraye
and fell grainy upon them. She felt it between her
ing went on and on, and there was now a high-p
whooping over the thick shouting of the *rurales*.
over abruptly when the horses were cut loose, and th
sideways in the sand, the impact throwing Ysabel
She fought to get to her feet, dazed with the suddenne

the door flap pulled back, she stood protectively, with anger, over the prostrate girl.

The voice was speaking rapidly in Spanish. She caught only a word or two and, dependent upon Ysabel, began in desperation to shake her. "I cannot understand what he is saying. Ysabel . . . oh please, Ysabel, pull yourself together."

The voice was slow, halting. "Make her stop screaming. She must stop or they will kill her."

She turned and stood upright. There was such a rush of relief in her that her mouth quivered into a smile, in a reflex action of which she was barely aware. "You speak English, boy?"

She crossed the wickiup to him and knew a small fear, a sense of having said the wrong thing. He was not a boy despite the slight build, but a man. She could not see his face well in the gloom of the place, but the black hair hung on his shoulders under the wide red band of flannel which bound it back.

"Make her stop," he said again.

"Yes. Listen." Oh God, the bond of language. This was no enemy, this man who could speak her tongue. She came closer to him. "Listen, you cannot keep us here." A faint light touched his face, pointing up a half-seen wariness, imperturbability, even surprise. "I belong to the officers at the army post. At Tucson. Do you understand that?"

He was silent a moment. She saw the flickering of his eyes. "To the white eyes at the fort? To the nantan?"

The words came out of her in a rush. She was incoherent. "What do you think they will do when they find where I am, they will come to take me back, they will kill you all."

Again she felt his hesitation. "You are not *Nakaiyi*, Mexican?"

"Of course not. I am Anna Stillman of Washington, D.C., and I am an American."

Again there was silence. Then he said, in a very low voice, "I am Joaquin."

It was disconcerting. The silence came around to her and she said finally, "Well, I am pleased to meet you." A wild desire to laugh overtook her but she steadied and said firmly, "You will take us to the army post. No harm will come to you if. . . ."

"You make promises for the white eyes," he interrupted harshly. "We are at war with the white eyes." He turned and went out.

Desolate, she dropped down beside the now quiet and exhausted

Ysabel. An old woman came with the darkness and brought a bowl of meat neither of them could eat and washed the blood from Ysabel's face. Flesh was expendable, but unblemished youth and strength were to be desired in a servant. Another woman, younger, came and pinched Anna several times, but Anna decided it was out of curiosity concerning her blue serge basque, which by now was in deplorable condition. She offered it. The woman laughed, rather bitterly. Anna tried to talk to her, tried to pry some Spanish from Ysabel. It was useless.

She kept her head. They had been offered food; Ysabel's wound had been washed. These were signs which pointed only to the good. In tomorrow's hopeful light she would be able to make her position clear, speak again with the man called Joaquin. That knowledge burned steadily, brightly. Outside there were sounds which spoke of drunkenness, a great scurrying as women came with the fermented corn. When the two squaws lay down and rolled themselves in old army blankets, she did the same, drawing a corner of the near squaw's blanket over her. She saw Ysabel, upright, with her head dropped back against the wall, and the numb lethargy came over her and she slept.

Tucson, within its dobe walls, was little and rough and ugly, as baked and dried out as if it had just been taken from an oven. Mean buildings were in various stages of piecemeal collapse, its corrals were broken down, filth littered the streets. Among those gathered to their fathers in the graveyard were two who had died of natural causes. The Old Pueblo was a pack-train center. Teamsters, emigrants, miners camped on its outskirts, and Conestoga, army, supply, and forage wagons floundered through it in a great turmoil of leaving and arriving. When it was dry a man could choke in the dust and when it rained he could drown in the potholes.

There were seldom more than twenty Americans in it; it was mostly Mexicans and Papagos sleeping in the sun, and a sprinkling of Apaches *mansos* . . . tame Apaches in whom was a craving for Mex-American food and American whiskey to the exclusion of everything else, including the making of war. They performed menial labor for the food and the whiskey, a thing which within the tribe would have subjected them to the cruelest ridicule. The more reliable and ambitious of them did scout duty for the army.

They were looked down upon by the army and derided by The People, which was what their true name, *N'de,* meant. Only their enemies called them Apache, enemy. It was good sport to get them drunk to stupefaction, and then sometimes the Mexicans quietly and permanently disposed of them: there was a bounty in Mexico on Apache scalps, although the taking of scalps was a thing generally beneath contempt to The People. The Mexicans with whom they had warred for centuries hated them, and they hated the Mexicans; their attitudes to one another were those of mutual cunning deceptions and distrusts, and, when the opportunity presented itself, total annihilation.

Ninety-four years earlier Tucson had been the Spanish presidio. When the Mexicans rebelled and drove out the Spaniards, the land belonged again, if not on paper, in fact, to The People. They ravaged and burned and raided from the eastern territory of New Mexico deep into Sonora and Chihuahua. Then New Mexico, which included that portion of Arizona north of the Gila, ceded to the United States, and the Territory was established, with Prescott as its capital. On a fair blue day in 1863 the Stars and Stripes rose over Tucson for the first time.

But there had been Americans there long before the war: miners working in small lone groups to open the copper mines, renegades and outlaws feeling themselves safe from the law in a lawless country, visionary men come to appraise the land for mail and passenger service to the Pacific coast. And the army, working against the overwhelming odds of the country itself and an adversary not only born and bred to near perfect guerrilla warfare but, since the first Spanish horse had fallen into their hands, probably the finest horsemen in existence. In the breadth of that gray strip of mountain and desert, only Tucson and, sporadically, little Tubac between the Old Pueblo and Sonoita, and a couple of heavily fortified ranches, had held out.

The war brought little action to Confederate Arizona, but it greatly reduced the army garrisons. The People did not understand the reasons for the white eyes' war, but they knew how this could come to be, for there had been a time long ago when they had not been united as a people, when they had fought to the death among themselves.

The white eyes' war left exposed and vulnerable the supply depots, the scattered ranches, the desert road, the settlers moving west, aiming to homestead in Arizona Territory or bent on reaching the golden lands of California and Oregon. The People were unopposed. They fought Union and Confederate alike, increased their driving raids into northern Mexico, came within the shadow of the walls of the Old Pueblo itself, drove off the troopers' horses, murdered without prejudice.

They learned quickly, when the war ended and the army returned in force, that this was to be a war of extermination . . . for them. They knew that all white eyes were not bad men, and this arbitrary sentence puzzled them; after all, they, The People, had made the original peace overtures when the white eyes first invaded their homeland. Much of their bitterness lay in the fact that the Americans and Mexicans had busily divided and apportioned and bought and sold this country and neither of them had bothered to ask The People whose country it was what they thought about it.

They had done their best, in the beginning, to keep the peace with the Americans. Some of them had even gone voluntarily on reservation ground . . . "the caged earth." There was no food on the reservation because the prime concern of the first Indian agents was profiteering. The People did not share this concern. They escaped before they starved.

Cochise's Chiricahua did not go on the reservation and they did not starve. There was dissatisfaction among the younger braves, but Cochise pursued a firm policy: he supplied the stage station at Apache Pass with firewood, and he built up a cattle herd, the first in Apachería for a people with no proclivity toward the agrarian. It was the most progressive and foreign step The People had ever taken, and it was inevitable that its imprint could not be permanently cast. The eager boy-nantan, George N. Bascom, late of the United States Military Academy, in one of the most atrocious diplomatic blunders ever perpetrated in Arizona Territory, invited the Chiricahua leader in under a white flag, accused him of the kidnaping of a half-Apache child who was actually taken by the Pinals, made an abortive attempt to hold him, and hanged three of his braves.

Then there was the bond between the tall many-bullet-scarred Cochise and the big-headed wise politician, Mangas Colorado, Red Sleeves. Mangas gave the *niña* of himself and his beautiful Mexican

woman for Cochise's second wife. Together they had been beaten
only once, when the soldiers brought the firewagons, howitzers, into
Apache Pass and blasted them into the rock which was their fortress.
They had never been caught that way again.

But Mangas had been tricked, too, by the white eyes' nantan
Shirland. Mangas, too, had learned to trust the white flag. They
were a people of total and enduring honor, and the symbols of
honor were also the symbols of trust. When he found he had been
taken captive under that symbol, the wise old man thought fatal-
istically that he might at least enjoy a good night's sleep, but even
that was denied him. The soldiers heated their bayonets in the fire
and placed them against Mangas's legs and spine. When he rose
with quiet dignity to protest, he was cut down by carbine fire. He
had tried to escape, the sergeant of the guard informed the in-
different Shirland.

The uneasy lot in life of chieftainship had fallen to Mangas's
able lieutenant, Victorio, and possibly there would be other able
men to take his place, which was also true of the Chiricahua. Cochise's sons could not be chosen simply because they were his sons,
but the signs pointed to his young Tahzay. And Cochise already
had within him the sicknesses which *Ysen* sends to signal the longest journey of all. Still, at this time, they were united, all the tribes
of Apachería, and joining them from time to time were small groups
of Navajo, whom The People called *Yutakah*.

If The People had had access to the record . . . the black writing
which the white eyes kept and which never failed to fascinate them
. . . they would have been astonished at the great volubility of
many nantans, but they would not have been pleased. With the
single exception of the Chiricahua Gokliya, whom the Mexicans
called Geronimo, and who had very early left his people to establish
himself as a lone-wolf war chief, there were few instances in which
a promise had been broken by The People. But there were many
instances in which promises had been broken, and the white eyes
could speak with the forked tongue in the words which they set
upon paper as well as with the words they honied for the councils.

The runners and vedettes came to tell The People a fresh new
flag of the white eyes had been raised in the Old Pueblo. Something had happened again: something to do with the chieftainship
of the land which the white eyes had bought without consulting

the Apache who owned it. Tucson was to be called the head of
the territory now, the capital, and there would be many more
white eyes, thousands of them, pouring in upon the stolen land of
The People.

Shafter went into an upstairs room over a saloon in the Buckalew
Block, had a drink, called for hot water, and shaved. He changed
into clean duck breeches, dark shirt, and leather chaleco, cleaned
and inspected the single Leech and Rigdon .44 he carried, filled
his cartridge belt and canteen, rigged a bedroll. Charley Tom, wearing a black slouch hat with the top punched straight up, sat on
the bed and watched him, then went down to keep an eye on the
army-drawn gear in the saddlebags. When Shafter came down, Obre
was leaning on the bar, waiting.

Shafter slung the bedroll over his shoulder. "They get the greasers
buried?"

Obre nodded. His lean face was alien solemn. "Willson was playin'
padre," he said.

"What?" Shafter said.

"He all of a sudden upped and said it wasn't right to get planted
without prayin' if you was a good mass-gone greaser. Said he'd
hate to think of 'em hootin' around in hell with their tails on fire
just because nobody prayed over 'em."

"Well, for God's sake," Shafter said. "Wha'd he say?"

"I didn't get much of it. I was too busy admirin' him. It sounded
nice." He looked at Shafter. "You figurin' on gone alone?"

"I was about to say you maybe didn't have anything else to do,"
Shafter said.

Obre looked down at the bar. "I think you're crazy, Shafter."

"Do you?" Shafter said.

"I think they're dead. Both of 'em. If the squaws ain't done it,
they're dead of fright."

"You are entitled to your opinion," Shafter said politely. He signaled the bartender. "Two beers."

"Beer?" Obre said. "Jesus, you are crazy, Shafter. What for in
hell are you buyin' dollar beers when you can drink two-bit redeye?"

"I feel like drinking beer," Shafter said. He put four fifty-cent
shin plasters on the bar and pushed one of the beers over to Obre.

"I'm steppin' high out of my way," Obre said.

"Drink it," Shafter said.

Obre was humble. The beer was warm gold in his mouth. That Shafter had asked him made him feel good. Then he thought of something. "Ain't you got Charley Tom?"

Shafter looked at him. "I like to know for sure Charley Tom ain't doin' any embroidering on what I say."

Obre accepted the responsibility of the trust with no change of expression. Not quite unconsciously his hand brushed back across the right twin of the low-slung Dance .36s he wore. The action was not lost on Shafter. "I reckon it's gone to be fairly peaceable where I'm headin," he said.

Obre accepted this also. He was a peaceable man, who liked to sit in the sun, work with the Dance revolvers, and do a little extermination work, which paid well, now and then. He frowned when Shafter said, "I wonder if Joaquin Mitchell's up there with Victorio."

Obre jeered then. "That half white eyes." He spit out something in Comanche. "Breed *Tá-ashi*."

"I don't reckon he could help his pa's fancy," Shafter said. He adjusted the bedroll. "Anyhow, I wouldn't count on him to give us a howdy."

Obre felt better. They rode out, toward Apache Pass, on the liquid light of a three-quarter moon.

Four

The men of The People were heavyheaded in the morning, having drunk too deeply of the *tulepah*. This they made by burying corn until it sprouted, digging it, grinding the mash, adding water, and letting it ferment. The white men and the Mexicans called it tiswin. It was like a weak beer and could be consumed in great quantities. They made also a fiery liquor from the aguave, the mescal plant.

The spoils had been distributed—the *Nakaiyi pistoles* and *carabinas*, the contents of the baggage, the horses and mules. These were divided not necessarily among their captors, but among those who most needed them, in an even, socialistic division. Victorio's Mimbreños would take most of the horses with them to Ojo Caliente or Santa Rita del Cobre. Cochise's Chiricahua had plenty of horses, which were not only essential to the raid but good to eat.

The men did not see the sunrise. Some of them went to the steam house and then plunged into the cold stream and sat in the sun and spoke to one another. The Stronghold was a fine place, as fine as any retiro in Apachería. There were solid battlements of insular ocherous rock rising out of the grama grasslands from which the Apache corridor led. There was good spring water, a stream, caves of pine and oak shade, grass. Birds sang here and the flowers came. On the lower elevations were scrub oak and manzanita, and higher, cypress made feathery masses and madroña grew. The ponies of The People followed centuries-old trails across the desert, then higher into the grass country and at last into the mountain fortress, the green island in the barrenness. From it, the Chiricahua commanded Apache Pass, between the Chiricahua and Dos Cabezas . . . the two heads . . . Mountains. From it, it was a near run into the land of the *Nakaiyes*, the Mexicans, their traditional enemies.

Cochise's band alone did not constitute The People. There were also Victorio's Mimbreños, whom the white eyes called the Warm Springs Apaches, for their territory centered at Ojo Caliente; they called themselves the *cihéné*, Red Paint People. The Gileños had their ranchería at the headwaters of the Gila River. The Mescaleros ranged beyond the Rio Grande. The Jicarillas lived in the New Mexican mountains, the Coyoteros northwest of the Gila, the Arivaipa in the northwestern mountains, the Tontos in the northern territory.

A scant thirty-five years ago they had all been together under one chief, Juan José. But Juan José was dead by the treachery of the white eyes, and The People now had their separate tribal chiefs. This was not a hereditary office. This was given for wisdom, bravery, prowess. This was given to the man who best provided for and guided the affairs of his tribe. Once the tribes had had both administrative and war chiefs, but with the rise of Cochise, who had been uniquely chosen both in one, the new order had begun to prevail. Eskiminzin of the Arivaipa was also such a man, and Victorio of the Mimbreños, for he was not only lieutenant but disciple of Mangas Colorado.

They sat on a ledge: Victorio, Mangas Chie, Tahzay, Joaquin, Delgadito. The loginess was working out of them, in the sunlight. Joaquin had not gone on the preceding day's raid, nor, disturbed by his new knowledge, had he drunk. This knowledge was now discussed, but Cochise said that the prisoners were Victorio's and he must decide what to do with them.

Victorio had a fine handsome face, aquiline, broad at the cheekbones, with large clear eyes. Since Mangas's death nearly seven years ago, he had demonstrated his superior talent for leadership. He was fearless in battle and much of Mangas's thoughtful manner had rubbed off on him. He did not act without full consideration. He was at war with the white eyes, but he wondered if this which had occurred was a good thing. The white eyes set great store by their women. And this was a nantan's woman. It troubled him; he eyed the younger braves morosely. Of the *Nakaiyi* woman there was no question. He had thought yesterday they were both *Nakaiyi*.

"Keep them," Cochise said finally.

"And what of the white eyes soldiers?" Victorio said.

There was an edge of humor on Cochise's thin lips. He was about sixty-four now, and there was much gray in the hair which hung on his shoulders. "Since when has my brother feared the white eyes soldiers?" he said.

They laughed. Feeling better in the sun, they were good-humored. Victorio said, "But the demand will come. For the

Nakaiyi niña it will be a request, and we will get good horses for her. The white eyes will not ask. Is that not so, Joaquin?"

Joaquin shrugged. There was a burning in him, as if he could feel his blood. "If we barter for the *Nakaiyi niña,* maybe we will barter also for the *niña blanca,*" he said.

Cochise shook his gaunt head. "For what, Joaquin? For peace?" The luminous eyes were dulling with his progressive illness. "I would say it raises me up to know there are still those among us who believe in this thing. As I did." He looked at his son, Tahzay, and at Mangas's son, Chie. "As your father did, Chie. As Eskiminzin still does."

"Joaquin has a reason of blood for seeking peace," Chie said.

Joaquin said very quietly, "If my blood runs thicker than yours, Chie, it is the strength of Mimbreño which makes it so."

In the stiff silence Tahzay made a joke, a pun upon the name of the liquor they drank, and upon the name of their brother tribe. "And if it runs hotter than yours, Chie, it is mescalero which makes it so."

They laughed. Chie said, "I meant nothing ill to Joaquin, but perhaps this is a hard thing for him, and if it is, that is the business of us all."

"Not so," Joaquin said. "It came to me that with the nantan's woman we might raise the soldier's pledge to stay out of the Mimbreño rancherías."

Then Cochise said, "It will not be that way, Joaquin. There is no peace to be pledged and kept with them. Juan José learned this. Mangas Colorado learned this, both to their deaths. I learned it, but I live, because I learned it in time. The white eyes make their promises for the joy of destroying them."

No one spoke, but they thought the same. What was bred in them, as a race, was a gladness in the fulfilling of their destined way of life: the way of war. War was necessary to a non-agrarian people, and when they had filled their wickiups and their bellies with its spoils they were content in the ways of peace. They were nomadic by nature, and what is to change a man's nature: the written law of another race? These things were deeply ingrained, inherent, in the philosophy, even the religion, of The People. Their way of life was often spoken of, discussed aloud, among them. They wondered if the white eyes had always conquered, had always endeavored to force their own customs and usages and laws upon the conquered.

There were good things in the white eyes' way, much that was advantageous to be learned from them. But this was a pragmatic thing which must be studied and absorbed, mold itself to the existing need and desire to learn, and which must not be thrust wholesale, with force, upon them.

Yet the white eyes were very brave. They fought like men, and they knew how to die. This was admitted by The People. They were unlike the *Nakaiyes*, who often did not die bravely, but screamed and pleaded. Sometimes captured *Nakaiyi* women were absorbed into the tribe, but this was the exception rather than the rule and was generally the woman's choosing, either as an escape mechanism which, while it did not free her from a life of servitude, nevertheless elevated her to a social equality, or from a prompting of the heart which induced her, quite simply, to adore her captor.

But there was little white blood here. There was as much white blood as could be measured in the veins of the Mimbreño Joaquin. There was a slight admixture, very ancient, of Pueblo and Pima, but they were a remarkably pure people and proud of it. Joaquin was not strange to them; yet today he felt strange to himself.

At Santa Rita del Cobre, in the Mimbreño ranchería, his mother had been sick for a long time. Victorio had said his mother might have the *Nakaiyi niña*, and he knew Victorio had done this thoughtfully. There was no way of knowing how much or how easily the *americana* woman might infect another who carried her own blood. Victorio skirted the risk. Yet under these peculiar circumstances it was good that one of his own could speak with the white eyes.

Cochise said again, "There is no assurance that I can find in this holding, but I would hold her all the same. They will miss her, at the fort. Let them make the first move."

"I do not want that move to be made, again, with the firewagons," Victorio said.

Joaquin looked at him. "There is a way to beat the firewagons. It is not to entrench ourselves behind rock. It is to go when the firewagons come."

"Joaquin speaks wisely." Cochise shifted, crossing his long thin legs more comfortably. "I think also there is wisdom among the white eyes. If they want this woman back they will not endanger her. They will come with talk."

Victorio made a sound of scorn. "I have heard their talk. First they will threaten. If all goes well, their word will be broken at the first moment it is to their advantage to do so."

"Then this must be to your advantage," Cochise said quietly. "Your position is very strong. You have the woman. If you must, you can take her where they will never find her. See what they have to say."

"And if they come with many soldiers?" Delgadito had also been beloved by Mangas Colorado.

"See, still, what they say. If it is not to your liking you can wait until the white flag is taken back and strike hard at the soldiers. Then there will be less of the white eyes here."

Victorio bent his head. He said, "There was a time when a *niño-nantan* struck while the white flag was still raised."

"Yes." Cochise's voice was dull with the old pain of that time of betrayal. "But above all things we will keep our word when it is given."

Tahzay said to Cochise, "My father, what do you think would happen if we . . . if, say, Joaquin . . . took the *niña blanca* to the nantan and surrendered her."

Joaquin stared at him. Tahzay was much like Cochise, not so austere, with a becoming gravity. Before Cochise could answer, Joaquin said, "The quick iron on my ankle, Tahzay, or a quicker bullet."

Tahzay glanced at Cochise. "What say you, my father?"

Cochise studied the grave narrow face. "I see what is in your mind, my son. I see it with pride. But as with all things which we attempt with honor, with these *americanos*, it passes somewhere beyond their understanding. I do not think they would take such an action as it was meant. I think, perhaps, they would say among themselves, the Mimbreños are afraid. The Chiricahua are afraid."

"Do not forget, Tahzay," Joaquin said, "the words I speak and the tongue in which I speak them do not make me a thing more than Mimbreño."

Tahzay's face was troubled. "But you have known nantans who would understand this thing, father."

"That is true," Cochise said. His voice was brittle. "I can count them by these two eyes in my head."

Victorio rose suddenly. With the toe of one deerskin moccasin he traced an aimless pattern in the dust along the ledge. "I will keep the *niña blanca*," he said. "I will let her serve Klishta, but I will let no harm come to her." He looked at Cochise. "You know the game we play, with the horsehide cards. Always there is the one card held to a purpose. Perhaps this card we hold may win the game for us. We will wait."

Cochise nodded. "Where do you go from us, Victorio?"

At this time Victorio was in no hurry to return to either of his main rancherías, at Ojo Caliente and the Santa Rita copper mines on the Gila. He had stalwart braves and good war chiefs. The spring raiding had begun and his people were becoming rich and satisfied with the spoils. There had been tribal matters to discuss with the Chiricahua chief, and for the men of the hot springs it was pleasant in the Stronghold. There was plenty of meat and *tulepah* and many squaws to work, and two adulterous divorced women who had been turned out of their wickiups with their noses mutilated were available for the asking of his younger men. Also, it was Victorio who had gone out for yesterday's coup, and he wanted a time to consider it. He said slowly, "I think to Santa Rita. What think you, Joaquin, Delgadito?"

Delgadito said, "I believe there will be fresh stock and guns there. We will go and take them." His eyes narrowed. In this time of The Leaves Coming there would perhaps be men at the copper mines and other men going into the hills to search for that useless yellow metal they called gold. He was moving on them, in his mind, before he left the Chiricahua Stronghold.

Outside Cochise's wickiup his young wife, the daughter of Mangas Colorado, warmed meat: the flesh of a spotted pony they had eaten of the previous night. There were no set hours for meals; food was always ready over the fire. The men sniffed the air. Cochise said formally, "My brother is welcome at this place for as many suns as he wishes to see rise from this ledge." He stood up. "Let us go and eat."

"*Enju,*" Victorio said. "Joaquin, you will speak to the *niña blanca.*"

Joaquin got to his feet and walked down through the birdsong and the sound of water, past the pitched wickiups, until he came to the doorway he sought. Anna had not been allowed to leave the wickiup; this she understood from the old squaw, who grunted and shook her head and pointed to the sunlight opening. When Joaquin entered she could not manage the smile she had depended upon, but sat wordlessly.

He stood looking down at her. She was sitting on the army blanket under which she had slept, a cavalry blanket with a faded yellow stripe. Her dark hair was long, well down her back, and quite straight, though it curled slightly about her face, where it was pushed back and away. Her dark eyes, set wide apart, were very tired, with something which was more than tired, and the color of her skin disturbed him, for he did not find it pleasant. For her part, seeing him fully for the first time, an awareness touched her which went beyond the surprise of his knowledge of her language. He was not tall and the slightness which had compelled her to call him boy the night before, wholly seen, was actually a lithe leanness. He looked Indian and he did not look Indian; in the earth color of his face the eyes were black lashed but quite blue. Yet she was not startled; a thing she could not understand or define rose in her. She felt it as a sympathy.

It was he who was startled. With the instinct of an animal he sensed this thing in her and was repelled by it. Uneasily he said, "What is wrong with the Mexican?"

She glanced at Ysabel, huddled asleep, as if dead, in the corner. She said, "She is tired out. She is afraid."

"And you are not afraid," he said. It was not an inquiry.

She lied. "No. Because you cannot keep me here."

"We will not talk of what we have already talked of," he said. "I came to say to you that today you will do as the women tell you. There are many things you will begin to learn."

She watched him steadily, but a tremor of desperation began to stir in her. She said, "Will you not sit and talk with me, Joaquin?"

"No." He shook his head. There was something so fiercely Indian about his face now that she could find no room for courage anywhere within herself.

"Then will you listen to me?"

"Be brief," he said.

She locked her arms about her drawn-up knees. "You are an intelligent man. You use my language well. I believe your chief must be an intelligent man." She ignored the yellow mockery which came upon his face. "They are not so different, your chief and my chief. If the wife of your chief were held against her will, what would your chief do?"

He said, "He would kill as many of those who held her as he could. But, concerning his wife, he would bare his breast and mourn her."

She drew a sharp breath. "I believe you will free me," she said.

"It is better not to believe this."

"It is something I know inside," she lied desperately.

He drew back. The superstition of his people was strong in him. "It is dangerous to say this," he said.

"Are you not afraid of my chief and his soldiers?"

"No more so than you of mine." Again he mocked her.

She changed her ground abruptly. "Very well. Then how am I to conduct myself? Until I am set free."

Again he drew back. Her sudden calm and her insistence bothered him, but his dawning response was that which he might have held out to a brave man. "Do as you are told and they will not beat you. In a few days' time we will be gone from this place and the white eyes will not find you." He saw the blood leave her face, marking it whiter than the snow which blanketed the upper reaches of the Stronghold in the desert winter, the time of Ghost Face, and he was satisfied.

She rose and came to him, as she had come the night before. Her face was a mask and her arms were rigid at her sides, but her lips were parted and she was breathing rapidly, angrily. She said, "Do you find it strange, Joaquin, that the Indian eyes are in my face, while yours is the face with the white eyes?"

Rage surged in him. For a wild moment he almost struck her. Again with instinct he knew that she expected this, perhaps even desired it: it was the one thing which curbed him. His father was dead, but his father had left upon him a color which was the color of sky. This was his shame and was not mentioned, indeed, was forgotten now among his own. He had been novitiate with boys his own age in all the games of skill and craft and war, and in that time the shame of the eyes had made him undertake, risk, more than other boys. He did not follow, but led, and the lance in his hands and the captured carbine had done their work of expiation.

She saw what she had done to him, but she did not see how much. With one hand still clenched to strike, he swung away from her. And she thought, with apology already forming in her, that she had done a stupid and unforgivable thing.

Charley Tom poked the horse dung apart with a stick and examined it. When he straightened, he fingered a bunch of sage; some of it was broken off, and when he crushed it in his hand the

smell of it came pleasantly. "Very fesh," he said. "Two three hour."
He walked ahead. "Bush bust on other side, too," he said. "Two
horse here, two follow. Pony lame here, toes go out."

Obre grinned at Shafter. "That makes five, mounted. We just
missed 'em."

"They just missed us," Shafter said. "On purpose maybe. What
do you think, Charley?"

"Know we here," Charley Tom admitted, preparing to mount.

"No kill Apache *manso*," Obre jibed.

Charley Tom shot him an evil glance. "Kill bassard Comanche,
maybe," he said.

Obre laughed. "Quit," Shafter said. "From now on we go easy,
but I want to make the pass tonight."

"Then what?" Obre said.

Shafter looked up at the mountains. There was a faint forbidding
quality about them which was for him part and parcel of their
compulsion. "Fire up and hold our ground."

"Ain't you gone to send Charley up there?"

Charley Tom wheeled and looked at him. Under the punched-
up black hat his face was angry. "You quit, Obre. John say quit."

Obre laughed again. Shafter said, "You'll go if I tell you, Charley.
Or nantan Degnan won't be passin' out the *dinero* this month."

"No whiskey," Obre said. "No *borracho*."

Charley Tom's sullen face turned away from them. Far off, left,
quail whistled. Shafter listened. The whistle came again. It was
quail. But Obre said, "Maybe we ain't gone to make the pass tonight."

"Maybe not," Shafter agreed.

"Maybe those five *Tá-ashi* waitin' ahead for us."

"Maybe," Shafter said. He was looking for signal smoke, for mirror glint in the mountains. Poppies lay crushed, like blood, under
the hoofs.

Charley Tom said he wanted to use his mirror and Shafter said
go ahead. Charley Tom halted while they went on, turning his glass
into the sun.

"How come you to swap horses?" Obre said.

"It ain' my nature to risk a good horse or a woman's reputation,"
Shafter said. "As a rule, you owe 'em both too much." He looked
straight ahead now. "You ever have to throw your horse, Ob?"

"Hell, mine continual gets shot under me," Obre said.

Shafter said, "Your horse gets shot under you, you're exposed too long. You jump and throw him and tie his legs together you got a bulwark from the minute you bend to grab that off fetlock till the minute he's down." He bit contemplatively at his lower lip; the gesture flattened the tapered ends of the blond mustache. He thought of the warm struggling body jerking under bullet and arrow, and your head pressed against the doomed belly which rumbled and fought to expel the bowels. Most Indians did not aim for the horse because they wanted it. Then again, most men did not want to be afoot in the desert. But sometimes the horse, the living breastwork, was all there was.

Obre knew what Shafter was telling him. He watched the land now. He liked the color and the hairy silken flowers on the cactus; yet they made him uneasy. The season and its riotous renaissance made him want something and he did not know what it was he wanted. Sometimes all his blood seemed to flow and concentrate in one throbbing center of his being. The feeling made him mad. But he thought, it was not knowing where the *Tá-ashi* were . . . the people with the turned-up moccasins the Comanches called them. He spread an icy coolness over the strata of pulsating nerve which lay close to the surface. Men said of him he did not have a nerve in his body. Perhaps because of this, rather than the manner in which he earned his living, men neither liked nor trusted him. This was a fact which did not bother Obre much; you couldn't eat another man's respect or fill the cylinders of the Dances with it. And if there were hungers of the soul, that was only right and due portion of mortal travail.

He thought they would make the pass that night.

Charley Tom rode up, still flashing his mirror. Nothing talked back to it but they knew the signal had been seen. Charley Tom had told them, three men, peace, Apache Pass. He rode ahead again, passing Obre with a sulky side glance. He found where the five mounted Apaches had turned off and gone into the hills.

Shafter rode steadily, feeling the old pull in him and trying to smooth it over by not looking up. He hoped they wouldn't hit any patrols out of Bowie, but if they did he had Degnan's written order, a terse thing which boiled down to: no interference. The smell of the crushed flowers lay in the air. Between his teeth, Obre whistled "Dixie."

Five

When they were brought from the wickiup the sun was shining strongly and The People were pursuing the ordinary routine of the day.

Children, nearly naked, were playing along the stream with small bows and arrows and pistols made from crooked branches. Men sat in the shade, in the sunlight, with their horsehide cards, making, repairing, cleaning weapons. Women were at work in and before their wickiups, cooking, mending clothing, making new clothing, weaving or twining willow baskets, molding or pitching their clay water *tus*. The older boys were gone, out with their instructors on training problems which were not games but matters of dead earnest. Sometimes the problems were deliberately laid out beforehand; one overlooked, upturned stone along a trail might mean a man's life one future day.

The faces of The People were good-humored, some overbroad with rather spread-out features, some sharp, aquiline. Many of the young women were handsome, with shy eyes, small in the soft deer-skin dresses which were hung with fringe and little bells. Their hair was arranged in the back on a hide frame, in a shape like that of a figure eight. The hair of the older women lay free. They did not make fine jewelry as the Navajos and Zuñis did, but they traded for it. Some of the men wore the breeches of the white eyes, but most wore breech clouts, with the two ends hanging long, and belted shirts. Their thighs were brown and glistening above the cuffs of the knee-high, turned-up moccasins. Always there was the headband, red or white or blue flannel or cotton, bound around the forehead to keep the free hair from their eyes.

The ranchería was neat and orderly, and quiet except for the low talk and laughter of the men, the women speaking among themselves, the children squealing under the trees, along the water. Dogs lay in the sun. Vedettes stood watch from the high points, commanding the desert below and the eastern and western corridors which led into the Stronghold. Horses and mules stood in a corral at the far end of the ranchería, though some animals were tethered near the wickiups of their owners. There were storage pits along the banks, lined with hide: they contained acorns and the nut of the piñon pine, beans from the long flat pods of the mesquite, juniper berries, corn, against the lean time when Ghost Face rose over the land.

Before the young squaw who was the second wife of Cochise's lieutenant, Pionsenay, came for them, Ysabel had wakened. For a troubled time her dark eyes were dull with the emotional exhaustion of many tears; then she recalled where she was and sat up, moaned, fell back again. Anna knelt by her side and examined her head. The ugly gash the ragged edge of the *tus* had made appeared without fever, but Anna knew it was going to scar. She told Ysabel only what Joaquin had said about the work they must learn; she was unhappy enough concerning other disclosures he had made without subjecting Ysabel to them.

Ysabel watched her with great eyes, glazed and unblinking. She said, "My head hurts."

"I know," Anna said gently. "Perhaps they will let us bathe it again." She turned Ysabel's head toward the light. The girl's long jet hair was tangled and knotted. "I don't think it's infected, Ysabel."

Ysabel's voice was breathy. "It feels so stiff. It will be there always, won't it? The mark of it."

"I can't tell," Anna said lamely.

Tears welled in the dark eyes. "Then if the Virgin is not kind to me, *Vírgen de la Engracia,* he will never look at me again."

"What?" Anna said. "Who will never look at you again?"

"Ignacio." She began to weep in earnest.

Then Anna cupped the wet cheeks and forced the dark head up. She was weary of carrying the whole load; she rebelled at carrying Ysabel, too. "You listen to me," she said coldly. Ysabel looked at her, shocked. "If harm comes to either of us, it will be because we bring it on ourselves. I'm as sick of your tears as these people are, and if you cry you will be beaten. Do you want to be beaten? Do you?"

"No," Ysabel whimpered.

"Then hold up your head. You said we were *mozas* now. Well, you are acting like one. What would your father and mother say if they saw you? Yes, and Ignacio. All the way here I heard you rail against Ignacio, and now you speak his name first."

Ysabel stared at her.

"There is a way for us to be, I am sure, and we must do it. We must not complain and we must do what we are told. We must make every friendly overture we can, but we must hold ourselves aloof. We must never show we are frightened, but we must never be proud. Do you hear me, Ysabel, can you do this?"

Now Ysabel said clearly, "Can you?"

And Anna said, sitting back on her heels, "I don't know." She watched the dark girl. "But I am going to try. And if you don't try also, I won't give a damn if you are beaten."

"You are very cruel, Anna," Ysabel said.

"Perhaps I am," Anna said. "But when I go out of here I want to go out as Anna Stillman, white, American, not as some broken-down squaw beaten and worked out of recognition." She stood up. "You do as you wish, Ysabel. I can't interfere and I certainly can't protect you. The only protection we have is our attitude, and the hope that the post will send someone for us soon."

Ysabel said, "When the troops come in sight we are dead."

Anna stamped her foot, impatient, disgusted. "Keep on like this, Ysabel, and from where I stand you are already dead."

"It would have been better if they had killed us, down there at the springs," the girl said dully.

"Better for you, I don't doubt that," Anna said brutally, "but not for me. I have my life and I'm going to do everything I can to keep it until Linus comes for me."

Ysabel struck back like a child, with pleasure and hatred. "You will never see Linus again," she said.

They watched one another, furious. Then Anna came and knelt beside her again. "Ysabel, I am sorry. We must stay together, we mustn't fight one another. Please, will you make an effort. . . . Will you try?"

Ysabel did not answer. Pionsenay's wife entered the wickiup and came to them. She took Anna by the arm. "*Venga*," she said. Her foot, in the soft high moccasin the women wore, drew back to kick Ysabel. Ysabel rose. Anna allowed herself to be led, but she said to Pionsenay's wife, "*Quiero Joaquin*."

Pionsenay's wife said nothing. The sunlight was blinding when they emerged; Anna was dizzy with its impact. "*Quiero Joaquin*," she told Pionsenay's wife again, insistently. The girl pointed. He stood near, talking with a squat, heavily built man. When he saw them he put his hand on the heavy man's shoulder, then turned to them. When he came, a wind swept through the green leaves stirring in the canyons and heights of the encircling rock. His moccasins were soundless. It was strange to see a man walk and hear nothing of his step.

Anna held back. Within her was not a pity for him but a hot despising of herself, and it was a feeling more shattering than fear had ever been. She did not look at him directly, but down at the torn hem of her skirt, so that she did not see that there was no anger on his face, only a stiff disinterest.

"Yes?" he said.

She locked her hands, so that they would not betray her. "Will you tell them that we must have other clothes. We cannot move in these; they are only for sitting. May we not have our baggage?"

"Your things have been given where they were needed," Joaquin said.

"Then you found the little gun. It is mine." She looked up at him and his face made her heart fail.

"It was yours. Now it belongs to a man who had no little gun." His eyes went beyond her, to Ysabel, examined apathetically the silken rag which was all that remained of her dress; his glance probed without compassion the marked, swollen face which had been beautiful short hours ago and came to rest on Anna again. "You will be provided for," he said and spoke to Pionsenay's wife rapidly in Apache. Anna caught her own name, the Spanish Ana. He and Pionsenay's wife went away and left them waiting. The men, laughing over their cards, did not look at them. The women, straightening from their cook fires, had distant eyes. The children made menacing motions with their small weapons. Ysabel took her by the arm. "There," she said, inclining her head toward a grassy space along the stream.

Women were erecting a wickiup. They had thrust long slender poles into the ground, every two feet or so apart, in a rough oval form. Then they had bent the tops of the poles inward and bound them together, leaving a small smoke hole. Now brush would be intertwined and woven between the bent saplings, and when the structure was solid it would be covered with bark and hides. The women worked swiftly, with great agility.

Ysabel said, "That we will do. And butcher for the hunting parties and jerk meat for them so that they will have strength to go against us even in the winter." Her voice was hard. "Do you still hold up your head, Anna?"

Anna did not answer. She watched the women, the easy relaxed men, the playing children. She watched a naked *niña* make a mud-cake. Another passed her carrying a doll made of wood and rags. When Pionsenay's wife came with deerskin clothing in her arms, Anna was fighting to stay on her feet.

Ysabel was right. The God of the Mexicans wrought miracles, but the God of the Episcopalians had not had the time or the inclination or the good sense to do likewise in centuries. She did not pray, but commanded Ysabel's God to do something. The first nostalgia sharpened all her senses to a point of pain: there was her aunt, arranging a vase of big pink roses in a clean and shining room. Major Shaw's nephew, desolated at her leaving, he said, swung her grandly down the floor of the ballroom, all of them laughing because she still held the silly little derringer in her hand. In a hundred ways and times and moments, Linus bent to her. There had been a ball, when they were children, a red ball, and he had rolled it across the grass to her and it had fallen in the lake when she did not stop it. A thousand miles, a thousand years away. . . .

She had been condemned. When they left this place, Joaquin had said they would never be found. And she began the futile search for a hope, however slim, however small, with which she might find strength for whatever lay ahead.

A vedette passed them, running. Victorio came up from the stream bank, walking quickly. The vedette spoke in a mixture of Apache and Spanish. Almost immediately Victorio signaled Pionsenay's wife. She handed Anna the bundle in her arms and they were again turned into the wickiup.

Anna stood holding the deerskin against her breasts. Her fingers were clenched hard in the velvet soft stuff. Two words the vedette had spoken made an aftermath of ringing in her: *ellos vienen.* They are coming.

Before breakfast there was guard mount and, following it, troop inspection. Colonel Walter Degnan went hard by the book, General Philip Cooke's *Tactics,* stretching the 10 A.M. drill for two hours once a week, a tough drill in the sun, but not as tough as it would have been for troopers green on drilling. When it was over there was a mass loosening of the hot gray flannel shirts. Because the collars of the shirts were only a foldover of material, the bandanna or handkerchief served as collar. It also kept dust out of the nose and mouth or, worn around the head, sweat from running into the eyes. After Degnan's drills it was used until it was a sodden crumpled rag, to wipe away the sweat.

Following noon mess there was an hour to get ready for personal inspection. It didn't give you much time to wash up, change clothes, polish buttons and buckles and all the other dabs of brass the army stuck all over you and demanded you keep like it had just come out of quartermaster's. The buttons you did in a hurry, sliding under them a thin flat-hinged board with holes for the buttons to come up through; you scrubbed them down with salt and vinegar water.

After that you were free to write letters or play seven-up or rinse out the gray wool socks Ma had knitted or pick up your clean clothes from one of the two enlisted men's wives who ran the laundry, or shine up your flat-heeled calf boots. Or you could sleep, like the Mexicans did, through the hottest part of the day. Or you could count over if you'd managed to save enough out of your thirteen dollars a month to buy maybe a bright striped or checkered cotton shirt, which the army for some mysterious reason let you wear in place of gray flannel during the summer months.

But you still had to be ready, no matter what you were doing. Generally, late in the afternoon, it was just stable inspection, and nobody got bothered by that except the men on stable detail and the horses, most of which were geldings because stallions and mares were too much trouble when they got to feeling loving. But every once in a while Degnan made it so rough it jarred your spine when you heard the bugle sound off, and you ran like hell for full pack drill.

That meant not only a precise six-thickness folding of saddle blanket and saddling up; that meant the whole works: filling the prairie belt which held your ammo by thimble webs, rigging your blanket with a change of underwear and sometimes a dog tent, and a canvas 'paulin to roll behind the cantle of the leather-covered McClellan, with your mount's feed bag slipped over one end of the roll. It meant complete saddlebag gear: curry comb and brush, extra ammo, spare horseshoe and nails, coiled rope, a four-teen-inch iron picket pin, flint and steel. And you never knew until you got there whether this was drill or whether you were going to move out. If it was the latter you had to draw rations, a pound of bacon or pork for each day's march, hardtack, coffee, sugar, salt, dried beans or peas.

You hooked up your thirty-six-inch saber, guard to the rear, stuck your Springfield .50–.70 Government into your carbine sling, holstered your Colt .44 butt forward on the right, snapped your canteen to a belt ring, and then you were ready. And the Old Man would go down the line, when you never looked sharper, and his eyes would apparently see nothing but the yellow half stripe bordered in red which said you had five years' service, and he would say, your chevrons are worn, trooper. Replace them. And you would wonder why the devil you bothered shining your boots.

There was one thing: they would have gone to hell and come back if the Old Man told them to.

After sundown dress parade there were still guard details and sentry and mess duties. But it was good when they stood under the flag and the coolness came across the land and the sky paled and then went the color of green apples along the broken skyline, sometimes after a sunset that was like something had set the whole of heaven on fire. It was very quiet on the post, and when the flag came down the bugle sang slow and sad and sweet. It was quieter than usual, because the men knew what had happened. They did not know precise details, but the rumor ran like a dust storm, and then it was no longer rumor but truth. Because of the Old Man, who was tough and smart and unerringly fair, and because of the son, who was a chip off the old block and got showed no favoritism whatsoever by his pa, there was a thing like a funeral in the offing hanging heavy here and clutching at men's hearts. Old Sergeant Stern, who had been at the battle of Apache Pass before he transferred to Degnan's command, had broken two second knuckles on his left hand, smashing it into a dobe wall.

Linus took it, upright and drained and sick, trying not to let it show. His troopers could not look at him; it was like looking on an ache that reached out and took hold of them, too. Degnan was tight-lipped and put them through full pack drill twice in two days, and they were glad for it.

Bleeker, with his sketchbooks, had gone with a patrol escorting supply wagons, east to San Simon, where the telegraph was. Linus went into Tucson on the second night. Men grouped and talked in low tones when they saw him; a few came, without questions, and spoke to him grimly, with sympathy. But he had no answer, and the eyes and voices of men ran along his back when he turned it, walking down the night street. He thought he was not purposely asking company, but he felt better when he found Willson at the bar in the Quartz Rock.

"Howdy, Linus," Willson said.

"*Buenos*," Linus said wearily, leaning on the bar. The bartender brought him a reddish bottle. "What's that for?" he said.

The man looked at it, not at him. "It's on the house, Lieutenant."

For a moment Linus thought of telling him he didn't need it or want it or what it implied. But because of what it implied he said, "Thanks, Bill." The bartender slid him a glass and he filled it, and Willson's.

"Christ, it's hot in here," Willson complained. He took out a grimy handkerchief and wiped his face. The place was full and noisy, and from outside, where a Mexican woman was dropping ropes of dough into oil, a stinking smoke filtered in. Three troopers were drinking in a corner, avoiding Linus' eye. Linus drank his whiskey and said, "They made it by tonight."

"Sho," Willson said. He looked into his glass morosely. "They prolly palaverin' right now."

"You think so." Linus watched his long sad face. The thought made him begin to sweat and itch, but there was something else, too, a kind of hopefulness that felt windy and clean.

Willson said, "Listen, Linus. John Shafter ain't Jesus Shafter."

"I never said he was," Linus said.

"Didn't want you thinkin' it," Willson said. Then he said, "How's your pa?"

"He's all right." Linus refilled his glass; sweat was running down his face now. A hand touched his arm and a voice said, "Lieutenant."

He turned. Will Oury was standing there, and the Mexican, Jesús Elias, and a burly Irish teamster named Kiernan. Oury said, "Is it true what we hear, Lieutenant?"

Linus looked at him, and then at the handsome affluent Mexican teamster boss and then at the red shock-haired, freckled Kiernan. "Have a drink, Will," he said. "What did you hear?"

Oury said, "We heard your fiancée was on that Mexican coach."

"That's right," Linus said.

"And a Mexican woman," Elias said.

"That's right. You gentlemen have a drink. It's on the house."

"Thanks, no," Oury said. "I'm not trying to horn in, Lieutenant. But I don't want you to think this isn't our business. It is." He pushed his hat farther back on his head, disclosing neatly combed gray hair. "It's the business of everybody in Arizona Territory."

"It helps to know you feel that way, Will," Linus said.

"We want to know what's being done about it."

"Everything that's humanly possible."

Jesús Elias struck himself softly on the leg with the rawhide quirt he carried. Under the brim of his big Mexican concha-ringed hat his eyes were very bright and alert. "It is the business of my people, too, Lieutenant," he said.

"We've sent word to Sonora," Linus said.

Oury was impatient. "I think you miss the point." He said again, "We want to know what's being done."

Linus said, "That's under army jurisdiction, Will. I don't have to tell you that."

Elias's bright eyes moved back and forth, from Oury to Linus. "That is why we want to know, Lieutenant. The military seem to be establishing some kind of secret routine here. We aren't happy with it." He spoke quickly, taking small frequent breaths. "The military is supposed to be protecting the Mexican population. That was a promise your government made to us."

Linus said evenly, "I'll tell you what, Señor Elias, you get together all your people strung out over Arizona Territory and put them in one place, and we'll detail a guard over them. Nobody said you had to stay here. There's no law you can't go back over the border."

Elias's face was white. "Are you telling us to get out?"

"I'm telling you that somebody's Washington pipedream underwrote that order. We can't any more protect you than we can protect our own."

"That's quite an admission," Oury said softly.

"You want to write a letter about it or something?"

Oury was angry. "I'm not looking for trouble, Lieutenant. We only wanted you to know we're ready to help out whenever you decide you aren't too proud to ask us. We think you need help."

"Yes," Elias said. "I told your father Amarillo was around. I don't see Amarillo in the post guardhouse."

"It's all those bucks he's got," Linus said. "How many would you say, Señor Elias, forty or fifty maybe?"

"Close to a hundred," Elias said tightly.

Willson had not turned around. He made a snorting sound. He had been with Shafter when Shafter counted Amarillo's ten prime head of warriors. When he snorted, Kiernan said, "Howdy, Willson. Where's your grayback compadres tonight?"

Willson still did not turn around. "Aw, shut up," he said.

Kiernan's broad face flushed and sprung loose. Then he laughed. "By God, ain't you the sociable one," he said. But he had said enough, that first time. Linus saw, right away, that Oury knew.

"Is John Shafter out for you, Lieutenant?" Oury said.

"I don't think I have to answer that, Will," Linus said.

"You just did." Oury's mouth was a thin line. "I want to tell you something. There are men who have been here in this country for a good span. Elias was here before the Stars and Stripes were."

"I owned this town," Elias said.

Oury went on in a voice as thin as he had made his mouth. "We expect to be here after you've gone. And we expect to see this territory so safe a kid can walk out any day, any hour, and pick himself a posy if he wants to."

"What you gone do," Willson said, his back still to them. "Kill off all the sidewinders?"

Oury was watching Linus. "There's a breed of critter crawls lower than a sidewinder. Indian breed. We're going to kill him off. Every last one of 'em. If it takes forever. I only got one thing more to say, Lieutenant. For a man ought to be going through hell-fire now you're right calm and smart. That don't ring true to a man of my mettle."

Elias was still bright-eyed, still switching at himself. "We want those women back, Lieutenant."

"We're going to get them back," Linus said.

"Are you?" Oury said. "With John Shafter? Does John Shafter know all there is?"

"No," Linus said. "He just knows a great deal."

"You are an impressionable man, Lieutenant. As I said, there are those of us here who belong here, who stick here. John Shafter is a renegade grayback reb who has been known to side with Indians and take their part. This man Obre has a streak of blood so black it could be nigger." He resettled his hat. "I expect you think you know what you're doing."

Willson turned around very slowly. He cocked his arms back and set his elbows on the bar. "What about me, Oury?"

"I wasn't talking to you," Oury said.

"If I warn't here you'd be talkin' about me. I'd tread easy was I you."

"Is that a threat?" Oury demanded.

"I got enough *dinero* to pass out to Obre for what he does good," Willson said. "Take it how you want it."

Oury said, "Willson, if you're trying to call me, you're going to find I'm almighty tough. And smart."

"Modest, too," Willson said. "I aim to be just like you when I grow up."

Kiernan burst out, thrusting his red face close to Linus'. "What are you, a goddamn Indian lover, too?"

Linus sized him up. He was a pretty sturdy boy, with a chest like a flour barrel. "I don't say my prayers to you, Kiernan. Why don't you get the hell out of here."

The bartender slid another bottle down the bar. "I don't want any trouble in here, boys." Linus glanced past Oury and saw the three troopers in the corner were tensed, unable to hear over the noise but looking their way. "No trouble," he said.

But Kiernan was saying, "One of these days somebody's goin' to whittle you down to a stub, shavetail. I hope to hell it's one a them Indians you love so much."

"Shut up, Kiernan," Oury said. "Would you care to make a little wager with me, Lieutenant?"

"No," Linus said.

The answer startled Oury. He took a step back. Linus did not even evince curiosity. To have asked the subject of the wager and then refused, Oury could have taken, but this thing was more insulting than anything Linus had said. Turning, he could not hold back. "If you change your mind, come around. I stand to make a pile on the bet you never see your woman again. And I expect you'll find out before then who your friends are."

"*Adiós*, Indian lover," Kiernan said.

They went out. Willson sighed heavily, as if it was an effort. "Goddamn," he said. "I am sure powerful tired of hearin' Indian lover, Indian hater all over this here country. Sometimes I wisht I'd of never left Texas." In the sad horse face there was something sadder, but no rancor. "That mule-dung pitcher, Kiernan. Some day

I'm gone to kick his goddamn teeth so far down his throat he'll bite hisself first time he goes to the outback."

"I don't get it," Linus said.

"How's that?"

"Will Oury. Elias. Sure, I can see what they mean. They have been here a long time, but they haven't got any claim on the place. They're important men here. They ought to be bigger."

Willson pondered. "I figure once a man's soul gits shriveled ain't nothing gone to make it grow again."

"Why do they hate Shafter?"

"They got to hate somebody. Wasn't Shafter it'd be somebody else. Shafter don't hold hisself mighty, but he won't git yeasty with 'em. That's the real reason. They set around and study who likes Indians and who don't. They're the original honest-to-God only good Indian dead Indian hombres."

"They really believe that?"

"Sho," Willson said. "A sight of men do. There's men likes Indians says they know 'em and men hates Indians says they know 'em, and they all talkin' hogwash. You can study on 'em and see how they run things, so's you can tell how to handle yourself with 'em and how to please 'em and how to keep from steppin' on their toes, but there ain't no way to know an Indian less you can git inside him."

The words made Linus shiver. When Willson went on, the shiver slipped into a racking chill. "The only thing you can perdict safe about an Indian is how unperdictable he is. You think you got it all figured exactly what he's gone to do and, by damn, he goes and does the exact rear of it. I never knowed whether he done it to confuse you or if he didn't know hisself what he wanted to do."

Linus was frowning. "But they're men. I believe they're rational men."

"Ain't said otherwise, Linus. I just go by the sum total that when they're peaceable they're as quiet a passel of hombres as you could want around, and when they ain't they're about the meanest critters you ever come acrost. I don't neither like 'em or not like 'em. Don't see no sense in doin' either. And when you start playin' around with that sum total, you know what you find out? You find out Oury's a stripe of the same cut."

Linus said, "You played it close with him, Willson."

"Close, but neat," Willson said. "Kiernan's drummed a near fight with Shafter a couple of times. He might be sorry if it rolls his way. He's got a power of weight there, but his brains roll round like tumbleweeds. He picks at me, too, now and then. I reckon either of us could take him in the long haul, fist-up style, but if he messes around Obre he's gone to have a lead breakfast."

"Elias puts him up to it."

"I reckon. That dude greaser can smell Indian a foot away. He's scared of Obre. That shows good sense. Obre's pa got kilt down to the Alamo three days 'fore he was borned, so he don't love greasers none either. And Oury, I reckon he warn't as happy as he might of been to see us rebs take Tucson awhile back, so he's got a nose for Confederate blood. He kind of snuffs us out for the simple joy of tellin' us we're Indian lovers. Ain't nothing lower."

Willson poured himself another drink. "I see a minute ago you wasn't a gamblin' man," he said, "but it might of been the comp'ny. You want to gamble with this critter?"

"Sure," Linus said.

"I will bet you, for nothin', that Jesús Elias and Will Oury are out to the post right now tellin' your pa how he's messed things up for certain and givin' him the benefit of their experience."

"My father can handle it," Linus said.

"You sure? I seem to recollect he took off after Amarillo when there warn't much call for it. And I also study your pa don't cotton to Shafter."

Linus was about to protest, but that was not fair. He looked at Willson squarely. "My father respects Shafter. He believes Shafter knows what he's doing."

Willson nodded. "I been wrong before. If I was you I'd watch Kiernan."

"He was drunk," Linus said.

"I don't think so. Them micks flush up when they git riled so's it's hard to tell."

"I'll watch."

"You leavin'?" Willson said. "You want comp'ny gone out?"

"I'd rather go alone." Linus hesitated. The questions were gray and burned as ash in his mouth, but he did not ask any of them. There could be only token acknowledgment. It was better not to let yourself think, if you could, of the three men camped in the pass and of what they might be saying. When he started for the door, the troopers rose but he shook his head negatively; he didn't need nursemaiding.

Outside there was commotion, laughter, and advice. An old prospector had tripped in a pothole. At its lip an enduring burro waited. The old man's eyes were shiny with outrage. Nobody moved to help him. Linus pushed through and hauled him to his feet. "Thanks, sonny," the old man said through a stained bush of beard.

"You hurt, grandpa?" Linus said.

"Takes more'n a sight of hole to bust me up," the old man said. "Yellowlegs, ain't ye?" He dusted himself off with short impotent swipes at his breeches. "I got me a little poke," he said. "Buy you a drink."

"You keep your poke," Linus said. "Just watch where you're going."

"Hell, I've fell in better holes most anywhere you could name," the old man said. "I mind one time in the Dragoons. . . ." He whirled on a grinning Mexican. "What in all-fired hell you toothin' at, you bug-eyed monkey?" He whirled back on Linus. "I tell you something, sonny. I ain't gone to buy you a drink after all. I'm gonna save this here poke and add to it and clean up sight enough to buy me some powder and blow this goddasted pebblo clear to Orygon."

Linus had him by the arm and was drawing him off. He thought the old man might be drunk, or maybe just older than the hills. The burro followed them, moving patiently under its load of gear. "What's your name?" Linus said.

"Cecil Horne. Mostly folks call me Cec. What's yourn?"

"Linus Degnan."

"Your padre the nantan out to the fort?"

"That's right," Linus said. "How long you been out, Cec?"

"A spell." He took off his hat. He looked as if he was trying to remember. "Wintered down on the Gila."

"You mentioned the Dragoons. Do you know them?"

You expected his voice to come out in a cackle, but it was strong and deep and booming. "Know 'em? Why, sonny, I know 'em like the hairs on my chest. All them hills. All this country."

Linus was shoving him farther off the street. "Do you know where Cochise holes up?"

The old man looked at him queerly. "Reckon so. I never had a invite in."

"How long you going to be around?"

"Not long. Few days, mebbe. I crave to bend my elbow and I'm short on vittles."

"Where are you heading?"

"I ain't studied on that yet."

"Will you do me a favor?" Linus said.

"Sure, sonny. You raised me up, didn't you?"

"Before you go, will you come out to the post and see me?"

"Sure," Horne said.

"It might be important."

"I figger so or you wouldn't say it."

Linus stood watching him. A few days. Shafter should be back, one way or another. If he was going to make it back. If he wasn't, this old man knew his way around every humpbacked cactus from here to New Mexico, or so he let on. There was a half-formed all wild scheme in Linus' mind. He held out his hand. "Thanks, Cec. You won't forget?"

"Sonny, if I had forgittin' habits I wouldn've lost meself years agone."

"You hang on that poke," Linus said.

"Don't sound like you trust me much," Horne said. "I'd like to see any buster git it away from me."

He turned toward the Quartz Rock. The burro lowered its eyes and shifted its slender legs and settled to wait.

Six

Shafter rolled a cigarette and lit it without bothering to cup the tip and lay back with his head on his saddle. The fire had died down for cooking, but Charley Tom built it up now with greasewood and let it get bright. The smell of cooking had died away; Charley Tom was scouring the frying pan with sand. "You're a hell of a cook, Charley," Shafter said lazily.

"Cook beef good," Charley Tom said. He was agreeable, because he wasn't anxious for Shafter to send him anywhere, any time. "Army no give beef. All goddamn time eat pig." He was mad there wasn't any jerky in the stuff the mess had given him. "Tell cook put pig in ear," he said thoughtfully.

Shafter lay looking up at the sky. There wasn't one star up there that wasn't fixing to swim down and fall right in your eye if you looked at it long enough, including the far ones you could locate out of the periphery of your sight but couldn't see when you looked straight at them. The moon wasn't up yet, but there was a spreading white glow that said it wasn't far off. Shafter posed himself a problem: say you could see, straight on, those far stars, instead of having to look for them sidewise. Would you see, if you looked sidewise again, more stars? And on and on, like an image within an image within an image. There wasn't much to reassure a man at the idea of stars piled on stars so far out you finally lost track of the whole thing; it could probably drive you loco if you thought about it long enough. He stopped thinking about it. He raised up and tossed Charley Tom the cigarette makings. "Very good, John," Charley Tom said. He was killing himself to be *simpático*. Shafter half wished he would be his natural sullen self.

They smoked without talking. They were deep in the pass, deeper than either Charley Tom or Obre liked, with rock shafting up on both sides. Nobody could have asked a better place to be snared like a rabbit. Shafter was staking it all.

Obre came in, the convex surfaces of his face glistening in the front light the fire threw on him. Beyond him a coyote made short yipping sounds and was answered in kind. Shafter turned his head on the saddle and said, "You lookin' for Indians, it's late for them."

"Indians, hell, I ain't keen on some sidewinder decidin' he wants to get warm with me," Obre said. He was looking up at the battlements which prisoned him here. He knew, as well as Shafter did, that they were watched. He would have felt better if he was sure of the number of eyes. He took the black Mex tobacco and paper from Charley Tom and rolled a cigarette, hunkering by the fire. "You ain't got the sense God give a vinegarroon," he said. "Boots off. Saddle ten feet off your horse. Belt unbuckled. You ever try to drag a gun out of a unbuckled belt?"

"All the time," Shafter said. His eyes were closed. "I should of brought a fistful of Degnan's cigars."

"Why sure," Obre said. "And a rocker chair and a chamber pot and a Mex *puta*." He inhaled deeply, letting the smoke out his thin nostrils. "I'll take first watch."

Shafter sunk his cigarette in the sand and rolled over in his blanket, pulling the saddle with him and shifting his gun belt. "Anybody drops in, wake me," he said.

"Ha, very good, John," Charley Tom said.

Obre breathed deep, hearing a wheeze in his chest from the hot harsh cigarette. "Go to sleep, will you, Charley. I won't let nothing get you."

Charley Tom rolled up with his hat on.

Shafter wasn't asleep. He heard Obre go around the circle a couple of times, checking the horses, coming back, smoking maybe to keep himself awake, although Shafter thought probably he couldn't sleep anyway. There wasn't any danger now. They could have been had, three hours ago, in still daylight. If it was going to be bad it would come at dawn. Otherwise, it would be full morning, or maybe they would be let sit on their tails here till they starved to death. When that happened it would be time to send Charley Tom up. He didn't want to do that if he didn't have to.

The moon came all of a sudden, like it had been jerked up on a string. It was better in a lot of ways, seeing the rock get silvered and pockets of light begin to deepen on the ground. The black rock got blacker in places, and in other places it looked as if you could shave in it, and the scrub turned furry, with its outlines blurred and softened. There were softnesses in this country. Some men didn't think so, seeing the endless scrub-dotted sand and windswept mesas and brassy sunlight. Most men like that didn't stay, but passed on to greener places and so never knew the miracle of the desert and the high wooded canyons and the lakes the sky dipped into. For some men, just that foreverness of sky and land was too much to bear, and they looked without belief and went away and the country never missed them. Right now Shafter had a feeling in him that when he ended it up it would be out here someplace. He had had this feeling for some time. Living creatures would live a little longer because of your flesh, and your bones would lie bleached and comfortable in the sand. In the spring maybe the bright young flowers would come around you and a spider might make a home where your brain used to cradle, and keep you company. You could always see the sky that way, the massed clouds passing the sun, the life-giving rains coming, the close stars pricking out one by one and springing in green clusters. It would be good. He wished he could be certain of it.

He wanted to find a woman and while he didn't overlook any possibilities it always turned out thin and hollow. If he only could, he reckoned he would set up a little spread and be easy for the rest of the time allotted him. He dreamed this always when he lay awake, but he dreamed it less and less with the months coming on shorter every circuit of the year. When he thought about a woman a restlessness like a burning lodged in him, so he could never think of any particular woman except the one he had been married to and known so little that sometimes the only thing he remembered distinctly was coming home after seven rotten months, in the middle of the night, shouting her name all the way up the path, and her meeting him laughing and crying and all the time him sort of wildly swinging and turning and working her back to the bedroom, like two people in a crazy dance. Then she died. It was a hell of a thing to leave a man with only that one clear memory. There was never anything more than that night and he had quit fooling himself there was ever going to be.

The moon seemed to be rising very swiftly, pushing stars out of its way.

It was still dark when Charley Tom shook him, and he knew by the chill sweet smell it was the darkness before dawn, and his watch. Charley Tom had built up the fire again, and he moved closer to it, running his tongue over his teeth and spitting to get the sleep taste out of his mouth. He pulled on his boots and buckled up and told Charley Tom to lie down and lie ready.

"You awake, Ob?"

"Most of the goddamn night," Obre said. He reached down and loosened the Dances and watched Shafter. It was cold, always coldest before sunrise, somehow. The moon was an old whitening husk and the stars were going off behind some changing darkness. The field of sky which had been black as velvet was a black with substance now, as if it had been pitched over. Shafter got out the big tin bucket and set it close to boil. He was going to make coffee. A lot of coffee.

There were maybe fifteen minutes, while the dark drained out of the sky, that he squatted motionless. The horses slept and there was a cold quiet like there must be at the bottom of a lake. Then birds began and a finger of sunlight moved tentatively across the east-facing rock and began to widen.

Obre rolled out. They had made it.

The sun was high when Charley Tom said, "They come now." Shafter lifted his head, as if he tested for a smell which was beyond doubt, Indian smell, but it was not there. Something had tipped Charley Tom, maybe the *simpático* he worked so hard for and never reached with white men, and it wasn't sound because there wasn't any metal on Indian ponies to bell on rock.

They came down the pass, mounted, at a slow trot, about ten of them, with no lances and no paint. Shafter stood up and waited. Within twenty feet of the fire they held the ponies in with the braided rawhide hackamores. Shafter put up his hand, flat out. His guess had been good: it wasn't Cochise, it was Victorio.

"Howdy, Victorio," he said.

After a moment Victorio said, *"Buenos días."* He moved his pony forward slightly. "Shafter?" he said.

Shafter didn't move. *"Sí."* He motioned to Charley Tom. "Tell him long time since we meet. Ask him if he remembers we passed through last year when he was at Ojo Caliente. Tell him we have plenty coffee."

While Charley talked that spitty-sounding talk with its heavy breaths and sudden glottal stops and peculiar softnesses, Shafter eyed the Apache cadre. He knew Delgadito and Pionsenay. Then, at the tail, he spotted Joaquin. When Charley finished, he said, "Tell them we are at peace but poor. No presents but plenty coffee."

Victorio dismounted and the bucks followed, handing the ponies over to one man. When they came to the fire, carrying their carbines, Charley Tom began to rack out the tin cups. "Sit," Obre said in fluent Apache. "We are happy to see our Mimbres brothers. Have coffee, make talk."

They sat. Victorio said, "You drink coffee first."

Shafter complied, burning his mouth. If the coffee was poisoned, he would drop dead before Victorio's suspicious eyes. Probably Victorio hoped he would. When he remained upright, cursing his scalded mouth, they accepted the coffee. He ignored Joaquin. Maybe Victorio had figured he was going to need Joaquin, but Shafter didn't push it.

When Victorio had finished his coffee he said, "Which way are you, Shafter, a brave man or a fool?"

Shafter didn't give him an inch. He spoke and Victorio spoke and Charley ran it back and forth. Shafter said, "You saw we came in peace. I don't break my word."

Victorio's fine chiseled upper lip lifted a little. "What do you want?" he said.

Shafter hesitated. Then he made a decision. He was not going to stand on ceremony. "A few days ago two women were taken off a stage at Dragoon Springs," he said. "One of them was a Mexican woman gone to Sonora. The other belongs to the army post at Tucson. We're lookin' for them."

There was silence. The bucks sat motionless, not even bending to their cups, or passing them, as they had done a moment ago. Shafter let his glance go over Joaquin and saw the light eyes as cold and clear and suave as a winter sky lock on his own. He thought he might find some betrayal in the half breed, but he figured not. Joaquin's padre was up in the Tucson graveyard, and Shafter remembered once Joaquin had come in to see where the old man lay. He seemed pretty white then; right now he looked more *Tá-ashi* than Victorio. Before he looked away he saw there was something in Joaquin's eyes after all. He could only interpret it as a sort of accusing, and he thought, don't look at me, boy, I didn't stud you.

When he had decided the silence was long enough, Victorio set down his cup. Shafter knew the silence hadn't been because Victorio was studying what to say, but just for effect. When he finally spoke, Shafter had to hand it to him.

"We have the women," Victorio said.

Shafter nodded, letting Victorio know he already knew this. He said, "There is sadness at the post."

Victorio smiled slightly. "And anger."

"More sad than mad," Shafter said. "The women are very young and come from a place where there are many nantans and thousands of white eyes. They ain't used to the ways of the *cihéné*."

"When The People are taken by the white eyes they are forced to learn the ways of the white eyes," Victorio said.

Shafter thought a moment. "But in their hearts, inside, they can't accept it. They can't change. The white eyes can't be Apache and the Apache can't be white eyes."

Victorio did not answer. His glance shifted and came to rest on Charley Tom.

Charley Tom talked rapidly on his own and told Victorio he was true Apache inside. Shafter missed it, but Obre laughed and Charley Tom looked at him with hatred.

Shafter said, "What price do you ask for the *niñas*, Victorio?"

"For the *Nakaiyi*, forty horses and twenty woven blankets. Six cases of cartridges for the *carabinas* and the mules to carry them. *Nakaiyi* silver for our women."

Shafter half whistled. It was a stiff price. The Mex girl's padre would pay it with joy, pay a hundred horses if he had to. And Linus would parcel out the whole United States Army without batting an eye. It was Degnan would have half a fit at the idea of this kind of barter. He said, "And for the American *niña?*"

"There is no price," Victorio said.

Shafter misunderstood him. His instinctive reaction was that Victorio was throwing the girl in for free. He felt a momentary surprise and then it came home to him and he could have kicked himself. When he spoke it was with a new hardness. "Maybe the *cihéné* don't understand. I ain't askin' for myself. If I wasn't here now there would be soldiers at both approaches to the Stronghold. This wouldn't be a good thing for The People."

"Nor for the soldiers," Victorio countered. "If there are as many white eyes in this country as you are so quick to tell us there are, you would need them all, including the old and sick. What man is this nantan that he would threaten such a thing?"

"A brave man. He wants this woman back. He is willing to pay any price you ask. He does not want to send troops against you."

"It is his death to do so," Victorio said.

Shafter knew what he was saying: it was the girl's death. But he couldn't let it pass. "The *niña* is to be the squaw of the nantan's son," he said. "She is very dear to him. He is rich and would not consider any demand you made too high."

"She is not for sale," Victorio said.

Shafter gritted his teeth. "Why are you willing to release the *Nakaiyi* and not the *americana?*"

"That is for me to know," Victorio said.

He made himself shrug. "The woman means nothing to me. I can't think what you might gain by holdin' her. Except maybe a lot more white eyes soldiers on your trail every time you move. The soldiers are like you when something happens to one of their own. They make up for it."

"The nantan's threat passes through me like the wind of the bean," Victorio said.

Shafter changed his tactics. "When do you go to Ojo Caliente?"

"As soon as the goods are delivered for the *Nakaiyi,*" Victorio said.

"Will you be ready to bargain again for the woman?"

Victorio said, "After she has become one of us, perhaps we will send her back to the nantan."

Shafter fought his anger. "What will your price be?"

"I have not thought."

Obre said suddenly, "The nantan will release any Apache prisoners in his charge."

Victorio swung his head and looked at him. "He holds no Mimbreños." He stood up. He was not without pity and he respected Shafter because he detected no sign of flinching, no lie, no show of anger in him. "The white eyes woman is well," he said gruffly. He could have let the nantan grieve but there was too much honor in him for that. "She does not lower her head."

Shafter watched him. To thank him for that small thing would be a weakness. He said, "I will give your word to the nantan."

"You know it is my word," Victorio said.

"Yes."

"Will the nantan know it?"

"I'll see he knows it."

Victorio stood looking at him. He was tall for an Indian, strongly built, with a settled muscularity. When he looked at Shafter he thought Shafter was a good man. He said, "Do not stay here in this pass tonight."

Shafter got to his feet. "We go now. We will bring the goods for the *Nakaiyi* in a week's time. After that, unless we are under the flag, if you see me again it'll be against you, Victorio."

"*Enju,*" Victorio said. There was a light in his eyes, almost a warmth. "It is not good that men must fight for no thing."

"I don't reckon we can call this no thing," Shafter said.

"I will single you out," Victorio said.

"I'll be ready," Shafter said.

Victorio was on the pony, knees bent to the wild sinewy thing. It was in Shafter to speak to Joaquin, but then he knew that there was nothing to say. Joaquin had been brought deliberately, but it was hard to say why Victorio went to all the trouble. No palaver with him, not a word spoken. Christ, it was frustrating not to be able to ask anything or request that some message be taken to the girl. He couldn't let himself do that.

They were gone. Charley Tom began to gather up the cups. It was impossible to tell anything from his face except that it looked natural again in its malicious sulky set.

Obre was saddling, his mouth tight. "Well, that tears it," he said.

Shafter was silent.

"Ain't you got no pity for that poor goddamn girl?" Obre said, suddenly on the verge of fury.

"Yes," Shafter said. "I got all the pity in the world for her, but I ain't gone to spend the rest of my life edgin' into Apache camps tryin' to talk 'em out of her."

"Nobody said for you to. That's the first time I hear you give way what's in your mind, Shafter, that big buck must've edged you up some."

"Hump it, Charley," Shafter snapped.

They kicked the horses out. "Old Degnan would turn green and breed maggots he could hear all them promises we made for him," Obre said. "Ain't nothin' gone to hold him in now. I lay you he hightails it right down to Ojo Caliente."

"They ain't gone to Ojo Caliente," Shafter said.

Obre shot him a sidewise glance. "What the hell you mean? He said he was, didn't he?"

"That's how I know he ain't gone there. If he'd of been gone there, he would of said he was gone to Santa Rita."

"You done that on purpose," Obre said.

"Couldn't you see he wasn't gone to tell us anything?"

Obre said apologetically, "Well, we got the Mex girl off. Can't say I'm exactly glad happy to think of comin' out here again."

"No law you got to," Shafter said.

"I reckon I will though," Obre said.

Shafter thought he didn't want to have to hear what Degnan was going to say. Degnan had had high hopes, and so did he, but neither of them were fools. It was Linus he didn't want to have to face up to. Linus could easy come a fool. That made a kind of hole in him, and he knew inside he was a coward for that. Plus which he didn't want anybody to put him in the position of having to say he thought Victorio was honest and just and subtle and intelligent and proud, not in that personal pride which makes a man so lowdown his own ma can't stomach him, but in the same manner of pride a lion takes because he's a lion or a Texican because he's worn gray. It wasn't so hard to separate pride in a lone ant of a man and pride in an idea.

He was tired, dead aching tired, and full of something he defined as anger, but which was really the sapped-out hollow ache of futility. It wasn't his fight. But there was the idea. Or maybe he meant the ideal. There was a fine shining empty word for you. Victorio was an idealistic man. So was Walter Degnan. There would be, between them, an unswerving abiding by the rules, dissimilar as the rules might be: Victorio's were more flexible and tended to work to his own advantage; Degnan, chafed by the strictures of a militant society, would adhere to his but work in little resiliencies wherever he could. Then, straight unwatered honesty. On that score, Victorio would have his heart cut out before he would deviate an inch, but Degnan might employ all sorts of harmless minor treacheries to gain honestly an honest end, and still stay within bounds. Honesty, after all, was how you happened to be looking at it, and from where. And bravery. Cowardice wasn't pretty, but bravery was mostly a stupid thing, and an odd thing, too, because it wasn't as a rule too self-sustaining and yet if you made a practice of it, or even evinced one instance of it, it seemed to sustain other people.

He wanted to remember that you couldn't pit these two men in these three things because one was a civilized man sprung from generations of civilized men, and one was a man about equal parts viciousness and generosity, with a salting of unalterable good sense. He wanted to remember that there could be no comparison and no compromise between men whose codes were at opposite ends of the pole, particularly when one wanted nothing more than to be left alone and the other could no more stand to be left alone than a longhorn in a twister. But his memory wasn't too good sometimes any more, and he thought maybe Victorio had the edge.

Seven

The water ran cold and swift here, but Anna did not dare go to the still pool, which was out of sight of the main camp. Wind was singing in the pines which lanced up along the canyon; the chalky trunks of the sycamore pressed close, hanging fragrant. Waist-deep in the water, she lathered her hair with the soapy white substance of yucca root, which was nearly as good as Pears' soap, and plunged in. When she came up, the soaked buckskin clinging to her, the children had lined the bank and were watching delightedly.

"*Hola*," she said, short of breath.

"*Hola*," they chorused back. They were quite friendly now, from a distance, regarding her with curiosity and amusement. Their mothers bathed in the pool and never with their clothes on.

Pionsenay's wife and Ysabel were up on the bank, grinding corn with stone metates smoothed and shaped by the running water. Neither of them appeared to notice her. Ysabel's face was badly sunburned; the creamy skin which had barely tasted sun was covered with tiny white blisters. Anna turned dark quickly, but her hands were raw and sore from the unaccustomed labor with primitive instruments.

The sun was on a long red late-afternoon glide down the sky and coolness was coming in from the high places. She waded part way out of the water and smelled the smoke of the cook fires and was hungry. Ysabel did not look up: her bent shoulders moved jerkily and her face, even from this angle, was petulant. She was very slow at any task she was set at, and there was no pretense about this. She never hung back, out of fear, but she never seemed to finish. One reason for that, Anna thought, might be that there didn't seem to be any foreseeable end to the work. Food was constantly being gathered and prepared, yucca stalk roasted and its flowers dried for sweetening, mescal crowns harvested and baked, firewood brought in: mesquite roots, which burned hot but slowly and died to a good lasting bed, clothes to be sewn, hides to be scraped, cooking vessels to wash. She had found that what you could learn at all you could master.

She was possessed of a childlike interest in the role she had been forced to assume, and the increasing reassurance that no physical violence was to be visited upon her served to encourage her. But she was homesick: not for the aunt's shining house, not for the sight and sound of city, but for the pueblo she had never seen, the bare army post which lay so near. They had taken on the proportions of paradise. She felt now that homesickness might be the most terrible sickness of all: it was capable of killing. In the night she thought, but Linus is down there . . . *he is down there,* and did not really believe it. She had not seen him for a year and yet it was as if she had only now been torn away from him. Then again, that flame of expectancy which the vedette had fed . . . the news of someone coming . . . had long since died to ash. Somebody might have been coming, well enough, but it had not been for her. What she believed was that if only she could also be assured that nobody was coming for her, ever, she would at least have something to accept. Acceptance was the essential thing. She could recall, as a child, a puppy which had inexplicably vanished, as if from the face of the earth. She was old enough to have borne the fact of its death, but she never knew, and she had been in anguish to know. The environment which had bred her had left her more practical than vulnerable, and she did not really consider her predicament cruel, but only absurdly ill contrived and stupid and inconvenient. She had even thought simply of attempting to walk down the corridor, out of this place, to see what they would do. But the thin red line which glowed jewel-like on Ysabel's forehead served notice that these people would brook no rebellion. As it was, she was afraid of displeasing the women, knowing they were wont to torment their female captives as a matter of course. That she had been spared was paradoxical, but she did not contemplate it too far and strove to maintain a balance between calm obedience and undismayed self-reliance which added up, in its own quiet way, to spunk.

Going home, a bird sang joyously. She whistled back, without thinking. Pionsenay's wife looked up at her and the children were momentarily silent, staring. She was abashed, who had only whistled at a bird. Struggling to braid her hair, she braced against the water. The current was very fast here. It was the pull of it which had first made her consider suicide. The arguments against this were that she knew Linus would arrive moments after they had recovered her body (if, indeed, they bothered to do so) and the fact that nothing really terrible enough to warrant suicide had happened yet.

She was not certain how many days she had been here, and Ysabel was no help. Ysabel barely spoke. Anna's patience was wafer thin, but she continued to press Ysabel. She knew the problem wasn't keeping up Ysabel's spirit, as Ysabel evidently had not been endowed with any: one would think she didn't care at all, and she cared so shockingly. Quite possibly the Lord did help those who helped themselves.

When she started out of the water, the children began to retreat, laughing. At her, she supposed, but at least they were laughing. She gave them simple greetings in Spanish and they responded, but her tongue could not seem to manage one slithery word of Apache. A little girl said, "Ana," and she said, "Si?" questioningly, and they covered their mouths and danced, teasing. Caught in the jostling merriment of his playmates, a little naked boy slipped off the bank and vanished from sight.

Pionsenay's wife screamed. Her rising was a blur across Anna's eyes before she let the water take her, too. It took her under and out, and she felt an insane moment of doubt that this thing could really happen. She saw the little brown body foreshortened in the water and queerly unresisting. She caught at his ankle and felt it slide out of her grasp, reached again, kept her hold, and fought to find the surface.

When she got her footing she was downstream, close to the shore. She staggered, only partly aware of men running and women crying out, ignoring a keening woman who grabbed for the child. Air felt good in her lungs. She draped the child over her arm, where he hung like a limp wet fish folded in the middle. After a moment, water began to pour out of him, and when that ceased he choked and screamed and she turned him upright. His eyes were wide with bewilderment. When she saw he was breathing normally again she swung him high over her head, until the screaming became laughter.

When she set him down she felt the quiet close around her, thick, stifling. Ankle-deep in the shallows, she saw the set male faces, and when she turned her head it was to Victorio's black attentive inspection. She could hear the wind in the trees and young leaves came down upon her head and she felt trapped between the water and the half circle of unmoving people. She came up and passed them, with her eyes down, and they parted silently and silently let her through. A woman held the clinging child. She went on to Pionsenay's wickiup. Changing into dry clothing, she cried for the first time.

She left the wickiup. Her nerves were hot, jumping. It looked normal outside, but there was still the quiet over everything. She went to Pionsenay's wife and Ysabel and took the grinding stone out of Ysabel's hands.

Ysabel's teeth showed. "How helpful you are, Anna."

She had reached a limit, beyond weariness, beyond anger. The only thing to do was treat Ysabel as if everything was perfectly harmonious between them, which was increasingly difficult. She was certain that Pionsenay's wife was aware of their discord; she saw how the Apache girl looked discerningly from her to Ysabel and back again. Also, Pionsenay's wife was evincing less and less animosity and Anna did not want anything to endanger so promising a potential. The Apache girl's face was always full of interest when Anna spoke. Ysabel did not even raise her eyes, although she let Anna continue with the grinding stone.

Looking at her, Anna saw the marked face and defeated eyes and ugly burned skin. She felt her heart move. She thought, she cannot continue like this. She will lose her mind, perhaps. And what will they do to her then. Because she has lost hope. Anna put down the stone. The woman and the little boy were standing just beyond a sycamore, watching her. She wished they would go away. "Ysabel," she said nervously, "what does she want?"

"To thank you," Ysabel said shortly.

"Oh. Well, that's silly. Anybody would have done it."

"Would they?" Ysabel said. "Isn't he a dear little child? He will grow up and murder your sons."

"It doesn't appear I'm to have any sons," Anna said. The hard stone of hurt rose into her throat. It came with wistfulness at first, then with an appalling urgency. For the first time her eyes clung, without any faith at all, in anything, to the serene puzzled gaze of Pionsenay's wife. "How long have I been here?" she said. The girl looked alert but uncertain. "Ask her, Ysabel."

"Thirteen days," Ysabel said. "Don't you know that? You must be content, Anna. My people say only those who are happy dispense with time. I know it to the second."

When the first of the night moved in from the canyons, Joaquin came to the wickiup. With him were Victorio and Cochise. They were sober and direct; she dreaded facing them. "They want to tell you they are grateful," Joaquin said. "The child is an only son."

She was shy. "He is all right?"

"If it was not for what you did, there would be mourning."

Their steady regard made it more than difficult; she could not look at them.

"They give you the freedom of the ranchería," Joaquin said.

Now she could look at him. For the first time, a long time, they held each other in each other's eyes, and she was shaken and spent in what she counted a victory with distinction, and one which she had in no way intrigued to make possible.

In the morning the stupendous thing happened: they came for Ysabel. Anna was stunned. It was young Mangas Chie who came, and while he spoke good Spanish and a little English he would tell her nothing. He talked to Ysabel and went away.

It was too much: she viciously begrudged Ysabel, hard and malicious in her resentment. Why Ysabel? Ysabel was sobbing great breathy sobs. What Anna had been convinced of was a void, a vacuum, and what Ysabel had doubted had transpired. The sequel to their individual reactions was so out of proportion that Anna lost complete control of herself; the injustice of it smashed and pounded and destroyed the core of civilized conduct and left her raging, without logic or reason.

She begged forgiveness for the terrible things she had said to Ysabel. She protested her intention in harassing Ysabel. She defended herself in things she had neither voiced nor executed, but only thought, and betrayed herself by doing so.

At the last, she pleaded with Ysabel not to leave her. This was the hard thing, the link broken. Never had she been so alone.

When she finished, Ysabel was shaking with emotion. Limp and stupefied, Anna clung to her hands. She said the same things over and over again, and there was something stiff and unyielding in Ysabel when she tried to embrace her, a spiny sharpness that had not been in her when it was most needed.

"Tell them to keep watch," she said. "Tell Linus. Tell them to stay close. If I know they are close. . . ."

Ysabel had already gone away.

"You'll remember?" Anna cried out to her.

"I'll remember," Ysabel said.

A long time afterward she realized that it had been humiliating, degrading, to behave so badly. If they had been able to ransom Ysabel, they would be able to ransom her.

As Shafter had surmised, Colonel Walter Degnan was an idealist. He was the product of an age, a society, and a profession which exalted womanhood, considered chivalry, next to bravery, the highest masculine virtue, and was prepared to die in the defense and preservation of both. His entire life had been what other men called successful: that is, by a chemistry of good fortune and intelligent application he had at no time experienced any particular or extended failure. He had married well and happily, grieved at the death of his wife, reared a son in his own image, or so believed, contributed with distinction to the incredible chaos of a major war, and come through each, seeing each in his own mind as a separate and individual partition of his existence, perhaps a better man. He had no true taste for war, as many good military men do not, but he was cool and practiced in the field and notably competent at the administrative end of the business, an art in itself which is without glory but essential. The war had been, for him, a catharsis, coming as it did hours after the only woman he had ever wanted had gone away from him. The death he saw in battle, those broken bodies, the flower of the nation, the eternal yearning youth with all its dreams gone down to dust, were outside the pale of grief, a never-to-be assuaged hurt carried in the heart like an old wound. Grief was for the gentle people beyond horror: his wife, and Anna's mother, and his oldest friend, Anna's father, who had outwitted Gettysburg and surrendered to an unmilitary finality named pneumonia.

He had been shaped, molded, by the gentle people, and because of them perhaps had learned self-containment in the times another man might fall apart under stress. He had an effective temper and he repressed it marvelously, on the outside, though he was often raw and bleeding within himself. What he strove for most of all was justice, but he was so constructed that it was sometimes difficult for him to hurdle the idea of the contiguous factors involved in the moral arbitration of right and wrong. Fact was what the face wore, and his first sight of Ysabel Vasquez prompted in him a justification for the complete and total destruction of the entire race of red men. Charley Tom was most readily available. He was spurred to strike down the *manso* scout on the spot. It was some time before he got a grip on himself. To kill Charley Tom would not be just, but the roaring campaign of extermination which rose scarlet in his brain was a vindication he must assume and consummate.

He had given Tony Bleeker free rein. Shafter and the correspondent were waiting, while he, Degnan, had an infuriating exchange with Obre.

"Come in, Obre." Holding open the door.

"That's all right," Obre said.

What in God's name did that mean? "Nonsense, man, come in, come in."

"I'd as soon wait," Obre said. He wasn't going to have Degnan do him any favors.

"I think you should be present." What did the gunslinger want, an engraved invitation? Goddamit, I'm doing him a favor.

Obre's eyes unnerved Degnan. It was monstrous for a man not to have two eyes the same color. "I don't reckon you need me." Bitter, amused.

"I insist, Obre. Come in, please."

Neither wanted nor needed, paid off and knowing it, Obre entered for the first time the sanctified realm of the colonel's office. He was uneasy and sat on the edge of a chair and, when he took off his gloves, Degnan saw the finest hands he had ever seen on a human being: separate engines of spare perfect potency, hard, smooth, aristocratic, tendons raised under the tawny skin, long straight tapered fingers with tended nails, powerful and absolute. The hands were an end in themselves. Degnan had heard you could judge a man by his hands. He saw now this was a myth.

The girl sat facing Tony Bleeker, but Degnan, behind his desk, could see, if he chose, her face. He did not choose, having seen her at too close quarters when Shafter and Obre brought her in. Earlier, her father, a handsome grandee of the old school, had arrived from Sonora. He had thirty *rurales* with him, in a gesture somewhat like that of locking the stable door after the horse has been stolen.

That he was not present now had been his own choice: he had spoken privately with his daughter and, having been assured that what he most feared might have happened to her had been a groundless apprehension, had gone off to the church to thank her name saint for his daughter's deliverance, pledge an annual gift to the glory of God if her captors were brought to immediate justice, and light an extravagance of candles to the intercession of the Virgin in the matter of Don Ignacio, who could no longer be held to his vow considering the distressing appearance of his betrothed. He begged that Don Ignacio remember that even Our Lord bore scars.

The girl was trying hard, Degnan thought. Occasionally she made reflexive twitching motions, as if her nerves were strung on wire. It was Linus she looked to most often; his face had the ashy look of bereavement and she was sorry for him.

The person she was sorriest for was herself, but this was in no way apparent. She had convinced Shafter. Her wan smile as Victorio handed her over, her uplifted head, her obvious fortitude, had impressed him. The girl was a thoroughbred and it showed. She moved with grace in the ill-fitting buckskin and she rode proudly, ignoring the men. Shafter could see that despite the sunburn she was a beaut. When that scar drew together properly it wasn't going to detract any as far as he was concerned; he thought it was going to be pretty interesting, exciting even. They left her alone with whatever she was thinking about.

She was thinking about a betrothal contract breached, a sizable fortune out of her hands, the possible impossibility of a passionate if innocent alliance with the magnificent stable boy. It took years to grow a beautiful face and only seconds to ruin it. That was the work of the devil and somebody had to pay for it.

Degnan was saying, "We know what an ordeal it is for you, *Señorita,* but if we are to prosecute this matter we must have all the information you can give us."

Linus almost interrupted his father. "How is Anna, Miss Vasquez?"

She looked at him. "She is well, Lieutenant. She is . . . perfectly all right."

That was when Shafter felt his ears prick.

She was looking intently at Degnan. "I realize you must ask me questions, Colonel. Please don't hesitate. I am ready to help you in any way I can."

Bleeker wrote four fat black words in his notebook. Wonderful courage. Complete co-operation.

"We are distressed to inconvenience you," Degnan said. "But it's important beyond measure to us."

"I know that, Colonel," she said.

"Will you tell us exactly what happened the day of the attack?"

"We were approaching Dragoon Springs," she said composedly. "I had just asked my *rurale* captain the time." Her voice faltered. "He told me and then fell out of the saddle, shot. The Indians attacked and the horses ran off with us."

"What did you do during this time?" Degnan said, biting out the words.

"I told Anna we must get on the floor so there was less danger of being struck."

"Were either of you armed?"

"Anna had a little gun. She had packed it in a valise and could not get to it."

Thank God for small handouts, Shafter thought. All she'd had to do was pop off some buck and she was a very dead girl.

Bleeker wrote, Fine state affairs young ladies armed, this advanced day and age.

"What happened then?" Degnan said.

"We reached the stage station and then they took us." Her face contorted.

"Just dragged you out of the coach?" Degnan said.

"Yes, Colonel."

"Excuse me," Shafter said, "but when we found the coach it was tipped over, ma'am. Were you in it when that happened?"

She looked at Shafter and felt a tremor of uncertainty. Her voice grew firm. "Yes. The impact threw me against the door and I fainted. I was unconscious until we reached their camp."

"What was their attitude toward you?" Degnan said.

Her smile was crooked, acid. "You see my face, do you not, Colonel?"

In the silence Bleeker wrote, On arrival deliberately disfigured.

"What did they do with you and Anna?" Degnan said.

"We were put into one of their houses. Anna cried and I tried to comfort her." She looked at Linus. His face was twisted. "At night one of the Indians began to drink heavily. He came in. . . ." She stopped, drew a breath, and contemplated her hands. "He began to beat me."

Linus was white. "What about Anna?"

"They did not touch Anna."

Shafter uncrossed his long legs and slid down on his spine.

Degnan was filled with outrage, teeth clenched. "Please continue, *Señorita.*"

"In the morning I was made to go to work. If I did not do as I was told I was repeatedly struck and beaten. I need not tell you I did as I was told." She held out both roughened, calloused hands to them, almost in a gesture of supplication.

Bleeker wrote hotly, Beautiful, defenseless, innocent slave.

"But Anna was with you all this time," Linus said. "You were together. . . ."

She put her hands to her face and began to cry softly. There is no awkwardness anywhere such as that which falls upon men in the presence of an anguished weeping woman. Oddly, it was Linus who was equal to it. He went to her and bent over her with the solicitous look of a lover.

"Whatever you believe is going to be difficult for us, we have to know." She raised her face to him; the tears were wet on her cheeks. "This concerns Anna," he said. "No matter what it is, I have to know it."

She whimpered it. "Lieutenant, I would rather die than. . . ." She shrank from him and then regarded him with what he recognized as an ultimate misery. "Anna has been well treated, Lieutenant. At first I thought it was because she is an American and they might fear the troops."

"Go on," Linus said.

"But it was not that. It was . . . there is a man."

"Go on," he said again, hoarse, thick.

Flies made the only sound in the room, a disinterested clamorous buzzing. Her voice was full of catches and glides. "She was given a choice, you see. What I did not understand . . . oh please, must I continue?"

"What didn't you understand?" If his father was still in the room, still conscious, Linus did not know it. He felt a ruthlessness like poison in his veins.

"Anna . . . at first she tried to help me and was very kind and protective. Then, later, when she went with him, it was all changed. She hardly spoke to me." She looked up quickly. "Of course they may have told her not to. When I left she kissed me, but when I asked her what message she wished me to take you she . . . she smiled and said there was no message."

"And what is this man's name?"

"I do not know it, Lieutenant."

After a long time Linus said, "Are you telling me that Anna is with an Apache buck of her own choice?"

She burst into tears.

Linus turned and left the room. Only the presence of men before whom he must maintain a rigid self-domination prevented Degnan, stricken, from following. When Ysabel continued to weep, he called a halt. The girl was in want of rest, and he was in such a state of agitation that he badly needed a drink. After the orderly had taken her to the quarters of the enlisted men's wives, he ordered whiskey. Shafter told him he had a pressing errand and set off with Obre.

When they had gone, Degnan said in a haggard voice, "Tony, I don't have to ask you not to. . . ."

"No, Walter," Bleeker said. "You don't have to ask me that." He was beginning to regret the telegram he had sent to President Ulysses S. Grant.

Degnan hauled a book out of his desk drawer; he had aged ten years in the last fifteen minutes, Bleeker thought. Bleeker was a younger man, but he had not been bound by the restrictions of army life. "Walter, does it occur to you to doubt this girl in any way?" he said.

"Of course not." Degnan was searching through the book. "Why should I? She isn't a stage actress, Tony, she's a sheltered child . . . you know how these Mexicans are. They won't let their girls walk from here to there without somebody in tow." He looked up sharply. "What makes you ask a thing like that?"

"Nothing really," Bleeker said. He reached over and poured himself another drink from the colonel's decanter. "Maybe it's something ingrained . . . in my profession you never take anything at face value."

"In my profession it's all you have to go on," Degnan said. "Listen to this: it's a War Department estimate of the number of lives lost and the amount of U.S. property this man Cochise has stolen over a period of eight years. I'm not citing what the whole nation of these devils has managed to do, I'm telling you about one man: Cochise. Eight million dollars' worth of supplies and horses and mules and gold and army equipment. Four thousand lives. Four *thousand*, Tony." He slammed the book shut. "We've spent nearly thirty-eight million dollars in an Apache extermination program, and every cent of it has been thrown away. Does it seem believable to you that a lone savage who never has more than three hundred fighting men in hand could accomplish such a thing, could trap us and halt us and stick us at every turn? That over two thousand United States cavalry and infantry and artillery are absolutely powerless against him? Do you realize there's not one mile of safe passage anywhere in southern Arizona? Tony, I am a reasonable man. I am accustomed to dealing with reasonable men. What in God's name is the solution?"

Bleeker said, "The estimate doesn't surprise me. Look at the country, look at the size of it. Look at your adversary. He not only knows his terrain like the palm of his hand, he can eke a living out of one square foot of sand. He turns and runs when the odds are against him. What I can't comprehend is the government's stand . . . thirty-eight million, as you say, for extermination. This is the War Department's dictum. Then, on the other hand, we turn around and devise a protection policy through the Department of the Interior. We can't do both, Walter, one cancels out the other, irrevocably. If it's to be war, the only solution is to get them to stand and fight, in the open. Which is absurd, *per se*. Why should they risk that when they can send out three men to terrorize an entire pueblo for a week? Why should they face up to us when they can lead us to believe they're planning a strike at, say, Santa Rita, draw us off all hot to defend it, and then hit Janos? You've a subtle foe on your hands, Walter, and one a lot more artful than you in every respect. And I don't think you are dealing with entirely reasonable men."

"You don't? You think with Oury and Elias that we are beset by a pack of animals and that the only choice is to methodically hunt them down and destroy them one by one?"

"No, I don't believe that. In the first place it's utterly impractical. Now Baylor's scheme. . . ."

Degnan was short with disgust. "John Baylor's scheme ruined him, politically and militarily."

"Which is to Jefferson Davis's credit," Bleeker said. "What would be your reaction if you learned that the Confederate military governor of Arizona Territory had issued orders to get all Apaches in under pretense of a peace treaty, kill every male on the spot, take the women and children captive? Yes, and detail that order to the point of issuing vouchers to defray the cost of the whiskey he planned to use in this courageous coup? God almighty. From there we progess to an eight-year period of tracking and pursuing and killing a single Apache here, two there, three here. Chipping, as it were, at a block the size of Superstition Mountain. Which is inhuman."

"Inhuman! Good God, Tony. . . ."

"Wait a minute," Bleeker said. "Yes, it's inhuman. Do you counter inhumanity with inhumanity?"

"I suppose not," Degnan said bitterly. "I suppose we're endowed with some sort of moral persuasion that we can't lower ourselves to the same level they operate upon. Therefore, if we don't wipe them out we must cuckold and flatter them with the most degrading kindness to attain our ends?"

"Kindness, no," Bleeker said. "I think you treat them with honor. It's the one thing they seem to understand."

"What are we doing wrong?" Degnan said.

"That's easy," Bleeker said. "Our so-called experts are so gravely in error in their approach. Half of them think of it from the standpoint of a red-white alliance, the brotherhood angle. It makes them all soppy inside. It's unrealistic. It's false. There's another faction which is going to effect the cure by understanding the Apache. This is equally unrealistic. Do you know why? Because they end up thinking for him, instead of with him. They can't think with him. Walter, you're dealing with a race which acts, in the main, on impulse. They're a steadfast race, yes: the wrongs dealt them smolder in them for decades, forever, for all I know. . . . They never seem to forget them at any rate. They're still avenging Juan José's death. Cochise is still avenging the braves Bascom hanged. Victorio's still avenging Mangas Colorado. This is the one thing they're constant in. Other than that, they are a mass of incongruities; so much they do is unpremeditated. Good Lord, we can't even understand their mental processes, much less undertake to deal with them on an intellectual basis."

Degnan looked down at the book on his desk. After a moment he rubbed his forehead wearily. "We can put five thousand troops in the field if we have to, and make not one inroad, nothing but dents, in an army of three hundred guerrilla fighters. Our entire westward expansion is at a dead standstill because of them. Yet we've managed to subdue other tribes. . . . Kit Carson had the Navajos signed and sealed with a minimum of trouble."

"The Bartlett Commission had the Apaches pretty well set up, too, don't forget that," Bleeker said. "It was working for a while."

"I know," Degnan said. "You're going over the Bascom story again."

"Not entirely. Bascom was the instrument, the flint that struck the spark, no question. But there are other factors: the main one, probably, is attempting to convert the tiger into a household tabby. Make farmers of people who have never farmed. Establish permanency for the nomad. Subdue a second nature which is warfare. Understand, Walter, they are not a warring race solely for the sake of survival. They take pride in warring; it's done with ceremony, it's near a religious thing with them. There's the sad rub."

"What?" Degnan said.

"The choice we give them. Either we wipe them out or they come to live with us in peace. Our way."

"Is there no other way?"

"No."

"And you believe that they can be assimilated into our society?"

"Admitted, instructed, left to continue as they are, in modified fashion. Assimilated, never. The entire structure of their society, moral, social, religious, whatever, is a world apart from ours. I don't think there can be an equitable rapport with them. Only a mutually advantageous resolving. It's a simple fact: we can't understand them nor can they understand us. Consequently we have no true base to spring from in our dealings with them."

"We have a military basis," Degnan said. "I can't concern myself with a philosophic approach; I'm under military orders."

"Why can't you?" Bleeker said, helping himself to a cigar.

Degnan looked at him from under lowered brows. "Because if I become involved emotionally with them—or in any way outside my orders—it's inevitable that I'll be remiss in my duty. I'm not laced so straight I don't know that, Tony."

"Good for you," Bleeker said, lighting the cigar. "Unhappily, there's got to be some emotional involvement, human nature being what it is. I don't like to see it become the clear-cut right or wrong type we seem to be developing. I don't know what the answer is. But I know it jolly well isn't what we're doing now. What good are your troops, as you say, against men who can disguise themselves as rocks and bushes and shadows, communicate by birdcalls, strike and slip away? There's nothing wrong with our cavalry . . . it does well what it was designed for, offensive tactical mass fighting. It's just that it's never fighting a mass. It's fighting ten, twenty, thirty individual men who are constantly on the move and rarely seen. We are never going to win them this way, Walter."

"Win them?" Degnan said.

"Win them. If we have the riches of Croesus and the life span of Methuselah, maybe we'll finish them with a one-by-one search and annihilation. But they can be won. They were won before. I wasn't here and I know you weren't, but I can remember when Cochise kept the peace. Indeed, when he was the only man of stature in the length of this country. When he gave his word, it made even the men who had talked him into it seem small by comparison. You see what we have done to an intelligent, honorable man in just nine years? I suppose I could be shot at sunrise for saying it, but neither are they wrong, merely because their thought processes don't ride the same groove as ours."

He shifted his portly bulk. "And here are the nantans in Washington who have never seen an Indian guiding all our destinies. As for you, Walter, I would say you are already emotionally involved. And to a point where your hands are completely tied."

Degnan shook his head. "I am not going to Washington with this. I am not even going upstairs. I'm going on my own."

"And what do you think this will mean for Miss Stillman?"

After a time Degnan said in a sick voice, "Under the circumstances I'm afraid I can't even consider that now."

"Ah, then you're not involved. You're making a military decision. You are also making a mistake." He studied the end of his cigar. "This man Shafter. What do you know about him?"

"Enough. He blew west after the war. A saddle tramp. He bummed around in the mountains for a while, prospecting. He and Willson. They picked up enough to live on evidently. Obre was with them, off and on, but he had a Gileño woman. . . . It's where he learned the jargon. Oury says they've never been in any real

trouble, except for a scrape Obre got into in Prescott. A paid killing as I understand it. The jury said it was justifiable homicide,
self-defense. But trouble or not they've got the earmarks. I don't
want you to think I'm not grateful for what Shafter's done. I don't
know any way to repay him. . . . I'm going to recommend a letter
of commendation from the War Department, but I have a feeling
even that will take him by the short hair." His eyes narrowed. "You
know what he said to me, right after I got out here. I mentioned
the Civil War. He said he 'reckoned' I meant the War for Secession
. . . that it wasn't a civil war, or a war between the states, but a war
for secession. He went on to inform me that the main reason there
was so much bad feeling was because we Unionists couldn't seem
to get it through our heads that the rebs never wanted any part of
us and never will. The whole business was as simple as that; it was
us that made it so complicated."

"You trust him?" Bleeker said with a small smile.

"Yes," Degnan said reluctantly.

"And you realize that he has done what no government agent or
army officer has been able to do in some years . . . actually effected
a personal communication with these people."

"What are you getting at, Tony?"

"Only wondering if you're going to continue to listen to him,"
Bleeker said.

"He won't come to me. He goes to Linus," Degnan said. "He
doesn't return my trust is what it amounts to. I can't shed any
tears over that."

"Where is Linus, by the way?" Bleeker said.

"He was Shafter's errand," Degnan explained quietly.

Bleeker sat back and watched him. "Listen to him, Walter."

"Why should I? Maybe Oury's right, maybe he is an Indian
lover."

Bleeker said, "It might be damned unfortunate if he lets you
down."

"Oh grow, my soul," Walter Degnan said.

Eight

Obre headed for town. Shafter, loping for the stables, hit it just right; with a certain adroitness in stops and starts, he intercepted the little Irish-laundress wife of Corporal Raphael Callahan, who was crossing the parade ground very trim in her striped skirts and big white apron, but rather wanton-looking for all that because of her mop of auburn hair, which was so curly it had a mind of its own and was generally, disarmingly, out of place. Shafter cornered her at the doorway to the laundry.

"Wait up, sweetie."

She pretended she hadn't seen him, tilting her head. "Well, if it ain't Mister Shafter himself," she said.

"How are you, Katie? I been missin' you."

"You're a liar," she told him.

"I got a lot on my mind," he told her. He trapped her by placing one arm out, hand on the dobe, between her head and the doorway.

"You oughtn't to do that, Mister Shafter," she said.

"Why not?" he said.

"I'm scared somebody'll see us and tell Rafe."

She was pretty nice; Shafter hoped Rafe Callahan appreciated it. "Come on, Katie, you like me a little, don't you?" he said.

She was a bundle of eagerness. "I ain't made up my mind. Let me out now. If Rafe ever. . . ."

He looked her right in the eye. "I kind of favor the direct approach. What's wrong with a little friendly palaver between you and me?"

She sighed. "All right. What do you want, Mister Shafter?"

"Katie, you have no goddamn soul." He looked at her admiringly. "Do me a favor?"

"I thought so," she said. "You do want something. What do I get out of it?"

"Anything you want," he said, grinning. "Anytime. Right now, just tell me one thing."

"You're a caution, John Shafter, and I shouldn't have nothing to do with you. What do you want to know?"

"The little Mexican girl," he said. "You helped her clean up and dress, didn't you?"

She was instantly sober. "That poor chick." Then her eyes blazed. "John Shafter, if you've got any idea. . . ."

"Whoa, sweetie," he said. "All I want to know is how bad she was marked up."

"You saw her."

"I ain't talkin' about her face. The rest of her. Was she bruised bad?"

"Bruised?" Katie said. "She didn't have a mark on her I could see. Nice smooth skin she had, but kind of skinny."

"Katie," he said, "I'll love you to my dying day. See you around."

"You're a liar," she said again, after him, wistfully.

Linus had about finished saddling up. Shafter jerked his thumb at two enlisted men on detail and they went out. He leaned on the wall and folded his arms and watched Linus, who, he was glad to see, was not in such a frenzy he wasn't doing the job just like he was going to stand inspection. When Linus didn't even look at him, he twitched a spear of hay out of a near-by bale and stuck it in the corner of his mouth. He said, "I reckon you know what you're doin', Linus."

The boy pulled a cinch strap up and buckled it. "Whether I do or whether I don't, what difference does it make?"

"To who?" Shafter said.

"What?" Linus looked at him irritatedly.

"I said, doesn't make any difference to who?"

"I haven't got time to talk to you now," Linus said.

Shafter hunkered down, putting his weight on one boot heel. "You know, of all the things those Apaches can think up, the one I like best is the one with the sidewinder. It shows a kind of well . . . niceness, you might say. Finesse, your pa'd put it."

Linus didn't look at him.

"They take this sidewinder, see, and they stake you both out, just out of reach of one another. Only they stake the 'winder on a piece of dry rawhide. It's kind of hot and bothersome out there. You're sure glad to see the sun go down." He took the straw out of his mouth. "Of course when the sun goes down there's considerable moisture in the air. Wets up that piece of rawhide. The snake's stuck at the end of it so long he reckons he might as well try it one more time, and this time that tether's stretched enough to make it worth his while." He stood up. "You prob'ly won't get that far, though. Speakin' of niceties, there's a couple of tricks those squaws can do might kind of make you wish you hadn't been born male."

Linus said, "You're wasting my time."

"I reckon you got some sort of plan in your mind," Shafter said.

Linus said, "You aren't going to talk me out of anything."

"Answer me one thing, Linus. I ever give you a turn the wrong way?" Shafter said.

"No," Linus said. "You never did."

Shafter said, "That Mex filly's a lyin' bitch."

He eyed Shafter deliberately across the cup of the saddle. "Thanks for the try, Shafter," he said.

Shafter shrugged. "Ask Katie Callahan."

"Ask her what? If you lie, will she swear to it?"

"Don't call me a liar, Linus, ever," Shafter said.

"I didn't, I was only asking. What's Katie got to do with this?"

"Katie just painted me the prettiest picture you ever saw of the little *señorita* without her shimmy. Nice and smooth, she said, without a mark on her."

Linus' face was still and watchful.

"We could go and ask her to strip down for us," Shafter said. "In case you wanted to see for yourself."

Linus said, "John, if she could lie about that she could lie about. . . ."

"Takes you a sight of time to get sensible," Shafter said. "What made you figure I didn't have an ace in the hole yet, you got to go off half cocked like that."

Linus put his head down. In the crippled, powerless gesture Shafter read a complete return to despair. He wanted Linus despairing, and flexible, as he was, rather than as he had been a moment ago. "Now let's you and me go find Willson and Ob and wet our whistle and talk this thing over. All right?"

"All right," Linus said. It felt, to him, as if he was going to spend the rest of his life saying all right to John Shafter.

Riding into Tucson, he decided maybe he ought to make a clean breast of everything. The way Shafter had stuck by him for no apparent reason but plain unvarnished friendliness made him feel a little ashamed for holding out. "I thought I had an ace in the hole, too," he said.

"You ain't got to tell me," Shafter said. He sounded uncomfortable.

"I thought I ought to."

"Some damn fool thing, I reckon," Shafter said.

"Maybe," Linus said. "Cecil Horne."

Shafter looked thoughtful but unconcerned. "Cec Horne's crazy," he said.

"I wondered," Linus said.

"They all are," Shafter said. "A little. Man can't spend all his days grubbin' around in the hills and having nothing to talk to but a donkey. It does something to him."

"Why do they do it?" Linus said.

"Half of it's gold. They're always gone to strike it rich. They never lose sight of that. They never fail the idea. Other half's they like it. There's worse things than not having to traffic with your fellow man all your days."

"They're of a breed, aren't they?" Linus said.

"Did you say breed or creed?"

"Breed," Linus said.

"Oh. I ain't certain what that means, Linus. That's twice now in two weeks I heard that word. Bleek said it, too. I expect what you think is, like, prospectors are a breed and Texicans are a breed and soldiers are a breed. Like everybody's got a category, you mean?"

"I guess so," Linus said.

"I don't hold much with such sayings," Shafter said. "It's like the owls who go around sayin', I might not know so-and-so, but I sure know human nature. What they mean is they think they're pretty sharp at sightin' down run-of-the-mill reaction. They never take into consideration the exception to their own rules, and there's mostly exceptions. I don't reckon there's any way to know human nature: it ain't a thing, like a tree or a river, it's got too much of the soul or the spirit or some damn thing involved in it for it to run true to any course. It galls me to hear a man holler human nature's black or white, with nothing in between, just like he might holler the desert's all gray because he doesn't see the colors in it. Strikes me as bein' about as uppity a thing as he could say." He gave Linus a rather vague smile. "I'm not sayin' it hurts to try and gauge a man's reaction if you got him mad at you or something, so you'll know how to meet it, but I do say you shouldn't ought to go on the assumption he's gone to do what you think he is, because surer'n hell it'll give the lie to the theory. For instance, you had it all figured what your girl's reaction was gone to be when she got taken by Victorio, and here you were dead wrong all the way because instead of bein' scared or sick or anything else, here she is takin' up with a Mimbreño buck."

"Good God, Shafter, if you say a thing like that again I'll knock you clean off that horse," Linus said.

"I ain't tryin' to torment you, Linus," Shafter said gently. "I'm just tryin' to show you what I mean." He looked into Linus' horrified eyes. "Now, what I think about the workin's of human nature is, something sure set that Mex girl up to take it out on your Anna."

"But what?" Linus said. "They liked one another enough to make the trip together . . . enough for her to invite Anna to visit her family in Santa Fe. It doesn't make sense. Look, Shafter, Anna is the kindest, most agreeable person who ever lived . . . you asked me what she was like and that's what I should have told you, agreeable. Whatever happened up there, I'd stake my life that Anna never said a mean word to her."

"Maybe she didn't have to," Shafter said. "When it comes to women, they not only ain't built like men where it counts; their heads are considerable different, too, or at least what goes on in 'em."

"You mean something might have happened to her when she got hit in the head?" Linus said.

"Not like you mean. That crack she took didn't quit when it hit bone. It went right on down inside somewhere."

"But what motive would she . . . ?"

"You name it. I say she's a little sorehead bitch with a man-size fret."

"But she wasn't faking anything," Linus said desperately. "She was crying. . . . She looked us right in the eye."

"I didn't say she was faking anything. I think she played it straight as she could long as she could."

Linus was bewildered. He trusted and believed in the honesty and virtue of the type of woman who had been gently reared, protected, in no way exposed to the harsher vicissitudes of life. There was still doubt in his mind. The only thing he did not doubt was

Shafter. "It seems to me you know a hell of a lot about women," he said.

"No, I don't," Shafter said thoughtfully. "The only thing I know is when a thing doesn't ring true. Not always, just when it doesn't ring true with a woman." He shifted. "Women are good liars as a rule. She had me sold. She could have carried it off, except for one thing. She shouldn't have said your girl was all right. She should have been smart enough to say your girl was in good spirits but crazy to get out of there, or that she was pretty busted up and gettin' her share of the rough gone. But she played it too hard, Linus."

"Let's talk to her," Linus said. "Let's break her down."

"For what? She'll stick to her story. She's got to. No way we can prove or disprove it." He looked at Linus. "You want Horne to sit in with us?"

"It's up to you," Linus said.

"Well, Jesus, Linus, don't shove it off on me, will you? I reckon you thought you were gone to let Horne take you up there so you could see for yourself. Go ahead, if you want to, I ain't gone to stop you. If I'd wanted to stop you I'd of kicked your slats in back at the stable and had your pa put you in irons."

"I owe Horne something. I asked him to come out and see me."

"It's all right with me," Shafter said. "Never know how good another man's ideas are till you hear 'em."

"One thing I'm curious about," Linus said. "When you went back out there, how come you didn't open negotiations with Victorio again?"

"No sense. He'd said all he was gone to say. If he'd wanted to say more, he'd of said it. You got to take his word, Linus."

"They operate so damn slow," Linus said. "That's the trouble. All that waiting around and taking days to make up their minds and not talking before they've smoked or drunk coffee or something. Just so you'll think it's too profound to be decided right off."

"It is, for them," Shafter said. All of a sudden there was something in his mind making him uneasy and he couldn't puzzle out what it was; he just knew it was something that didn't feel right, didn't belong there. It had to do with sorting out how much was fact and how much was fiction in the glib account the Mexican girl had given.

"One thing more," Linus said.

"Linus, will you just clamp your chops for a while," Shafter said. "I'm tryin' to think."

Now. Like: what if it was true about Linus' girl, and he'd come a cropper on this one. Like: the girl might be kind of woolly from the experience and not know what she was doing. Like: the girl might be a strange sort of tramp to begin with . . . he had known some strange tramps with some strange tastes. But he was only casting for answers, to beat down the indefinable thing that was gnawing away inside him. Then he knew what it was: it was the word breed. It hit him like a falling feed sack. Joaquin. He thought about it and began to get phenomenally thirsty, as thirsty as he had ever been in all his life. He felt he had been let in on something he didn't want in on; he felt he was a damn fool but he couldn't shake it. Maybe that mixed-up half white eyes would want him a white woman. It surprised him he hadn't thought of it right off, when the girl came out with that choice bit. Shafter, old horse, you are slipping. The years are creeping up on you. You were never very bright to begin with, and now look what's happening to you. Ma told you you got kicked in the head by a mule when you were a mite. Should've known it would catch up with you. Changed everything. Inside, he didn't believe it, but his record for being right wasn't one hundred per cent or anywhere near it. If it turned out to be anything like that, Linus wasn't gone to have to hear it from him, that was certain sure. The trouble was, his mind was a big blank. He had to figure how he could get hold of Joaquin, because that was the only thing left to do.

In the afternoon, early, a party of twelve Chiricahua ran into a fifteen-man patrol headed into Tucson from San Simon, carrying dispatches for the garrison. Actually they had not run into it, but had watched its progress for some time, from the moment the first dust rose on the horizon until the pacing horses crossed the vision ant size, and at last, when they picked their way through the rocks of a malpais, where Pionsenay had decided to take them. He was interested, if not in the sergeant at their head, in what might be in the leather *aparejos* the sergeant carried: white man's writing it would be. Joaquin would tell them what was written there. He was also interested because this would be a fine little coup close to home; there were already three raiding parties out, two big ones over the border in *Nakaiyi* country, and one east in New Mexico Territory.

There was nothing wrong with his attack, but the troopers were Apache wary. Pionsenay's first shot nicked the sergeant in the leg and dropped his horse. The sergeant was pretty cool; he stopped to unstrap the *aparejos* before one of his troopers picked him up in a neat mounted recovery. Pionsenay had the edge, behind his rock, but the troopers dashed out of the malpais and into the open, barely wasting a shot on the entrenched Apaches. The horse holder came up with his charges, and Pionsenay followed the detail for a time, whooping it up and firing at them, but when the troopers answered with the big .44s that could bowl over the tusked *monstruo* the old men whispered had lived here a million harvests ago, Pionsenay drew off. He had been racing behind and alongside the detail, and when he turned, one of the soldiers fired and Klishta, who was beside him, fell dead on the ground.

It was bad because he hadn't taken a horse or downed a trooper, and he had lost a man. Klishta would be avenged by his brother, but Pionsenay felt responsible for what had happened.

The wailing women began when they entered the main camp. This was not Cochise's only stronghold, but it was the largest and the favorite. The braves who were not out with war parties were all here now, as were all the women and children. When Klishta's squaw saw her husband's body hanging on the pony, she went into her wickiup and cut short her hair and the hair of her children. They mourned, huddled together. After a time they removed from the wickiup all the things which belonged to them, but left within all the things which had belonged to Klishta, all things he had owned or used or touched: implements of war, clothing, blanket, pallet. With a brand from the cookfire Klishta's squaw fired the wickiup, and when it began to burn steadily, the dry brush crackling as it consumed all that was left of her man, she called to her his dog and cut its throat. It did not struggle and made no sound, merely sinking down and snuffing in perplexity at its blood running. Then it died. The men prepared the body, braving the spirit of the deceased. When they reached the grave site, far up in a rocky cavern, the oldest son, a boy of thirteen, placed the muzzle of a carbine against the ear of his father's favorite horse and blew out its brains. Dog and horse were buried with the man, all *tats-an*, all dead, to be with him in the paradise underground to which the ghosts of dead comrades would bring him. No one, man, woman, or child, would go near his resting place again, and his name would not be mentioned, ever, for fear of offending his spirit, which might for some time be in close and watchful visitation. The war parties would provide now for his family, and in time his brother might take the widow as his wife.

Pionsenay was deeply depressed. Since the captive woman had come, he had shared the wickiup of his older wife, leaving his girl squaw alone with the white eyes. Although aging, he was a good and experienced war leader. He not only felt accountable for the death of Klishta, but because he had returned with nothing to show for the foray. He began to drink *tulepah*. Before the fire, where his young wife and the *americana* girl were cooking, he drank deeply. Cochise came and put his hand on his lieutenant's shoulder.

"It happens so, Pionsenay," he said, using the informal language.

"It was foolish," Pionsenay said. He looked up and saw that Victorio was coming also. He remembered when he had walked hard and assured and in his prime, as Victorio walked now. Victorio had captured many horses and two women and received a fine ransom and not lost a man. "It was foolish," he repeated. "We should have had them trapped in the rock, but they ran through and fired at us from the saddle."

Victorio was hunkered, on one heel. The long solid muscle of his thigh swelled like a rolling of water. "They learn from us then. When they stand, they stand well, but they are not too proud to run."

Pionsenay regarded him glumly. Victorio was the Mimbreño chief, and he could analyze and instruct, but he was still a pup to Cochise's lieutenant. Pionsenay made a growling sound and flung out his arm. Anna jumped and ran for more of the corn beer, passing it now to Cochise and Victorio also. When she handed the *tus* to Victorio, eyes on the clay jar itself, he did not take it immediately, but only touched it, so that she did not dare release it for fear of dropping it. In the hesitant time she raised her head and met the steady unimpassioned look of him, directed upon her own. He saw how quickly she took in her breath, but the approval stamped his aquiline face when she did not draw away from his regard. He took the *tus*. He said to Cochise, "This woman saved a child of the Chiricahua. I remember this. I thought perhaps it would be well to return her to the white eyes in payment. Now your brave is dead. Let her pay for that."

Pionsenay said, "You pay no price for my mistake."

"Are we brothers or do we dispute like women?" Victorio said.

"He will be avenged," Pionsenay said.

Cochise was provoked, intervening. "His brother will pay. This is not your debt, nor yours, Victorio. This is my law on it." He looked at Victorio. "Is it in your mind that the soldiers will sit in their blue breeches and make no attempt to recover the *niña?*"

"I want to draw them out," Victorio said. "We will be equal to them. We will fight well to show them they cannot have her back. But first we will tell them this."

"Tell them?" Cochise said. "What are your thoughts?"

"We will tell them that had they not killed your brave they might have ransomed the *niña,* but now this will not be."

"Who will you send?" Cochise said.

"Joaquin," Victorio said.

"To the nantan?" Cochise was shaking his head. "The risk is too great."

"To the man Shafter," Victorio said. "He is with the nantan in this; let him carry the word. He is brave and he does not speak with a forked tongue. He knows also when not to speak." Victorio drank again. "I have spoken with Delgadito and Joaquin. We are not going to Santa Rita as we planned."

"Why this change?" Cochise said.

"The man Shafter is clever. He says nothing without reason. He asked when we went to Ojo Caliente. This was done for a purpose. When I told him, he knew that we would go to Santa Rita. Let him think this. We will go to Ojo Caliente. This wolf will show he can run with all wolves."

"*Enju,*" Cochise said. "But they will strike you at both places. Do not weaken your rancherías."

"We do not take the *niña,*" Victorio said. "We will leave her here until they are convinced we no longer have her."

"If they believe she is dead their anger will be for us here then," Pionsenay warned.

Cochise laughed. "Let them come out in anger. I will show them what a fight is. And if I am slower than when the blood ran thicker, Tahzay will take my place. And you with him, *camarada.*" Again he placed his hand on Pionsenay's shoulder.

Pionsenay felt better. The heavy thing in him was lightened. Victorio was right: a life for a life. The *niña* for the child, but now the *niña* for a dead Chiricahua.

Joaquin splashed up through the shallows on the black and white Appaloosa. The men had been in the deep pool, and he was half naked, feeling the sun against him. It was still cool for swimming and the stroke of the sun was a physical thing, fragile but solidly golden, softness with substance. Pionsenay's wife and two other women looked from the narrows where they were soaking willow withes and Anna glanced up from under the hanging branches of a sycamore. He slid off the horse and came toward her, into the dappled pattern of sunlight which lay among the leaves.

"What are you doing?" he said.

"Splitting willow for them."

He stood watching her. His shoulders still glistened with water. "Do you find it difficult?"

"Only monotonous." She spoke almost abruptly. She knew she would end by saying the wrong thing, would send him away. Her own language tasted good on her tongue and she wanted to use it. "What is her name, Joaquin? The girl."

"Pionsenay's wife? Nuadin."

"I never know what to call her." She tried the name and could not master the explosive sound of it.

He remained standing. He said, "You do that very well." She could not tell if there was mockery in his voice. "You are very clever."

He was not mocking. She looked up at him directly. "Why do you say that?"

He dropped down beside the bunched split willow, on the grass. "We watched to see when you would be sad. Like the Mexican girl. You're strong, for a woman. We know the Americans are brave, but we didn't know about their women."

To her dismay she felt tears well in her; she bent her head and bit at her lip; his steady scrutiny lay upon her like a touch. "I'm not brave, Joaquin. I'm lonely and tired and homesick."

"It doesn't show."

She looked at him almost with pleading. "Joaquin, you are the only hope I have."

"I am not named hope," he said rather flatly.

"Yes, because you will talk to me. You will tell me things."

"What things?" he said.

"Anything . . . I don't know, anything," she said on a lowering note of depression. "You don't know what it is to be lonely."

He leaned back on his elbows. His skin was very smooth and tight over a slender muscularity which had barely settled into its determined mold. "Yes, I know," he said.

She risked it. "You are part white, aren't you?"

"Half. My father came out with the Ewing Young Company. Then he was a guide for the mining men."

"He taught you English."

"He and other men. I was with him much of the time."

"Where is he now, Joaquin?"

"Dead. In Tucson. In a fight with some drunken Mexicans."

"Oh. I am sorry. And your mother?"

"At Santa Rita."

"Have you brothers or sisters?"

He shook his head. He was shifting restlessly now. "Only my mother. But that is not where I am lonely. Nor here. With my father I was lonely. I was always lonely with white men."

"But why?" she said.

"Because when a white man says half breed he can put all the contempt in the world in his voice." He half smiled. "I have the misfortune of your blood. With my people, here, I am worth a little, to myself and to them. With my father's people I was not given a choice." His mouth was a little grim. "Now I have the better half of two worlds."

She put aside the knife and the lengths of pliant willow. "Joaquin, I am afraid of making you angry."

"Yes, you could do that," he said with faint humor.

"I don't want to."

"For you, or for me?"

"For us both. If you're angry you won't talk to me and I need you."

"Say it," he said.

"You could pass as white."

For the first time he laughed. "What's so good about being white?"

She was taken back. "Well, what is so good about being Indian?"

"When you've been here awhile you will answer that for yourself.

Do you know how many of our captives, given the chance, ever really want to go back? I don't want to be white."

She was offended. She got on her knees and looked down at him. "So you torture and kill and use your blood as an excuse? Joaquin, do you know what they did to those Mexican soldiers? They burned a man. Burned him."

He said, "Have you ever seen Apache scalps on Mexican and American saddles? Have you ever seen them geld and flay our wounded? Or what they do to our dead if we don't recover them?"

"But one does not excuse the other," she cried.

"Forgive me. I did not understand that we were looking for excuses."

"But you are white. Nothing can change that."

"I have already changed it. It is not spoken of here."

"And that changes it," she said. "Just don't talk about it and it won't be. If you never mention it, it will go away."

He put his dark head back and the laughter came full in him. He felt a wild, nervous elation quivering under the surface of passions, reflections, conceptions he had long ago disciplined himself to suppress. She amused him, because he saw that in spite of her fear of angering him she was filled with small flames which nothing could extinguish. She was silent. He picked up a length of willow and tapped her suddenly on the cheek, lightly, with it. "And you could pass as Mimbreño."

Now she would amuse him further by telling him in kind that she did not wish to be Mimbreño. While he waited for the predetermined response, she dropped her hand, palm up, on his bare chest, fingers curled inward. Her hand was hard and calloused where the raw places healed. The shock of it took him off balance; it was as if he had been struck, and the impact jolted him in the pit of his belly and spread tenuous fingers along his thighs. But she was only intent, bending over him; her face was the face of a child.

"Look at our skins, Joaquin. There is no difference now." She took her hand away. "And if someone struck off our heads this minute they would see that blood is the same color always. No one would say this is white blood and this is Indian blood."

"Are you trying to say it doesn't matter?" Joaquin said.

"I am saying it. I think you are too proud, Joaquin."

He was frowning. "You don't know what you are saying."

"I do know," she said. "It's things like this, this talk of blood and race and pride that have got both of us in the muddle we're in now. And selfishness. And we keep on in this way. You kill us and we kill you, and neither of us moves one step forward or one step back. Neither of us tries to understand the other. I think there is a core of great stupidity in men, with their pride. . . . I think somehow men carry a thing with the potential of good so far that it becomes the end in itself. Yes. All the ills we bring down upon ourselves are there in the name of pride." She made a little hissing sound between her lips. "All the cruelties and outrages and evils, in the name of pride. So that it never matters how terrible, as long as the pride remains intact."

"What would happen to a people without pride?" he said. "How long would they survive? My people have eaten pride and breathed pride and clothed themselves with pride when there was nothing else."

"And warred with pride and killed with pride and refused, with pride, to live in peace."

He corrected her. "Refused, with pride, to give up our lands. Is there still pride in your people when they consider the ways they have taken to steal our lands?"

"I wonder if they do consider," she said then, quietly. "I never did. We would read in the newspapers what you were doing to us, here, and think only that you were wrong in not allowing us to pass and to settle. Wrong, never wronged. But there are men who believe you are wronged, Joaquin, there are white men fighting for you."

"White men who never saw an Apache camp."

"Yes. But that doesn't prevent them from wanting to try. Maybe they'll do everything badly, but they try. They want to help you. I don't think you will let them help you."

"No," he said, again with the half smile. "We are too proud."

Pionsenay's wife came and looked at them and picked up a bundle of withes. She looked longest at Joaquin, sprawled on the grass. She went away again. Her round face, totally unreadable, awakened in Anna a new knowledge.

"If you feel so strongly about your blood, Joaquin, you must know that you are a prisoner, too."

His eyes were closed. He said, "I would rather be prisoner here than free dirt in Santa Fe or Tucson or Prescott."

She put her arms around her knees and watched him sadly, studying the semi-Indian modeling of his face now that his eyes were closed and he could not observe her. "Was it so bad in those places, Joaquin?"

"It could have been worse. My father wouldn't let it be as bad as it could have been. Maybe it was harder for him than for me. Nothing was easy. I took my novitiate with Victorio's boys and then I went with my father. We both thought it would work. My mother said it couldn't, but neither of us believed her." He opened his eyes and sat up. For a moment he felt her hand burning against his flesh again, but when he looked she was only sitting quietly, in an attitude of listening and sadness. He was galled and sore, furious at himself not only because he had told her these things but because he recognized the need to talk to her, to use the language, to be with a woman. The thickness which closed off his throat was the white blood rising, and he fought it with the only weapon he had, a harsh rejection of her. There was something soft about her after all and it was tearing at him, smashing him all up inside. He rose and could not even say her name, by which other men had called her, but said hoarsely, "What do you think of this place in the rocks?"

"It is beautiful here, Joaquin. No wonder your people love it. Yesterday when we were in the heights the whole desert lay under us, and it was miles and miles of flowers, as far as I could see, and the mountains in the distance and the trees below us."

He saw the curiosity come into her face then, and he gritted his teeth. He said, "It's well you like it here because we are not going to leave it after all."

"Not leave it? But you said. . . ."

"Victorio goes. You stay."

The curiosity fled. Desperation came into her eyes; he wondered what had been in her mind that she should react in this way. "Why must I stay?" she said.

"I have a mission for Victorio. After that maybe you will go."

She was relieved. At least they were not going to keep her powerless to communicate. "What are you going to do?" she said.

He wanted to tell her, bluntly, in a need which was, he knew, part the wildness of the only blood he would recognize and accept, and part something pulsing, driving, nameless. But his voice came out sterile and subdued. "I am to tell your man we cannot let you go. Because the troopers killed Klishta."

She stared at him. Then she was on her feet. "But I didn't kill him! I had nothing to do with it!"

Whatever he could say now must be either insensate, hacking, brutal, or weak and compassionate. There was nothing in-between. When he swung up on the bare back of the Appaloosa, he heeled it viciously in the ribs. The desire to hurt someone, something, to strike out blindly, to mitigate his very existence in some inexorable and venomous measure ran in him like quicksilver, and the unavailing senselessness of this was only a spur, roweling the flesh which he had believed inviolable and whose unconditional defenselessness he now perceived and identified. In the camp he went into the wickiup he shared with Victorio and Mangas Chie and Delgadito and got the Mexican carbine with the silver inlay on the stock and, without speaking to any man, went into the high places.

Nine

Victorio walked along the bank in the gentle purple rising of the evening, with the cook smoke aromatic and pleasant in the nose and the people relaxed and contented in the clear sweet air. He walked alone because he was thoughtful: he had in his mind many memories, and he wondered if it was a sign of age. No. This he rejected, almost with anger. He was as handsome and strong and lithe and quick on his feet as a panther. He was respected, admired, emulated, loved by his people, although he knew that no man would take, for his people, the place of Mangas Colorado. It was upon his own privilege he dwelt now: he, chosen by Mangas, pupil of Mangas, confidant of Mangas, and, at the last, bowed to the ground in love and loyalty and grief at the heart-stopping thing which had come upon Mangas, walking where Mangas had walked, chief of all the Mimbreños.

Tonight the responsibility of his trust lay upon him in a sharpened awareness. He felt that he would never be what Mangas had been; perhaps never what Cochise had been, though there was still time to test this. Where Mangas had been constant in his belief that diplomacy, tact, judiciousness, wisdom comprised the only course to pursue in dealing with the white man, Cochise had been inconstant. A comparison of the two greatest men of their nation was perhaps unfair, but it was also necessary to a chief striving to attain for himself the best of both. Cochise was a superior war chief. This had not been so of Mangas. Cochise was a good politician. Mangas had been a superb lawyer, judge, and jury. While Mangas had continued to live in unalterable fidelity to his code, Cochise had warred with phenomenal success and, in the propitious times, armed himself well with the honor and honesty which characterized Mangas.

Cochise was, in many ways, a disturbing man with whom to talk. He had been early imbued with a fatalism which ran darkly in him even when he warred most brilliantly, and this fatalism had to do with the conscious perception that the day was rapidly nearing when his people must go to live with the white man. He had known this since the first Americans entered his lands; even at the height of his magnificence, both in battle and as administrative chief, that black aching cancer had grown in him. He had tested this knowledge, and the test had failed through betrayal. But he had never ceased thinking in this vein. His theory was not complicated: we are outnumbered but not yet outwitted. As long as it is possible, we will hold out, and when it is no longer possible we will capitulate. The word surrender did not enter his mind.

Over the years he had impressed Victorio with this consuming passion, until Victorio, too, was swollen with it: the passion to do what was right for his people. His latest talk with the Chiricahua chief had given rise to a recurrent despondency. Because he knew Cochise was right. It was Mangas who had been wrong. No, perhaps not wrong, perhaps it was the time which was wrong, Mangas too visionary for the time.

Victorio stood quietly, watching a first star swim toward him from the great spaces where White Painted Woman, the Virgin of his people, lived young and beautiful and free with the son who had been placed in her by no man, but by a single pure crystal of dew which dropped upon her body. White Painted Woman had been with him always, had ridden at his side into all danger, and guided him at the council fire. She was his medicine. He wished that she would give him some sign now, to ease the sadness and lift his heart.

Mangas and his eternal, damned trust! Victorio's eyes were filled with the pain of an old day when he had been young and had gone with Mangas, unarmed and alone, to a camp of the white eyes in the hills. Why had Mangas done this foolhardy thing? Because Mangas trusted. Because he wished to tell the white eyes that he knew where there was a rich vein of gold, useless to the Apache, and to say he would take them to it. Victorio had not gone into the camp, but had hidden outside it by Mangas's order. He heard, when the bearded white eyes accused his chief of preparing an ambush. He saw, when they seized his chief and bound him and whipped him with harness straps until his broad aging back was a bloody pulp. When they cut him loose, Victorio took him to a cave high in the hills and bathed and treated the terrible surface which had once been firm intact flesh, and there they had lived until the flesh healed, and Mangas had sworn him to secrecy. Mangas had never gone naked again, and his people had never known, until he died, the shame which lived in him. It was a shame which Victorio had shared, until there were times he could feel, almost with joy, the hot running of blood, the agony of flesh flayed to the bone.

Why did not Mangas learn? Why had Mangas clung still to the belief that the white eyes were good people, that peace could be secured? Because Mangas still trusted. He went again, and this time there was the final whipping: the heated bayonets and the body torn with lead, and, finally, decapitation. Victorio was sick with the ultimate degradation: it had come to him that the head of his chief was sent to the city of the great nantan, in the East, and that the brain within it was said to be of abnormally large size. It was enough to make a man wither and weep. Mangas martyred to what end? Cochise embracing and speaking this same ideal, but tempering it with action, resistance, until resistance was no longer possible. Victorio thought, if this has been planned and I am to be the result, the finish, the tool of the plan, then *Ysen* must take me by one hand and White Painted Woman by the other, for I cannot be both men; I can only profit from both men and be myself.

It was not always best to remember. Only the good things should be remembered. Perhaps there was a sickness in him, and if this was the case he must submit to treatment by a medicine man. Certainly something was running in him green as gall. When he walked farther and Delgadito came to him, he voiced another thing which disturbed him.

"Where is Joaquin?"

"He took his horse and went up." Delgadito looked his chief in the eye. "Joaquin is troubled."

"He has not come to me," Victorio said.

Nuadin, Pionsenay's wife, passed close to them and stopped. She had overheard. "Today Joaquin laughed with the white-eyes *niña*," she said. "They were lying in the grass."

Victorio said, "Gabble, goose, gabble with all geese."

She laughed and went on; Victorio's eyes narrowed, watching her; something in the set of head, the curve of flesh, had struck him with mournful reminiscence, so that he thought of the narrow face and the flesh of the woman in his own wickiup, and of his sons who were long out with a war party.

"Will you speak to Joaquin?" Delgadito said.

"Joaquin is as my own now. He is my own. He will speak to me."

"And if he does not?" Delgadito persisted.

"He will come to me," Victorio said.

"All men of us come to you with our troubles," Delgadito said. He paused. "Where do you go?"

Victorio looked at him. Then his face, with the elegant aquiline nose, turned away. "The trouble is not my own," he said.

"No." Delgadito was humming and stinging like a black hornet. "You are not to have troubles of your own. You are only to carry the troubles of us all."

Victorio bent, picked up a stick, and, squatting, drew it through the dirt. "What am I to do, Delgadito, brother? I have taken my people where there is no turning back, by the holding of this *niña*. I speak to Cochise and he says, sometimes with laughter, sometimes sadly, let the troops come. He knows, as I do, that we will fight the troops." He rose. "But let me ask you, is it not better when we do not fight the troops?"

Delgadito said waspishly, "So thought Mangas Colorado. He is not here to say this now." His eyes were wild and bright. "Do you believe we can drive the troops forever from our lands?"

Victorio shook his head. "They are too many. Not only too many but too brave. Cochise believes it is all over for us." His voice was bitter. "Then we will become women. Then we will dig and haul wood and hoe the fields. Women. Women." He spat into the dirt and hurled the stick from him, toward the water. "Cochise banishes Geronimo from the Chiricahua because Geronimo will not keep the peace. But this was only when Cochise wished to keep the peace. Now it is different."

"Geronimo is still not welcome among us," Delgadito said proudly. "Nor will he ever be, with me."

"Nor with me," Victorio said. "Nothing of that man is fair or true or honest, and the tongue in his mouth is the tongue of the serpent. The bitter medicine is now Cochise's . . . to see his own son Nachise with this man. Nachise has chosen. But what is the choice of our people? Do we become a tribe of Geronimos, striking, running, hiding, starving? Or do we go and become women?"

"This I do not understand," Delgadito said. "This is better kept for the council. I wish to fight the troops, anywhere, at all times. I will not die in the fields, and I would rather know a lean belly than beg the beef of the white eyes agents. What is in my mind is the now, only the now, and the here, and I will not look for tomorrow until it comes."

Victorio smiled suddenly. "You are right, Delgadito. It is better to die in battle, clean and free, than to grovel in the dust. I want peace, but they will not let us have it. I want peace, but I want it on my terms." He thought a moment. "Joaquin is wise. He takes his troubles away to fight with them."

"Will you do the same?" Delgadito said.

Victorio said, "Leave me now, brother."

The old medicine man, Nockahoto, had only just come in from one of the sacred medicine caves and was smoking before his wickiup. Victorio came up to him and said, "I need you."

The old man took his pipe out of his mouth and turned his head. Of his right eye there was nothing but a milky, bluish surface, like a mushy membrane, and the frame of this curved nothing was pushed and pulled within the surrounding flesh. A horse had stepped upon his face when he was very young. But he had the sight of three men in his remaining eye, because he practiced the great medicine.

Nockahoto was a sachem of distinction. He fasted interminably, sometimes appearing barely to keep body and soul together. He spent much time alone in the high places and was known throughout Apachería for the quality, length, color, and content of his dreams. No sachem surpassed him in the reading of signs and omens, and he had once been adept at fire-swallowing. This he no longer practiced, for his chest had become rheumy. When he spoke, he cleared his throat. "Where is your hurt?" he asked Victorio.

Victorio shook his head. "There is something in me, Father."

The old man pursed his lips. The eye glimmered whitely. "Something lives in you," he said. "What form has this thing taken?"

"That is why I come here," Victorio said. "I only know that it is feeding on my brain and drinking my blood."

Nockahoto rose. "Come," he said. Victorio followed him to the medicine wickiup. Inside, the old man lay down, flat upon his back. "Think of this thing which is in you," he said.

For over an hour Victorio sat motionless, thinking of Mangas and of Cochise and of the thing inside which fed upon him, while the sachem slept. Finally Nockahoto sat up. He moved not with the hesitation of old age, but with deliberate slowness and ceremony. He studied Victorio. Then he said, "Have you heard an owl hoot near you?"

Victorio shuddered and shook his head.

"Have you eaten of our brother, the bear, with whom we have a never-ending truce?"

Victorio said firmly, "Never."

"Has lightning struck beside you?" Nockahoto said.

"No," Victorio said.

"Has any living animal shown itself your enemy?" Nockahoto said.

"No," Victorio said. Then he remembered something. "Wait. On the raid . . . at the springs. A horse kicked out at me. His hoof touched my leg with its iron."

Nockahoto got to his feet. "The horse sickness is in you," he pronounced. "I dreamed of this, and in my dream I told it that it must leave you. I will not call the devil dancers. This sickness answers to me alone."

The words made Victorio tense with fear. The old man moved into the shadowy corner of the wickiup. The blind eye was so white it appeared to flare in the gloom. While Victorio watched, Nockahoto took the buckskin medicine shirt, slipping it over his head carefully so as not to disturb unduly the magic which lived in his hair, picked up a bag of hoddentin and the four medicine cords, and returned to the sick man. "Lie down," he said.

Victorio obeyed. The old man sat cross-legged at his side. Victorio kept his eyes on the medicine shirt, which was ornamented with the symbols of those crawling things which contain the witching serum of death: rattlesnake, tarantula, scorpion, and the good things which *Ysen* had given his people to sustain them and their lands: sun, moon, star, rain, cloud, rainbow, mountain. Nockahoto opened the buckskin bag and took from it a pinch of the yellow hoddentin, which he sprinkled on Victorio's breast and belly. Then he began to sing in a low, cracked, phlegmy voice.

He was no longer Nockahoto, the medicine man. He was a divine power, strong and terrible, and no sickness could stand against him. He felt his divinity run with great force in his arms and legs; he felt his shriveled old body grow strong again, and in his chest was a burning as if he had swallowed the fire, as he used to do.

While all this holiness surged and brimmed in him, his voice never lost the low, steady controlled tone, but remained even and unvaried, and at last became bell clear, and all the cracks in it drew together and mended.

When he took the beautiful medicine cords in his hand and began to swing them over Victorio's breast, Victorio felt a hot liquid rushing in him which could not be contained and burst forth all over his body in a warm, profuse sweat. He was instantly weak and trembling, as if the old man had sucked away all his stamina and virility and taken them into himself. Something was churning in his belly, rushing from wall to wall of him, a struggling, caged thing pressing against his bladder and forcing his heart out of its accustomed place. The sickness was growing to its fullest dimensions, raging and desperate, as Nockahoto's medicine began to sear and pull at it. It beat its head against Victorio's brain, fierce thudding beats, and its feet dug deep into the groin as it lengthened in its pain. Victorio could see nothing now. He felt his mouth fall open and tasted the horse medicine, the eriogonum, when Nockahoto placed it upon his lower lip. The sweat still poured from him, running wet and sticky upon his face and bathing his body. The roaring in his head was the furious roar of the sickness, which could not protest with force enough to drown the pulse of Nockahoto's song of exorcism.

Suddenly Victorio felt a horrible thing: the huge frenzied form inside metamorphosed and became a sickening slippery boiling mass, as if his guts had torn loose and were writhing bloodily, like a ball of snakes in the spring. The mass rose into his throat, and he could not breathe. Just when the last of his air was gone, the thing fell back inside him again, deeply. There was a bursting of light in his head and then the mass slipped away, first explosively, then softly, draining, oozing out of him with his sweat. In harsh and brilliant hues he saw now tremendous paintings on red rock, and these paintings were of himself and of his people. They were on the caged earth, in a place where it was not good, and they fevered and grew ill. The pictures followed one another in bright continuum. They had left the caged earth and gone to war again. Several times this scene was repeated as he and his people came and went, from freedom to the caged earth and back again. Then he saw depicted men carrying the gaunt dead body of Cochise. They were

lowering it by ropes, with horse and dog, into a hidden crevice in
the rock. Here was Mangas's head: the enormous brain was bursting from it, streaming matter and pus and tissue. And at last there
was himself, alone in the rock, and men coming. He strained to
see, and they were not men of the white eyes, but soldiers of the
Nakaiyes. He killed many of them. Many. He looked into a small
round black hole, which was the barrel end of a carbine. He stood
upright and felt his heart blown out of him, circling into the wind,
whole and free forever, and it winged like a bird down the canyons and across the meadows of sand, into the place where the
warm springs rose, and there it came to rest.

He lay in exhaustion. The sweat began to dry, prickling against
his skin, and out of his weakness came a relief so towering, so
potent, that he almost forgot to breathe in his gladness.

Nockahoto saw the breathing pattern stabilize. Then he sang,
quietly, the final song, in praise and gratitude.

> *The horse of the sun is a yellow stallion.*
> *The place above his nose is of the mist;*
> *His ears, like young lightning, move back and forth.*
> *He has come to us.*
> *The horse of the sun is a yellow stallion.*
> *A blue stallion, a black stallion.*
> *The horse of the sun has come out to us.*

Victorio slept. Nockahoto sat by him unmoving, unwilling to
loose his hold on the holiness which had come to him, letting it
slip away gradually, as the sickness had slipped from Victorio.

When Victorio woke, it was late and he knew many things. He
turned his head and saw Nockahoto and the reflection of the fires
outside. He was ravenously hungry; when he tried to walk he staggered in his weakness.

"*Ysen* grant you a long life," he said in a tired voice.

"And you," Nockahoto said.

"How must I pay you?" Victorio said. The savory smell of cooked
meat dizzied him, sweeter than the rosy perfumes of a hundred
señoritas. He was drunk with the smell and swayed.

"I will take your red *Nakaiyi* horse," Nockahoto said.

"That is a big payment, old man," Victorio said.

Nockahoto's dead eye glittered, almost with emotion. He said,
"That was a big sickness."

Corporal Rafe Callahan was up and shaving long before reveille. It was cold, with the dawn just beginning to break. The heat of the day, which adobe held, had cooled in the night, and he shivered, stripped to the waist, with his suspenders hanging. The flame of the oil lamp was tremulous in draught.

He shaved with care. He had stable detail today. The last time he had stable detail the Old Man had come around, out of nowhere, looked at him, and said, "When you've attained the rank, eminence, and age of General Crook, you have my permission to grow a beard, Callahan." Which was letting him off easy, but humiliating. He was tired this morning because he had slept badly, and to cap it, Katie had slept badly, too. That had him all worked up, because he wondered if his restlessness was keeping her awake because her restlessness was keeping him awake or what. He threw caution to the wind and took a vicious swipe at himself with the razor, but nothing happened except that a gob of soap slid off his jaw.

Katie lay propped on the pillow, watching him. She had taken the long sleeves out of her nightdress, and her bare arms, white with red freckles, lay outside the blanket. Sometimes he looked at her, in the mirror, and sometimes he studied his own black-Irish, good-looking face. When all the soap was gone he said, "How come you to twitch around like that so much last night, Katie?"

She ran her fingers through her unruly auburn hair. "You kept me awake," she said neatly.

"The hell I did, you kept me awake," he returned. "Worse'n a flea on a griddle."

"I don't know, Rafe. You acted funny when you came in. Like you had something on your mind."

"So'd you," he countered, wiping his neck with a clean towel.

"Only thing was on my mind was you had something on your mind," she said.

He cursed. "Don't married folks never have no sensible conversations?" he said.

"You used to tell me when something was bothering you," she said.

"So'd you," he said again.

"I'll tell you if you'll tell me," she said.

He picked up his shirt and slipped it over his head. Then he came and sat on the edge of the bed. They looked at one another:

Kate always looked mighty nice in the morning, he thought, because she had all that natural color in her cheeks and her lips, and the freckles stood out on the bridge of her nose. "Honest, Katie, it ain't nothing personal. It's comp'ny business got me worried."

She gave her head a little toss, against the pillow. "Rafe, I bet you Bess Layden and me between us hear more comp'ny business in the laundry than you hear all day mountin' guard."

"You know me, Kate," he said. "I ain't the best soljer in the world, but I try, huh? I don't go courtin' the Old Man, but I always treat him respectable and by the book. I mean I don't go out of my way to get in his way, see? Well, now I don't know whether I ought to put myself under his thumb long enough to tell him somethin'."

"Tell him what?" she said. "You ain't goin' to tell tales on anybody, are you?"

"Hell no," he said impatiently. "It ain't that. It's just that last night . . . well, you know Sarge Stern and me, we took a note in for the Old Man, to give to that Oury. And then Sarge got drunk. Real fallin'-down drunk. He's goin' to have some head this morning."

She was bored. "And if you think the colonel don't know that already, you're crazy. What's he care, anyway?"

"Let me finish, will you? When we come out of town, 'long after dark, about eleven it was, I would've swore there was a Indian right outside the main wall, about fifty–sixty feet from the gate."

"Oh, Rafe." She made a show of pushing him away, half turning on her side.

"You know it all," he said. "Women know it all." He started to get up but she turned back to him.

"So there was an Indian outside the gate. That lousy place is full of Indian. And Mexicans. And lice, and dust. And drunks."

His face softened. "I know, Katie. This here's a tough tour. But don't you worry, now, we're savin' pretty good, and I ain't one of these here professional army men. Soon's this is over we're goin' where it's green, you and me." He patted her arm, and while she did not draw away he was somehow hurt at the listlessness of her flesh, the lack of response. "You listen now, Katie," he said. "You know what kind of Indians you see in Tucson 'swell's I do. You see them Papagos, don't like to wander round much for fear of the

'Paches, and you see our scouts, but you don't see 'em skulkin' around the walls out there."

Dawn was breaking grayly. Through the single window with its oiled-paper pane there was a lightening; the paper turned from ash to dun. She wanted to see the day come; she wanted to put her fist through that awful oiled paper and watch the sun begin to hug the mountains.

"You listenin', Katie?"

"Um," she said, yawning.

"This Indian. He was flat against the wall. Not really standin' there." He shook his head. "It's hard to explain . . . the way he was standin'. When we come up on him, he turned like a god-damn cat and was gone. Just vanished. So I yelled and took off down the wall and there wasn't nobody there. Nothing. And Sarge not only didn't see him, the minute I yelled and rode off, he fell outa the saddle, right on the ground, and I couldn't hardly get him back up again."

She laughed. "So you're afraid to tell the colonel because you think he'll say you had one too many, too."

"No, I ain't," he said. "I'm clear . . . there's lots of folks can vouch for me. What I'm afraid of is makin' a fool of myself. Sayin' I saw a Indian, like that. Sure, it sounds crazy. But then, after what's happened . . . the lieutenant's girl and all, I keep thinkin' I maybe ought to tell him."

She nodded, but her mind was elsewhere. "I think you're makin' something out of nothin', Rafe. How could there be any connection?"

"You don't think I ought to tell him?"

She shrugged. "What does it matter? Tell him if you're goin' to lose sleep over it."

He sat pondering. Then she put her hand out, almost timidly, and stroked his wrist with the tips of her fingers. He had forgotten, until she did that, until she said, "Rafe, I been a good wife to you, ain't I?"

He said with quick Irish humor, "Far's I know."

"Oh Rafe, you know what I mean. I ain't asked for nothing much, have I?"

He was already drawing away. She was going to ask for something, and he was trying to hang onto his money, and hers, her laundry money, saving hard for the green place in the future. "We ain't spendin' no money," he said in a tight voice.

"Money? It ain't that." It came out in a rush; her eyes were shy and beseeching. "Rafe, would you grow a mustache?"

"Grow a mustache!" He stared down at her. "Grow a mustache. What for, for Chrissake?"

"Because. Because. . . ." Her unblinking gaze was fixed on his upper lip. "Because it would be pretty."

"*Pretty*." His face was twisted in bewilderment and disgust. "You mean to tell me you laid there all night botherin' about a thing like that? You mean to tell me?"

She nodded seriously. He stood up. "Well I'll be damned," he said. "I'll be teetotally damned." He sat down again, groped for his boots, pulled them on, and swiped at them with the towel. Any other morning she'd give him hell for that, but this morning she didn't seem to notice.

He didn't say anything more. When he started for the door she sprang out of bed and did what she had wanted to do ever since they moved into this adobe room. She put her hand clean through the oiled paper and tore it loose. She was just in time to fling both arms around his neck as he cut the corner of the building. He groaned, trying to untangle himself. "Good God, Katie . . . in your nightgown . . . let *go*, will you?"

But she was only saying, "Oh thank you, Rafe, thank you," and he was saying despairingly, "I didn't say I would, I didn't say I would."

He got through guard mount, mess, and inspection. Sergeant Stern, looking like a sick pig, told him to take the Old Man's gelding up to commandant. But he was still worried. "Listen, Sarge, you remember that Indian last night. Outside the wall. You saw him, didn't you? Just before you fell off your horse."

And Stern was shouting at him. "What Indian, you lousy yellow-legs? What Indian? What horse? I hear you say again I fell off my horse I'll have your stripes, you moth-eaten bastard dog soljer, you grass-eating goat, you muck-drinking coyote. I'll rip them stripes off and shove 'em down your gullet. One more word you'll draw striker duty, you flea-bitten snake turd."

Rafe Callahan went off with the Old Man's horse. Someday there was going to be a law made. Against sergeants. Someday there wouldn't be any more sergeants. The Old Man was waiting, with

Linus and two orderlies and a clerk. Callahan held the horse for him while he mounted. When he stepped back he saluted and turned up his chin, so the Old Man could see how nice and clean-shaven he was.

Degnan realized he wanted to say something. "What is it, trooper?"

It was on the tip of Rafe Callahan's tongue. That he wanted to report he'd seen an Indian, an Apache, hanging around the wall of the Old Pueblo. Yes, and the Old Man would say, why in hell didn't you tell me this last night, Callahan, and maybe there would go a stripe. He said, with the blood flushing his neck, "Sir, Corporal Raphael Callahan requests the colonel's permission to grow a mustache."

Degnan looked at him. He said, "Trooper, you have my permission to grow another head and a set of horns on it if you wish."

When he went back to the stable he saw Katie skipping across to the laundry with a basket held before her. She was whistling like a jay. By God, there not only ought to be a law against sergeants. There ought to be one against colonels. There ought to be one against wives.

Joaquin was two nights outside the walls of the Old Pueblo. Mangas Chie and Ponce had come down with him, but he did not want them, and they waited in the foothills, in a near-blind arroyo from which ran only a rocky corridor wide enough to permit a horse to slip through. That first night Joaquin stood near the gate, but far enough from it to give himself the length of wall to cover retreat. He wanted one man: that piece of slime who called himself Charley Tom and wore a punched-up black hat. He would trust no one else, and yet he did not feel Charley Tom entirely trustworthy.

There were many sounds, in the night, inside the walls. Horses clopped, and mules. Wagons rumbled. Men called and sang and talked and there was light and companionship here, except for him. There was the smell of the pueblo, of oil and frying and animals and dung, a smell sometimes dry as dust and sometimes fat, as though with the oil, and this smell hung constant. The smell of men was more transitory and was dispersed into the night, but he could smell white men. They had a strange flat dead smell.

All night no one came out of the pueblo but the two soldiers.

Before dawn he went into the draw and ate and drank with Chie and Ponce. "There was nothing," he said.

"No man moved?" Chie said.

"No man I wanted." He drank water from a cavalry canteen. "Two soldiers came out. I think they were drunk. There was a break in the wall, a rotten place. I went through it and waited on the other side."

"Ai, I do not like this," Ponce said. "It may take a long time. There is danger in this, Joaquin."

Joaquin spat between his teeth and said nothing. He slept several hours. That night he went down again, and again he had to fight Chie and Ponce to keep them where they were. He understood: they wished to have a hand in this and they did not want to have him exposed alone. But they had to understand, too: Victorio had singled him out, and the risk was his personal possession. Then there was something struggling in him he could not tell them, because he did not know himself what it was. He only knew that he must do it if it took a whole harvest of nights.

Early he saw the Mexican, Jesús Elias, with three of his teamsters, ride in from the army post. Elias's saddle was deeply carved and mounted lavishly with Mexican silver, a great weight upon his horse, and his jacket was crusted with silver and his hat ringed with it. They were heavily armed, all of them, and Elias's pistols had silver on them, too. Joaquin would have given an arm to take him.

The desert night was blue. When the air stirred around him, the smell of the town was lost in an odor of flowers, space, dust, dry coolness. He followed the moon shadow along the wall. There were citadels of cloud in the sky, and the faint wind had swung south. At times it died to nothing, and he could sense the thirstiness of the land. There was rain ahead somewhere, not close yet. It would prolong the desert bloom, and in the high places the springs would grow fuller and the streams swell. He was a fool to let his senses go soft and ripe, but he thought of the high places, where he had gone in the night, without a word to any man, building his small fire at the mouth of a cleft in the rock, watching the stars bud and burst out of the sky.

Within these walls his father lay, who was white. Where are you now, old father, with the suffocating wooden box rotted away around you, and your flesh eaten to bone, and perhaps even the bones scattered away from the amusing pattern in which nature originally arranges them? His father had loved him, of that he was sure. It was comforting to be loved, but it was difficult also, because of the demands it made upon one. No one made demands upon him now, least of all in the name of love, the unreasonable. He had loved his father, and the loss had left him dry and hard inside, where he knew that for his other father, for Victorio, the grief of loss would be a hot wet thing, not of tears, but a bleeding inside. He had thought of his father that night alone, and of many things. He had thought of the times he had been with his father, until always someone, some prospector or miner or teamster meeting his father again would say, so this is the boy, eh, Dave, and appraise him, and it would begin: Dave Mitchell's in town with that breed kid of his, Jesus, blue eyes and all. . . . No Mimbreño had ever called him breed, or white eyes, and when he went out with the instructors he made himself the best of the students, so that no upturned stone, no track, no broken twig, no tuft of fur, no print of moccasin escaped him. In the games he had held a hot stone in his armpit the longest, and in the wrestling he had once let a boy break a finger before he would yield. When his novitiate was over he had gone alone with nothing but his bow, not for two weeks, but for three, and on the first raid in which he was allowed to participate (in the first four he had been horse handler) he had ridden down a Mexican with a pistol aimed at him. The coup was sung on their return, incorporated into the endless annals of the bravery of their people. Victorio's pride had been quiet and intense, and this was the thing of importance.

His father came for him again. In Prescott a drunken miner buying drinks said, *don't give that goddamn Indian no whiskey.* He was a man then, and he nearly had to fight his father to keep from taking the miner. In Santa Fe, in a stinking filthy room behind a saloon, a voice outside yelled, *the girl's got an Indian with her,* and broke into laughter, and the girl was cowering half naked against the wall and screaming. *Indian, Indian, get out, get out, don't touch me, get out.* He remembered the oily glistening swine outside who waited for her and his hands closed around her throat and cut off her voice and she slipped to the floor, frantic and flopping, like a chicken with its head wrung off. He stopped before he killed her.

The others were worse. There was a woman who called him, my

poor boy. When her husband butchered she cooked him a beef
heart. The kindness, the pity so passionately misdirected that it
assumed a quality of sacrifice, made him shrink and sicken.

And there was no woman, except for a girl who had taken her
puberty rites before he left Ojo Caliente. He did not have enough
horses for her, and he did not really want her, except out of a superficial need. The first stirring of anything in him had come like a
blow. Adept as he was at reading signs, he could not read this.
No, that was not true, he could read it but he did not want to.

What are you doing?

Splitting willow for them.

He did not think of White Painted Woman or of *Ysen*. He said,
God, help me.

When the moon moved, he slipped again through the break in
the rotten adobe and was inside the wall. There was a stable here,
roof half fallen in, with several tethered animals. He searched out
a hobbled horse. It was the horse Charley Tom had ridden into
Apache Pass. Joaquin could have picked out the horses of Charley
Tom and Shafter and the quarter Comanche anywhere, anytime,
because that was where his eyes had been when these men came
and while they spoke to Victorio.

The horses sensed him and moved and settled again. Charley
Tom's horse blew and flapped its lips. Joaquin went around it,
crouched, palm on its muzzle; on its off side there was a pile of
dried grass. He gave it a handful and slid in behind the grass and
waited.

He did not wait long. The *manso's* tall black hat blocked out an
area of sky, and Charley Tom came, singing under his breath, to
get his horse. He sang in a tedious unmusical mutter. *Qué es mi
vida preguntías. . . .* Joaquin took him from behind, around the
throat, with one arm. He let him see the knife. For a long time
there was no sound but Charley Tom's breathing. Then Joaquin
said, "Someone asks what is your life, brother?"

Charley Tom breathed, "Joaquin."

"I know what your life is. It flies away."

The *manso's* eyes were on the edge of the knife. "I do nothing,
Mimbres."

Joaquin said, "Yes, you do something. You do it for your people."

Charley Tom sagged. The knife went away, but Joaquin did not
release him. "Get me Shafter," he said.

Charley Tom said, "Not know where Shafto is."

Joaquin put his knee in the *manso's* back and pushed, pulling back at the throat. There was a cracking sound. "Get me Shafter," he said again.

"Shafto with the army now," Charley Tom said. He expelled his breath in a short hard gasp. This time he felt one of his ribs break away. Almost sobbing he said, "Shafto with nantan's son."

"Where?" Joaquin said.

"Drink whiskey."

"Get him," Joaquin said. "No nantan, no breed Comanche. Only Shafter. Outside the wall." He freed the *manso* with a wrench. Charley Tom stumbled but remained upright.

Joaquin said, "Traitor. Tame one. Jackal without pride. Listen, if there is anyone but Shafter outside that wall, do you know where you will be? With Chie and Ponce. They have planned a new thing to do with you if I do not come back. It will be a long slow thing."

Charley Tom said, "*Sabe, me,*" and was gone, bent a little with the ragged pain in his side.

Joaquin slid in behind the grass again and waited. He figured close to half an hour by the stars before he went back out through the break. From the corner he looked the length of the wall. Far down it he could see the single cherry glow of a cigarette. He made the sound of a night bird, sleepy, chirruping, running liquid. The glowing tip of the cigarette lowered and floated toward him.

Ten

Shafter came along the wall, keeping close to it, with one hand on the butt of his gun. He didn't figure Charley Tom had any cause to lie about anything, but he didn't trust anybody. That was the first thing you learned in the desert country: not to trust anybody. Indians were born knowing it; white men had to learn it. The ones who hadn't learned it in time were dead. At the end of the wall the shadow was purple and dense. Shafter, too, could smell the rain coming, a long way off. He stopped. He didn't even have time to sense anything before Joaquin was facing him, with the shadow wrapped around him like a blanket. Shafter spread his fingers and let his palm lie on the upper surface of the gun butt. He said, "Howdy, Joaquin."

"*Buenos,*" Joaquin said in a low voice. "Speak Apache, Shafter."

Shafter shook his head. "Not good enough, Joaquin. You speak English."

Joaquin said, "The *manso* says you are with the army now, Shafter."

Shafter was surprised. "With the army. No. He must've meant I was with Lieutenant Degnan."

Joaquin caught something in the voice, something which told him Shafter would have no part of the blue uniform; he remembered the horse soldiers in gray, with the hats like the one Shafter still wore. "The army hires you?" he said.

Shafter began to feel irritated. This personal palaver was cryptic, leading nowhere, and none of it was the boy's business. It was mystery enough for him that Charley Tom had come larruping in, in a lather, all hunched up and holding his side and motioning to him by violently jerking his head. He whispered five words. "Mimbres outside wall. Want you." Shafter kept his face bland because he knew Linus was watching. "Who?" he said. "Joaquin," Charley Tom said. "You come alone. You no come alone they kill me." The toughest part was saying casually to Linus and Willson and Obre and Cecil Horne, "I got to see somebody. Be back later." It was tough because, while Obre's blue eye was closed against the smoke of his cigarette, the black one was wide open, fixed on him, and because Linus' face, which was very thin and severe these days, wore a quick overcast of suspicion. He said to Joaquin, "I don't work for the army. The lieutenant's my friend." And said no more, because this was Joaquin's shot. Bide your time, *amigo*, I got all night, and all day, and you only got to dawn. He flipped his cigarette butt and took out the makings for another, and Joaquin said in the same low voice, "I will smoke with you, Shafter."

That was admitting you didn't have the makings yourself, but you had to admire the boy had got around it without begging. Shafter handed over paper and tobacco. The boy didn't show off about it either, rolling the cigarette a little awkwardly and using both hands to do it. Shafter studied him: he was a pretty cool kid, and once in a while he did something human-acting, like the awkward rolling of the cigarette, with the lip between the teeth in concentration. There was only a faint doubt in his mind about what the kid wanted. Either they were ready to negotiate for the girl, or it was that blood would tell, or was thicker than water, or some damn thing. With that uppermost in his mind he said, "I reckon you'd like to go up and visit with your pa awhile, Joaquin."

Joaquin was off-guard. "Why do you say that?"

"Only reason I know of you'd take a risk like this. Look, anytime you want to go up there and see him, I'll go with you."

Joaquin stared at him. Shafter meant it. He said, "I have your safe conduct in Tucson, Shafter. Are you so tired of living?"

Shafter smiled a little. "I'll tell you, Joaquin, I ain't as big as some or as small as others, but by God if a man wants to visit with his pa I aim to see he does it. It's a free country."

Joaquin was going to say, free for who? but he didn't let himself. Again Shafter had taken him off-balance, and it was not that he did not want to thank him, it was that he did not know how. He found himself suppressing the longing to go to his father's grave. Apaches did not visit with their dead. There was the cast-off shell of a boy named Joe Mitchell in that grave and he did not want to come within a distance where the dust of the shell might gather and rise and choke him. Yet the thing which impressed him now was that if he said, yes, that was what he wanted, Shafter would be game. He knew that he did not need to put this to the test; he knew that in Shafter was an inherent thing which was not pity,

but a fairness not only for him but for all men. This was a rare
thing. His own people did not have it, and there appeared to be
little of it among white men, although they talked about it a great
deal. When he had smoked the hot fast-burning cigarette he said,
"I did not come to visit my father, Shafter. I came for Victorio."

Shafter moved closer into the shadow. Now he could see the
boy's face, mobile, still young, neatly cut, but with the youth going
out of it rapidly. In another year it would begin to look as if it had
been chiseled from a butte, and the slenderness would ripen and
anchor in the deep-chested, wiry, near-perfect physical construction of the Apache. Blood told here all right; he bet Joaquin could
do fifty miles a day without any trouble at all. He bet Joaquin was
right on the edge of his life and feeling his oats and making some
final decisions. He bet John Shafter was a lot righter than he figured
he'd been. He bet he ought to drink more and think less.

Joaquin said, "Victorio has grown fond of the nantan's girl."

Again Shafter smiled, but now it was wry, cynical. "Victorio has?"
he said.

The boy's expression did not change. "The girl is content with
the Mimbreños."

"Is she?" Shafter said. But he couldn't keep it up. "Who the hell
you playin' patty with, Joaquin?"

Joaquin said, "You know what this girl did, Shafter? A little boy
was drowning and she went after him, where the water was strongest."

Shafter waited.

"My people were very much affected by this. She is free to come
and go as she chooses in the ranchería."

Shafter took a deep hopeful breath, but there was a foreboding
looming heavily in the back of his mind. "Is that what you came
to tell me?"

"No," Joaquin said. "I came to tell you that troopers coming in
from the east killed a Chiricahua chief. So Victorio has changed
his mind." A bleak coldness touched him and whispered along the
ridge of his spine. This was hard: this was harder than he had
thought possible, with Shafter just standing there, looking at him.
There was a thing in Shafter's face that made him writhe inside
and pulled him toward the man against his will. He said harshly,
hating to be harsh, "The girl stays with us now. Victorio wants the
nantan to know that he will never give her up. If the troops come,

he will be ready as he has never been ready before. And Cochise with him."

Shafter kept his grimness contained. After a while, hearing only the boy's uneven betraying breathing, he leaned back against the wall and put his hands in his pockets. When he slouched like that, his eyes were nearly level with Joaquin's, their locked glances in a pocket of light. He had a thousand things to say, and all he had to say wrong was one word. He hedged.

"You want me to tell the nantan this, Joaquin? Why me?"

"We trust you," Joaquin said.

There by God was a dubious honor. It warmed him.

"Because I think you are my friend," Joaquin said suddenly.

Shafter reached, again, for tobacco and silently handed it, again, to Joaquin. He said, "You think I can be your friend and the lieutenant's friend, too?"

"Yes," Joaquin said.

Shafter considered. "All right. I'll go along. Does one friend make it so bad I got to go to the other friend with something that's near gone to kill him?"

Then Joaquin said, "That is what friends are for."

"Friends are honest with one another."

"What do you want to know?" Joaquin said. He tensed, the last of the sentence slurred, and then Shafter caught it, too: movement, behind him, along the wall. "Wait," he whispered, but Joaquin had already fallen back into shadow. Shafter knew; for a moment he was wildly angry, then he felt a quick surge of fear. "Linus," he said, "move easy, you don't want a knife in your gut." He spoke quickly to Joaquin and there was sweat in the palms of his hands. "Charley didn't talk. I reckon he just knew, when I went off. Maybe you'd like to tell him yourself, Joaquin."

Joaquin was burning. There was a curiosity, a need like the need of water on an August day. But there was also the need to loose something of the innate ruthlessness which even blood could not water down. He wet his lip, seeing the hard-set face of the nantan's son, almost as white as the wall with the moonlight on it.

Well, here I am between my two friends, Shafter thought, not without humor. I'd just as leave be between two cougars. He said, "Unbuckle your belt and drop your gun, Linus."

"Not until he drops the knife," Linus said steadily.

He had barely finished speaking when Joaquin flung the knife into the sand, almost at his feet. It startled him, but he did not flinch. He felt, when the buck stepped out of the shadow, that something whole and absolute was happening to his life in this moment, some final decision shaping up out of the night. He set about trapping it the only way he knew. He said, "I'm Lieutenant Degnan." He held out his hand.

Joaquin looked up. He was half a head shorter than Linus. He read with accuracy Linus' face; he saw that every grain of human rejoicing in this man had been poisoned by sorrow. For this, he knew, he was required to be exultant. But where there was no seed, nothing would grow. He kept both hands straight at his sides, and, after a time, a long time, Linus withdrew his hand. He never took his eyes off Joaquin, even when he asked Shafter, "Can I talk with him?"

"I reckon you got to ask him that," Shafter said.

Joaquin said, "I will speak with you." He hesitated. When Linus thought he was finished, he added, "Lieutenant."

Shafter was watching Linus; he didn't figure Joaquin needed watching. They might be of an age, these two, but Joaquin had himself under curb and Linus would be quick to champ the bit. It wasn't until Joaquin said, "lieutenant" that Shafter thought something had come into his voice. What? A peculiar inflection which was neither ironic nor condescending, but almost as if it were shot through with envy.

Linus had dropped his .44 and was facing Joaquin, maybe seven or eight feet between them. He already knew about the white blood, he could see it, but he had not been around Shafter so long for nothing. He was going to deal as Indian as he knew how.

"We want to thank you for freeing the Mexican girl," he said.

Joaquin said indifferently, "She was worth a great deal. We have been paid."

"We want to know your terms for the release of my . . . for Miss Stillman." His voice shook a little.

"There are no terms," Joaquin said.

"Does your chief know that my father and I plan an all-out offensive against him?" Linus said.

Joaquin smiled a little. "Tell your father to hurry. Victorio sweats to meet him."

Linus' hands had begun to clench and unclench; he couldn't stop it. "What is your reason for holding Miss Stillman?"

"Shafter knows," Joaquin said.

Linus rasped the words. "The Mexican girl did not tell the truth."

Joaquin was disinterested. "That is not my concern."

"The Mexican girl said Anna was living with a . . . with one of your men," Linus said thickly.

Joaquin said, "I am the man."

Linus flung himself in a furious tackle. Where Joaquin had been was only night, and he came up against the wall half crouched and hung against it fighting for breath. There was nothing left but the long knife in the sand, picking up moonlight. He came up on his feet and swung with all his weight at Shafter, belting him squarely on the side of the jaw with such force that he nearly shattered his fist. Shafter staggered and went back on the wall with a grunt. He had been hit too hard to have it hurt. Before he could make a move, Linus hit him again, just under the ear, and a redness exploded in his head. It cleared a little, hazy and gray behind his eyes, and he heard himself saying, "Don't make me do it, Linus . . . don't make me do it," but blacking out under the boy's steady effective attack, falling even under the impact of the voice, forged white hot but methodical:

"Goddamn you, Shafter, you lied to me."

Shafter pushed himself off the wall and Linus hit him in the belly, doubling him up. Before he could connect again, Shafter grappled with him and at last managed to bring the blade of his hand down on the side of the boy's neck. Then he was holding Linus' limp full weight and staggering again with it, and he let Linus down and stood there, blowing like a spent horse.

When he got his wind back, he picked up the knife and went down the wall and found the break by the stable, but he knew even then that it was no good. Joaquin was gone.

He sat down and rolled another cigarette and waited while Linus struggled to make it back. Nice friends you got, Shafter. A few more nice friends like you got here and you will be laying inside with Dave Mitchell and the rest of those gut-shot, neck-stretched hombres didn't get to die a natural death. Jesus H. Christ. The trouble with your friends is they got too much grit, too much sand, and all you want to do is lie down somewhere.

Linus sat up and put his head in his arms. Shafter said, "Are you listenin' to me, Linus? All right, goddamit, don't answer. I told you not to call me a liar. I didn't lie to you. I got to admit when we were ridin' into town that day I did think about the half breed. But I didn't see any sense courtin' trouble till we knew for sure."

Linus said hoarsely, "What am I, a blasted baby, you can't tell me these things? Who the hell are you, thinking things that maybe mean life or death to me?"

"I ain't anybody," Shafter said. "Now that you ask. I didn't think you had to ask. But if you want me to shake off this load of yours I been heavin' around, you just say so."

"That night," Linus said. "You and Horne . . . all of us. You and your ace in the hole. Wait, you said. Just wait. That's some ace, Shafter. Even a coyote can wait. It doesn't take any strategy, any planning, waiting. You got Horne so worked up he wouldn't have taken me from here to Bowie."

"So now you got something to go on," Shafter said. He leaned down and passed over the knife. "Here."

Linus looked up at him and took the knife. "There's no sense apologizing, is there?'"

Shafter rubbed his jaw. "Not unless it makes you feel better."

"There's only one thing going to make me feel better," Linus said. He held the knife by the wrapped rawhide hilt. "It's when I put this right in that half breed's heart." He got to his feet groggily. The lock of hair fell over his forehead and he almost lost his balance when he bent to retrieve his hat. "What in hell did you hit me with?"

"Pick up your belt," Shafter said. Linus did. When he straightened he felt Shafter's hand on his shoulder. "Linus, if you feel that way, go ahead. Sink it in me if you got to." His voice was not easy now, but darkly compassionate. "Will you spend a little time lookin' at your belly button?"

"What?" Linus said.

"I mean it," Shafter said. "I mean do you still want your girl? Ain't it maybe been spoiled pretty bad now?"

"I'll show you," Linus said. He was very calm. "I'll show you and I'll show her. I'll make it up to her, every minute of it."

"Look a little longer," Shafter said.

Linus was silent. Then he said, "What is it, Shafter, am I stupid?"

"No," Shafter said. "Just bewildered, like the rest of us, I reckon. You want me to say it for you?"

"No," Linus said. "I know what you're going to say . . . what you want me to say. You want me to be logical and reasonable and look at this objectively. Well I can't. And it hasn't anything to do with age or experience or anything else, except love." He was stoic and unembarrassed. "I love Anna. If you think for one minute that I'm going to consider any possibility that she doesn't want to leave there, you're out of your mind."

Shafter nodded. "All right. You know how you got to feel. Just don't run wild on me, will you?"

Linus looked at him, but he didn't say anything. They started down the wall and turned into town. Almost immediately Charley Tom got up from the ground, where he had been waiting, and came to them. He still walked hunched up, holding his hand over his rib cage, just under the heart.

"Thanks, Charley," Shafter said. "You better go home and let the post surgeon see what he can do for you."

Charley Tom shook his head. "No ride out. Maybe they out there."

Linus pulled up short. "Would they do that?" he said, hoping they would, itching with what Charley Tom had suggested.

"Christ almighty," Shafter said. "Who'd ever thought I'd of ended up wet-nursin' a couple of idiot papooses. Charley, you wait and ride out with the lieutenant."

"You're coming, Shafter?" Linus said.

Shafter shook his head. "No, I'm through now, Linus. I'm up to my neck. Dead weight."

"But you can't just. . . ." Linus said.

"Who can't?" Shafter said. "You think I ain't got anything to do but ride around the edges of your pa's blue coat?" He caught himself. "I'm sorry, Linus, I know you're askin', but it ain't enough."

Linus felt pinched. He knew, clearly and without question, exactly what Shafter meant, and he was a little astonished at his own perceptiveness. His asking wasn't enough. But if his father asked? And how to get his father to ask and make him believe it was his own idea?

In a rough house without any door a Mexican girl got up enough energy to lunge away from the dobe frame and sway off the step toward them. She was slight and rather sickly-looking and had doused herself with some sweetish scent which assailed the nostrils nauseatingly. "*Hola*, Shafter," she said, her head on one side.

"*Buenos,* Paquita," Shafter said. "I'm powerful tired," he informed her. They went on, past doorways where Mexicans sat in the dirt before mean hovels, and a few Indians, Papagos, starred the darkness with their cigarettes. The tower of the little church loomed on the sky, the bell silent and black in the arch. Some men moved toward them, and one of them broke away, ahead, and Cecil Horne's old basso rumbled, "That you, Shafter?"

"What's the matter?" Shafter said.

"Come on down, sonny," Horne said. He took off his hat and beckoned with it. "That Irish bullwhacker's pickin' on yore buddy agin."

Shafter said, "I had all I want for tonight, Cec. Willson can take care of himself."

Horne chuckled. "I dunno. Looks a mite slow to me. He don't hardly say a word."

"Well, he ain't takin' anything, is he?" Shafter said.

"Nope," Horne said. "That mick come up right when Willson was fixin' to take a sip out'n his glass. Butted into him and upsot it. Willson, he don't even study him, he jest waits till the mick gits his shot sot up and reaches acrost the bar and grabs it and drinks it hisself." He was grinning like a wolf. "The redhead spouts off like a whale. Willson, he still don't say nothin'. They's quite a crowd eggin' 'em on."

"Let's go bust it up," Linus said. He was flushed and sweating.

It didn't look as if there was any stopping it. Men were milling, laughing, yelling, when they reached the Quartz Rock. Kiernan and Willson were out in the street now. Kiernan was swaggering, throwing his weight. Willson looked unutterably sad. Elias stood at the rear fringe of the crowd with two of his teamsters, a Mexican and a Californian named Logan, backing Kiernan. Nobody was backing Willson, not even Obre, who stood at the far end of the building, leaning on it with his thumbs hooked through his belt. Shafter shouldered through the milling men and signaled Willson with a lift of the head.

"Here's the Indian lovers," Kiernan said. "All of 'em. They look pretty white on the outside, don't they?"

The Mexicans cheered. Willson sighed. "Howdy, Shafter. Where you gone at?" he said.

"To bed." Shafter didn't look at Kiernan. "Come on, I got something to tell you."

Elias edged in, behind Kiernan. "He stole your whiskey, Kiernan. Are you going to let him do this?"

Kiernan concentrated on the problem. It did look as if Willson was just going to go off and leave him standing there. "Hell no," he said. "Hey, Willson, you owe me for a redeye. You ain't goin' nowhere till you pay me."

"Here's an I.O.U.," Willson said and hit him on the side of the head.

Kiernan went down and bounced back again. "Why, you lousy grayback, you done it now for sure."

"Just payin' my debts," Willson said, looking sadder than ever and throwing up both hands when Kiernan came at him.

Shafter reached out and caught the teamster by the collar of his duck shirt. "Break it up, Kiernan. You had it coming."

Elias interfered quickly. "Keep out of this, Shafter. It's not your fight."

But Kiernan had turned, his rubbery face red with anticipation. "Sure it's his fight. I'll take you on anytime, Shafter. I'll take on any Indian lover."

"Go to hell," Shafter said. "You comin', Willson?"

"You yellow-bellied sidewinder," Kiernan said. He swung his head and gestured at Linus; he was balanced on the balls of his feet, his barrel chest and enormous shoulders straining. "Him, too. Yellow stripe on his pants and one down his back."

Linus dived at him with clean, obvious joy. Shafter stuck out his foot and tripped him and Linus went down. The Mexicans cheered.

"Take him, Kiernan," Elias said.

Kiernan made a rush at Linus and Linus got him around the ankle, prone on the ground, and pulled him down. Shafter moved in then, but something hot and stinging caught him around the chest like a coil and held him. The Californian, Logan, had snaked out his teamster's whip. Shafter yanked hard and pulled Logan off-balance, dragged the whip out of his hand, and slugged him with the loaded butt. Elias began to stamp his feet, shrieking like a woman. Kiernan and Linus were writhing in the dust and Linus was getting the worst of it. Within the circle somebody hit somebody else, but it came to a dead halt because nobody could watch two fights at once and do either of them justice. Kiernan jumped on Linus and Shafter went in and booted him hard in the backside. Kiernan grunted and lunged up on his knees. Somebody fired a gun, the sound half lost in the uproar. Along the wall, near

Obre, Cecil Horne sat down suddenly, with his legs stretched out before him.

Kicking was fair. Kiernan stood up to let Linus have it and Linus reached up and grabbed him in the groin. Kiernan went up screaming, but Linus held on. Then he saw the short knife in Kiernan's hand, and he let go and rolled away, putting everything he had in it.

Willson moved, too, when he saw the knife, and the Mexicans pushed in behind him. It was going to snowball bad, Shafter saw. But he didn't count on what stopped it. Obre stopped it, stepping into the circle with one gun drawn. "Who shot Horne?" he said. He didn't shout, but his voice carried.

The circle began to spread, to pull back, with the first pressure of silence weighing on it. Kiernan was doubled up, groaning; Linus was on his feet, his lip split and bleeding. Again it was Shafter who cleared through. Horne was still sitting quietly against the wall. Will Oury was bending over him, so Shafter couldn't see the bearded old face. But when Oury straightened, he could see the hole in the forehead.

"What happened, Shafter?" Oury said.

"Wild shot, I reckon." Shafter bent and felt for a heart beat where there wasn't any. As soon ask a dobe wall who fired it.

"Who started this?" Oury said.

Elias was tightlipped beside him. "The Indian lovers, Will, who did you think?"

Then Obre said, "Nobody's got to hear any greaser lies. Kiernan started it and Kiernan's gone to finish it." He moved toward Kiernan slowly, but he was smiling. "Stand up, Kiernan." Kiernan straightened. Obre put the Dance back in its holster. He said, "Kiernan, a long time you want to fight Shafter. You want to fight Willson. I ain't see particular you want to fight me, so it's fair. All them names you call other men guts me. I know it ain't your fault, I know you get put up to it every time you go round to collect your pay."

Kiernan was staring at him.

"You want to use the knife," Obre said. "Comanche is very good with the knife. Very good."

Kiernan cursed him.

"Hold it," Oury yelled, but Shafter backed him off. "You hold it, Will. You want to see justice done, send Elias in there."

"I ain't goin' to fight you, you red nigger," Kiernan panted.

"You are gone to fight me," Obre said. "Because if you don't, I'm gone to kill you. I'm gone to kill you anyway."

Kiernan screamed, "Elias, you goin' to stop this?"

Elias was silent, taut as a pulled wire. Shafter reached over and unburdened him of both silver-mounted pistols.

Kiernan was edging around the inner lip of the circle, trapped, trying to pull away from Obre. Obre didn't move; there was no place for either of them to go. Obre said, "The knife or draw, Kiernan."

"You ain't got nothin' against me," Kiernan said.

"Sure I do. Wasn't for you that old man wouldn't be dead now, likely. He was a pretty good old man. He don't deserve to be dead."

"Fight me fair then," Kiernan screamed.

Obre looked down at his hands in the black gloves, turning them over and examining them as if he could see both back and palm through the supple leather. "I didn't hear the lieutenant say that when you pulled the knife," he said gravely. He took off the gloves and tossed them to Willson.

Kiernan stood up very straight. He threw the knife away. His voice was raw, resigned. "Your way then. Maybe it's time somebody spread you, Comanche."

Beside Shafter, Elias drew a long breath of relief. Kiernan was good with a gun, as good as any teamster on his run, and he knew a couple of fast tricks.

Obre knew all the tricks, but he used only one. He had never filed the sights, as many did, so that they would not trip clearing leather, but he oiled the insides of his holsters. He liked to sight when he fired, and he was expert at angle sighting from any level he could set his eye. Within ten yards he would not have an opportunity to aim, and he figured Kiernan at six or six and a half yards from him. He never fanned his guns either, not even in practice; it tore them up and busted them apart too quickly, and it was show-off stuff and not his way. The first shot had to count; he never figured on another chance. Nor had he slip-hammered the Dances, or any other gun, not since he was a kid, kicking a can along in the dust with a ripping barrage of shots.

There was one thing: there weren't any triggers on the Dances.

He found long ago there was no sense doing in two hard motions, cocking, pulling, what you could do in a sole practiced one.

It took a long time, a lot of training, to learn you didn't need a trigger or a trigger finger, to master letting the hammer slide off the joint of the thumb so oiled and slick the aim didn't flicker a fraction, to co-ordinate every individual specific move in a series of moves into a smooth cohesive whole. The skill did not, with him, rise particularly from speed in drawing. It lay rather in an uncanny ability to compute the error factor in another man, another man's guns, a sixth sense like a built-in calculator, so automatic that it was like the flawless operation of a faultless machine. It had to do with the inherent, mostly overlooked thing which, coupled with speed and accuracy and perhaps more important than both, made the edge between the mere marksman and the valid gunfighter: the sheer gut to stand up to another gun.

Kiernan used the old trick, without any warning. He flipped his holster and fired upward, out of the end of it.

Obre felt three things. He felt the thong which tied down his right holster bite into his leg as the sinew jumped under it. He felt the drag of the Dance, low on his hipbone. He felt the wind of Kiernan's shot run along his temple.

Kiernan had another chance. His gun was half out when the flat Dance slipped into Obre's deliberate hand and the hammer slid off under the thumb like hot grease. Obre shot him. He fell face down.

The Mexicans cheered everybody. Elias shouted, "I'm going to prosecute you, Obre. You won't get away with this."

Obre ignored him.

"Give me my guns, Shafter," Elias said. Shafter handed them over. Elias was white and shaking. "No Indian's going to gun a white man in this town," he said.

Obre pushed past him. His nerves were quivering like fiddle strings. The greaser was a sore loser. Obre could be a sore winner: he nearly turned on Linus when Linus followed him; he didn't know which was the most trouble—your enemies or your friends. Elias's idea of prosecution would be to dry-gulch him the first chance he got.

Nobody went near Cecil Horne but the four of them: Obre, Shafter, Willson, Linus. Oury was riding out, settling his big gray hat furiously. "You're through in Tucson, Obre," he called.

Obre told him what he could do to himself. Elias and Logan moved off with Kiernan's body. Shafter lifted Horne's slight wiry bulk and took it into the Quartz Rock and put it on the bar. There wasn't anything to do, but you had to do something.

"I got his gear in the back room," the bartender said. "His donkey's down to Harter's."

"We ought to check his stuff for kinfolk," Shafter said.

The bartender let them in the storeroom and pointed out the worn saddlebags. There were no letters, no papers. Nothing even to identify the man, verify his name, prove he had ever existed. But Shafter got up with something in his hand. It was small and roughly circular, hung with what looked like frayed black hemp.

"What is it?" Linus said.

Shafter said, "Apache scalp."

There were five of them.

Linus stumbled out, not looking at the old man on the bar, the hands which had panned for gold and gentled a burro and taken scalps crossed on the breast. Some wag had put a half-empty glass of beer in the stiffening fingers. Outside, Linus unknotted his handkerchief and tried to wipe the thick blood off his lip, but it had dried and crusted.

Shafter came out, rubbing the back of his neck. "You all right?" he said.

"Sure, I'm great," Linus said. His voice was caustic. Then he said, "This is a rotten country, Shafter. This must be the rottenest country that ever was."

Shafter said, "It's only men are rotten, Linus."

"This country makes them that way," Linus said.

Shafter looked at him; there was something hard and biting in him now. Shafter thought it was like a thirteen-year old whose voice had been halting and cracking and riding up and down the scale and all of a sudden became firm and settled in its own special adult pitch. It might ripen and broaden, but it was set for good, just like a fried egg.

"Isn't it ever any bigger than this?" Linus said.

"I reckon not," Shafter said. "Unless it's happening to you."

"It seems as if it ought to be more important. The most important."

"It ain't though," Shafter said. "How's your lip?"

"All right. One of my back teeth is loose."

Shafter said, "Linus, whatever you liked about Cec Horne didn't

make him good. Five Apache scalps don't make him bad. There
ain't ever anything that's all of a piece."

"Nothing?" Linus said.

"Nothing."

"I was afraid of that," Linus said.

Shafter watched the chrysalis fighting its way out of the hard
shell and thought, so this is how it happens, who had never seen
it happen because you didn't know when it was happening to you,
just as Linus did not know it now. Shafter thought it was kind of
sad to ride into a town one man and ride out another, never even
being able to realize and savor and hold the moment you broke
free, the moment you knew for certain you had your whole life in
your hands and that you could do with it not just anything, but
possibly everything you wanted to. Man was a lot like the desert.
The sun rose and it was harsh and stark. The sun kept circling
and the light shifted and there were new and brilliant shadings,
finer colors showing, coming out little by little, and at last, when
the sun was downing, the priceless gentleness, the quiet luster came
into its own, and no matter how austere the next sunrise, you
remembered and you waited and, sure enough, the radiance was
there.

Eleven

All the strangenesses were crowding upon Anna. The nights were deep, silent, no hour distinguishable from another; she slipped into them out of routine and weariness, without rest or comfort, promised temporary oblivion from which she must rise to face another morning. The days merged into one another, steady, golden, rain-washed, cloud-filled, skied-over blue, the hours, like the hours of the night, empty of all determination.

Her hands would pause at their work. She had only just come here, it was yesterday the big Mexican horse had picked its way up the corridor from the desert. No, she had been here weeks, months, years, forever. Somewhere in the remote dimension there had been a girl named Ysabel, her only friend. Somehow she had got Ysabel confused with her mother, who was dead. Her mother had come here with her. She could barely recall her mother. At times there was not even the mercy of oblivion, and she woke uneasily from dream and fell back powerless into another world where two children played in the dirt along a river. She was one of the children. There was mud on the edges of her skirt. This reference was persistent. The other child was a boy. She could not see his face. Behind her closed eyes the struggle would begin to block out everything but the face which did not come, except, at times, set at some exact, withdrawn angle, or in a certain thoughtful and to her unnatural expression which it appeared to assume through habit, never full and clear in her mind. She could only say his name and never really see him.

In the morning she was drawn, sane, wistfully thankful for the sun, for the presence of human beings with whom she had nothing but the most elementary existent material contact. She could say then, calmly, I cannot remember Linus' face.

Nuadin would see her frown, eyes slick and frantic with the effort to recall, and her face would implore. She liked the *americana* girl and she did not want her to be sad. She wanted her to be one of them. Anna talked to her in disconnected bursts. She said, It's not being here that's the trouble, not at all, it's only I can't reach out and touch you. Don't you see? Not just that I can't talk to you except for a few miserable words of miserable Spanish, but that we're so completely outside one another. I can live as you do, by your customs, there's nothing so difficult about that, it's only an adjustment, and share your food and your fire, and I suppose learn your language, but I can't reach you. And you can't reach me. You can't understand that I'm completely, absolutely alone, just as if none of you existed at all. It's not your fault. . . . I like you, Nuadin, truly I do, and I shouldn't like you to change and I want you and your people to be free and happy, but I want to be free and happy, too. The only way to solve it is for me to be born with you, and it's too late for that, it can't be done. I suppose you think it's selfish of me, but I have to have someone. Everybody has to have someone. Nuadin nodded. The words were alien, ugly to her, but matter-of-fact and without complaint. Clouds were burning across the sun. She pointed them out to Anna. It was all she could offer.

Joaquin came back. Some of the women were down on a lower slope of the mountain, scraping fresh hides. He went to Anna before he went to Victorio. Her breath caught and made a little clicking sound when she saw him. Her heart was hard and painful. But both Ponce and Mangas Chie were suspicious and displeased when he stopped. They rode on, up.

"I am glad you are back, Joaquin," she said.

He did not dismount. He looked to find some sign of what had made her glad of this. The women went on with their work, stolid, incurious. The sun beat strongly here, and it was hot and glaring even where the brush made balls of shade on the ground. She moved close to the horse. His face was rigid, almost wary. When she said, "Are you all right?" she saw the glint of his teeth between his lips.

He said, "Your man is going to fight for you, Ana. That seems to be his only greeting."

"Oh no," she said weakly. "No, I don't want that."

"No?" he said. "Why not?"

"I don't want anyone hurt or killed because of me. Can't they understand that. . . . As long as he's known me, he should know that."

He did not answer.

She bit her lip. "It isn't me, really, is it? It's that Victorio is trying to prove something, and I am only the pawn."

"Pawn?"

"A piece in a game we play . . . the piece of least sacrifice." She put her hand on the strong-muscled ridge of the Appaloosa's neck. "You saw him, Joaquin. How . . . how is he?"

"How am I to know that? He came where he was not wanted and spoke to me."

"But how did he seem?"

"Angry at hearing the truth."

"Why do you do this to me?" she cried. "Can't you tell me anything? It means nothing to you, and I have to live on the scraps you choose to pass out to me. Do you want to see me cry, is that it? Well, I won't, and I can't; there isn't a drop of moisture in me anywhere. You are drying me up, and I will turn into a husk, a leaf, and I will blow away in the wind. Joaquin!"

He looked down into her face.

"Help me, Joaquin. Please."

A thin flame flared in him. "How?" he said.

She was shaking her head, advancing the ultimatum. One dark braid swung forward on her breast. "Go away. Stay away from me. Go with Victorio. Or be with me."

He rode on.

She stood with her head bent. Soon Nuadin came and touched her arm. The work was not finished. Anna said, "I am coming. I am coming for the last time."

Victorio had been out on a training problem with some of the boys. When he saw Joaquin he came at a half run, taking Joaquin by both shoulders. "How did it go? Chie and Ponce?"

"Well," Joaquin said. "It was not difficult."

"You saw Shafter?"

"And the nantan's son."

"Ai, you did not go to the post?" Victorio said, surprised.

"He came to me," Joaquin said, in a voice which implied he had had some control over this. With Victorio, rather than with Anna, a single panel of the tableau was graphic for him: the fair hair and height, the prestige of uniform. And of blood. His lip curled. "He is not afraid. Only like a bear who has sat in a bee's nest. They are coming out against us. You will be watched."

"*Enju,*" Victorio said. "We will go now, I think."

"I will stay," Joaquin said.

Victorio looked at him. Then again he put his hands on Joaquin's shoulders, hard. He said, "*Ysen* gave man other men so that he would not be alone."

"When it is time for me to speak, I will speak," Joaquin said.

"I will wait," Victorio said.

"The man Shafter is my friend," Joaquin said.

The smile was barely discernible on Victorio's mouth. His regard was the same as that which he placed upon his sons, no more, no less. He said, "The strongest of things gives way. Take a wall of stone, Joaquin. The crack begins in it, and every day the crack becomes a little wider, a little longer. Do you know what causes this? The wind and sand and sun and rain, which are the friends of the wall. In time the wall falls to its friends."

"You are my father," Joaquin said, lifting his head.

"May it always be so," Victorio said.

Late in the afternoon the small raiding party came in from New Mexico Territory. They had no captives, but there was plenty of plunder, horses, clothing, *americano* tinned food, some guns. The celebration began at once. By dark the men were bloated with *tulepah,* and when the first stars came the warriors stamped in the circle, telling in formal improvised song the interminable details of the exploit, citing their own courage and that of their comrades. Two white men were dead and a house had been burned. The account was repetitious and became highly colored, embroidered with exaggeration as each warrior contributed to it. The old women drank also, and a few smoked. The women of all ages danced alone, and then with the men, the young girls shy in choosing their partners. Anna sat at the far rim of the circle and watched. The dancing was uninhibited even within its ritual confines, then decorous and rather stately when the women joined in. The drum was so monotonous and steady that it drugged her. Joaquin sat by Victorio; she looked often at him but never once caught his eye.

When the men were glazed of vision, alternating between stupor and bursts of noisy enthusiasm, she got up and went down into the

wickiup and pulled closed the hide door. The drum went on, insistent, and there was laughter and the stamp of feet and the glare
of the fires, but it was dark here and silent. She made herself wait.
No one came. They would be up most of the night. She wished
upon them all a great drunkenness. She slipped out, crossed behind the ragged groups of wickiups, and began the long walk down.

In the beginning she moved with caution, fearful of dislodging
stones. Then sound and light began to recede like a wave pulling
out and dying, and the dark and cold closed in upon her.

There was no moon; the stars were hazy and indistinct. The cold
was sharp as a blade. She was walking the last hope, blindly,
ignorantly, unaware of distance, danger, anything but the retaining
of, if not sanity, identity. There were things here which loved the
night—reptiles, furred creatures; rain coming, day coming, no
water: the detached realities. She was not guided by recklessness
but by some hard, unthinking, driving stupefaction. No, not hope
after all. All that was left of hope was a shred, hanging.

The eyes learn darkness. Rocks loom blacker in the planes of
night, brush assumes its own disparate contours, the trail takes on
a flat firmness without obstacle. She walked steadily, mechanically,
out of a necessity greater than reason.

The night moved and spoke, but she was not aware of the
presence of fear until she realized that her heart had been pump-
ing brutally and had only now quieted enough for her to breathe
normally, without strain. If her flesh crawled, it was with cold. She
was without madness, without terror, simply and quietly fixed on
course, moving away.

The vedette came to Cochise. "The white-eyes *niña* walks out,"
he said.

Victorio rose unsteadily; he was drunk. He cast about for Delgadito, but Joaquin stopped him.

"Let her go," Joaquin said.

Victorio swayed, uncomprehending.

Joaquin said, "It will teach her what she will not learn any other
way."

Victorio sat down again. His laughter was thick and grating.

Joaquin turned to an old squaw behind him. He said, "Bring my
horse."

With some part of her she realized, without any deep consideration, the deceptiveness of desert distances. A mountain, which an
hour's walk might bring you to, never came any closer. At times
only a full day of traveling brought it closer. But it appeared within
touch, and there was a shimmery lake at its base. Only when it
rose near enough to reveal the baked arroyos and sandy humpbacked rises of its foothills and the lake dissolved into the clarity
of the atmosphere which had been responsible for the deception
did the senses accept the great and grand swindle.

The sea of the desert was as endless as the seas of water and,
to some, as lonely. Only the practiced eye, marking beyond the
apparent sameness of land, acknowledging and reflecting an inner
passion for distances, saw that the sameness was camouflage, responded to the chameleon-turning splendor where the scarlet and
black and mauve and gold shifted down the blue mountains and
across the pale sand. Within the obelisks of rock, in the high places,
there was security. Sanctuary waited in the higher mountains where
the lakes glistened, the swaying pines towered, the lush green meadows rolled with wild flowers. No element of survival came to offer
assurance where the stones ended and the sand began; yet from the
heights, looking down the snaking valleys of the mountain chains,
beyond the misting alabaster, amethyst, jasper, sapphire, smoke,
pearl, the heart rejected even the suggestion that there was nothing here.

She thirsted for the waste which promised heat without shade,
fire without food, mirage without water.

Sometimes she stopped, not to rest, for she was hard, tough as
rawhide now, but to listen. There was the sound of insects, night
birds, the lithe dog-like little coyotes shouting distantly to one another. These were sounds to which she was accustomed. The trail
went down and down, into the darkness. That illumination which
lies upon the desert even on moonless nights, as if the sand had
imprisoned and held the daylight and mirrored it back into the sky,
pointed the broken line where the mountains moored on the murky
arch of distance.

She walked nearly what was left of the night, coming to the
foot of the corridor, where the palo verde guarded the washes
and gave its yellow scent to the dark. There was water here, but
she did not know it, keeping her mouth from drying with a small
flat stone on her tongue, wracked with the cold although she sensed

the not inconsiderable warming of the air as she came nearer the desert floor. A corner of the sky was lifting very faintly, like old dirty canvas tearing, revealing the advance of a cheerless gray dawn. The little spherical saucers of the cholla were heaped one upon the other.

She was tired and she did not want the day to come. Would it have mattered if she had stayed up among the rocks, praying concealment until another night? She did not think so. Not to men who knew by a single grain of dust on rock that that rock had been passed over.

She did not know when she was first aware of the quiet, skin-shod walking horse. A sensitivity not yet completely numbed told her that it was there, that something was wrong, that she was not alone. The sky threatened, merciless; the trembling fatigue in her legs unbalanced her. In the first colorless light she turned her head and saw the horse and walked petrified, resigned to the rush and pain which would be the lance, barbarous and final, and willed her heart to stand and meet it. There was only the pacing horse, at her left and slightly behind her. Steeling to the torturous waiting, she turned her head again and for a time did not know Joaquin with the heavy plaits of hair lying against the gray cavalry shirt.

She looked away and stumbled on. The horse moved slowly beside her.

Birds were singing. The pacing horse went with her. In the first patches of soft sand which studded the hard-packed earth she sank and stopped. The horse stood. She was no longer cold, but shaking, inside, with a violence like a rushing black wind. She took ten more steps, and the horse moved again. The audibility of the day was inchoate, desultory, and there was no air to breathe in the savage vacuum.

Then she stopped and turned full. She did not speak, nor did he. There was nothing to say. She crossed to him. There was nowhere else to go. When at last he reached down, she put her foot on his instep and swung up before him. He pulled the horse around.

The weariness became very keen and salient, almost a stimulation, unbearably pleasant; it was flowing like water, sweetly and easily, with a calm force beyond all power to arrest. Under its placid gliding she was whetted, honed to a fine edge, turned on the wheel of some total, willing vulnerability which drew, towered, crested, broke, releasing a warm honeyed foam in her, as if her blood frothed, the myriad shining bubbles ascending, bursting, along the yielding passages of vein. The column of her throat grew round and hard as marble, swayed upon a tremorous base, lost its balance; her head came to rest against him. She felt his mouth, taut, feverish, just above her temple. The slack gait of the horse cradled. The first rain, soft and light as fog, drifted on her uplifted face, half-closed eyes, submissive hands.

In the wash the palo verde hung the more brilliantly for the early grayness, the more lustrous deprived of an overwhelming sun. The misting rain leant intensity to fresh virescent grass blurred with milky petals, sprawling thickly under the trees, up the cut banks, to the edges of guardian rock; a vague and argent light opaqued whatever world lay beyond this. She knelt where the water ran floating the spent florets of the trees and drank from her hands until he stopped her. The Appaloosa, grazing, had flowers on his lips. Still on her knees, she pressed close and hard against him where he stood; when she felt his hands she thought he would lift her, but there was no rising; there was the inescapable convulsive delirium of the sinking, the drowning. The rain, webbing fragilely the starved young flesh, was lambent with some mellowed coolness, silken and pliant, speckling somberly on the rock. A bird flashed, under the crown of trees, over them and was gone into the morning.

Twelve

An old man once said you could gauge just how rapidly you were getting old by how much longer it took you to lose your temper, how much easier you felt about things which, earlier, would have caused you excessive bother, how much oftener you shrugged off even major annoyances. The old man had got to be a general and was retired on a nice pension which guaranteed there wasn't much about to bother him. I am not an old man yet, Walter Degnan thought. Not, at least, if that old fool was right. I can lose my temper with the best of them. I seem to be too right-muscled to shrug well. And the only thing which distinguishes me from a mad bear at times is that I am in complete possession of a very civilized thing called control.

But he was barking. "All I want is yes-and-no answers," he said.

"I can't give you yes-and-no answers," Linus said. "It wouldn't be fair." He was sitting in the corner, in the round-seated chair Tony Bleeker favored. His father, who had been pacing the cage of his office, stopped short and leaned against the edge of his desk. His face was troubled. He felt for his son a sympathy which bordered on tears, and which he could not permit himself to offer.

"Linus, can't you get it through your head that I have to make a report of this . . . that your name has to appear on that report? What do you think I'm going to do, slant it so you get the clean end of the stick?"

"Of course not," Linus said. "Father, what I wish you would get through *your* head, once and for all, is that there's a limit to what you can do here. I understand that technically this area is under your jurisdiction. Elias and Oury understand it . . . they demand it. But how in hell are you going to stop these things? What are you going to do to prevent it—divide the garrison, put ten men here, ten there, strengthening nothing and weakening everything? Somebody gets shot up or killed in Tucson every day of the month. This is no exaggeration. There's nothing you can do about it."

"You are not involved in it every day of the month," Degnan said.

"Look, Father . . . this was bound to come. Kiernan, Logan, all of them, have been asking for trouble."

"From you?" Degnan said pointedly.

"Yes, from me," Linus said.

"Since when?" Degnan snapped. "Since you've been bumming around with Shafter. This is not solely your business, Linus; it's mine, too. I happen to be your father. I have got to know exactly what happened."

"You mean Elias didn't tell you?"

"Elias told me. Oury, too. I want to hear it from you."

"Sure," Linus said. He was irritated. "And I'll tell you what I want. I want you to bring John Shafter in here and ask him. I want you to ask Obre and Willson. I want to see who tells the lies and who tells the truth, and I'm the only man who can point out the difference for you."

Degnan said wearily then, "Don't fight me, son."

"I'm not," Linus said. "You're fighting me."

Degnan lowered his head and looked at the floor. "Will you tell me, as you saw it?"

"I'll tell you as it happened," Linus said. "It started one night over the bar, right after we found out about Anna. Just Willson and me. Kiernan was insolent. I took it. Last night I wasn't in the mood to take anything." He licked the split lip. "I wanted to fight."

"You wanted to go into Tucson and disgrace the entire garrison," his father said. "You had a caprice, in other words. As ranking junior officer of this post you had to lower yourself to exchanging blows with some sweaty Irish teamster. And when you get your brains beaten out, your Comanche friend jumps in and guns him."

Linus smiled a little. "Is that Elias's story?"

"Linus, Jesús Elias is a sane, intelligent, responsible man. He is a gentleman. Do you understand what I'm saying?"

"I understand you aren't eating any part of the cake but the icing."

Degnan made a gesture of total exasperation, throwing both arms toward the ceiling. "What is the use? You're going to sit there and defend Obre in spite of everything."

"No," Linus said quietly, "I'm not going to defend Obre. Unlike you, I'm not going to judge him either."

After a moment the colonel nodded. "I won't interrupt you again."

"All right. It was like this. Kiernan got rough with Willson, but Willson hit him first. One of the teamsters wrapped Shafter up in his whip. . . . I think Elias's men were going to take the four of us; I think that's what Elias had in mind. First Kiernan called us Indian lovers; then he called me yellow, so I went for him. Shafter, damn him, tripped me, trying to stop it, I guess. Kiernan pulled a knife on me."

"What?" his father said. "What?"

"Elias forgot to tell you?" Linus said. "Somebody in the crowd fired a shot, just feeling his oats, but it got Horne in the head. Then Obre came in and broke it up. Kiernan had all the chance in the world."

"Is that so?" his father said. "All the chance in the world against a man who makes his living with guns. Elias says Kiernan never got his gun out."

Linus said, "Kiernan fired out of his holster. Did Elias say that?"

"No," his father admitted. "But I don't think it makes any difference. Did Obre or did he not tell Kiernan he was going to kill him?"

"He told him."

"Then it was deliberate. Premeditated. What was Horne to him?"

"I don't think Horne was anything to him, Father. I think he'd just had all he could take, like the rest of us. I think what he really wanted was for it to be Elias, but Kiernan was the best he could get."

"You tell me this," Degnan said. "You sit there and tell me this."

"I think a man has to stand and fight somewhere along the line," Linus said. "I think it's contemptible beyond measure for any man to want to hurt another man because his grandfather happened to be an Indian. I think the crime lies in any man having the right to provoke another beyond endurance. You can put that in your report, for me. You can also put in that if anything happens to Obre there's only one man responsible for it."

"Elias has asked me to bring Obre to justice."

"Military or no, I doubt if you can legally do it," Linus said. "What do you want to do, bring him in and try him? I won't let you do that, Father, I'll risk my neck to get him out. He did as much for me in Apache Pass."

Degnan said on a wavering note, "Who am I to pacify, you or Elias, and how? I can't make it right with both of you."

"Don't make me laugh; it hurts my lip," Linus said cheerfully. "I don't think you can satisfy either of us. But when you write that report, be sure you say that I did it for the honor of the U. S. Cavalry, which is very proud of the stripe on its breeches. And will not be told it's got one down its back."

Degnan smiled a little. Then his face stiffened. "I'm going to accept your version, Linus."

"That's damned white of you," Linus said, grinning.

"Linus, for Christ's sake, will you stop all this! I will even accept that your . . . your rebel friends were perfectly blameless in this affair, if that's what you want. But I have got to have your word that you'll stay the hell *out* of trouble. There was no reason for you to become involved in this."

"There was some reason," Linus said, "but it was kind of personal and I probably shouldn't have gone so far with it, especially as I about knocked Shafter's head off a little while before."

"Good God," the colonel said. "I give up. How many people were mixed up in this war of yours in the course of the evening? Surely not Shafter?"

"I'm afraid so. He was very decent about it. After that Mexican girl told us about Anna, I was going to try and get up there alone . . . to the Stronghold. I thought Horne would show me where the corridor is. Shafter talked me out of it. He said the girl was lying about Anna. She hadn't really been beaten, you know, Father. I didn't want you to know it."

"Why not?" Degnan said. He was beginning to feel totally incompetent, not only at his job but at the entire business of living.

"I thought it would only complicate things for you," Linus said.

Degnan was struck by the unimpassioned tone Linus had taken. The business of Anna had affected him badly; he did not sleep well and he found himself becoming harsh with his men. It came to him now that this was the first time he had seen his son reasonably calm and willing to speak freely, but he was confused by Linus' immediate reaction and approach. He tried to maintain a similar calm, but his voice came out a little flat.

"As you now see fit to dispense all this information which you've obviously felt I was somehow not mentally or emotionally prepared to take, may I ask how I have earned the privilege?"

"Well," Linus said, "it was that I had a little talk with the buck Anna's supposed to be living with."

Walter Degnan went and sat down at his desk and put his head in his hands. "Linus, I am about at the end of my tether."

"Me too," Linus said. "You want to hear the rest of it?"

"If you can spare it," his father said.

"He came down . . . the half breed you've heard Shafter mention. Charley Tom came and got Shafter. It looked strange to me, so I tailed him. I was pretty worked up when I realized what was going on. He told Shafter the detail coming in from San Simon killed one of their chiefs, so they weren't going to let Anna go. I told him we were going to open a full-scale campaign against them. Which appeared to make him happy." He stopped and regarded his father, who was now staring at him with a look bordering on the unhinged. "He's only a kid . . . maybe younger than me. A pretty ruthless kid. Good English. Chip on his shoulder. He really twisted the old knife."

"What knife?" Degnan croaked.

"That he had Anna."

"Merciful God, Linus." Degnan got up and then sat down again. "He tells you this. You go out and fight people. Did it occur to you to come to me, that this was the time for us to be doing some good hard planning?"

"I thought about it," Linus said. "But I figured you'd be planning on your own. We agree we can't just leave Anna up there with them. But you see, you're all hot to ride out and start shooting and Shafter wants to wait until they move out of the Stronghold, and I think you're both wrong. And this kid, too, I think he's wrong. What I thought I should do is take Victorio's word for it that Anna's all right."

"All right?" Degnan said incredulously.

"Sure. I mean I guess Victorio's an honest man. Shafter says he is. What would he gain by lying about it?"

"And in the meantime Anna is to be exposed to . . . ?"

Linus laughed. "Father, do you honestly believe one word of that? Do you?"

Degnan sat staring at him.

Linus said, "That little Mex rattler comes in here and turns us all upside-down, and if I'd ever known it when she talked she wouldn't be in Sonora now; she'd be staked out on an anthill. Apache *el mismo*. We all believed her. Except Shafter, at first, he had to think about it. And all the proof I need to know it's a lie

is for this half-white son of a bitch to come down and tell me."
He stood up, cocked the soft black hat far back on his head, and
came to look his father right in the eye. "Father, if somebody came
and told you that about mother, would you believe it?"

"Of course not," Degnan said wildly.

"That's what I mean," Linus said. "So anytime you want to sound
Boots and Saddles, I'm real anxious."

Degnan leaned back in his chair, gripping the arms. The boy,
his son, his junior officer, United States Military Academy '68, future well assured, had rather neatly turned the tables on him, and
on Shafter. He did not like the idea of this, although he felt somehow compensated that Shafter had been excluded. Something, he
realized, had happened to Linus; it was almost a physical meta-
morphosis; he seemed easier, more relaxed; yet he was reflecting
a new and shiny steadiness, an overt optimism. Walter Degnan
felt a rush of emotion, a feeling that of all things in the world now
he wanted to, had to, see his son go on and on, up and up, and
Anna with him, and all this foul, onerous business overcome and
forgotten. His enthusiasm for Linus' revealed, inner, personal
knowledge broke its bounds. His boy was right, right all the way,
and all of this was going to be something they looked back on
and . . . well, if not laughed about . . . at least discussed naturally
and without any tears. And Anna. Of course she would be all right,
sensible girl that she was; good, honest, poised, sensible Anna, who
would know how to handle herself if she happened to fall in with
all the demons of hell. Right now he had to do something for
Linus, something to show him.

"What do you think Shafter will take to go out with us?"

Linus was shaking his head. "He won't go, Father. He'll tell you
in detail what the half breed said, but he won't go."

"How do you know?"

"I asked him."

"And what did he say?"

"Precisely, he said he was not going to ride around the edges of
your blue coat."

Degnan flushed. "He did, did he? Well, if he feels that way I
can't change it. What do you think he'd do if I asked him?"

Fall over dead, Linus thought. "I couldn't say, Father."

Degnan looked off at nothing, through the smoke screen laid by
his cigar. "I would like him along. He knows this man Victorio and

from what you say he's more conversant with the situation than I am." His voice was dry. "I think I'll ask. For the hell of it, you might say."

"What about Willson?" Linus said. "What about Obre? Obre speaks Apache like. . . ."

"I have nine Chiricahua scouts who speak it like the natives they are," Degnan interrupted. "I did not say I was going to take on that entire lot of renegades."

"You better ease up on that, Father," Linus said calmly. "Leave that word to Will Oury. Just because a man's politics don't jibe with yours doesn't make him a renegade. I think you'd better bargain for all three of them."

"Bargain?" The colonel's eyes narrowed. Then he looked down at his hands. "I see. You're going to beat me out with this, aren't you, Linus? If Obre is riding with Colonel Walter Degnan, it will make my stand in the matter of Kiernan obvious. It will also place Obre, to all intents and purposes, under the protection of the United States Government."

"Father, I wouldn't be surprised if they make you a general one of these days," Linus said.

Degnan was torn. Whatever he owed Shafter was so intangible, so nebulous that there was no name for it. At first he had thought the Texican's appeal, for his son, had been the glamorous false façade of the forbidden: the fast gun, the easy living, the pulling up of stakes whenever you felt like it, the sense of total freedom from any physical ties whatsoever, the complete divorce from all responsibility. The flaw in this theory lay in the fact that Shafter never really did anything; he was simply around, never drunk, never quarrelsome, never saying much, and you said good morning to him and went on and didn't think about him until the next time he happened to be around and you said good morning to him again. That there was about him a certain authority, decision, even perhaps command, might easily stem from his appearance of equanimity and patience, which implied that he had learned some trick of self-mastery. Degnan had even considered that perhaps Shafter was offering his son something which he himself was not offering, but that, of course, was nonsense; he was far too intelligent and disciplined to let himself dwell on such self-pitying vagaries. So what was it? So simple an explanation as that of human fellow feeling, that Linus might stand in Shafter's mind for something

Shafter had never had and never would have, did not occur to him.

"Father," Linus said, "you're keeping Shafter waiting."

"He's alone?" Degnan said.

"Willson's with him," Linus said.

"I'll talk to them."

"I'm going out with Bleek," Linus said. He didn't want to be there if Shafter refused, and Bleeker was one of the few people around with whom he could talk about this thing. Bleeker was toying with the idea of a short story about it for *Harper's* magazine, pointing out the violent ends which resulted from racial discrimination in a polyglot society in a crude frontier settlement under martial law. He was unhappy that he had not witnessed it personally and was depending on Linus to furnish the information for his accompanying sketches. A simple matter of changing names, a text thundering with indignation, the moral pointed that a war for racial equality continued. You're stretching it, Linus had told him. Bleeker admitted that he was, but it was the occupational disease which provided his living. Trundling along with his big sketch portfolio, he reminded Linus that to a good reporter every stone in the path had a story to tell, and Linus grinned and told him, look at this one, Bleek, you're right, a horse passed over this one.

Shafter and Willson were in the outer room. When Linus came out, Shafter shot him a questioning glance, but Linus looked noncommittal and passed on. Degnan came to the doorway. "Good afternoon, Shafter. Willson. Come in, will you?"

They came in. Willson said sadly, "Howdy, Colonel," and reached for the proffered cigar.

"I understand from Linus that you are fortunate to be alive today," Degnan said.

"I don't reckon it's bad as all that, Colonel," Shafter said. "I hope you weren't too hard on the lieutenant."

"Not hard enough," Degnan said. "From his account he managed successfully to play the fool from first to last. He, however, seems to feel he was entirely justified."

"Personally," Shafter said, "I think he showed a hell of a lot of self-control. Been a simple matter of a fist fight, Colonel, there wouldn't have been anything to it. It was them wanted to play rough."

"So I understand." Degnan looked at Willson pointedly. Willson's grave horse face, wreathed in fine Havana smoke, was disarmingly benign. "You struck the first blow, Willson?"

"Just grazed him," Willson said. He coughed self-consciously.

Shafter saw the spark of laughter in Degnan's eyes. "You got to report this, I reckon, Colonel. I take it Linus told you the whole story."

"You mean about the Indian?" Degnan leaned back in his chair. "Yes. These redskins seem to think they can get away with just about anything they set their minds to. I wouldn't be surprised to see them swarming over the walls of Tucson. Well, we're going to change all that." He leafed through the papers on his desk and came up with an envelope. "This is a telegram from the President," he said.

He read it aloud: "Make every effort to secure the release of captive women. Full authority given under special-sessions act of War Department to carry operations to absolute extreme. You are authorized to draw troops from area posts if necessary. Orders to this effect being forwarded to General George Stoneman, Fort Whipple, commanding; Forts Bowie, Grant, Crittenden, McDowell, and reservation agents in Arizona and New Mexico Territories. Department urges total warfare, treat whenever necessary, annihilate when possible. Unremitting summer campaign with all available forces to be initiated at once. Confer with Stoneman. All post commanders in area subordinate to Colonel Walter I. Degnan, commanding. Ulysses S. Grant, President, U.S.A."

After a moment Shafter said, "Excuse me, Colonel, didn't you misread something there? What was that about treating again?"

Degnan scanned the telegram. "Treat whenever necessary, annihilate when possible."

Shafter said, "I reckoned you read it backward."

Degnan was frowning, chewing at the inside of his lower lip. He hashed it over. Should it read, "Treat when possible, annihilate when necessary?" Good God, had some idiot garbled the thing? He remembered what Bleeker had said: the War Department and the Department of the Interior were certainly at loggerheads, pursuing blindly their opposing policies. It looked as if poor old Grant was caught squarely in the middle. No doubt this order came directly from the War Department, with Grant's signature merely an official sop. He threw the telegram down in disgust. He said, "Orders or no orders, I was about to start out on my own. Now the decision is out of my hands."

Shafter didn't say anything.

"Now," Degnan said. "About the Indian. Linus tells me he delivered a message from Victorio. They're playing an eye for an eye, is that it?"

"That's it," Shafter said. He didn't know how much Linus had told his father and he didn't want any misunderstandings.

"And this buck gave Linus to know that Anna was his share of the booty."

Shafter relaxed. "Yes, sir. I want you to know that was why Linus was. . . ."

"And I want you to stop defending Linus," Degnan said. "I'm damn certain that under the circumstances I would have done the same." His index finger shot out at Willson. "And not waited for you to start it either, Willson." He swung around in his chair and looked at Shafter. "After you brought in that Mexican girl, Shafter, I decided that it was my duty to press these people despite what happened to Anna." He linked his hands on his desk, looked down at them. "You can see that this was a difficult decision for me. I welcome this order from Washington."

Shafter nodded. "I don't think you got to worry about Miss Stillman, Colonel. What you'd ought to watch for is maybe bein' able to surprise some of the women. . . . They'll be out harvesting pretty soon. You might find her, like that. She might be with 'em just waitin' a chance to get out."

Degnan's head shot up. It was the kind of thinking he desperately needed. Shafter seemed consistently to think of things, little side angles, which did not occur to him. He said, "What do you mean, not worry about her?"

"Joaquin ain't gone to let anything happen to her," Shafter said.

"You mean this English-speaking half breed? How can he protect her?"

Shafter made the familiar little gesture with his upper lip, flattening the blond mustache. He felt puzzled. "Colonel Degnan, this boy is just as white as you are, one whole half of him. His pa was married as legal as an Indian marriage can be, down to Ojo Caliente. The boy's been kind of pushed around from pillar to post, raised hard, never really findin' his place. Bein' Joe Mitchell didn't work for him. Bein' Mimbreño does. It ain't usual, but it ain't unheard of either. . . . Obre knows a Gileño girl is half white. If he's taken a shine to your girl, ain't no law gone to stop him."

Degnan was leaning back in his chair again. "Has Linus discussed this with you?"

Shafter was uncomfortable. "Here and there," he said hesitatingly.

"Perhaps you should know that neither Linus nor I believe a word of this cock-and-bull story," Degnan said.

Shafter looked at him for quite a while. He said, "I reckon that's your affair, sir."

"You believe it," Degnan shot.

"It ain't my affair," Shafter said again.

"You're dodging, Shafter. Well, I want to tell you something. When Linus talked to me today he was different; his entire attitude was different. I don't know how to describe it. Steadier, perhaps. More assured. I think his realization . . . no, belief, that this is a superb piece of Apache trickery made that difference. I am going to support him in it until I know the reverse to be a certainty. I trust you to do the same."

Shafter said, "I always figure to do right by Linus."

Degnan's small silence made the remark enigmatic, somehow unfinished. Then he said, "As I see it, Linus is at a very critical point in his life." Degnan rose, half came around the desk, stared at the ceiling. Shafter was aware of the trim, clean-cut, upturned profile. "A great deal hinges on the outcome of this, Shafter. I think you understand what I mean when I say that Linus' future is hanging in the balance." He turned and faced Shafter. "And as for my girl . . . for Anna, I would rather have her decently dead than existing under the circumstances which have been indicated to me."

"Excuse me again, Colonel," Shafter said. "There's a lot more than indication here. Like I say, it ain't my affair, but I reckon if it was my son I'd rather have him face up to the truth right off."

"Ah," Degnan said, leaning back against his desk. "So you do believe it. Well, Linus is not your son, he's mine, and I'm going to play the game his way." He slumped suddenly, as if the air had gone out of him; his eyes, fastened on Shafter's, were despondent. "John, many a boy has ridden into manhood on the crest of the most blatant self-deception."

Shafter's eyes narrowed. The Old Man knew, understood, a lot more than he'd thought. He was surprised again when Degnan said,

"I regret that Linus dragged you men into this business. I was off on a wild-goose chase, as you know. If I'd been here I couldn't have done a quarter of what you did. I hope you're not going to let Linus down, Shafter."

"I don't reckon there's much I can do now, Colonel," Shafter said.

Degnan said nonchalantly, "I need a couple of men to take over my Apache scouts. I want an interpreter I can trust."

Shafter looked over at Willson. Willson looked back, ground out the butt of his cigar, and reached for another. Shafter stalled. "I can't say for Obre, Colonel."

"You can answer for yourself. So can you, Willson." Degnan shook his finger, giving the words emphasis. "Look here, Obre's in trouble if Jesús Elias wants to press this. No matter how Elias does it, through the law or on his own terms, he can make it damned hot for Obre."

Shafter began to ease up. He had the upper hand and knew it. He felt the last stiff muscle unknot. Willson said, "How much *dinero*, Colonel?"

"Scout pay plus a bonus at the end of the campaign," Degnan said.

"Cigar now and then?" Willson said. "Seein' as how they don't seem to stunt my growth none."

"You drive a hard bargain, Willson," Degnan said. "I'll take it."

Shafter looked at the thick gray ashy tip of his own cigar. He could Jesus-well live without it. "I'm gone to drive you a harder one, sir."

Degnan said, "Name it."

"If I join you," Shafter said, "and you see me holdin' up one finger, it means I got to go."

Degnan laughed, but rather mirthlessly. "And two fingers?"

"Then I quit cold," Shafter said. "It's this way: Victorio and me, we sort of agreed if we saw one another again one of us was gone all the way west. Or maybe both of us. I wasn't braggin' to him, I figured I owed your girl that much, and I reckon he did, too, because he took me up on it. I expect you know they call me an Indian lover. I been called worse. I met some Indians I liked a sight more'n some white men. So if I can see to it, I ain't gone to let anything happen to Joaquin."

"Are you saying that this half breed's a friend of yours?" Degnan said.

"Not exactly," Shafter said. "I'm a friend of his."

Degnan thought about it. There was some current here which was too strong for him; for the moment he wasn't going to get caught in it. He said, "That's a personal matter. That's up to you. Are you hired, Shafter?"

Shafter said quietly, "All right, Colonel."

"You, Willson?" Degnan said.

Willson nodded soberly.

"You'll speak to Obre?"

"I'll give him the message," Shafter said.

"Good," Degnan said. "Now I'm calling a council this evening. You be here. You feel free to offer any suggestions that you think will give us the upper hand."

"Colonel, the only suggestion I can think of, offhand, I'll give you right now," Shafter said. "It's that the U. S. Cavalry ought to do less open fighting and more dry-gulching."

Degnan looked blank.

"That's when you're on the outside lookin' in," Shafter said. "Ambush. Like the Apaches do. Every time you get a chance. You let 'em into the hole and then you close in."

Something crossed Degnan's face, a shadow almost of physical pain. "Like the Crater," he said.

Shafter looked at him from under lowered brows. "Were you at the Crater, sir?"

"At it?" Degnan said. "I was *in* it." His face was grim. "And you, I take it, were outside it?"

Shafter made a sudden explosive sound of laughter. "I'll be damned. I must of missed you, Colonel." He rose. The laughter never reached his eyes. The words brought to him the screaming inferno of that not-so-long-gone July day, with the Yankees trying to claw their way out of the pit they'd blasted in a literal last-ditch attempt to make it into Petersburg, the reb artillery smashing them to pieces, the reb infantry shooting, clubbing, bayoneting them to death from the rim of the ragged hole. All the violence of the war had been contained, for him, in those hours, ghastly beyond belief; yet when he tried to remember, all he could see was the torn flags cutting swaths of faded color in the pall of acrid smoke. He felt not a rapport with Degnan, but an unavoidable kinship.

It was as if a chance acquaintance had suddenly upped and revealed he was your outhouse cousin. You had to accept him and while you were trying to make up your mind whether you liked him or not you still had to be cordial and polite to him. And all the time you wanted to ask to see his birth certificate.

At the door Degnan said, around his cigar, "By the way, Shafter, my given name is Walter."

So he felt it, too. The unwilling outhouse cousins. They shook hands. Outside, stepping into the silky afternoon sunlight, Shafter had the feeling that he had done this once before, every word said, every move lived earlier, so that he could have told exactly what Willson was going to say.

"Tough old bastard, ain't he?"

"He's all right," Shafter said.

"For what's he want you to call him Walter?"

"I wouldn't know," Shafter said. He let out a piercing whistle, between his teeth. Across the parade ground, Katie Callahan ducked her head out the window of the laundry room and waved to him. Rafe was coming up with their horses, so she stayed where she was.

"You seen the Old Man?" Rafe Callahan said. Without waiting for answer he added, "The grapevine's got it we're really goin' to put on a campaign. All stops out."

"I wouldn't know," Shafter said again.

They mounted up.

"Say, Callahan," Willson called back, "I shorly do like your mushtash."

The motionless saguaros in the long veiling shadow were turning dark. Just about all that was left of the spring breeze humped down out of the foothills and went floating off toward the arroyo, between the banks. Flowers were beginning to die in the dry wash. Linus had fallen asleep with his hat over his eyes. When he sat up and looked over Bleeker's shoulder he saw that Bleeker had drawn, with infinite detail, a buxom feminine figure in spangled tights, black stockings, and a massive coiffure.

"Nobody said you had to stay out here," Linus said.

"To the contrary, I did it from boredom, not out of salacious meditation," Bleeker said. "Do you think she's got too much hair?"

"I think she's got too much everything," Linus said.

"Callow youth." Bleeker tore the sketch in half and gave it to the breeze. "I pray some lonely buck puts that back together." He took out his watch and looked at it. Then he stood up and dusted the seat of his pants with his hat. Despite the portly figure, the knickers, the almost finicky neatness, he was cool as ice and ready for anything; chances were, Linus thought, a man would call him tenderfoot just about once. Bleeker gathered up his notes and sketches while Linus caught up the horses. When they reached the bottom of the slope, Linus pulled in abruptly. "Wait, Bleek."

Bleeker waited. "Ah yes, dust," he said calmly.

They sat there while the dust got bigger and closer. "We should have headed for the wash," Linus said.

"Too late now. Let's just wave and say *buenos*."

Then Linus said, "It's Charley Tom."

The *manso* was riding hard; his horse was lathered. "Good I find you, 'tenant," he said.

"What's up, Charley?" Linus said. "You been to the post?"

"Come up from south," Charley Tom said. "He Finds Honey comes. We meet. Big news."

"What in the world is he finds honey?" Bleeker said.

"One of our scouts. He's been over the border a hell of a long time," Linus said. "It's how they get their names . . . from something special they did." He leaned toward Charley Tom. "What's Honey got to say?"

"Two big raiding parties come up. Very big, maybe one hund braves. Make good strike on *Nakaiyes*."

"A hundred!" Linus whistled. "They've got men to spare then. Where are they now, Charley?"

Charley Tom jerked his head. "South. They move very slow, camp at night."

"How come?" Linus said.

"Honey say very big party. Maybe two hund horse, much gear, captives. Honey say carrying big everything." Charley Tom flung out his arms. "All *Nakaiyi* everything: serapes, silver, chili, corn, flour, guns, mules. Honey say count six *muchachos* for Apache no have *muchachos*. Parties meet over border, travel together. Camp very cautious. Many vedettes. Split herds at night so get away quick with them."

"Good work, Charley," Linus said. "Let's head for home."

He feels fine now, Tony Bleeker thought. He's already started to let off steam, and he needs it. And I'm no Indian fighter, but so have I, so have I. . . . He began to sing, and pretty soon Linus joined in. They made it ring across the end of day, out of the dust which rose around them.

> Oh, roll your tail,
> And roll it high;
> For we'll be angels
> Bye and bye.

"Not this horse," Obre said. "Are you crazy, Shafter?" He pitched his boots into the corner and lay back on Shafter's lumpy unmade bed, smoking, arms under his head.

"I might be," Shafter said. "You're always tellin' me I am." He didn't look up from the table by the window; he was sitting far enough back, though, so that he couldn't be seen or sighted from the outside. He had the Leech and Rigdon gutted and was beginning to strip down a Henry .44 carbine.

"I was figurin' on pullin' stakes," Obre said. "I was figurin' on maybe lookin' up Little Fire for a while."

"I ain't got any Little Fire," Shafter said. "Anyhow, she's probly got some Gileño buck by now."

Obre smoked, undisturbed by the prophecy. "Those army scouts know what they're doin'," he said finally.

"Degnan didn't say contrary," Willson said. "All he said was he wanted somebody he could trust to do his palaverin'."

Obre didn't answer.

"I didn't tell him you was as untrustworthy as they come," Willson said.

Shafter finished dismantling the Henry and bent over, out of his chair. "Now where the hell'd that pin go?" he said. Willson got down on his hands and knees and located the pin, under the table.

"If you two ain't a picture," Obre said. "You aim to put on Yankee blue?"

"Aim to wear just what I'm wearin'," Shafter said, unruffled.

Obre felt the old curiosity, as strongly as he had felt it that day riding into Dragoon Springs. "Aim to dance to a bugle again, the two of you? Aim to get that girl back?"

"Aim to try," Shafter said.

Obre contemplated the ceiling. The remains of generations of dead flies graced it. Water stains mapped it brown. It was going to be kind of lonesome in this part of the world. Not that he ever needed anybody, he believed, not knowing that his feeling Shafter needed him constituted a need of his own. He couldn't shake the feeling Degnan was a favor-giver. He reached over and snubbed out the cigarette on the floor and examined his nails. He knew he was making excuses. What was really in the back of his mind was that if Elias had anything hasty planned for him, he didn't want Shafter and Willson involved in it. He was even fooling himself that Shafter didn't know this. Nothing was bothering him . . . not Elias, not Kiernan, not Degnan . . . except himself. The only pay he'd received in over a month was the pistol he'd taken from the dead *rurale,* and you couldn't say he'd earned that. Not that he wanted money; the only thing he wanted was not to see, after five years, his family breaking up. Like they were marrying and moving off. And here the kid, this Linus, had somehow got in the family, by adoption, he guessed, and it was kind of small when you were rearing a kid not to see him through. At least until he knew his left ear from his right.

"You know," he said, "I bet you're right, Shafter. I bet you Little Fire's even got herself a *niño* by now."

Shafter didn't look up. He fitted the tubular magazine back under the Henry's octagonal barrel.

Obre said, "If you can quit fiddlin' with that thing for five minutes, how about givin' me a haircut."

"Who's gone to see you?" Shafter said.

"Why," Obre said, "the way you talkin' now, just about everybody in the whole damn world. Whole passel of U. S. Cavalry. Christ knows how many *Tá-ashi.*"

Shafter was relieved; he hadn't thought there was much chance Obre would take the job. It wasn't only you liked having a gun around you could really depend on; it was mainly he would have felt hollow as a pit, after all this time, without the man behind it.

Thirteen

"There they are," Willson said. "This here might be the shortest campaign gone." He was mildly, almost curiously, optimistic.

Shafter didn't answer; he suspected Willson probably wanted an answer.

"They not know we watch. No see us," Charley Tom said.

Shafter got to feeling nettled: all this whistling in the dark. "There ain't no way to keep a whole passel of cavalry stashed away, Charley," he said.

They lay in the rocks, looking down at the camp spread under them, backed up against the foothills. The last edge of the sun was lipping over the mountains, the light going fast. The stillness that was always so loud and clear to Shafter was touching everything with its wings. Below, one day out from home, the war party was staked for its last night on the desert.

There were a lot of bucks down there, and they weren't risking anything. They were camped against the foothills because of the escape trails they could use if they had to. Up and out. No fires. The big herd was split into groups of fifteen, twenty, ready to be taken out, rushed up some twisting rocky route. An old insurance and a good one, Shafter knew. It would be tough deciding which group you were going to chase. Every group had its handler on guard. They would move out about dawn, never placing the herd in a mass, spreading out the pack horses. Not a man down there didn't know what he would do if the time he had to do it came.

Shafter thought they must be dying to cut loose. Two parties of fifty bucks each, making ceremonies and dancing themselves up to fever pitch, tying on their hoddentin bags, packing their fancy medicine hats and fire drills, checking over carbines and lances and the shields which had been prayed over, setting out at last for the plunder, the prize. And all of it done by rite and rote, even to the palaver, a special warpath argot they used at no other time and by whose confines they were rigidly bound. Off to some town where the men would defend and die while the stock was run out and the women and children taken. Maybe to a rancho where the *caballeros* fought off Apaches as part of their regular chores, and there were fine Spanish horses in the stables. And home again, with the sacrifice of the empty saddles, but the game won. Vengeance on the ancient, traditional enemy. A way of life.

Charley Tom and Honey talked low and rapidly to one another. Shafter was squint-eyed even though there wasn't enough light left to salt the vision. It was more an unconscious gesture, habit. Under them, clear and distant, a child wailed, a long, longing sound that slivered the stillness and hit at the base of the spine.

Willson started. "Jesus, those pore kids. What they want with 'em anyway?"

"Year's time they'll forget they're Mex," Shafter said. "They grow up good Chiricahua. Or they get ransomed early. It ain't so bad for the kids. They really love those kids." He pushed himself back on his hands, rolled over behind the crest of the rock, and sat up. "You mark how those herds spread?"

"Sho," Willson said. "You think I just been layin' here wool-gatherin'?"

"Charley," Shafter said.

Charley Tom inched down to him.

"How many of those horses can we run out?" Shafter said.

Charley Tom looked at him and shook his head. "No good, John."

Shafter said, "Me, you, Willson, Honey. Obre. That's five. Who else?"

"I ain't that light on my feet," Willson said.

"You ain't got to be," Shafter said.

"I ain't that light in my head," Willson said.

Charley Tom was adamant. "No good. They get us all, John."

"Who else?" Shafter said again.

"Tlodasay," Charley Tom said then. "He Talks Crooked."

Shafter sighed, almost in resignation. Hell, he was hired. You're hired, you do the job. He had to talk to Degnan.

The garrison was bivouacked three miles off, on high ground, with no fires and the horse picketed close. Degnan hadn't had time to confer with General Stoneman or wait for the two companies of the Tenth coming in to reinforce him. When Honey and Charley Tom reported in, he figured he had the big raiding party under his thumb. But he wasn't going to jump the gun; he was going to play the element of surprise for all it was worth. There were troopers huddled all over the place when Shafter gave a sentry the countersign and rode in; just huddled, not smoking or talking, just waiting, under the last light that was going out like a final, snuffed candle. Shafter dismounted and turned to find Linus at his elbow.

"Find anything, Shafter?"

"Nothin' I didn't already reckon on," Shafter said. "It looks pretty good." He qualified it apologetically. "Maybe."

Degnan walked up. Shafter thought he seemed nerved up, close-grained. "You found them," he said.

"We found 'em," Shafter said. "It might go slick, Colonel. If you can move. It's gone to take some movin'."

"Where? How?" Degnan said.

"About three miles out. They're humped up against the hills, with the herds split. If you come on 'em on the straightaway, they'll tail it into the mountains. But if you. . . ."

"Yes, I see," Degnan said. "If I can get a force into those foothills. Charge them on the flat and then cut them off when they make for the hills."

Shafter said, "I don't want you thinkin' it's gone to be easy."

"I never look for it to be easy," Walter Degnan said. "We'll have a try at it."

This assurance was beautiful to hear. The same old damn-Yankee assurance which had come close to wrecking John Shafter's life. "Wait awhile," Shafter said. "Near dawn. While it's still dark. I want to run off the horses. That'll be your signal."

"You want to what?" Degnan said.

Shafter said, "I want to panic 'em. Run the horses out. Then you hit 'em."

"You think you can do it?" Degnan's voice had quickened.

"Colonel, I only got a notion," Shafter said. "Where's Obre?"

"Here," Obre said. He had come up behind Shafter. "They got dogs down there?"

"No," Shafter said.

Linus said, "Why dogs?"

"Dogs are bad," Shafter said. "They don't travel with 'em as a rule. Dogs bark. Mostly they're trained pretty sharp, but you can't stop 'em barkin' once they make up their minds on it." He turned to Linus. "I got to have light. Make me a blanket shield, Linus, and get me something to write on."

The little fire rose, under the shield. It would have to be fast, before they choked to death in the smoke. Shafter laid it out for them, where the herds lay. When he finished, when they had it stamped on their minds, he said, "Who's got a bit?"

Someone, some hand in the dark, passed the coin over. "We flip for the inner herds," he said.

Obre said, "I'm handlin' one."

"I said we flip."

Charley Tom and Obre drew the two inner herds. Charley Tom made a fatalistic utterance in his own tongue. Obre rose, satisfied. Nobody was doing him any goddamn favors. They killed the fire and flung blankets, dispersing the smoke. Shafter sent Charley Tom after Crooked and went for the dun. There would be six of them riding back to the bluff, sweating out the meat of the night.

"Shafter," Degnan said. He waited. He stood with his hand on the dun gelding's nose; the solid flesh was warm and alive; the gelding swung his head and sunk his lips in Shafter's neck, without nibbling.

"What time?" Degnan said.

Shafter said, "You just got to lie ready. If we can work it the way I'd study to do, there won't be any shooting. But you'll hear it all right. If it goes. Just remember these are fightin' bucks." He pulled the dun around. "One thing more. There's women and kids down there."

Degnan held out his hand. "Good luck, John."

"You, too," Shafter said. He couldn't bring himself to the familiarity. "Good luck, Degnan."

When he mounted, Linus was at the stirrup, but he didn't offer his hand. "I guess it's a hell of a time to be thinking," he said.

"Depends on what you're thinkin'," Shafter said.

"I was thinking that this seems a little . . . what? Not unreal. A little silly?"

"Try sorry," Shafter said.

There was an urgency in Linus' voice. "John, listen, I have to tell you. I have to thank. . . ."

Shafter cut him off brutally. He felt brutal. "Hang it, Linus, I ain't got time to palaver now."

Willson came up, mounted. "Looky that," he said. "The colonel give me a cigar and I'm too spooked to smoke it."

"It'll taste fine around noon tomorrow," Shafter said. For a flashing second he almost reached out and touched Linus, and he was surprised that the touch would not have been on the shoulder but on the cheek, as you might touch your own kid when he was saddened and quiet. He turned away.

The impossible thing would be to get into the herds. The herds would sense them before they got anywhere near, and horses were like people, scared of things they couldn't identify. They had to come in upwind and hope the vedettes, the red animals, wouldn't spot them through scent. They couldn't all make it. He figured, with luck, that Charley and Honey and Crooked, the birds of a feather, might. Maybe Obre, but he had the longest, toughest way to go. Willson was sometimes too steady, too phlegmatic for his own good, and as for himself . . . well, a lot depended on how bad you wanted a thing. Sometimes you wanted it so damn bad the very spur tripped you.

He didn't try to sleep. The scouts were sleeping like cats. Apaches could sleep anytime, anywhere, building and conserving their strength for whatever they had to face. He lay flat on his back. There were all those stars, swinging at different depths, dry and hard and cold, sharp as knives. He had always liked looking at stars, ever since he was a child. Not that he thought anything particularly about them, except that they were a long way off and, for him, singularly beautiful. When the bad times came along, the peak times, the death times, it was good to know the stars were there. They were always there. All he had was stars. He never wept inside himself any more, but he never fought the circling tightness that coiled in his chest either. And he had begun to taste hate for what was ahead, what was to be ahead for the rest of his days, the killing, the gravitating to the killing, the accustoming without struggle to his portion in a country where life was cheap as sand. The restlessness, the sense of loss and emptiness swelled in him. He was a killer. Obre was a killer, and Willson. Ah, but so was Walter Degnan; so was that kid he felt he couldn't let down. So were a million men who had never taken a life. A killer sleeps in all of us, maybe. God, what a legacy. To form in every one of us a killer. To give us the power to turn the killer loose.

He watched the stars move. Then he turned over on his belly and fixed his eyes on the eastern curve of sky. Thanks to that legacy and an army of Walter Degnans and the shrouded arms of death which had reached out and taken the girl even while he held her, he was here. Waiting to release the killer.

Dawn was making a small sign, not visibly, but by feel, smell in the air, a glinting fresh coldness. The stars were skidding off the sky, blowing out. Working down the face of the bluff, on the eastward end, Shafter killed a vedette. It was fast, silent: a quarter of the way up the buck was standing, maybe watching over the sleeping camp, maybe watching nothing. Shafter spotted him bulking and had no time even for thought. He could not move soundlessly; the buck turned on him at three, four feet, throwing up his carbine, but not out, across his chest, in a startled protective gesture, and Shafter clubbed him in the head with the barrel of the Leech and Rigdon and, when he was down, broke his neck with a single blow of the butt at the base of the skull. It didn't even wind him; he went on, sometimes inching on his belly, sometimes crouched, half on all fours like an animal.

Once rock rolled on the far plate of the bluff, but he heard nothing. They were all on their own. Obre and Charley Tom had gone down first with a good headstart: they needed it. If they got through, got in, Shafter hoped they wouldn't start things too soon, before he and Willson and Honey and Crooked made it, but they wouldn't be able to wait. He didn't tell them anything. He didn't say anything. The only thing he did was socket the Henry on the old McClellan and put his hand on the gelding before he turned him loose. It was quiet; he didn't like it this quiet. Not that he felt anything was wrong; it wasn't that kind of quiet. It was the kind made you feel you were all alone in the world.

He hit the bottom of the bluff. Way off at his left, black on black, he thought he saw Willson for a moment, but it might have been a trick of light. He never got on his feet again, not until it was all over. It almost astonished him that it had been so quick, so easy, and that he was right on the fringe of the camp. He began instinctively to regulate his breathing: in deep, filling his lungs, out long and slow, with the sound filtered out of it. He could measure progress in inches if he wanted to, and the quiet was broken. He

could hear breathing, rustling, the odd, nondescript stirrings of
sleep.

Dead ahead a horse whickered. He froze, close enough to hear his
man making a fast round when the herd pricked and swayed. The
biggest obstacle was that man, the horse sentry, who would be
close to being a horse himself. All his senses were so sharp they
hurt, but he was not conscious of any particular fear. Prone on the
ground, he could see the horses, silhouetted high above him, beginning to settle again. He started to inch in.

The shot came from ahead, to the right, where Obre should have
been. Almost simultaneously there was a blast of squealing and
the drum of hoofs. He crouched and ran, dodging crookedly, throwing himself at the near horse and making it up on the second try,
getting one leg over but hanging offside, with the horse between
him and the handler. His leg felt as if it would tear off with the
strain. The wild Confederate yell broke in his throat and rocketed
crazily into the night and the horse was moving, terrified, head
thrown back, eyes white and rolling, drawing the herd off with it.
Over its croup he got one blurred sight of the handler, running;
then the herd went over like a wave, cresting for the hills.

First off he heard only the yelling of the bucks and a few spo-
radic shots and the thud of hoofs as the herds went out. Then, almost incongruous, a steadying note in the chaos, he heard Charge
come rolling out of a bugle in a great golden clear swell. It sounded
good. He'd forgotten how fine Charge sounded, how your heart
speeded and grew and threatened to suffocate you when the faith-
ful, unwavering staccato beat of it blared out: only three reiterated
notes staggered and spaced, ringing pure and true as sunlight, cutting sharp. It did something appalling to him, hacking him to the
bone, so that he felt an insane desire to turn back, directly into
the spreading cone of sound. For a moment all his nerves hung by
a thread; then, calming cold, the underlying grimness and meaning
of the command struck him like a blast of icy wind, and the grimness was shot through with a great depressing sadness.

He swung up on the horse and kept the herd running, giving
the horse its head and letting it find its own way up the treacherous
rocky bluff. It steadied under the pressure of his knees, going up
and up, and all he knew was that the night was full of sound, behind him, voices crying under the slump of guns. Ahead, on the
surface of the sky, he could see printed the running shapes of horses.

He wondered who was up there. Linus, he bet. The Old Man would have gone in with the charge. Linus would be dug in up there to pick off the bucks if they tried to make it out.

Then a funny thing happened. All of a sudden there was the dun gelding, running at his side like it had been waiting for him, and he knew he had made it up the bluff. Dawn was coming in on the heels of a freshening breeze and he saw the Henry poking up out of its scabbard, the shallow cup of the worn McClellan, the patient profile of the dun, as it ran with him.

From the top of a hill he looked down into a little sparsely grassed valley lying at the base of a chain of hills. Scattering down the slope into it was Willson, hunched up on a scrubby pony so small Willson's legs were near dragging. The breeze swung kitty-corner and lifted the brim of Shafter's hat and blew away the last of the night and he could see the unlit cigar clamped dead center in Willson's mouth. He reached over and grabbed the cantle of the McClellan, pulling both horses to a stop, sliding off the slick bare back, yelling down the slope.

"Willson! Turn 'em loose! Let 'em go!"

Willson's grave, cigar-studded face turned to him. Then he threw a leg and hit the ground running. The two herds began to spread out and stand, blowing.

"Thought you said there wasn't no dogs down there?" Willson said when Shafter reached him.

"Dogs?" Shafter said blankly.

"Didn't you make out the one I was ridin'?"

Shafter didn't smile. "You see Ob?"

"No," Willson said. "There was one shot, was all. That triggered it. You have any trouble?"

"It went all right. You?"

"Easy," Willson said. "Except for that damn dog." He regarded the stunted pony morosely. He put his hand on the rump of the horse Shafter had ridden out, grasped its mane, and swung up. "You gone to wait here?"

"I don't want to get caught in a crossfire if Linus starts shooting things up," Shafter said.

The scattered shots sounded far off now, blocked by the hill. A band of horses burst over the brow and flowed around them, and Charley Tom and Crooked followed. The horses had eased down now; they began to crop when they hit the thin grass in the valley.

Shafter took Charley Tom by the arm. "Obre?"

"No see Obre," Charley Tom said. He was grinning broadly. "Obre shoot Chiricahua or Chiricahua shoot Obre."

"How the hell do you know?" Shafter said.

"Not deaf," Charley Tom said. "You quit, John. You hear, too." He rubbed his arm when Shafter released him.

The four of them crossed the little valley and started up the far hill and that was when Shafter saw he had made a mistake. The trim mounted figure which cut out to intercept him was pure Degnan all right, but it wasn't Linus; it was the Old Man.

Shafter wasn't good at concealing his surprise. It was always disconcerting when you had it fixed in your mind just how it was going to be and then it proved different. The Old Man was holding himself like he was laced up in steel stays. Only the timber of his voice gave him away.

"Beautiful, Shafter, beautiful. By God, it was something to look down and see those horses come over the hill. You men all right?"

Shafter side-stepped him. "I figured Linus would be dug in up here, Colonel."

"You figured wrong for once," Degnan said. He was actually on the verge of chuckling, Shafter thought. He could feel his mouth grow taut; he wanted to reach out and smack Degnan, and Charley Tom along with him. But Degnan went on with that spilling excitement all over him.

"There hasn't been a buck up this hill, Shafter. Linus must have mopped up down there. We aren't waiting. We're going down and see."

"I'll go with you," Shafter said.

"That's not necessary. You've done your share. More than your share, Shafter."

Shafter looked up. Honey was coming in from the west side of the cut, leaving his scattered herd behind him. Shafter said, "Colonel, Obre's still down there."

Degnan looked at him. "All right, let's ride." He lifted his hand and Stern waddled into sight. "Get 'em moving, Sergeant," Degnan said. "Willson, keep track of these horses. Keep 'em together." He eyed the herds. "We're going to have them on the way back to Sonora before nightfall."

They mounted up. Behind them the troopers filed out, leading their mounts, and Stern's impatient bawl filled the clean morning

air. Fall in. Prepare to mount. Degnan set a good stiff pace riding
back.

From the bluff where he had spent the night, Shafter looked
down at the Apache camp. In his mind's eye was mirrored the
neat, spare, silent, sleeping quarters, so that it was something of a
shock to survey the total shambles that lay under him now. The
troopers were standing, walking around, like they owned the place,
which they did, and you could see there were hardly any Apaches
in any condition to stand up. Why was it, whenever they lay around
like that they looked like bundles of old clothes? Shafter rode on,
after the elated colonel. When he reached the mess, riding through
and over heaps of Apache dead, he stopped the first trooper he
saw.

"Where's Obre?"

The trooper, heavy-set and grizzled, looked at him without recognition or comprehension.

"The interpreter," Shafter said.

The trooper was too old to be here. "The real dark one with the
funny eyes?" he said. He turned and pointed.

Obre lay against the rump of a downed horse. A cigarette balanced on his lower lip and he gestured with one hand, effusively,
argumentatively, at a tall bony-headed man, the post surgeon. Shafter rode on over. When he got there he saw Obre's chaleco was
wet and black with blood.

"Howdy, Shafter," Obre said, one eye closed against the smoke.

"What the hell happened to you?" Shafter said.

The surgeon turned. "Is this man a friend of yours? If he is,
you'd better talk some sense into him. He won't let me touch him."

Shafter dismounted. Obre made a move to sit up, chewed at his
lower lip, spat out the cigarette, and fell back. "High in the shoulder," he said and coughed. "The bastard had a carbine on me before I made the herd. You want to get rid of this for me?"

"Him?" the surgeon said. "Him?"

"Why'nt you go give yourself a pill," Obre said.

Shafter had already split his shirt and was examining the hole
the carbine ball had made. "It ain't much," he said.

"That's what I keep tellin' pill peddler here. Would've done it
myself but I couldn't quite reach."

The surgeon threw up his hands and walked off. Shafter burned
some gunpowder on Obre's knife. Troopers passed him, one sup-

porting a sullen Apache with a broken, bloody leg. Shafter pried the ball out. Obre cursed and sweated. Linus and Rafe Callahan came up when Shafter finished. Shafter figured on saying congratulations or something, but it came out lame, and he felt twice as awkward when he saw the lack of triumph, the near dismay, on Linus' face.

"You hit bad, Obre?" Linus said.

"She just whistled past me, Lieutenant," Obre said. He was extra polite because of Callahan standing there.

Linus stripped off a glove and wiped his forehead with the palm of his hand. "Well, we got them all. They were too confused to get on their feet."

"I reckon you'll find a few of 'em got out, Linus," Shafter said. He wanted to say something more, something that would take the pressure off. "Your pa was sure took with the way you handled things." But that maybe only made it worse, judging by the boy's shadowed eyes. And of course a handful of bucks sneaking out past the Old Man in the hills, in the dawn, was inevitable. It was just as well they'd split the force; the whole kit and caboodle ramjamming in here and they'd have been killing their own. "What's your casualties?" he said.

"The same old one," Linus said wearily. "Bleeker's horse. Obre's lying on it."

"Bleeker. His horse got shot?" Shafter said.

"They never get shot. They just seem to give out somehow."

Shafter looked around. Bleeker was squarely in the middle of the ruined camp, bent over his sketchbook. "What he'd ought to draw sometime," Shafter said, "is a fat man gone down on a slowly sinkin' horse."

That made Linus smile, but rather bleakly. He looked at Shafter and a small light came into his eyes. "We've got a prisoner," he said. He pulled his glove back on. The gesture was cool, professional, matter-of-fact. "And wait until you see me make him talk."

Again Shafter glanced over the blasted, ugly spot. Buzzards were coming in already, circling in ever-narrowing planes, hovering, silent, hungry. Walter Degnan, struggling with his bad Spanish, stood talking to the two Mexican women. One was buxom, gray-haired, voluble; the other a girl about the age, Shafter guessed, of the little glib-tongued Ysabel. The kids, all boys from maybe six to twelve, huddled against the women. The girl was weeping. The woman's face was greasy with emotion; her hands were never still.

And close to a hundred dead bucks splattered all over the place.

The depression which had settled on him, racing the herd out of this place, began to creep heavily into his mind again. He needed to let Obre know he was glad things weren't as bad as he'd thought they might be; he needed to make Linus smile easier; he needed to tell Degnan what a good job it had been all the way through. But there was a sour taste in his mouth. He looked back at Linus and their eyes locked and he knew that they felt in that instant the same dissatisfaction, the same sense of futility. Regardless of what had happened to him, Linus didn't like this. Shafter had never liked it. And it was only the beginning. A good roaring success of a beginning.

The rest of the summer was going to be hell, no two ways about that. A campaign undertaken where and when it could be, boiling up out of the heat, with the troopers frying in the sun and the horses going bone-slung and spavined; the thick gray dust over everything, the water hot and slimy in the canteens, the metal of gun and saber too hot to touch, the desert sucking out every last drop of moisture, the dry air burning in the lungs. Shafter knew how the troopers would look in a month's time: no more polish on the brass, no more blacking, patched pants, blue overjackets chalky with dust, shirt open at the neck and the V of the neck burned scarlet, stubble of beard itching fiercely through the sweat, constant trickle of salty water down the spine, sweat in the eyes, stinging, blinding; drag-headed horses pushed to the limit of endurance, fire in the throat for cool water a never-ending torture the scummy stuff in the canteens only intensified, lost spurs, dropped blankets, forgotten picket pins. Even Walter Degnan wouldn't be able to keep up the spit and polish in a month's time. The devil himself wouldn't force these men to do or be other than what they did or were. Or would be. Christ, he must have been out of his head to say he'd go along with it.

Linus turned suddenly, breaking the meeting of eyes. His down-drawn mouth was as bitter as if he had read Shafter's mind. "Callahan, pick up Layden and the remuda and cut out a mount for Mr. Bleeker."

When Callahan rode out, two troopers passed him coming in. One of them carried a narrow flag in a saddle socket. They were

the advance of the long dusty line which would push through the
summer under Degnan's command.

Bleeker came to stand beside Shafter. "Here comes the Tenth
Nubian," he said.

Shafter squinted and saw the veteran Negro cavalry rising out
of its own dust.

Change. The fruit of five years' change, rapid, inexorable, the
sort of change a man reckoned as improbable. Shafter licked his
lower lip and tasted dust. He never took his eyes off the long line.
Well. There was Fox P. Canby, used to belong to old Grampa
Virgil, just over the hump from the Shafter spread. No surprise.
No surprise at all. Fox P. Canby, looking as if he was dropping
over to borrow a harness strap, except for the triangular Company
C guidon riding limp above his forage cap.

"Howdy, Shafter," Fox P. Canby said, in passing. Just like that.
No mister. Shafter.

"Howdy, Fox P.," Shafter said.

Degnan was going out to meet the white captain leading. Stern
began to bawl orders concerning catching up mounts, rations, hitch-
ing mules, saddling up.

Shafter reached in his pocket and took out makings and began
to roll a cigarette. He didn't even turn around when the shot
sounded and Linus came barreling up from the fringe of the camp
and went past him on the run.

The single Apache prisoner had lifted his guard's .44 and in a
highly unorthodox move killed himself.

Fourteen

The wind died when the sun went down. Far up the trail, Anna saw Nuadin begin the ascent from the few bunched wickiups on the lower level. She pretended not to notice, hoping Nuadin was bound somewhere else. But the girl's singleness of purpose was obvious, even from here. Anna did not raise her eyes when Nuadin paused.

"*Donde está Joaquin, Ana?*"

It was frustrating to be unable to lie in any tongue. No, humiliating. "*No sé,*" she said. It was true; she did not know. Her voice sounded sulky in her own ears, and her face, when she turned it up to Nuadin, felt round and heavy as a moon. Nuadin was cheerful, good-tempered, consistently childlike. "Chie," she said and pointed back down the trail. Anna nodded but did not get up, and after a moment Nuadin started down again, still looking unaccountably cheerful.

The season of Large Leaves was waning into Large With Fruit. The summer had passed more quickly than any summer Anna could remember. Victorio had gone back to Santa Rita nearly four months ago, but Chie had come twice with messages for Joaquin. This would be the third time he had come. It was dangerous; the bluecoats were everywhere, swarming like flies. . . . She shut off thought and flung down the strip of deerskin she had been working, away from her.

And Joaquin not here to meet him. Twice now he had gone off without telling her where, or why. The first time he had been gone two days. He was astonished at her anger. He had been hunting, he had a good young deer, he had anticipated her approval. But she met him on the verge of tears. It struck him as strange and touching and amusing. She should know by now that the men went away often, sometimes for weeks at a time, and returned to their wickiups as if they had never been gone. The poor white man, he said, tied so fast to his woman that he must account for every moment away from her.

But it was something more than this, and he knew it and concealed his amusement. Her face, when she lifted it, was wet. He kissed her. He remembered many things he thought he had forgotten, and he felt his selfishness had reached a limit. There wasn't any telling how far she might allow her selfishness to go. Moving with her into the shadowy circle of the wickiup, he admonished them both.

"Ana, we can never have any bad feeling between us. There's nothing worth it. You're here and I am here, and it can happen that one or both of us is not here, and if that happens all things have to be right with us."

She nodded, downcast. He was practicing patience. "Here," he said. He put his hands on her shoulders. "You wouldn't lie to me, Ana. Would you lie to yourself?"

He knew what she would say. No. But he also knew that everybody lies to themselves. His face was grave and intent. "You say to me, Joaquin, I love you, I want to be where you are. And this is true. I know this. But this is only part of it. Perhaps the smallest part."

This frightened her. "What do you mean?"

He hesitated. "It is hard to say it. Sometimes I think, this girl comes to you because she has no one else. She is accepted among your people, but not at ease with them. She never forgets how quickly they are capable of killing. She does not trust them. She cannot talk to them. You must be here to talk for her. To talk with her. This is a very strong thing. Maybe stronger than the thing she calls loving." She tried to interrupt. "No, don't talk, Ana. There's nothing wrong with feeling this way. It would be the easiest way to feel. I can see this." Again he hesitated, speaking slowly. "How am I to know what you still feel for this soldier? Or to blame you for it? How are you to know yourself?"

He expected her protest, but it did not come. She brought to an end the myriad small torments which had lived with him all summer. "A great deal of what you say is true, Joaquin. I shouldn't like to be here without you. I'm afraid of when we will have to go to Santa Rita. Yes, I am unhappy sometimes. Not for myself, but for the people who care about me. If I could only tell them that it was all right. They wouldn't believe it, of course, but it would mean so much to me. They couldn't accept any . . . any of this. They could not accept you. Maybe they could not accept me now." Her voice hardened. "No, *would* not. And there is one thing more. I don't ever want to say this again. All my life I loved Linus. Now I do not love Linus. I think of him. I will probably always think of him and despise myself."

He felt miserable and wildly ecstatic, all at once. "Ana. . . ."

"Please. You thought about this all summer and I didn't know it. But I have to know it, because I belong to you."

He said, "Yes, you belong to me, but I do not own you."

She half smiled. "You own whatever you hold by right of possession."

"Ana," he said. "Ana. . . ." Still holding her, still looking deeply at her, with the thick warm longing beginning to swim up between them, around them.

Then Chie came. He came not as the son of Mangas, rich and bearing gifts, with escort, but alone, traveling spare and light, and in paint. He had been at war since the summer began and had never fired a shot. The white eyes soldiers had not come near the Mimbreño ranchería at Santa Rita, although they were out everywhere else, Apache hunting, striking very hard, and making long pursuits, Chie said.

He was very hesitant with Anna, practicing his little English and wishing she would teach him more. For the first time he liked her, liked the sound of her laughter, liked her ease and quietness. For the first time he knew that Victorio had been right. For the first time he knew the wisdom of Victorio's sanction. He remembered his own disapproval, and Ponce's and Delgadito's, that Joaquin should take a white girl. They did not mention Joaquin's father. It was as if Dave Mitchell had been born dead. And there was no word for marriage. Two people went with one another. Victorio said, Joaquin is still my son. If he wishes to go with the *niña blanca*, then I wish him to go with her. I will practice avoidance with his mother if he wishes. This perplexed Chie. A husband belonged to his wife's family in their matriarchal society, but he could not look upon his mother-in-law. Some of the young men were becoming restless with this restriction, which was designed to develop great physical agility if nothing else, and here was Victorio reversing the practice in view of the fact that Joaquin would have no mother-in-law to avoid. Ponce, who had nearly broken a leg once getting out of his wife's mother's way, felt deeply enough about Victorio's decision to go home and strike his wife twice on the shoul-

der. This was unusual of him and, when she questioned him, he
struck her again for good measure. He had not seen, as had Chie,
Victorio's sadness under the stern exterior. But from the moment
of that pronouncement he, Chie, had been high in Victorio's favor,
and when the time came that a *mensajero*, a permanent messenger,
must be selected, Victorio chose Chie.

All the way Chie looked for soldiers, but there were none. He
would have been fiercely glad to lie above some rocky defile and
snap off a few, even at the cost of his own life. The loss of the
fifty Mimbreños in the spring raiding party rankled and smoldered
in him. The nine who made it to the Stronghold had been Cochise's
men. Chie noted that a good percentage of the Chiricahua women
were carrying children. Conceived before the raid, deliberately.
Destined for the raid, in future.

Chie enjoyed shaking hands. This practice, which had been in-
stituted by the white eyes and demonstrated at their councils, had
never become widespread, but Chie, like most of his fellow braves,
was prone to indulge in it when he felt occasion demanded; mostly
to show he had attended a council or two. He shook hands with
Anna, in an unexpected gesture through which she could hardly
keep her composure. She hoped he would not progress to any further demonstrations of familiarity, even though she knew that whatever kissing went on with these people was furtive and occurred
only casually between couples considering going with one another.

The evening was cool, yellow with the promise of stars. Joaquin's
wickiup was pitched far up the trail, away from the main camp.
Anna and Nuadin and two other women had put it up, but it had
been Cochise's thoughtful choice of location: farther from the water
perhaps, but isolated. They seldom saw Cochise any more; his illness progressed slowly but steadily; he spent his time either sitting
before the fire of the third wife he had lately taken or huddled
with Tahzay and his war chiefs. The wickiup was pitched close
to the rock wall. A crooked sycamore which appeared to grow hori-
zontally out of the rock stretched over it, and pines needled up
the canyon, closing it in on three sides. The wind came strong and
warm sometimes, following the smooth path of the canyon, clinging in the pines, and the pines were thin and warped with it.

Joaquin and Chie were sitting close to the small fire. The sky
stretched wild and red, a different red in the spectrum from that
of the red rock, so red it stained the red rock gold. The light was

slick and glistening, falling off dense as the perfect parallel ranks of cloud piled one upon the other, darkened and changed. Anna came to sit in the doorway when a last crimson line of sky thinned into night and a first star thickened and cleared. Only then did Joaquin break off the soft clicking tongue he spoke with Chie. Then the talk was clumsy with Spanish and English and Apache, and Joaquin repeated for her what he knew she could not understand. It was important to him that she understand.

The People still spoke of the spring ambush which had taken their men. Spoke, but mentioned no man's name, and the women still mourned at Santa Rita and Ojo Caliente, Chie said. Joaquin glanced at Anna, but she remained silent. Yes, she could remember: those nine men, three of them dying of their wounds, staggering in on foot, the wailing of the women which had gone on and on until Anna covered her ears with her hands and wished to scream, to drown out the sound. They did not dare go back for the buzzard-torn dead, even at night. Had not the white eyes begun the attack at night? And the dead braves would not rest quietly, but must become ghosts, walking at night, unless in the rocky clefts they could find their horses, killed and placed for them, to ride into the forever country. The air was hot and thick with the smoke and smell of burning wickiups. Remember? She would never forget. That night of the survivors' return, with the women and children crying their pain to the sky, she had gone to the stream for water. Numbed by some emotion she could not identify, did not try to identify, she had only dipped the *tus* when she started back in a terror which turned her flesh to liquid. One of the homeless, the nameless, one of the wandering ghosts rose almost at her side. Still kneeling, she stared up at it, on the edge of fainting.

It was Cochise. Stripped naked except for a narrow loincloth, he stood rigid upon the bank. The wavering reflection of the fires shimmered like blood on his scarred, gaunt body, still powerful and long limbed, only hollowed and marked with the rages of time and war and chance. He did not see her. He saw nothing. His face was so twisted with the agony of his grief that it was like a mask, the mouth contorted as if by some dread crippling, the eyes so sunken there were only two black pits, without light, where they lay; the once taut flesh over the high prominent cheekbones fallen, over the crumbling ridge of the jaw. In that tortured face the broken mouth writhed, cruel beyond the cruelest thought, but vulnerable, weak, deformed in an anguish which was crushing the heart, sapping the last reservoir of power, speeding the dark force of death. Suddenly he raised both arms high over his head, hands clenched into fists. The surge of motion pulled his whole torso upward, as if he strained with all his strength. The rib cage gleamed white, every flat curving bone alive and separate; the lean muscle running from the outer edge of the armpit into the shoulder sprang out like rope uncoiling. From the broken mouth burst a cry which brought tears to her eyes. His hands fell lifelessly. She could see the sweat beading his nakedness, beginning to run, big drops, like rain. Then he was gone.

Half the night she lay awake, staring out at her fire and trying to understand. Beginning to know. Beginning to build the will to fight what she saw would be the worst hurdle among many hurdles for herself and for Joaquin.

He could not go out with the war parties. And she knew no way to stop him.

Chie brought the thing which stopped him. There was only one thing which could stop him: Victorio. It was why Chie had come. Victorio had said that Joaquin must not leave the Stronghold until he was sent for, until it was safe to come to Santa Rita or to Ojo Caliente. This word was a law, and if it was disobeyed, Victorio could no longer recognize his son.

Joaquin relayed this noncommittally. If he champed at the bit, it was not apparent to Anna. He ate, slept, hunted, went out with Pionsenay to set up training problems. Cochise had lost nearly one sixth of his effective fighting force, but Tahzay was out, crazy for revenge, hitting at the troopers wherever he could and fading back into the Dragoons. Cochise's mouth never lost its bitter down-drawn line; the time for capitulation was closer at hand than he had believed; Tahzay could accomplish only a strike-and-run delay of the inevitable. And from his older son, the violent, brooding Nachise, who had walked out with Geronimo, there came no offer of assistance, no word, no sign.

Unknown to Anna, Joaquin had broached the subject of his participation only once to Cochise. Cochise cut him short. "Say this to my war chief," he said. Tahzay refused. Tahzay was young and wise, and his face was becoming the face of his father and his mind the mind of his father, but his soul was still in the making, still in the molding for the responsibility he knew would be his when Cochise passed, and his soul screamed for vengeance. "Give your strength for Victorio," he said, his lean, mobile face dark with blood, haggard with sleeplessness and his own thoughts. "I will give mine for my father."

Joaquin did not take this as final, but Chie's arrival put an end to the matter. Yes, Chie said, Victorio was strong and well; his, Joaquin's, mother had had a little spell of sickness but it had passed; she had a *Nakaiyi* woman to wait on her now. Chie was restless. His face was alternately depressed and eager. Anna was thankful he had removed his paint; the most benign face became hideous under the bizarre, significant stripes of black, yellow, vermilion. Chie seemed to feel unclothed without it and wanted to talk mainly of the misfortune of the massacre.

Victorio had suffered a blow comparable to if not greater than that of Cochise. But. . . . And here Chie paused, giving the words emphasis. The soldiers had made no attempt to attack at Santa Rita and Victorio was so indecisive about sending out his war parties that hardly a man had left. This, when retaliation was demanded. Victorio argued that the summer harvests were approaching and he needed his men to guard the women on the outings for which they would have to travel far enough to set up camp. There was dissatisfaction among the young braves; some even talked of walking out. It took a man of Victorio's stature to hold them in. And they were not happy.

Then Chie said, "The soldiers do not come to Santa Rita because they believe your *niña* is there."

Joaquin was frowning, but he shook his head in assent.

In the doorway Anna crossed her arms and gripped herself, not cold but shivering.

"What I think they will do," Chie said, "is fight us through the summer and then they will try to talk to Victorio again." He leaned forward and tapped Joaquin lightly on the knee. "Listen. They are certain your *niña* is with us. They still will not risk her."

"Let them think it," Joaquin said. His voice sounded weary suddenly. "Let them think whatever they want to."

"We have seen the soldiers," Chie said. "But far off. Many of them are black men, Negroes."

"Tahzay says the Negro soldiers are very good," Joaquin said. "He says there are men with the army who are not soldiers."

Chie's laugh was a quarter grunt. "*Enju*. Their parties are split so: the old nantan sitting highest, but he does not always sit; sometimes he gets upon his horse and leads. Then there is a white soldier, a *capitán,* with the Negroes, and the young nantan with some whites and some Negroes, and a fat man who does not fight but makes pictures." Chie spat in a motion which was like a snake striking. Anna drew back instinctively. "And the *mansos.* And the three *de la ciudad.*"

Joaquin lifted his head. "What three?"

"The *rubio* you spoke with . . . Shafter. And the Comanche with the quick pistols. . . ."

Joaquin interrupted him. "Shafter? With the soldiers?"

Chie said, "Tahzay did not tell you? It was he who ran off the horses at the *emboscada.*"

"He does not ride with the troops," Joaquin said. His voice sounded thick.

Chie was impatient. "You speak as if you had not talked with any man here, Joaquin. No, the young nantan led the troops. The young nantan came in out of the dark to butcher us like deer."

Anna closed her eyes. A rough edge of stiff skin, stretched on the door pole, dug against her cheek, the quick hurt of it comforting. Her mind went ragged and thin. Linus, Linus, I want a thousand, a million miles between us, Linus, for I am a coward. . . . She half rose to go inside, but Joaquin stopped her.

"Stay, Ana." His voice was harsh.

She stayed. She was half afraid of him now, sensing the squall blowing up. She willed Chie away. Whatever this was, she wanted her own chance to heal it.

But Chie was rooted. He, too, was a little angry now, at Joaquin. "If you listened to any promises Shafter made at the walls, you are a fool, Joaquin."

Anna caught her breath. She saw Joaquin's spine stiffen as he straightened, but he was not looking at Chie.

"Shafter made no promises," he said.

"Shafter is no different from others of his color who promise," Chie said.

Oh Christ. Victorio, and now Chie. Why could they accept nothing? Why were they so strong and he so weak? Their strength lay in their refusal to accept any word, any part, any promise of the white eyes. He felt a faint hollow nausea; he felt if he ran a knife along a vein now his blood would come white.

But he found strength. The doubt receded. He could remember Shafter's voice: the lieutenant's my friend. But Shafter was his friend also. He had not said he was Shafter's friend. There was strength in that.

Now, more than ever, he wanted to get out. He needed Victorio, he had not seen his mother in weeks, he missed his own people of the hot desert country. He told Chie what he must tell Victorio: that it was time for them to leave, that they would travel at night, that no matter what the troops did or did not do, his place was with Victorio. He glanced at Anna. Chie was to say Ana felt the same. When Joaquin rose, he put his hand on Chie's shoulder. "Tell him I will risk nothing and everything to come."

But when Chie came the second time he did not mention, before Anna, what Victorio's answer to this had been. He came to say that Joaquin's mother was dead. The devil dancers had come in, but she had died the moment they went away. Joaquin owed two horses, which Victorio had given. Down the trail from the wickiup he and Chie spoke briefly, and then Chie was gone. Anna could say nothing. She could not remember her own mother, and sorrow is not as elastic as it sometimes appears to be. She anticipated Joaquin's leaving now, his need to be alone, and was uneasy when he stayed close to the camp, half dogging her footsteps. It made it worse. She could only feel sympathy for him, not for an Indian woman she had never laid eyes on. Watching him hunched against the rock wall, rolling a cigarette, eyes shadowed, walking in some corridor of recall where she was an alien, she thought, and what am I to be to him now, mother besides all else, and found a small truth. Of course. Of course. When he came in she touched his hand wordlessly, letting her fingers lie on the smooth inner skin of his wrist. It was the first physical touch between them since Chie left. It absolved her and gave to him the first small measure of consolation.

He did not mention leaving the Stronghold, so she surmised that Victorio had refused his request. But she wondered how much Chie had said out of her hearing, for Joaquin told her they would have to take whatever stores they could with them when they did leave. It would not be right to go home with nothing, dependent upon his people for their food. She planned accordingly, working at curing

and storing. Now there were new winnowed seeds and berries, early
grape, drying before the wickiup. She crushed and dried rasp-
berries, forming them into sweet dry cakes. She would go with
Nuadin and some of the younger women to harvest wild potatoes.
Joaquin brought in plenty of meat and he helped her with the
butchering and preparation of the flesh, although she guessed he
wouldn't have liked to be seen at it.

She had been out with the women and gone up alone, leading a
scrub pony bearing panniers of chokeberry, when she found Joaquin
had gone. The fire was out, and a soft wind was bending the pines
a little, and she stood by the dead fire and knew. There was nothing to tell her but the feeling, the growing rapport with him which
had instilled in her some sixth sense. It was not merely that he was
not here, in the ranchería, but that he was gone and would not be
back that night. And it was not the loneliness. It was a wanting
more than physical or mental, a yearning so totally unreasonable
that she knew with a certain terror the total unreasonableness of
love. Her need, in that moment, standing before the empty wickiup,
was the need of desperation.

That night Tahzay came in. His party had taken and killed four
troopers of a detail dug in near Cienega Springs. The celebration
went on into the dawn.

And it hurt her that Chie should come, for the third time, with
Joaquin not there, and that she must say she did not know where he
was.

She went to meet Chie. She started down the trail as he started
up, and the despondency which had lain in her two days was swept
away by the knowledge that she had lived this, in its entirety, in
some other dimension of time. She had seen Chie before, coming
up this same trail, with the sun striking off the water and the thin
white streams of cook smoke rising behind him into the sweet clarity
of the air. The bend of his knee as he stepped, the set of his head
were so familiar to her that she stopped dead in her tracks, and
this, too, she had done before. It was not simply that she had seen
Chie come up like this in the past. She had seen him in this exact
attitude. She thought, now a bird will sing, and had barely finished
thinking it before the little reedy voice piped from the tip of a
canyon pine. The abiding belief in the supernatural which was so
much a part of The People reached out for her, but she sloughed it
off, for this was something beyond the supernatural. The heart-

stopping thing was not that it had happened before, every minute detail of it, but that she had seen it happen before.

She was so stricken by the experience that she was not even surprised that Joaquin came back almost within the hour. He was on foot, with a bundle strapped over his shoulder, and the Mexican carbine swung from his hand. Because Chie was there he said little to her, only a quick greeting as he stowed the bundle, in its deer-skin wrapping, far back in a corner.

She did not eat until the men had eaten. Then she settled into the late afternoon, letting it wrap her in its warm golden light, unthinking, content because Joaquin was back, the moment of Chie's arrival forgotten. Across from her, not even speaking with Chie, Joaquin was working steadily with his big skinning knife at a perfect forked branch of cottonwood. She watched him, chin on her hand, and after a time lost interest in what he did, studying his face. The lowered angle of his head threw the high cheekbones into sharper relief; the precisely carved mouth was set, but once or twice he caught his lower lip in his teeth, in concentration. Under the dark bar of brow, she could not see his eyes and he did not look up, and when he bent his head lower over his work a coarse black plait took even the line of facial bone from her.

Chie rose, as if something in the girl's face had disturbed him.

"¿A donde vas, Chie?" she said. Her voice was husky, as if she did not really care where he went.

He said, in English, "Come back," and went down the trail.

Joaquin laid the forked branch beside another which might have been its twin. It was greasy smooth, but he had left an odd projecting knob on it. He picked up two flat boards, sleek and burnished as shot silk. Now she was curious, seeing him begin an intricate rawhide lashing of the boards between the forks.

Then she said, "What are you doing, Joaquin?"

And he said, "Making you a saddle."

She half laughed. It was some trick he played. "A saddle. But I have no horse."

And he said, "You have a horse."

She looked around the little clearing. "I have? Where is it?"

"Chie brought it," he said. "It is a gift from Victorio." He looked up at her. Some passing shift of light made his eyes so blue the color was almost unnatural. "For you to ride home on."

She took in her breath. This was why Chie had come then. The excitement was strong in her, and the recurring dread. "When?" she said.

"As soon as you've finished with the harvest." He stood up and went to the water pit, a shallow depression in the ground whose base was a stretched hide. From it he took a rough rectangle of wet horsehide. When he came back he said, "We are going to Ojo Caliente."

She watched him lay his awl in the red hot ashes at the fringe of the fire. "Is it far, Joaquin?"

He had begun to stretch the wet hide over the frame. Now she could see how cleverly the projection simulated a saddle horn, one upended trunk a cantle, the smooth boards skirts. "It's a long way . . . farther than Santa Rita. Chie says the war parties are forming at Ojo Caliente. Victorio has already gone up." He looked up from the difficult work of stretching the wet hide on the frame. "Ana, whatever you're thinking, don't speak of it now. It isn't the right time."

But she was beginning to be sick inside. "What do you mean it isn't the right time!"

"It isn't. I can feel it," was all he would say.

These little superstitions no longer angered her, but neither could she treat them lightly. She watched his hands, thin, flexible, small-boned, smoothing, shaping, working the wet hide. When he pushed the hot awl through the stuff, a little steamy sound escaped. She saw what a perfect thing this would be when the hide dried and shrank to the frame. It seemed a tremendous amount of work when there were saddles enough in camp . . . more saddles than horses, she supposed. And it was difficult only to sit and watch, with the sick feeling working in her and so much left unsaid. Because he did not feel it was the right time. She made the effort. "Can't you just get a saddle somewhere?"

"No," he said. "I want to make it for you. Go and get the bundle I brought in."

She brought it to him. When he unfolded the hide she saw two skins, neither of which she could identify. She lifted the upper one, a tawny fur the color of old buckskin. It was harsh and thick, a prime fur, and when she ran her hand over it, it tipped up silvery and shining. "What is it, Joaquin?"

"Mountain lion," he said. He reached over and took it out of her hands. "I tracked him a full day before he went into a tree."

"But he isn't any good to eat," she said. "Nobody eats mountain lion."

What began as a smile became a grin. "Always thinking of your belly, like a good Indian. No, he's no good to eat. But his skin is a . . . what, I don't know the word. It's good luck. It's the best luck we can have. I wanted him for your saddle." He looked at her now without smiling. "I want you to have good luck, Ana, always. Do you think that's foolish . . . that the skin can bring this for you?"

"No," she said. "No, I don't think it's foolish. No more foolish than carrying the hind foot of a rabbit." She touched the other fur, very like deer, but blotched and spattered with near-black spots. "And this?"

The hot awl hissed at her. "That I have only because I took the lucky skin first. That is deer."

"Deer? Spotted like this?"

He said, "You know how sometimes a man will have something wrong with his skin. Or some other . . . some. . . ."

"Deformity," she supplied.

"Yes. Animals have it, too. They are rare. Very valuable. I want you to work this for a gift."

"For Victorio?"

"No, for Tahzay. You must give it to him yourself, Ana. These people have been very good to. . . ." He stopped, not looking at her but more watching, reading, her face.

"You were going to say they have been very good to me," she said. The little irony was there; she could not help it.

"Yes. And to me. When Tahzay is chief of all the Chiricahua, I want him to say this skin was given him by a woman of the Mimbreños."

She was silent, still holding the spotted deerskin. She begged, prayed, to feel the importance of this and knew that she could never feel it as strongly as Joaquin did. The difficulty lay in trying to fathom what was of importance. Sometimes such small things, such trivia, loomed like a mountain in the Indian mind. "It is beautiful," she said, because that was what he wanted to hear.

"I will help you with it," he said.

"No, I want to do it myself." She saw his quick glance of ap-

proval, both at her offer and at the practical query which followed
it. "And what have you done with the meat, please?"

"If you keep on, Ana, you'll be as fat as that old squaw that
couldn't see over her own belly and fell off the cliff last spring."
But he said, "I would not eat the flesh of a deer marked like this."

She went to work on the hide, scraping off the scraps of clinging
flesh with a knife and then placing it in the water pit to soak.
It would need a day, she thought, before it could be properly
stretched and pulled into softness. It would be good not to have
to wrap it around a tree and scrape off the hair. The hair was much
too fine to remove. It darkened as the water covered it. Some of the
women boiled and steamed the deer's brains and worked them in
the water pits before they put their hides to soak, but she had not
been able to bring herself to this, and, as far as she could determine, the slimy mess didn't add a thing to the ease of working the
hide.

When she returned, Chie was coming up the trail, leading three
pack mules and a handsome little paint mare splotched chestnut
on gray. The mare's mane was gray-white and very long and over
its forehead tinkled a silver *naja*, shaped like a crescent moon lying
on its points, and from each point hung a row of three small delicate
silver balls. It was the sort of trapping belonged on a big powerful thoroughbred or Arab, but Anna was delighted. The mare was
gentle but frisky; when she threw her head the pale mane flew
and rippled on her neck. She did not like the smell of the cougar
skin and protested by shrieking and kicking out as if she would run.
Chie laughed. "She will go like the wind, Joaquin." He gave Anna
the quirt, not rawhide but braided horsehair in the Mexican fashion, the butt loaded with iron, as heavy a sap as any man could
reasonably handle. She held it in her hand. It had belonged to someone, some man, some Mexican . . . and the horse. . . .

Already some of the men were starting up to them. There was
the news of the cougar skin, for one thing. *Ai*, that Joaquin, all the
luck was going his way these days. And the paint mare. They were
covetous, envious, loving the paint horses more than any other because of their coloring and speed and endurance. They fondled the
mare and made her nervous. They examined the half-finished saddle critically; not all of them could make saddles, any more than all
of them could make bows or arrows or use a fire drill. If they had
known Joaquin had a gift for this and saddles were needed, he

would have been pushed to death making them, just as they pushed those among them who were clever with the arrow reed and the bow wood. They grunted approval. Their hands went over and over the tawny good-luck skin, and Joaquin had to tell them twice, three times, how he had run the cougar down and treed it and shot it out of its crouch on a limb. Then the women came up, mostly to see the skin. Anna took Tayanclee's boy, who had nearly drowned, and set him upon the back of the paint mare and led him up the trail, and the men laughed and nodded. The child came back alone, jogging the mare and gripping her with his little legs. Anna went to cover the water pit so that no one would see Tahzay's spotted hide.

The women, too, were critical. They went over Anna's stores, sober-faced, talking at, rather than to her. Had she enough lip fern and cota bark for tea, enough green yucca, enough sweet dried yucca blossom, enough thin sheets of mescal fruit glazed with its own sticky juice, enough algerita jelly, enough mesquite bean for flour? She watched them helplessly. She had more than she knew how they would possibly carry with them, and the potatoes yet to come, but Nuadin seemed dissatisfied. She went down to her own wickiup and came back with a handful of pressed sunflower blossoms. Elbowing the other women aside, she placed the faded things on the center of several stacked datil fruits crushed into crackers. Anna understood at once. It was to make it look pretty. The women eyed her and shook their heads. She did not know how to make her food look pretty, poor thing. Then the women got into an argument. They began to push Nuadin and Tayanclee, and Anna got out of the center of it. She wanted to call Joaquin, but he was surrounded by the men and boys. The best she could do was listen. At last it made sense: it was the potato harvest. They were trying to decide when to go out to dig the species potato, which they would boil fresh with their meat and grind into flour for the time of Ghost Face. The uproar died as quickly as it had begun and the women turned and looked at Anna. Even the men were quiet, and the mare, with the little boy still upon her back.

Joaquin said, "They know we are to leave this place, Ana, and say that it is for you to tell them."

"I?" she said, laughing. "But I know nothing about it."

"Set them a day."

She thought. Well, they were to leave, let them be about leaving. She looked at Nuadin, who was her closest friend here. "*Mañana*," she said. "*Mañana por la mañana*."

And all the women looked at one another as if to say, that is just what I said, tomorrow morning, and none of you would listen to me. Still laughing, Anna caught Joaquin's eye and saw that she had not only pleased the women but him; that her decision told him she was eager to go. To go home. And after that, after The People had gone back down the trail, he could think, dreaming, of nothing else but Ojo Caliente and the long autumn days coming and the people he knew and loved and the pleasure of bringing Anna to it all.

The simple words, the simple resolving of so simple a thing as digging a few potatoes, awoke something in him which was like a glow, tender and strange and welcome. He felt it showed, like a light upon him, and he scarcely cared if it was noticed. He talked for a time with Pionsenay, after dark, and, when he returned, laid out the hide panniers which the scrub pony would carry in the morning when Anna went out with the women. When the first curve of moon rode up, he scattered the fire and left the ashy, charred, red chunks of the underbed to pulse and flicker in the darkness.

Anna was asleep, but very lightly, for her breathing was shallow. When he slipped out of the gray trooper's shirt, she turned in her sleep, one arm over her head, the blanket flung half away. For a moment he only watched her. The first intrusion of night light, halted by a barrier of rock and tree, seemed pale and without strength, but it slid through, past rock and tree, played tentatively along the ground, then settled into a steady flooding, wide but wan. When the thousand little nerve ends of him began to move and assert themselves, he became almost painfully aware of her skin, and he remembered that morning after her coming when he had found it so unpleasant, when the very whiteness of her face and the darkness of her eyes had repelled and infuriated him, when the hand dropped upon him had made him shudder. And burn. Like a man with a taste for the bitter, a man who cannot get enough of the thing which tortures him even while he yearns for it. There was a word for this, he supposed. He didn't know what it was. Now her skin was as dark as his own, except where the light lay across her shoulders and the lifting curve of one firm, almost immature breast that the sun had not touched. In that light there was a quality of luminescence over her, even in the shadowed hollows, like the glinting in the sun of first frost, the luster and bloom which powdered the wild grapes greening along the water. He was full of the good thing of going home together, that most basic need and joy in man. He was full of her, but no longer with the dominating will to possess which had overpowered him in the beginning, now with a fixed and almost obstinate steadiness, looming more and more constant, immutable.

He did not touch her, but something crested out of him, a silent communication which reached and found her. She would have to have been formed of stone not to feel it, and she sat up suddenly and he felt her full and warm against him, not surface warm, but warmed all the way through with that heavy, luxuriant warmth of sleep. The sound she made was almost a sigh, and he thought then that she had slept deeply after all and that she had dreamed. He was afraid of dreaming, afraid of the things which were in the mind, beyond reach or control, and it was an effort for him to breach the gap between what he knew to be natural and what the disciplines of his mother's people taught him were unnatural. As he wanted the luck of the cougar skin for her, he wanted also that she should dream only the forever good, the forever happy, the impossible. She was still stupefied with sleep, limp against him, as if her body had no will of its own, but her face turned and lay against the thick cord in the side of his throat, and he felt her breath come unevenly, as if she were fully awake and did not want to be and he thought that he could give her this bequest of dreamlessness, of good, of assurance, of security, where no misunderstanding dwelled, where none of the ubiquitous deadly venoms which poisoned every day of human existence would ever gather and collect, where nothing of the stupid dullnesses of human relationship would ever form and mature. He thought this savagely, and with the awful innocence of the wholly innocent, and his belief in the future was contained in these self-pledges born in the mind as if created for the first time, but older than the thrusting mountains, which are fundamental to all loving and which lie slightly, only slightly, over the thin dividing line between hope and despair, on the side of hope.

Fifteen

Fox P. Canby sure hadn't lost his touch with sowbelly. He could even make sorrel taste a little like greens after he'd fatted it up some. He discoursed on the advantages of dropping an eggshell, which he didn't have, into the coffee, but it was the best can of brew Shafter had had in years.

Fox P. did grumble about the fires though. Shafter was too dogged relaxed; Shafter acted like he didn't care about nothing, or was raised up out of stone, or both. Although Fox P. wasn't as nervous these days as he used to be. He'd had enough of sand and dust and grit and being shot at to take them for granted. And Shafter was careful where he fired up: in a draw or arroyo. But it still threw light. Fox P. was joining the growing rank which thought and said, or thought and was afraid to say, that John Shafter was loco. Fox P. thought that just because an Indian hadn't attacked at night before was no guarantee he wasn't going to do it eventually. Tomorrow night. Tonight. He also wished that Mr. Obre would not whistle "Dixie" or "The Yellow Rose of Texas" or "Lorena." No matter how soft he whistled, it always sounded to Fox P. like it could be heard for about forty miles.

Mr. Obre usually whistled while he was doing his exercise in the evening. This was a funny sort of twisting, throwing thing he did with his shoulder and arm, to limber it up after the carbine wound started to heal. The arm would be as deadly good as new. The idea made Fox P. stop and meditate. What happened was, the day after Fox P.'s company reached Degnan's command, Fox P. happened to oversee trooper Callahan come up to Mr. Obre and overhear trooper Callahan say, grinning, "Now they broke up your gun arm, Comanch', I'll match you," and reach right across his own belly and go for the forward facing butt of the service Colt. It was all in joke, for an audience, and it backfired clean, because Mr. Obre had that left Dance in his left hand before Callahan ever cleared leather. Fox P. chuckled when he recalled Callahan's face. Fox P. oversaw and overheard a lot of things. Like Callahan's wife coming out to hug him and tell him how glad she was he was back safe and sound, and all the time, over his shoulder, looking at John Shafter. Lordy, it wasn't such a complicated life after all; things was pretty, purely simple if you kept the skin of your eye peeled.

Fox P. lighted up his pipe and looked over to where Shafter was whittling a stick. The night was so clear you could see the massed clouds, almost as white as in the daytime, spreading across a deep blue crystalline sky. Shafter was hunched against a boulder; he didn't look comfortable. He didn't look, either, quite the same as Fox P. remembered. Heavier through the shoulders and yet leaned up to a point where you liked to maybe offer him a square meal, and the lines coming in the face not only the pleasant squint lines but marks showing plain there were things a man kept inside himself which worried and pained so bad they burned right straight through and traced themselves on the outside and lay honest in the eye.

It was peculiar how it was just like Shafter knew what he was remembering: how both of them used to look, and be. "How's Grampa Virgil, Fox?" he said. "You ever hear from him?"

Fox P. shrugged, as if what he was going to say didn't matter, but all the time he knew it did. "He dead," he said. "Just laid down one morning and died."

Shafter wasn't surprised. The steady hands went on with the whittling. Grampa Virgil'd been old when he was a youngster. "Was he sick?"

"Not so's you could see it," Fox P. said. He took the pipe from between his teeth and looked at the scarred bowl. "Sick inside maybe. He never did feel rarin' to go again after them 'baggers tried to buy him out for a sack of goobers and he had to run 'em off with a rifle." Shafter's smile was faintly ironic. "And you know what that old coot done?" Fox P. said. "He tole me, and he tole Jessie Bell Huggins he craved to be laid up there on that south bluff . . . you mind where I mean?" Shafter nodded. "Man tell you where he wants to lay, you'd ought to lay him there," Fox P. said. "They was only me and Jessie Bell. We drug him up there hangin' over the orneriest mule you ever see, Shafter. I felt for that mule. Grampa'd got powerful with fat. And you know, we got him up there and laid him in the box and started to dig, and no matter where we touched the spade it was the solidest rock God ever made. Jessie Bell was trompin' on that shovel and cussin' and sayin' Grampa done it deliberate, and how he'd ought to be over in the wood lot with your folks. I tell you it was all ornery, Shafter, the mule and the rock and Jessie Bell, all of it."

"I take it he's buried shallow," Shafter said.

"He's where he wanted, though," Fox P. said.

"I hope you burned down the house," Shafter said.

"I sure didn't leave it for them 'baggers," Fox P. said.

Pretty soon Shafter said, "You look right fine in that blue coat, Fox."

Fox P. laughed. The size and whiteness and display of teeth in the shiny face were enough to give a man a start. "It ain't bad for a body with no strings. Better than gone north and gittin' industrialized. You mind how they crammed that word down our throats, Shafter?" He stood up. "This nigger don't aim to git no closer to a steam whistle than the old *Cocopo* takin' us yellowlegs up the Colorado."

"I remember you used to call me Mr. Shafter," Shafter said.

"That's right," Fox P. said. "And I remind you used to call me Hey."

Shafter smiled, without irony now, so kind of pensive that Fox P. felt a sadness beginning to mush up in him. He came and stood looking down at Shafter. "Ain't you never gone back, Shafter?"

Shafter said, "What for?" He tossed the stick into the fire.

"Mostly a man hankers to see the places he's left something of himself," Fox P. said.

"Man's a fool then," Shafter said. "There ain't any way of pickin' up what you left and stickin' it back on yourself."

"Some tries."

"Fox P., tend your own goddamn oats, will you?"

Fox P. went and sat down again. Outside the ring of light there was a sharp click of sound and he straightened, but Shafter never flicked an eyelid. Obre got so restless he liked to take a round now and then; he was carrying Shafter's Henry, and it sounded as if he'd levered it. He didn't fire it, though, so Fox P. settled back and went to smoking again. "You callin' me like that," he said, "I remind how I remarked to myself you was the last person I figger to find associated like you is presently associated."

"I got to eat," Shafter said.

"Does you care how the food is cooked?" Fox P. said.

"I don't aim to see the *Tá-ashi* runnin' off our women."

"I believes you," Fox P. said.

"You do? Well, it's a damn lie," Shafter said. "Truth of the matter is, I'm a hero. A one hundred per cent cool-headed, iron-nerved hero."

After a moment, Fox P. said, "You mind, Grampa Virgil took good care of me?" His voice was limned with hurt. He wasn't bitter and he was discomfited at the bitterness of other men.

"I mind," Shafter said absently.

"He was a good old coot. He had me and I had him, and we was all they was, for many a year."

It was true. Shafter looked up at him. Fox P. and Grampa, alone on that shabby hardpan farm, year in, year out. It might've, must've got so one couldn't walk over the door sill without the other. Maybe they hated one another's guts, but they wouldn't get along without one another. Whatever Fox P. said now, it must've blasted a hole a mile high when the old man died.

"We was good friends," Fox P. said.

"You reckon to go back?" Shafter said.

"Nope. I was one of them tries, and I couldn't stick the pieces back on neither." He sat up straight. "But maybe you got to go back at the end. Maybe somethin' comes and tells you to go back. Like I ought to go back and make 'em shovel out the rock and put me in by Grampa. Like you ought to go back to that wood lot and lie with Miss Lissy."

The tightening of Shafter's mouth, almost a grimace, stopped him. Shafter said, "I been loning it too long now, Fox. I'm gone to lone it all the way home."

"You ain't a loner," Fox P. said. "You got Mr. Obre on the right and Mr. Willson on the left."

"I could sit square in the middle of a howlin' herd and lone it," Shafter said.

"That's true," Fox P. said. "How you account for that?"

"I don't. I don't account for anything any more. I'm just glad to see the sun come up."

Obre came in and stood to the fire, warming up. "Thought I heard you gettin' ready to trigger off out there," Shafter said.

"You look real panicky," Obre said. "Some damn bird raised my hackles. Where's Charley?"

"Layin' over the other side of the ridge. He's spooked."

Fox P. laughed. It was a rich, full, bass laugh. "That's two of us spooked. How far you figger to go tomorrow, Shafter?"

"Just mosey along some," Shafter said.

"I can't hardly wait," Obre said. "My rump feels like two cannon balls."

"Whose watch?" Fox P. said.

"Mine," Shafter said. "Then you, then Ob. I want to get out by dawn. Any coffee left?"

"Half a pot," Fox P. said.

"Swill it," Obre said. "I don't aim to wake up up to my neck in a anthill."

They turned in. Shafter poured himself a can of coffee, threw his blanket roll against the boulder, lay the Henry close, and made himself comfortable. The troopers had been riding him about that Henry. It was true it wasn't the smoothest thing in the world to handle, loading as it did through the muzzle; and it wasn't too high-powered either. Its range was a thousand yards, but you had sixteen shots at your trigger finger, and if you were any marksman at all, you had sixteen dead whatever you were shooting at. Shafter wouldn't have traded it for ten .50–.70s. Obre was beginning to favor it, too, which was odd because Obre never put any dependence on anything but the Dances. The Henry was like safety in numbers: sixteen rounds right under your thumb. Shafter looked over to where Obre was rolled close to the fire. That was odd, too: ever since that Apache horse handler had got in his licks, Obre had grumbled, off and on, about being cold. He was the man of most acceptance Shafter ever knew, so maybe he was entitled to encourage a minor complaint or two.

He finished the coffee and thought back. He had been passing the time of day with Katie Callahan, three days after the colonel dry-gulched the war party. Degnan was getting set to ride over to Whipple for his delayed conference with General Stoneman; the accompanying detail was shining up; Linus was behind his father's desk studying a set of maps; Captain Tremaine of the Tenth was trying to get his Negro cavalry bedded down in close quarters; Sergeant Stern was gloriously drunk in Tucson; Rafe Callahan was trimming his mustache; Jesús Elias, with a jingle of silver, rode into the post.

"My God," Degnan said, peering out the window of commandant. "I haven't got time to talk with him now."

"I've got all the time in the world," Linus said, getting to his feet.

Degnan took one look at his son's face and reached for his hat. "On second thought, I'll do the talking," he said.

When he went out, he walked right past Shafter, leaning up against the blistered-paint siding, near the door. He didn't see Obre, sitting in the shade of the wall, down by the laundry, with that look on his face like a hunting cat which pretends drowsiness but all the time is crouching, inside, hair-triggered to jump.

"Good morning, Elias," Degnan said.

"*Buenos días*, Colonel." Elias looked leisurely down at Degnan, faintly patronizing, before he dismounted. He stripped off a soft glove and offered his hand. "My congratulations, Colonel, on your victory."

"Thank you, Elias. Let's hope it sets the pace for the summer."

"Let us," Elias murmured.

"Will you come in?" Degnan said. "I'm afraid I'm rather pressed for time. . . . I'm on my way to Fort Whipple."

"My business won't take long," Elias said, smiling. His handsome face was composed, assured. He looked straight into Degnan's impatient and somewhat vague eye. Then he turned and looked back out of the cantonment. Two men were riding in, out of their own dust. Then he looked past Degnan, at Shafter. "I have a warrant for the arrest of this man Obre," he said.

Degnan made a sighing sound. "Obre is recovering from a wound," he said. "He's in no condition to ride off this post, and, even if he were, I'm afraid I can't let him go."

Elias's face showed nothing but that pleasant, supreme assurance. He put his hand out, on Degnan's upper arm. "Colonel, you and I have been friends now for a long time, no? You aren't going to tell me you refuse to release him into my custody?"

"Yes," Degnan said, "I'm telling you. Who issued the warrant?"

"Judge Holbein."

"Judge Holbein hasn't been in this territory for weeks."

"Logan rode a long way to get this warrant, Colonel. I want this done legally. I deplore mob violence. Obre is guaranteed, on my word, a fair trial in Tucson." He removed his hand from Degnan's arm and reached for the whip at his belt. "See here, Colonel, you know what happened in this case as well as I do. My teamster is dead. My teamster was murdered."

Degnan's half smile was lopsided. "This is the attitude in which you plan a fair trial?"

"I am not on the jury. I give you my word Obre will remain in jail until Holbein gets here."

"I can't accept your word, Elias," Degnan said.

Now the whip began, softly, switching at the high Mexican boots. If there was any change of expression, it was an almost imperceptible narrowing of the eyes. "You cannot take my word?"

"I didn't mean that the way it sounds," Degnan said. "Your word is good with me. What if some of your Mex . . . your friends take him out of the jail before Holbein gets here?"

"I will not let that happen," Elias said, like God.

Against the wall, Shafter began to feel sore. The Old Man better say something more than this pretty soon, or he wouldn't be able to keep out of it. Then the colonel said, "Well, I'm sorry, Elias, but you can't try one of my men under civilian law. Obre's under contract to me as interpreter."

"So I understand," Elias said evenly. "But he is a civilian with the army. This is another matter entirely."

"No, it's not," Degnan said bluntly. "Obre is under military orders and answerable only to the United States Government."

Logan and a skinner named Auden pulled up behind Elias. They didn't say anything. Logan had a long length of rope coiled over his saddle scabbard. He sat forward, leaning on his pommel. He looked down the line of buildings to where Obre sat, looking half asleep.

"In that event," Elias said, "I feel I must make a report to some higher authority. I am going to bring this man to justice."

Degnan took six long strides forward. His hand shot out and touched, barely touched, the coiled rope Logan carried.

"Is this what you're going to bring him to justice with, Elias?"

"It is customary for teamsters to carry rope," Elias said in a voice loose with boredom.

"All right," Degnan said. "I'll tell you what you do. You make your report to a higher authority. Why not General Stoneman? Report Obre. Report me. State that, as you say, we have been friends for a long time. State that I told you, publicly, before anybody here who cares to listen, to get off this post and not to return unless you care to make a social call or to inform me of a need for military assistance."

Under the smooth dark skin there was a whitening of Elias's face. "Are you ordering me out of this cantonment, Colonel?"

"I am," Degnan said.

"You refuse to recognize Judge Holbein's warrant?"

"I do," Degnan said.

"You will not release Obre to me?"

"Not by a damn sight," Degnan said.

Elias mounted very deliberately. He looked down at Degnan. "I regret that this terminates our friendship, Colonel."

"That choice is your privilege," Degnan said.

Elias wheeled the big white horse and rode past Logan and Auden. Turning, Logan spat in the dust at Degnan's feet.

Stamping back to commandant, Degnan noticed Shafter for the first time. His forefinger stabbed the air. "Bear witness if you have to, John."

"Sure," Shafter said. He didn't feel sore now. He felt a kind of admiration for the blunt-spoken damn Yankee.

"I don't want Obre off this post," Degnan said.

Shafter pushed the battered Kossuth hat back on his head. "You better make that official. Nobody's gone to hold Obre in he don't want to be held. He might be cool-like, but he ain't always sensible."

Degnan nodded. It was the first time he had not felt a surge of distaste for the man who had gone into the Apache war camp apparently without a qualm, and who had been his lone casualty. He thought of that day in his office when he had first seen Obre's fine-boned hands, and he thought of those hands useless. No. He could not do Obre any favors. "Tell him it's an order," he said.

Shafter went and hunched against the wall on one heel, beside Obre. They watched the detail ride out with Degnan at its head. Then Shafter said, "Orders are we stay here."

Obre's face was darker than usual. "Wha'd the greaser want?"

"He didn't say to me," Shafter said.

"Your ears were stickin' straight out."

"I reckon he wants to take you out and string you up," Shafter said. He didn't turn his head, looking steadily out at the disappearing dust of the detail flooding up on the flats, under the burned blue-brown hills.

"Look," Obre said, "you and Willson keep the hell out of this."

"Sure," Shafter said.

"I had all the favors done me this year I ever want done me."

Shafter nodded.

"I don't owe nobody nothing."

"Sure," Shafter said.

"Is that all you got to say?" Obre said.

"I ain't aimin' to hassle with you, Ob," Shafter said. "I don't think Degnan's doin' any favors, though. In the beginning he was, maybe. For Linus. He'd of done anything for Linus. Now maybe he's learnin' something. He don't know it yet. Maybe I'm learnin' it along with him."

Obre grunted. "Learnin' what?"

"That nobody can do everything there is to be done all by himself, no matter how bad he wants to."

"I already knowed that," Obre said.

"You sure don't act it sometimes."

Obre sighed. "He ain't a bad gringo." He looked quickly at Shafter. "For a bluecoat, anyways." He stretched out his legs. "I reckon from now on, just to keep the record straight, I'll do the favorin'."

"All right," Shafter said. "Only don't make out you can handle Elias alone. Even if you can."

"You ride into town and bring me some clean duds," Obre said noncommittally. "And don't start no fights."

"I never started a fight in my life," Shafter said.

"You finished considerable."

"It ain't the same."

"How long we got to hang around here?"

"Till he gets back from talkin' to Stoneman. Then maybe you and me can do it my way." Shafter stood up. "You start thinkin' Indian, Ob. Think on the harvest, and what they're gone to be harvestin' where."

"You think they gone to let her loose for that?" Obre said.

Shafter said, "I reckon Joaquin don't aim to starve."

"If I could find her," Obre said, "that breed *Tá-ashi'd* sure have a long hungry winter."

Walter Degnan returned from his conference with General Stoneman with a certain light in his eye, a certain spring in his step.

Stoneman, who had taken command of the newly formed Arizona Department in April, looked like the man for the job in every respect, a regular meteor. He had the background from which to project himself: west with the Mormon Battalion, citation for valor and brevet commission out of the War between the States. He was afire with plans and projects. He was going to save an economy-minded government millions in the western campaigns. He was already investigating all army contracts and uncovering an unprecedented amount of graft. He was preparing to discharge every extraneous government employee. He was getting along with the Indian agents, a minor miracle in itself. And no more loafing for troopers not in the field; he had them digging irrigation ditches and erecting new quarters on the posts. With what he was saving, he was certain he would win approval of his plan for the construction of permanent roads in the territory. And he was certainly killing Apaches. His enthusiasm infected Degnan. They saw eye to eye, and their meeting was a simple matter of confirming one another's viewpoint: push hard as often as we can. It didn't occur to anybody that Stoneman might be pushing too hard.

"It sounds like Christmas," Tony Bleeker said. He was preparing to go over to Camp Grant and visit there for a time. He was lacing up a high boot, one foot braced on a chair. "Do you think it will have any effect on the desertion rate?"

In the fettle he was in, the question was a wet rag in Degnan's face. "Why do you take these negative attitudes, Tony? I tell you the man is the best thing that's come our way in months."

Bleeker turned around and stood upright, puffing a little. "I only ask because this post, Colonel Walter I. Degnan commanding, is minus one trooper, one horse, one saddle, one blanket, one set saddlebags. . . ."

"Who?" Degnan said.

"A man named Sawyer. It seems somebody told him he was going to have to dig ditches."

Degnan looked thoughtful. "You might not believe this, but I've never had a desertion before. Anybody looking for Sawyer?"

"Sterling Sergeant Stern. The lieutenant got the desertion report while you were out. The number of men who do not want to fight Apaches has shot up like a prairie flower."

"They'll get Sawyer."

"Maybe. But I rather think I can see him sluicing gold in Cali-forn-i-ay and laughing maniacally at the thought of his thirteen-dollar-a-month compadres."

Degnan threw down his gauntlets. "I suppose there's a total on the desertion figure?"

"I believe the lieutenant said eighty-six, in the territory. For the fiscal year, that is."

Degnan was chewing at his lower lip. "High. Too high. But they'll see. Things are going to get better by the day with Stone-man here. Where are you off to, Tony?"

"Camp Grant," Bleeker said, looking around for his hat. "I hope you won't be out another horse by the time I get there."

"It won't be comfortable at Grant. I hear it's pretty run-down. They ought to do something about it."

"Lieutenant Whitman has promised me all the redeye I can gurgle my way through," Bleeker said. "It may compensate."

"You're coming back, Tony?"

Bleeker hesitated a moment. Then he said, "Yes, Walter, I'm coming back. I wish I could say I didn't want to leave. I wish I could say I want to go out with your troopers and write and draw my head off. But I don't. I've got a pretty strong stomach, but I don't particularly want to see what's ahead. I want to see you suc-cessful in your main mission, but I don't want to have to face Linus, or you either, when the rest of it fails."

"You mean Anna?" Degnan said.

"Yes."

"You don't think we can do it?"

"We?" Bleeker said. "Put it this way. If it can be done, Shafter will do it. And he hasn't got a prayer."

"He bides his time," Degnan said, rather stubbornly.

"Don't we all, Walter?"

Degnan said, "It's a rotten thing I can come home feeling on top of the world and a five-minute conversation with you breaks my ankles." He sat down. "You might miss the biggest story of your life, Tony."

"I'll risk it," Bleeker said.

Degnan turned toward the open door of his office and called. "You still there, Shafter?" Shafter came to the doorway, carrying his hat. He looked uneasy, withdrawn.

"I suppose you heard," Degnan said.

"Matter of fact I did," Shafter said. "I ain't long on meanderin' once I get set. And you asked me to wait."

"And what is your opinion of Mr. Bleeker's appraisals and decisions?"

"I reckon he's still kind of innocent and tenderfooted," Shafter said, amused.

Bleeker was ruffled. "Shafter, I am not a gambler, but I'll make a wager with you. I'll give you till the end of the campaign and you name your price."

"I could use a new pair of boots," Shafter said.

"The price of a new pair of boots you end the summer empty-handed."

Linus came in and slapped a folder down on his father's desk. His face, when he turned it to Bleeker, was haggard, and the lock of light hair fell forward. "You gentlemen have no sense of decency whatever," he said. He meant it; his voice was strained, taut enough to snap. "If you need boots, Shafter, I'd be happy to advance you the money out of my pay. Bleek, you need a vacation."

Bleeker was pained and sober. "Linus, I'm sorrier than I can say. I never thought of it that way."

Degnan was exasperated. "What way, for God's sake? What are you talking about?"

Linus wheeled on him. "You need some rest, too, Father. I resent this entire conversation. Now you've carried it far enough that I must protest that Anna is worth rather more than a pair of boots."

Shafter said, "Linus. . . ."

"Shut up, Shafter. I don't want your apologies." Sweat had sprung out on his face. He was rigid with rage. Well, he was right, Shafter thought. Maybe it had all been innocent, but the innocently dealt hurt was always the greatest agony. He could have bit out his tongue; he wished Linus would turn on him as he had done at the wall, physically, and with the will and strength to punish.

Linus gained control of himself quickly. He was holding out his hand to Bleeker. "*Adiós*, Bleek. Regards to Lieutenant Whitman."

"Thanks, shavetail," Bleeker said. "All the luck in the world." He went out.

Before his father or Shafter could say anything, Linus picked up the folder again. "These are the new maps, Father, just in from the survey detail. Incidentally, the detail lost four men at Cienega

Springs. Chiricahua. There wasn't much left to identify." His voice was matter-of-fact. "I know where I want to go and how many men I want. Half Tremaine's troop if I can have it."

"It's yours," his father said in a tight, aching voice. "Are you going to hang around Cochise territory?"

"I'm playing a hunch," Linus said.

"Santa Rita?" his father said.

"A hunch is all I have," Linus said. This time it was a confirmation.

Degnan nodded. "We're all playing hunches." He looked at Shafter. "What's yours, John?"

Shafter felt like his clothes didn't fit him. He wouldn't look at Linus. "Obre pretty well knows the harvest areas. I reckon you can spare us. Willson'll be back from Sonora in a jig, and I understand you got some new Tonto scouts comin' in. You don't need us and you can spare Charley."

After a moment Degnan said, "Yes, I can spare you, I guess. We're all to be spared now." He considered. Willson had gone into Mexico with the detail returning the stolen horses. As soon as he got back he could be placed in full charge of the *manso* scouts. And Shafter's plan would get Obre out from under Elias's determined eye for the time being.

"I want one more man if it's all right with you," Shafter said. "I reckon you'll have to deal with Captain Tremaine." He told him, and Degnan called an orderly. "Tell trooper Canby to report to commandant."

Trooper Canby lost no time reporting. As he was clean of conscience he felt no particular trepidation at the summons, but his face nevertheless reflected an inner thoughtfulness and diffidence. His salute demonstrated proper military form, but there was about it a rhythmic, loose-jointed stylelessness.

"At ease, trooper," Degnan said. He indicated Shafter. "This gentleman has made a request for your services."

"Yessir," said Fox P. Canby cautiously.

"Just a minute," Shafter said. "I don't want Canby unless he's willing."

"Willing?" Degnan echoed. "He's under orders. Trooper, you're under orders."

"Yessir," said Fox P. Canby, even more cautiously.

"You still cook, Fox P.?" Shafter said.

"Yessir," said Fox P. Canby emphatically.

"And it's better'n gettin' shot at," Shafter said.

"Yessir," said Fox P. Canby, even more emphatically.

"As it is," Shafter said, "the grub rustlin' is certain and the gettin' shot at probable."

"Yessir," said Fox P. Canby dispiritedly.

"You want to pull stakes with me and Obre?"

Fox P. looked helplessly at Degnan, at Linus, at the wall. Then he said, "As you is giving me a choice, I would be a low-down skunk if I stayed put. When is I solicited for?"

"Tomorrow night," Shafter said. "Two pack horses and all the grub you can get on 'em. Extra ammo and blankets."

Degnan scrawled an order to Tremaine and dismissed Fox P. Canby. He wanted to discuss this with Shafter in detail, but he knew Shafter well enough by now to know Shafter probably didn't have any details to discuss: he always seemed to strike an idea and then let it work for itself. Also he had his hat on and was turning to Linus.

"You off duty?"

"Sure," Linus said.

"You want to ride into town with me?"

"Sure," Linus said.

Shafter couldn't read his eyes or his voice. He cocked his hat and looked at Degnan. "I'll see you before I pull out," he said, and then it just slipped out, easy as if it had always been used, always been there: "*Adiós*, Walter."

Nobody could argue summer wasn't coming in like an exploding firecracker, only hotter. Shafter untied his scarf and wiped his face and neck with it; it came away wet and gray. In the fierce lengthening sunlight of the afternoon heat waves shimmered at the bases of the burning hills. But all that tortured vegetation was holding water; here and there the ocotillo flaunted a rag of blossom red as blood, and there were patches of staghorn still cottony in the sand. The sky was as blue and clear as sapphire, a heavy dark depthless blue, like a deep glassy lake, holding piles of rich cloud. Everything went on forever: sand and sky and cloud, everything blue and gray and white in the afternoon light, with the occasional thin scarlet flower catching the eye and holding it.

A road runner legged it across their path, looked at them suspiciously, and went its ridiculous way. Shafter coughed, and it speeded up, racing along on its skinny stilts.

"What did you say?" Linus said.

"I didn't say anything."

"I thought you said something."

"I coughed," Shafter said.

They didn't speak again until Linus said, "How does Obre feel about Elias?"

"I wish I knew," Shafter said.

"I wish to hell he'd go to Mexico."

"Obre?"

"Elias."

"He won't. He's a big man here. *Muy grande.* Bigger'n Obre. Goddamit, I never object to a fair fight, but I get mad when they sneak up on you."

"I feel the same," Linus said. "Always fight them fair is my motto, in fact. Hide in the dark and slice them to ribbons but do it fair."

"Jesus, I reckon I make everybody cantankerous today," Shafter said. Then he said, "I aim to drink some beer in the ole saloon and I would be proud if you'd join me."

"Sure," Linus said.

"Linus, I reckon I'd ought to. . . ."

"You'd better not," Linus said.

"What I was gone to say was, I reckon I won't be seein' you for a spell."

"Well," Linus said, and then was silent. Shafter wondered what he was thinking. Pretty soon Linus said, "I'm surprised every time I think of all the things I regret in my life."

"What things?" Shafter said.

"Maybe I could worry it down to being born at all, but you haven't made me that cantankerous yet. I regret I dragged you into this. If it hadn't been for me, you'd have gone on long ago . . . maybe to all kinds of good things."

"I already had all the good things," Shafter said. He reined in the dun suddenly, the very action bringing Linus to a halt, and leaned forward on his saddle. "What do you regret, Linus? That you're responsible for my bein' here, or that I'm here?"

Linus watched him. He said, "It doesn't sound like you, making talk. You have no more call to ask that than I have to answer it. You give me hope, John."

Shafter sighed. "My feet hurt," he said. "It's on account of they're made of clay."

"It's not fair, what I did to you," Linus said. "I know that now. No man ought to ask so much of another."

Shafter studied him. There was a new and somewhat terrible pride in the young face, and yet it was a pride, Shafter knew, of which Linus was totally unconscious. He said, "I'll quit when you quit, Linus."

"I'll never quit," Linus said.

Shafter thought about it. He knew Linus meant it. He said, "The condemned man wants his beer."

They rode on. Shafter said, "Would you quit if you had proof?"

"Proof of what?" Linus said.

"At this point, proof of anything."

Linus said, "I'll quit when I have proof she's dead." He never moved a muscle and his face was so quiet it struck Shafter as almost dreaming. It made Shafter realize that probably there was a plane in any sustained shock in which the nebulous quality of dream was equally sustained. It was tremendous that Linus could cling to any hope at all, either in the time of dream or in the vast and awful time of reality. Having forgotten what hope was, or rather having nothing in particular for which to hope, Shafter was disconcerted at the idea that another human being found him capable of dispensing it.

The Old Pueblo lay naked in the sunlight, naked block and rectangle and square of shadow shifting solid with the running of the sun, falling dark without coolness along the ground, hugging the crooked adobe façades. Everything was of a form, wall and town: no roundnesses, no softnesses, stark line, sharp corner, up and down, parallel, so you almost looked longingly for some small formlessness to break the pattern. It wouldn't be any good talking in town, so Shafter said now, "If your hunch plays out, send somebody to look for me, will you?"

"We won't meet at Santa Rita?" Linus said.

Shafter shook his head. "Not unless I got to. I said what I said at Apache Pass so Victorio would know where I stood, but he wasn't talkin' through his sweat band about wantin' my gizzard. You watch out for him, Linus. He's got an awful good thinkpiece. If you go nosing around the Mimbreño rancherías, that's gone to be something you both understand."

Linus said, "This man Canby. You knew him before?"

Shafter nodded. "He grew up with Texas all around him. Now he can't shake the dust either."

They entered the town. "Go on," Linus said, "I've got to see somebody."

Shafter didn't think this sounded square on all sides, but he let it ride. You could carry nursemaiding just so far.

And he could remember now, having spent the summer with Obre and Canby and Charley Tom, riding what he knew was the last hope and growing harder and tougher and older and more alone inside himself, that his final word to Linus had been a selfjudgment.

"While I'm gone," he said, "you now and then think on the fact that the good Lord, for reasons known only to Himself, made more horses' asses then he did horses."

Half a mile out of the post, the search beginning, the chico from the broken-down *zapatería* in the Old Pueblo intercepted him. No, there was no mistake, the boots were for Señor Shafter, very fine brown boots with a wealth of intricate stitching, a hell of a hole in a cavalry lieutenant's thirty-a-month. Inside the left one was a piece of faded brown paper with Linus' scrawl on it: *Here, damn you. If you have to walk anywhere, anytime, I wish you blisters.*

Right then he left off for the first time sort of worrying about Linus and began for the first time to sort of worry about himself.

The summer became, in its way, a nightmare for the searchers. There were periods when they might have been alone in the world, days when they simply sat tight, long hours in the saddle. Sometimes they restocked grub at a ranch and found they were hungry for companionship, and their hosts, Mex or Irish or just plain Yankee, were equally hungry and wouldn't let them go and wanted to give them everything but the outhouse. They were scouting, Shafter always said, and neither Fox P. Canby nor Charley Tom knew any different. Fox P. figured there was something more than that but didn't ask, and Charley Tom had his suspicions, which were correct. But always, when they hit the ranches or the forts they were scouting, and there was Degnan's order to prove it.

They could count the Indians they'd seen, at close range, on the fingers of one hand. One night, on Obre's watch, there were suddenly three Indians on the fringe of the fire, silent, out of nowhere.

One moment there had been nothing but the darkness beyond the flare of firelight and the next they were standing there, bringing Obre's heart into his throat and his hand, quietly, gently, to the stock of the Henry. They were Tontos. They wanted grub. After they were fed they begged cigarette makings. They wanted whiskey, too, but Shafter said there wasn't any. They didn't believe him and he knew it. They slept and pulled out at dawn. Obre didn't talk much to them, but he let them know he could handle their tongue as well as they could, which might have accounted, in part, for their restlessness. A few days later, in the foothills, riding up through a boulder field, they came without warning on two old squaws sorting roots in the shade of a big rock. The squaws stared up, apparently emotionless, trapped, resigned. Shafter took in the squat, tired bodies, the broad flat faces, the impassive eyes. He bowed slightly from the waist, tipped his hat, and rode on.

And they could feel the eyes, perhaps not so impassive now, upon their departing backs, and Fox P. thought he could hear the whistle of arrows and squirmed in the saddle.

Every hour Shafter was prepared to dig in and fight and it never came. It made him relax to a point that Obre thought was carelessness and gave him time to think about how it was going for Degnan and what Linus was up to. "Watch the summer go," he said one morning to Canby.

"Shadows gettin' long," Fox P. concurred. He had an idea they might be going home, because Shafter seemed to have drawn them through a huge circle and was now coming around again on the perimeter. But Shafter didn't say. He was remembering how it was in the mountains, with a single leaf or two fluttering down, slow, but letting you know what time it was getting to be, and the blue water lying bluer and the first color beginning to glint in the trees. He could smell and taste the end of summer, a drowsy, sirupy, yellow heaviness in the air that made it hotter than hell. He felt let down, not because he hadn't found what he was looking for but because he realized another season had swung the round and the only thing he had to do now was pick up his pay. He figured it might be pleasant to go to Mexico and lay down and drink some tequila and pretend he was a deaf mute.

It was a fine morning, but Obre ignored it. He was fretting about how Willson was getting along, mulling over what scraps of news they'd had about a couple of nasty U. S. Army–*Tá-ashi* encounters.

Also he said it was getting colder every night and he reckoned at
this rate he would be laid out froze stiff as a board before the first
of October.

Nearing noon, climbing in the silvered grasslands, they came on
Charley Tom lying behind a ridge of red stone. He didn't turn
around, but he raised his hand in a gesture both signal and summons.

Well, it couldn't last, Shafter thought. They hadn't had to run
yet, but he was sure leaning on his luck. If it was a war party
Charley was studying, they'd have to backtrack and hope they
could get out of sight. When he dismounted he was conscious of
being tired and sore and gaunted, and he let his hand lie on the
dun and saw the dun was the same. He decided when he joined
Charley that if the whole Apache nation was before them he would
just lie there for a month or two anyway. He dropped down and
looked and didn't say a word even though Charley Tom was looking right at him now.

He counted eleven squaws, six horses, and two mules. And there
wasn't one shred of optimism left in him, and when he spoke it was
in a tone of genuine curiosity.

"What are they doin', Ob?"

"Diggin' spuds," Obre said.

"Lord," Fox P. said. "That's more ladies than I seen in a month
of Sundays."

"Believe me," Obre said, "they ain't ladies." He closed one eye.
Shafter, damn him, trying to make him believe Little Fire had
gone off with some Gileño buck. . . .

"Any bucks ridin' herd?" Shafter said.

Charley Tom shook his head.

"They're pretty far out to be alone," Shafter said doubtfully.

"No guard," Charley Tom insisted. "I watch a long time now,
John."

Shafter studied the women. It was a very smooth operation. One
bunch was digging and the rest were sorting and loading the panniers. He could see little blue and white patches, spears of blossom
on the solanum, the potato flowers. It was kind of pretty, the
women moving with an unself-conscious animal grace, some of
them slim and little and lithe in skins, some making a vulgar splash
of color in skirts of traded-for or stolen dry goods. There were some
old squaws out there, but there were some young ones, too. He

found he was straining his eyes, willing one of them to make some motion, perform some act, which was alien to the picture. They seemed happy. At least they were chattering away, although that was something women seemed to do even if they were unhappy. A clean, high burst of laughter reached him once and he wondered which of them had felt good enough to make such joyous, lighthearted music. A girl's laughter. My God, how good a girl's laughter could sound.

Finally he said, "Well, there's only one way to look 'em over."

"They prob'ly all armed with something, even if it's only a stone in the hand," Obre warned.

Shafter said, "Get rough if you have to, but don't shoot anybody." When he stood up, his legs ached.

"Are we gone to flush those quail?" Fox P. said.

"Yes indeed," Shafter said. "But you can't have any of 'em. What we are lookin' for is a white girl. She might be a little sunburned, but she won't look like the rest of 'em."

"Merciful God," Fox P. said. "I did have my wonders."

They rode out at a steady pace, without a word or a hail. It happened just as Shafter knew it would: the women caught the sound of the hoofs and turned and looked, and they, too, were silent, but they broke and ran. Charley Tom veered off, riding for the bunched pack animals, to shoo them off. But how those women could run. The young ones were like deer, and they were smart, too, running a staggered, crazy course.

Shafter stung the dun into a gallop. Running footraces was the prime sport of Apache women, and it was not unusual for them to outrun their men. The old squaws would drop behind quickly, but the girls could take them a long sweet chase and when one was cornered like as not she'd have a knife ready and wouldn't have any scruples as to using it. He fought the feeling that the whole thing was loco: despite his instructions to Fox P., there wasn't any way of telling whether a girl was red or white, or Chinese for that matter, unless they could round up every last one of them. He was thinking it when he pulled up beside a girl who made the mistake of veering toward him when she should have swung away. He saw her face tipped up to him, a face as Indian as a face could get, the eyes wide with fear, and then, with bewilderment as he rode past her, involuntarily pulling his neck into his shoulders as if he expected to feel a knife in his back.

Then he laughed. He couldn't help it. It was as if the sound of the girl's laughter he had heard awhile back was bouncing off him. He thought it might be the funniest thing he'd ever get to see: the four of them trying to ride down that scared covey of squaws; everybody, horses and all, zigzagging around like they were drunk, and underlying it the tragicomedy of the terrified doe-swift women who knew only too well why *americanos* chased squaws and would fight to the death about it.

He rode past another girl, who flung a stone at him. Her aim was bad, but he ran out of range anyway and did the only thing he could do. He sucked up all the air that would fit in his lungs and shouted Anna's name, twice, as loud and clear as he could make it ring.

Sixteen

Anna was loading the panniers on the scrub pony, wedging potatoes firmly against one another, when the four horsemen swept around the end of the ridge. At first she thought it was some of the men, come to stand guard. When she saw, with a stab of dismay, that they were not Apaches, she stood stupidly, both hands still stretched to the pannier, watching. Nuadin's excited whisper went clean through her.

"Vaqueros! Vámonos!"

But she did not move until Nuadin dragged at her arm, and then it was only to back away from the pony. They could not be white men; they were still too far off to be identified. Then she saw the faded blue of Fox P. Canby's uniform, and she ran.

Nuadin was already far ahead. Anna wanted to call to her and could not make a sound. She saw Nuadin sprawl suddenly and roll to her feet and go on as if it had not happened. Anna ran too hard and sensed she could not keep up the pace; she did not know how to breathe correctly or how to regulate her stride, letting the thigh muscles do the work; she ran with her whole body, and worst of all with her heart, which within a few minutes felt as if it would burst wetly out of her throat and nostrils. She did not look back.

The frightening thing was the blind wild panic, for she did not know what she was running from or where she was expected to go, and at the speed Nuadin was traveling it would be impossible to keep her in sight for long. Inside, intuitively, she knew that something was happening which threatened her particularly and which therefore threatened Joaquin. It was this awareness which gave her an endurance and cleverness far beyond the point at which she should simply have dropped in her tracks. She stopped gulping air as if she were drowning and tried to breathe steadily, but the pain in her lungs and the massive swollen mountain of her heart, struggling to break open, were beyond bearing. It was almost with relief that she heard her name called, and the word sounded strange, harsh, and ugly in her ears, after the soft Spanish pronunciation to which she had become accustomed.

She came to a tentative halt, more in obedience than anything else, for she had learned a great deal about obedience. Her head fell forward and it seemed to her that she stood for minutes, fighting for breath, with one hand clenched into a fist against her side, moving spasmodically, as though to crush the ache. But she stood for only a second, and, while it felt to her that she had stood quite still, it had been actually only a moment of hesitation before she was running again, a dragging slow run now, with the heart gone out of her, exploded and drained away. The hoofs thundered up and the horse pulled abreast and she looked into the rough stubbled face and heard the same voice which had called her name and stopped again.

"Are you Anna Stillman?" Shafter said as calmly as he could. He didn't want to scare her.

She made a sound for the first time. Shafter thought she was trying to speak, but she was not. A hideous broken sobbing poured out of her, a long incoherent protest which was wordless and toneless and barely human. She swung on one heel and began to run again.

Shafter was taken back, but he knew he shouldn't be. He moved with resignation and patience; he could let her run herself out and it would be over, but he didn't want to risk it when he didn't know how close they might be to a guard party. He cut her off without any trouble, leaned down, caught her around the waist, and kicked the dun into a long lope. There was no way she could match the horse now. Her feet left the ground and Shafter flung her awkwardly over the dun's withers, as if she were a sack of oats.

When he turned he saw Obre and Charley Tom were still chasing squaws, just for the hell of it; they quit when they saw him turn. He took Anna by the shoulders and pulled her upright before him. She slammed an elbow into his chest so hard she nearly knocked the wind out of him, and then she was fighting him, half slipping off the dun, and the dun was side-stepping nervously under them both. She felt none of the horror and disbelief she had felt when she had been dragged against the Apache pony, but a wrenching bone-deep rage and desperation.

Shafter managed to twist one arm behind her, so that she cried out and slumped forward with all the fight gone out of her in that one second of pain. Tears of weakness and exhaustion were running down her face. It was discordant, false, to have the man's voice saying so close to her, "Easy, little lady, I don't want to hurt you."

The other men were coming up, so that there was only one thing left for her to do. She sat upright, both hands on the dun's neck, holding her body erect and away from Shafter's, and she looked straight before her and tightened her lips. But she saw, out of the corner of her eye. Oh God, a Negro cavalryman, probably a deserter. And the dark, dark man in dusty black, with his lean saturnine face and savage smile. And the Indian. But he looked Apache. It was to him she spoke, coldly, hopelessly.

"*N'de?*"

Charley Tom dropped his eyes and did not answer. And the man holding her said again, "Easy, easy," and the horse began to move.

"Let's get out of here," Shafter said.

Fox P.'s voice was uneven. "Straight home, I hopes."

"Straight home," Shafter said.

"You think we gone to make it?" Obre voiced his never-ending doubt with elaborate carelessness.

"We're gone to find us a hole till nightfall," Shafter said. He glanced at Charley Tom and Charley Tom pulled out, back up the ridge. Those squaws would hit a vedette somewhere close, and the word would go on, by mirror, and there would be a war party on them before they knew it. For the first time Shafter began to feel the raw edge of his own nerve; hell, the whole summer had been easy in retrospect. They would have to hit rock quickly, in an effort to wipe out their trail. They had been the hunters for a long time, and now it would be their turn to play the hunted.

But he did one thing first. He unsnapped his canteen from the saddle ring and nudged Anna with it. For a long moment she looked down at it, trembling with contempt; then she took it in both hands and drank deeply and heard him say, "Good girl."

They rode hard, following Charley Tom, who was as skilled at erasing track as he was at tracking. Anna was in fresh agony: the McClellan's high wishbone pommel cut into her spine and she found herself clenching the dun's flesh to keep her balance. When she slipped, Shafter slid his arm about her and she suffered this, too, straining away from the relentless jarring of the pommel against the tender ridge of bone.

Charley Tom found them their hole, high up in an escarpment

dotted with clefts and caves. It was bare, empty, forbidding, and he only pointed to it before he turned back the way they had come with a sweep brush of pine dragging over his horse's rump. Halfway down he dismounted and began to slip the soft deerskin moccasins over the horse's feet.

Obre struggled through the rocks first, poking in and out of the clefts until he found one to his liking. The dun fought his way up gallantly, very tired and unhappy with his double burden. They hurried the horses into the cave, but before Shafter dismounted Anna pitched off, landed on her feet, and fell against the dun. She and Shafter stared at one another. She knew now who he was and it shook her to recognize a man she had never seen.

"You're Shafter," she said.

His forehead crinkled quizzically. "What? How do you know?"

"Joaquin," she said and buried her face against the horse.

Shafter touched her shoulder. He was more than ill at ease; he was deeply disturbed; he searched for some word which would reassure her. "Miss Stillman, please don't cry. We're gone to take you to Tucson safe as we can."

She raised her head and looked at him. Behind her, Obre and Fox P. edged for the cave opening, Obre's face dark and set, Fox P. head down and embarrassed. Anna waited until they had gone out, but when she tried to speak her voice emerged a hoarse whisper. "Safe to Tucson. And where were you when I needed you? Where were you last spring? Where were you when they let Ysabel Vasquez go and held me up there?" Her eyes were wide and clear now, with anger. "What makes you think I want to go to Tucson? What right have you to tell me where I must go?"

"Well," Shafter said. He was stumped. He took off his hat and held it in both hands and looked down at it. He said, "Ma'am, I am right sorry to cause you all this trouble. We been lookin' for you all summer. There wasn't any way we could force Victorio to let you go last spring." He raised his eyes to her and felt as if he wanted to go and hide his head. Why, she was only a little, little girl, and as always with a child he knew it was impossible to determine the depth and extent of its suffering. He tried to be gentle and felt he was only clumsy. "We knew how bad it must be for you, up there, and there wasn't anything we could do but wait. You got to understand that. It was bad for the people were waiting, too, you know." He stopped. He wasn't going to mention Linus.

She watched him for a long moment, seeing in his face strength and decision, tolerance and ruthlessness. His eyes were very kind; they were the eyes of a man she knew she could trust. But she marked also the set of his mouth. "Mister Shafter, I appreciate this . . . whatever you think it is you've done for me. But I have no desire to go to Tucson. I would like to be allowed to go home."

Shafter took three steps forward and grabbed her by the arms, hard. "Let me tell you something, lady. I may be a hired hand in this Yankee army, but I ain't riskin' my neck out here for the money. I got a friend has been half out of his mind over you, and what-ever I did, whatever I do from here on in, is for him. Now you tell me you don't remember his name!"

He thought she was going to fall to pieces, right there before him. "I know. Please don't go on, because I know. But I have to go back."

"Back?" he said. "Back? To what? That murderin' bunch up in the Stronghold?"

"Mr. Shafter," she said, "I am Joaquin's wife. I thought you under-stood that."

He was beaten. He was beaten right out. He released her. "Look," he said helplessly, "look . . . yes, I know that. I mean, we pretty much knew it. But you just don't see. . . . I don't know how to make you see. . . ."

She took pity on him. "Oh, but there is nothing more to see. Why must you complicate everything? You told Joaquin you were his friend."

"I'll do anything I can for Joaquin," Shafter said.

"Then give me a horse and let me go."

She was insane, that was it. But he knew it wasn't so. He tried to contain himself. "Miss Stillman, this ain't the first time I've seen a thing like this happen. But it was always with people had been with the Indians years and years and had forgot any other way of livin'. No, that ain't exactly true. A lot of 'em didn't forget. They didn't want any other way. But I never saw anybody had been with 'em a scarce six months eatin' their heart out to stay." She did not seem impressed by what he said; he read her reaction as in-difference, to him and to his gratuitous sermon. He plunged on. "I rode a few scouts where we received Indian prisoners. I know what I'm talkin' about. There was never one woman had been taken and forced. . . ."

"Forced?" she said with a thin smile.

His patience snapped. In that instant he disliked her intensely. "Lady," he said grimly, "I ain't gone to listen to the story of your life and I ain't gone to tell you mine. The only thing I want to get straight with you is that you're gone back to Tucson with me. After that you can sashay out with every buck from here to the Gila if you're of a mind."

All the color went out of her face. He saw a long shudder, like a convulsion, rack her, and he saw her hatred of him flare in her eyes.

Obre slammed into the cave at a run. "They're comin'," he said.

Shafter reached for the Henry, but he never stopped watching Anna. "You take the horses back far as you can. Wet their lips but don't use more'n a drop of water. And you keep quiet, because if I hear one little sound out of you I'll stun you with the butt of this rifle. Our lives depend on it, and if you think I don't mean it, you try me."

She loathed him. She swung away with the dun, catching a glimpse of Obre's surprised face. The cave was high and shallow, and she led the dun to the far wall, unsnapped Shafter's canteen, poured the hot alkaline water into her palm, and passed it over the dun's muzzle. She did the same with the other horses and stayed with them, raging and impotent.

Fox P. and Obre were belly down on the lip of the escarpment, sheltered by boulders, when Shafter joined them. Way off, down the snaking valley, he could make out the fast-moving cloud of dust which signaled riders. "Where's Charley?" he grunted.

"Cuttin' 'em a trail to get lost on," Obre said.

"Jesus, that *manso* ought to be drawin' colonel's pay," Shafter said.

"What's the matter?" Obre said, looking straight ahead. "Don't she like you?"

"I reckon not," Shafter said briefly.

"Excuse me for mentionin' it, but you ain't got much manners. My ma'd ever heard me talk like that to a lady she'd of boxed my ears."

"Yes?" Shafter said, almost politely. "Well, you watch her, on account of I don't trust her." And he thought, poor Linus. After all this, poor Linus. And he also thought, God, or *Ysen*, or White

Painted Woman, or whatever it is rattling around up there, if that party strikes us, don't let Joaquin be among 'em.

There were nine bucks in the party, but they never got close enough so he could recognize any of them. They swept off around the far end of the escarpment and rode on. Charley Tom had out-done himself, wiping out the trail, cutting a new one, vague but dis-cernible. He really had the dirty end of the stick, Shafter thought: he had to lead them blind and then find enough cover to save his own hide.

"Take the first watch, Fox, in case they double back," Shafter said. He got to his feet and he and Obre moved into the cave. Anna was still back against the shadowy gray wall. "Miss Stillman," Shafter said, "we are gone to travel all night and we are gone to travel hard. You better get some sleep now." He unstrapped a rolled blanket from one of the pack horses and tossed it to her. But she made no response, letting it lie where it had fallen.

Just before dark, Fox P. brought her some cold biscuit and dried meat. He was timid and anxious. "I'm sorry there ain't any coffee, Missy," he said. "It would do you good, some coffee. But we can't fire up. I'm terrible sorry."

She saw his concern, and his kindness. "It's all right. I haven't had any in so long I've forgotten what it tastes like." She looked at him. "You're Tenth Cavalry."

"Yes, ma'am," Fox P. said. "Now how'd you know a thing like that?"

He thought her half-seen face was wistful. "I know a little about the army."

"Well," he said. "Well. I am Fox P. Canby, ma'am, and if there is anything at all I can do for. . . ."

"Fox," Shafter said in a controlled, carrying voice.

Fox P. jumped, but when he got there Shafter was standing in the mouth of the cave and all he said was, "Moon's clouded over. Looks like our luck's holdin' too good."

Charley Tom made it back after dark. He was gloating, not just because he'd done better than he thought he could but because he figured Shafter couldn't get along without him. They left behind, in the cave, everything that could be spared. Shafter cleaned one pack horse of everything but a blanket, and this he spread over its back. They had unsaddled to rest the horses through the remainder of the day; now, saddling, Obre said, "Who's riding blanket?"

"She is," Shafter said.

"The hell she is," Obre said.

"You want to give her your saddle?"

"No," Obre said.

"Then quit askin' questions."

"You son of a bitch," Obre said blandly.

Fox P. straightened from tightening his mount's girth. "She's welcome to mine," he said.

Shafter said, "You think I resigned from givin' the orders here?"

"Nope," Fox P. said. "I think you are just what Mr. Obre said you are."

In spite of himself, Shafter grinned. What really struck him as funny, though, was that before he could make a move to stop it, there was Charley Tom lugging his saddle over and throwing it up on the pack horse. He didn't say a word, and Shafter didn't say a word. When they were ready, Shafter went to Anna. He couldn't see her now in the dark. He hated to say anything in front of the men, and they knew it. Obre pulled them out, Charley Tom riding blanket. Then Shafter said, "Miss Stillman, I don't know how you feel about givin' your word, or breakin' it either, but if you tell me you'll stay with me and not try to make a run for it, I'll take your word. Matter of fact, I'd appreciate it. It ain't gone to be too pleasant a trip as it is, and I'll take every scrap of co-operation cheerful."

She did not answer. He could hear her breathing. But he sensed that she was no longer angry. There was a quietness about her which bordered on resignation. He knew, too, that she could hate him without anger, coldly, deliberately, but her hatred of him did not seem important. What was important, what was always most important, was your own self-respect, your own peace of mind, the squaring of your own conscience. He said, "If I was double-jointed I'd kick myself clear back to Texas for everything I said to you."

She came close to him. "Don't apologize. It was my own fault. Both of us might have been calmer, perhaps, but it was my fault."

He breathed a little easier, but he still did not completely trust her. He said, "You get any sleep?"

She shook her head, then, realizing he could not see her, said, "No. It doesn't matter. Mr. Shafter, I would like to tell you something. It won't take long. I told Joaquin that the one thing which bothers me is that I can't tell my . . . my family that everything is all right, that I am happy. Now I will have that chance, and I suppose I should thank you. But I was wrong. This will only make it so much worse for Linus."

Shafter was moved. "I reckon we all make our own circumstances, Miss Stillman. You made yours by gettin' off that overland coach when you knew you shouldn't. Linus is makin' his by refusin' to let you . . . and me . . . alone, when he knows he should. But when a man tells me he ain't gone to quit till he knows his girl is dead. . . ."

Anna said, without emotion, without a trace of self-pity, "Oh God, I wish I were."

Shafter was horrified. All his mistrust of her drained away. He realized that through all this he had thought only of Linus, whom he loved, and of Joaquin, to whom he was drawn by chance and by his own reluctant admiration for the boy's stand. Had he, had any of them, really given a thought to the girl, or to what she might feel and want?

In the dark, quite by accident, he touched her hand, and, once he had touched it, he took it and held it. It was a slim, hard little hand, calloused over. "It might seem kind of funny my sayin' no-body'd ought to wish themselves dead, because one time I wished that for myself. Some don't grow out of the notion. I did. You got to, too. I'd ought to tell you, I reckon, you're gone to find Linus some changed. Some . . . well, fittin' his britches now, and that's all for the better. So if you and him and Joaquin are all sensible folks, there ain't anything to prevent you from workin' things out." He looked upward in the dark. "Nothin', that is, except a war gone on and no way to communicate, and the fact that prob'ly none of you is half as sensible as I hope you're gone to be."

She made a small sound he thought might be laughter. A good omen. "Mr. Shafter, there is nothing in our circumstances about which we can *be* sensible."

But, he thought, she at least would be mighty canny to deal with, because she showed him right off how her mind was working. He helped her into Charley Tom's saddle and when she was settled she said, "You have my word, by the way." Then she said, in a voice which charged Shafter's very bones, like a bolt had struck him and gone shivering down his spine, "Where do you suppose Joaquin is now, Mr. Shafter?"

"I reckon he might be staked out somewhere, tryin' to track us," Shafter said uneasily.

"I don't think so. He knows there is only one place you can take
me. He will reach Tucson before you."

"And if he does?" Shafter said.

She said quietly, "He will wait for me."

The night was torment. Having refused sleep when it was offered, she was now not allowed it when it forced itself upon her.
Time and again her body fell forward, so that there was nothing to
prevent her from collapsing except that bone-jerking return to consciousness which arrived always at the precise saving moment. She
hovered in some dark unpleasant dimension in which she never once
fully slept and which pressed thickly upon her when she fought to
stay awake. All things were cast and molded in alarming dispropor-
tion in that murky world between waking and sleeping, all sad
thought sadder, all desperation more desperate; her muddled mind,
in the grip of the false perspective, could not rest and accept the
reality, but was overactive, reaching, grasping, building, sinking.
Once, paralyzed with cold, she saw it was not Shafter beside her,
but the dark man called Obre. Without speaking he gave her his
blanket, which she wrapped about her and huddled into, moving
on like some shapeless old squaw. They walked ten minutes out of
every hour to relieve the horses; the horses were all they had to get
them through. She did not walk, but stumbled drunkenly, hanging
to the horse's coarse tangled mane. Long before dawn her bones
pulled apart, disintegrating into a painful jelly. She cried quietly,
having found the final depth of exhaustion. She ceased to care
about anything, and she knew, dimly, the danger of this.

The best Charley Tom could find was a draw, high in the hills,
but it was heavily strewn with boulders at one end. In the cold
rosy gray dawn Anna slid from the horse and dropped into a dead,
unmoving sleep from which she did not awaken until mid-afternoon.

Water was very short, so short that Charley Tom and Fox P.
had gone up into the heights to search for it. She was gritty with
dust and travel, but there was no help for it; the fine alkali was
lodged in every pore of her body and the salt of dried sweat was
crusted and hard upon her. She itched. Her eyes were so irritated
she could scarcely bare to open them. Yet to close them was only
to move the particles of dust across the aching surface of the eye-
ball. She saw the men in a new light, barely recognizable as men,

rough, dirty, bearded, burned, hollow-eyed, worn, weary to the depths of their souls.

Because water was short, she bred an immediate, insatiable thirst and the stone in her mouth was useless. She could not choke down the hard biscuit, and when Shafter finally passed her his canteen she resolved to take no more than a swallow. She was humiliated when she could not stop herself and he had to take it away from her. It killed her to watch him dole out water to the horses. Yet once the small amount she had drunk settled in her, the saliva came back into her mouth and the stone kept it coming.

Obre lay guard at one end of the wash, hatless, just under the dry crumbling lip; he had had three hours' sleep. Shafter, stretched at the other end, had had none. She moved quietly up and dropped down beside him. He didn't look at her, but he said, "You feel better?"

"Yes," she said. "I'm sorry about the water."

"That's all right," he said. Now he looked at her. Now she did not look like a child. She looked thin and old and tired; the narrow little face was mostly huge dark eyes. She wasn't what he would call pretty. There wasn't a trace of that pure, perfect classic beauty, nor even the frank, wholesome natural type of good looks; yet he thought he would look twice at her anywhere she passed. Even under the fatigue there was an intensity, a passion, a vividness which arrested him. The features were delicately set but there was a vital ardent force in the spare line and curve of bone which was singular and immediately attractive. He wondered what she had looked like six months ago, and he saw she was tough in the sense he liked a woman to be tough: resourceful, practical, and courageous up to the point where the dream behind the eyes began to dominate and they melted under its impact and you could do whatever you wanted with them until the every-day reality began to build up and assume control again. He said, "When did you quit bein' scared up there?"

She was frowning, as if she were thinking back. But she did not have to think. She said, "When I heard English spoken. It was like hearing music in the middle of nowhere."

"But you were scared."

"Yes. Terrified. Trapped in a ring of wolves. I thought they were going to torture us."

Shafter said, "I take it you don't exactly look on 'em as wolves any more then."

She looked at him quickly, but his face was turned toward the motionless, silent land below them. "I think of them as people, Mr. Shafter."

"Do you know what would of happened to you if it hadn't been for Joaquin?"

She still watched him. "Are you trying to suggest that I might be calculating enough to go to any lengths to save myself?"

He grinned then. "Maybe I am. I wish you'd tell me it ain't any of my business. Trouble is, it seems to be. I reckon I never did know what a meddlesome hoss I am." He swung his head and met her eyes soberly. "And I reckon you really do hate me, don't you?"

And she said, "Yes. In a sense I hate you more than I believed it possible to hate. You have disrupted my life, and Joaquin's, and now you will have caused Linus more unhappiness than he ever could have known if you had stayed out of this."

"Well now," he said, "I don't know. I recall one time, when I was a little shaver, I had a cat just disappeared into thin air. Wasn't till I'd walked my feet off lookin' and drained my soul off prayin' that my pa told me it had fell in a well and drowned. I hollered some, but at least I knew."

"With me it was a dog and I never knew," she said. Then she said, "You're very inventive. It's sentimental and I don't believe a word of it."

"No," he said, "it's gospel. And it ain't sentimental. It's the hard facts of life. It was my first lesson in not bein' sorry for myself, and there wasn't any reason bein' sorry for the cat; it was dead."

She said in a tight little voice, "You're a fake, Shafter."

He laughed. He felt a rising sadness in him. It was odd she looked so sad, as if she mirrored what he felt.

"Haven't you any family?" she said.

He shook his head.

"What will you do, after you take me back?"

"Push on," he said.

"Is that what you want?"

"It's what I got." He shifted, leaning his chin on his raised arm.

"First you have to see Linus through, is that it?"

"We been friendly," he said.

"You won't see Joaquin through?"

He was silent for a long time. "I don't know what I can do for Joaquin."

"Can you think of nothing?"

"He never asked."

"I see. Pride takes strange forms, doesn't it? I ask you then."

Again he shook his head. "I don't want you to. I think I pretty much understand you. That's more'n I did yesterday."

"What an offensive thing to say," she said, surprised.

"No, I didn't mean it to be. What I meant was, I understand you mean to renounce your own people, but you don't intend to accept the Mimbreños. You think that you and Joaquin can sort of live in a world of your own, in-between."

"Renounce? I can't do that. Joaquin doesn't feel that way."

"How do you feel?"

"I don't know." She closed her eyes, confused under his probing.

"We're at war with Mimbreños. You're gone to go and live with the enemy. You can just tear yourself up and go live with a people different from you as day is from night. With the people who are torturing and killing your people." He didn't want to look at her but he had to. Her face was warped, her mouth twisted.

"You are saying that this is insurmountable."

"I ain't sayin' that. I'm sayin' it seems so." Again he shifted, half turning on his side now. "You know, I first met Joaquin down at Ojo Caliente. Little over a year ago. Things were fairly quiet down there, and we were passin' through. I knew his pa well enough to lift a glass with. I talked to Joaquin then about comin' where he should be. It wasn't any good." Shafter's upper lip was compressed. "You see, it ain't as if his pa was just a saddle tramp. He wasn't. He had a university degree and a big appetite for livin'. He was pretty good all around, and the only thing he left behind him was Joaquin."

"What are you trying to say?"

"Can't you get him out of there?"

She shook her head. "How can I make him what he is not?"

"What does he figure his chances are if he stays with Victorio?"

"What are his chances if he leaves Victorio?" she said, and he saw that Joaquin's grinding, obdurate resentment was beginning to rub off on her.

"Has he been out with the war parties?" Shafter said, and knew instantly that he had dealt her, without meaning to, the hardest blow of all. Before she could answer, he pressed his advantage. "If you talked him out of that, you could talk him into anything."

She sounded shaken. "I didn't talk to him about it. Victorio wouldn't let him."

He half whistled. "Victorio? He's gettin' to be the most unpredictable cuss I ever came across."

She was hurt, wide open, and she flared at him. "Have you no sensitivity at all? Do you think it's only that I care about Joaquin's danger? Do you think I don't care that he may go out and kill Linus or Uncle Walter or trooper Canby? Or you?" Both her hands were clenched, flat on the ground before her. "Do you think I am merely a thoughtless, headstrong woman who's going to have her way in the face of everything?"

He didn't answer. Then he said, "You got to realize that Linus and the colonel ain't gone to listen to any of this. That you got no more chance of gettin' out of that army post than you had of gettin' out of the Stronghold."

She looked him right in the eye, direct, determined. "If you believe there are people who can't find their own way, who can't live above and beyond the circumstances that surround them, you're wrong. And if you believe that anything short of chaining me to a wall is going to keep me from going with Joaquin, you are wrong again." She reached over and put her hand on the stock of the Henry. "Why don't you get some sleep and let me watch for a while?"

He passed her the rifle. He said, "Annie, yes, I think you are gone to have your way in spite of everything." He went right off to sleep.

Shafter had it tentatively figured what procedure he would follow when (and if, his mind kept warning) they made the post. He had a natural abhorrence of the scene, the drama, the calculated effect, particularly if he was personally involved, so he had no intention of riding right in and delivering Anna. That wouldn't be fair to anybody.

To begin with, the girl's appearance, while it meant nothing to him, was bound to cause distaste and speculation. Only the practiced eye could have sighted he wasn't coming in with some captive squaw. The first person he wanted to see riding out of the cantonment was Katie Callahan, with soap, water, and some clean clothes and foofaraw of the sort a lady would wear. Second, he wanted Linus. Nobody else. This, of course, was providing Linus was home. He had a feeling in his bones that this was the case. He didn't know the date, wasn't even certain of the month, but from where he stood the summer was mighty dead, and, if he hadn't got his head shot off, Linus would be back.

Since he was still in command of this expedition, he did not concern himself with discussing it with Anna, although he did get around to mentioning it to Obre.

Charley Tom and Fox P. had got back with water and everybody'd had their fill. Shafter felt, if not another man, restored with some sleep and plenty to wet his gullet. He and Obre talked up at the end of the dry wash, and Shafter finished it all up with a punctuation of jut-jawed decision that wasn't entirely in character and which gave Obre a moment's pause.

"Then you pick up Willson, see, and find out what he wants to do. I'm gone straight in to town and hitch up my gear. Let's get the hell out of here."

"Ain't you forgot something?" Obre said.

"If I have, you tell me."

"Well, by Jesus," Obre said, "if I was gone to bake a pie I'd surer'n hell put the crust on before I poked her in the oven." He sensed there wasn't any easiness in Shafter right now and his own gall was up. They'd always got along, and Obre not only didn't feel like a fight now, he didn't feel like talking at all. He also was fond enough of women in general to feel that if the namby-pamby eastern daisy who had turned out to be just the opposite of what he imagined was giving Shafter trouble there was a reason for it. He said, in a voice which made it plain that was the end of it, "I aim to trail with you, Shafter, but I ain't gone nowhere until I tell Linus *adiós* and shake the Old Man's hand."

Shafter got up and went to check the horses. He invented several excuses to himself for Obre's attitude, but there wasn't any excuse to be made for unadorned decency; it stood by itself.

It was along about midnight when they came down out of the hills outside Tucson, Shafter and Fox P. and Charley Tom fanning out ahead, Obre holding Anna back until they were sure it was all clear. Shafter hated that long bare stretch in to the post, but it had been fine to look down from the hills and see the light pinpointed far out, in the Old Pueblo: dabs and sparks of steady gold glitter-

ing in the thick blue darkness, the warm, pulling, exciting light
making you forget for a minute the ugly dusty hole of a town.
And way off to the left, on the flat desert floor, the post was lit up
like a Christmas tree.

When they pulled in closer, Shafter realized some sort of hoedown
was in progress. A real *baile*, with that guitar-happy Mex music
pouring out and plenty of lanterns and candles and lamps. He knew
that any excuse would provide the spur for what passed as a good
time most anywhere in the world: music and dancing and some
extra-fancy food and drink. Out here it was the only way there was
to get away from the heat and filth and sweat and loneliness and
boredom for a few hours.

Except for the music and laughter, it was all pretty quiet, though,
not like the normal three-times-a-year stamp at the ranches, when
the herders managed to get together and yell their heads off and
knock themselves cold with *vino*. He was thinking you could certainly tell this was a U.S. army post, all right, with everything
slightly, annoyingly slightly, on the decorous side, when he ran right
into Sergeant Stern checking his guard mount in the dark. "Who
goes there?" Stern said.

"It's me, Shafter," Shafter said.

"What's the pashword?" Stern said thickly.

"Aw, for Chrissake," Shafter said. "It's me 'n Canby. Come on,
Stern, let me off this horse."

Stern came closer. He was considerably thinner than Shafter remembered, like he'd had a long, sweaty summer. "Hello, Shafter,"
he said. "When'd you get back?"

"Right now," Shafter said. "Listen, is the lieutenant here?"

"He's inside," Stern said. "You want me to go tell 'em you're
here?"

"No," Shafter said. "Don't tell anybody. You know where Mrs.
Callahan is?"

"You been gone too long, Shafter," Stern said. "Where do you
think she'd be with this birthday party for Cap'n Tremaine goin'
on?"

Shafter dismounted. Sure. Where would Katie be? One of the
two women on the post. Her feet would be worn to the ankles by
morning, just from dancing. He said, "Will you go in and get the
lieutenant for me without disturbin' anybody else?"

But Stern came closer. He had the temperament of a lonesome old woman. "You didn't find her, did you?"

"You gone to do me that favor or not?" Shafter said.

Stern humped off. They waited, with the music coming out to them, and the light, and the buzz of voices, low and constant as bee hum. Fox P. said, "I'm real thirsty tonight," and made a sort of gulping sound.

"Go on down and get cleaned up," Shafter said. "Maybe somebody'll give you a glass of water."

Fox P. laughed mirthlessly and started off toward quarters. Shafter called after him. "Fox."

Fox P. turned, but they couldn't see one another.

"I'll be seein' you," Shafter said, but he didn't think he would.

"Don't doubt it for a minute," Fox P. said. "I don't know what I has to do to get shook of you, Shafter."

The music kept right on, and the big rectangle of yellow light spilled out on the ground, and he saw Linus in the doorway of commandant; didn't really see him, but knew by height and heft that it was Linus, with Stern in tow. Linus came off the single step quickly, but then he stopped and said something to Stern. Shafter couldn't hear what it was, but Stern went off grumpily in the other direction. Shafter started to hold out his hand, and before he finished the move Linus had grabbed him hard by the shoulders and for a time, in the dim plane of light, Shafter thought he was looking at the Old Man.

"Think I ran out on you?" Shafter said.

"No," Linus said. Shafter had the feeling he was controlling his voice by clenching his teeth. "No. I'm glad to see you, Shafter."

"Well, how are you, boy?" Shafter said. "How's everything at Santa Rita?"

"Nobody there but some old women," Linus said. "How's everything wherever the hell you were?"

"Better'n I reckoned," Shafter said.

Linus said, "Shafter," and stopped. He took his hands away, but he kept watching Shafter's face, trying to read it. "Some days I hoped and some days I couldn't make myself hope. Some days I thought about you as the man who never makes a move without asking questions, and some days I thought of you as the man who never asks a question, who just makes the move. I killed three Apaches this summer, Shafter."

"Well," Shafter said, "that's good for you but kind of hard on them, ain't it?"

Then Linus burst out at him, all his control swept away. "You found her, didn't you? I knew it the day you rode out of here."

"She's up in the hills with Obre," Shafter said. "I figured it would be hard gone to just drag her in here for all these damn Yankees to stare at. Here, why'nt you borrow Charley's horse?"

"No saddle," Charley Tom said, rather loftily.

"Welcome home, Charley," Linus said. "You all right?"

"Very good," Charley Tom said. "Very tired, very firsty, no saddle."

Linus went off at a run for the stable, and Charley Tom followed him. Shafter was standing with his hand on the dun's nose when a couple of troopers came out and wandered off into the darkness, not seeing him, and then the girl's figure cut the light and Katie emerged, laughing, and stood on the narrow stoop a moment and then started for the corner of the building with her face turned up, as if she needed the air. Covered right up to the ears practically, too, Shafter saw, in some sort of modest checked stuff, with that wonderful red hair all over her head as usual. He had a sudden crazy urge to skin up behind her, and he couldn't stop it. His eyes felt as if they were burning and bloodshot, and he was actually moving when Rafe Callahan jumped off the step, mustache and all, and went roaring off, calling, "Katie, Katie," into the night.

Shafter said aloud to himself, "You ain't collected your pay yet, you bum," and got back on the dun and pretty soon Linus came up the line, saying hello to people and smiling just like nothing was happening and then they were moving off into the cool fuzzy-starred desert and the light and sound and warmth faded out behind them and were gone.

Shafter let Linus set the pace. Linus never said a word until they hit the first upswing of the foothills; then he said, "How is she, Shafter?"

Shafter said, "I didn't think to ask her." He meant it to be light and easy, but it didn't come out that way; it came out dead serious, so he said, "Linus, I might as well tell you now, you got trouble."

"My middle name," Linus said. "Linus T. Degnan. *T* for trouble. It's true about her and that half breed then?"

"I reckon so," Shafter said.

"It always was true?"

"I reckon so," Shafter said again.

"Where is he?"

"I ain't got any notion," Shafter said. But he bit his lower lip; he had a feeling Anna's confidence in Joaquin's reaction was pretty much justified; after all, by now she would know him better than anybody, even Victorio. He was gripped by a desire to turn his head, to look around him, to assure himself that he was still secure and upright in his saddle. His eyes felt now as if they were bleeding.

Half an hour later he pulled up and let out a low sloppy whistle that might have been a bird, but which sounded more like a man making a sound like a bird. Obre whistled back, faultlessly. When they reached the cut between the hills, Linus swung ahead, not seeing Obre until he had rounded the flank of the hill, and then almost riding him down. The stink of unwashed flesh and worn filthy horsehide hit him like a blow in the face, and he hated the night because it cut off his sight like a comfort bundled over his head. He passed Obre and said, "Anna?" questioningly, almost sternly.

Her voice was the same as he remembered. She said, "Here, Linus," and the horses bumped awkwardly against one another and pulled away again, and he reached for her hackamore to hold the horse in. He sensed that Obre was gone, leaving them, but he could think of nothing to say and the stink was still in his nostrils and he felt a great and terrible exhaustion, a coming to naught, a finality more final than death itself.

He said, "Where is your hand, Anna?"

Silently she held out her hand. He found it, fumbling, and locked it in his own. Her fingers were stiff and tensed; he could feel the blood beating hotly through them. He said, "Let's go home now."

Seventeen

Nuadin's remorse was loud and honest. Pionsenay would have beaten her, but the women were a wall of resistance even he did not attempt to breach. Tayanclee said stubbornly, "It was not Nuadin's doing. She did all she could. The girl was too long in beginning and she does not know the manner of running. You are fortunate your wife is alive and untouched. Men are fools, like the coyote."

And Nuadin sat with her face in her hands and rocked to and fro and moaned.

Joaquin questioned her closely but she knew very little, having been faced with her own course of escape. It was an old squaw who had dropped out of the race early who described the abductors to him.

Cochise came up to the wickiup with his long, faintly dragging stride. He had had an ill omen, a very bad dream; so bad, in fact, that not one detail of it stood out clearly in his mind; it was all a hazy swirling of color filled with the menacing, indistinct forms of *ghons* and animals, and he had waked from it perspiring and feeling rather ill. He was almost brusk with Joaquin, and he used the informal speech.

"It was the man Shafter?" he said.

Joaquin nodded once in assent. His face was so hard Cochise thought of the rock battlements around him, and there was no blue left in the eyes; they were black with anguish.

Cochise said, "How many men do you want?"

"None," Joaquin said.

"You forget that you are only one man," Cochise said.

"You forget that half of me is made to walk with the white man," Joaquin snarled.

Cochise's smile was thin. "Let me see you split yourself, then, son of my brother." But he knew Joaquin's mettle now, for his second wife had been held prisoner the day the boy nantan Bascom had betrayed him. He said, more gently, "Do you think that one half of you will take you anywhere?"

"I know it will not," Joaquin said. "But it will take me where I want to go this one time."

"You are not in a good position to avenge this," Cochise said.

"What is avenging?" Joaquin said. "You speak always of avenging. Does it raise the dead? Does it return the stolen?"

Cochise felt a little chill around his heart. "It serves nothing to run and die for what is gone."

"I am not ready to die," Joaquin said harshly. He looked down at Cochise, seated near the doorway. Cochise saw him stiffen suddenly, as if a pain had gripped him unaware. Well, what man did not have pain, of the body and of the soul? What man came here knowing at the moment of his coming that all pains pass, that the fire and ice and water and air and stone and seed of which man is forged have shaped him to take the crushing blow and stagger and fall and rise again. And forget.

But the pain of remembrance was too fresh in Joaquin's mind. Cochise saw him take his lower lip in his teeth.

"What is it, Joaquin?"

"It is my tongue," Joaquin said bitterly. "It will not lie still. It says things foolishly." And what had it said to her: if the wife of one of ours was taken, that man would bare his breast and mourn her. Women remembered; oh God, what long memories women had, not like a memory at all, but more some point of referral. He went down on one knee, before Cochise.

"You have given me a home here."

"You did not have to ask," Cochise said.

"I ask something now. Give me your wisdom."

There was a small spark of light in Cochise's eye. "For this, Nockahoto serves."

"No," Joaquin said. "Not the wisdom of the dream or the touch between man and *ghon*. There is another wisdom. In the head. In the heart. Born in the blood. Listen. Mangas Chie and I will go, with all that is ours and all that is my girl's. I am going to the town and I am going to take my girl back. For this I do not need your men. I need only my father's speech in my mouth. I need only to say with my father's speech what is truth in any man's tongue. I do not need to avenge, I do not want to kill. Tell me this is right."

Cochise's eyes were stone now, dull stone, but his brows rose. "It is nothing to tell a man what he wishes to hear."

Joaquin was silent. Then he sat back slowly. "But a man must act with honor."

Cochise shrugged. "What other way is there, for you, Joaquin? And how many ways for the white eyes? You made your choice too long ago. My older son, Nachise, chose and cannot return to me. You chose and cannot return to the blood of your father."

Joaquin said, "Shafter will listen to me."

Cochise said, "If all white eyes were Shafter, we would hold our land and be at peace forever." Then he said, "Where is your anger for this man Shafter?"

Joaquin shook his head. "I have no anger now for any man. Only for whatever has let this happen."

"Have no anger for *Ysen*," Cochise said.

"God?" Joaquin said. "God is dead."

"Your God may be," Cochise said imperturbably. "*Ysen* lives." He crossed his legs. "There is a white man who felt as you feel now, while you slept with his woman."

"I know this. Why else do you think I have no anger?"

Cochise said, "It will give me pain, when I must tell Victorio you are dead."

Joaquin stood up. "At least I will lie with my father."

"No Mimbreño will lie in that town," Cochise said steadily. "Your body will not be dead. You will rot in the iron *brazalete*. That is the death a man does not rise from. So, Joaquin, you cannot go and be a white man. You can only go and pretend to be a white man."

Mangas Chie stooped in the doorway. Joaquin said, "Chie, do you come with me now to the town, or do you go to Ojo Caliente?"

Chie looked at Cochise, whose first wife was his half sister, and at Joaquin, who was favored by Victorio. He said, "I go with you."

They came down with the pack mules, Anna's paint mare, the Appaloosa. The mules were loaded, but the Appaloosa carried Joaquin's fire drill, lance, shield, carbine, ammunition.

Cochise embraced Chie. "Be it well with you, son of my brother," he said formally. He turned to Joaquin.

Joaquin was holding out the still-wet spotted deerhide. "This is Tahzay's," he said, "from my girl." He felt his face begin to crack at the edges. He was aware of the thinness of Cochise's arms about him, and he turned away to Cochise's first wife, Mangas Chie's half sister.

"Burn my wickiup," he said. He swung up on the Appaloosa. He knew he would never see Cochise alive again.

They rode down, out of the Stronghold.

Walter Degnan was as close to having a fit of nerves as he had ever come in his life, and the only solution seemed to be to sit with his head in his hands. Fate, singular, had become fates, plural, and they were all in a vast conspiracy against him.

A reconnaissance detail coming in from Ord's California Division had had a fast and furious battle with a superior force of Apaches, led personally, they said, by Tahzay, and had limped in badly routed. . . . They had nine wounded in hospital and Bonehead Gribbons, the post surgeon, was on the jump. Tlodasay, whom everybody called Crooked, had come in from a scout with the hacked-up body of the deserter Sawyer, who not only had not made it to California, as Bleeker suggested, but who had not managed to put twenty miles between himself and the post.

And then there was Fox P. Canby, coming in as if he had never been away.

Formalities had been dispensed with, up to a point: the post was only three-quarters garrisoned, as Sergeant Hubbel of the Tenth was out with a pursuit detail, but every one of Tremaine's troopers had come in to drink to the captain's anniversary and watch Mrs. Callahan and Mrs. Layden swing around with the officers, and then with the troopers, and to admire the two dark-eyed *señorita* sisters who had ridden in from Tucson trailed by a pigeon-breasted old duenna who looked as if she would like to dance, too, if somebody would ask her. Fox P. didn't know the barriers were down, though, and he went right up to Captain Tremaine and saluted and said he was glad to be back and he wouldn't say no to joining in drinking to whatever it was everybody was drinking to.

Degnan spotted Fox P. right off. He had been sitting with the duenna, a grandaunt of Ochea, the Tucson *comerciante,* bending a polite ear to her running stream of inanities, and he looked up and there was Fox P. Canby. He shot up out of his chair, remembered, bent to the old lady, said, "Pardon" too loudly, and went up to Fox P., who already had a glass in his hand and had to shift it to his left in order to salute. Degnan didn't acknowledge the salute;

he looked strained and grayish, like a sick man would look, and he said, "Is Shafter with you?"

"No, sir, Colonel," Fox P. said. "Leastways he was with me, but he ain't with me now."

"I can see he is not with you now," Degnan said. "Where is he?"

"He went on an errant, Colonel. He's comin' back. Like always."

Degnan said to Tremaine, "Excuse me, Arthur," and went out.

He went across the cantonment to commandant. At the doorway he called Linus' name twice, but there wasn't a soul in the office. He went in and sat down at his desk and heard the music floating into the night and waited. He developed a tic in his left eyelid.

It was over an hour later he heard somebody coming and a shape went past the window, so he got up and leaned out and looked. It was Mrs. Callahan, running rather awkwardly in narrow-heeled shoes, with a shawl clutched around her shoulders. She disappeared in the direction of quarters. Just going home, he supposed, but then he wondered what for. It was still early, and she was young and had been enjoying herself. Unless Gribbons needed her. No, she hadn't been headed toward hospital. Then the suspicion clouded up in him. He crossed the compound, into a quieter sphere of the night; the married men's quarters were separate from barracks, next to officers' quarters. When he reached the dobe hallway, a lamp was burning and Shafter came toward him, throwing shadow big as a mountain on the wall, and said, "Howdy, Walter."

Degnan's smile was brief, tight with his suspicion. He held out his hand. "Glad to see you back, John. Where is she?"

Shafter indicated the closed door of Callahan's quarters. "With Katie. And Linus. She's pretty beat out, Walter."

"I expect so," Degnan said. But he moved for the door. Before he could knock, it opened and Katie looked out. "John Shafter, will you please see about some hot water before I . . . oh, excuse me, Colonel Degnan." She held the door open for him. "Come in, won't you?"

He went in and stopped and held out his arms. "Anna?" he said. "Anna. My dear child."

She came into his arms obediently, wearily. He was stunned, sickened with the smell of Indian, so distinct and strong that he had to force himself not to draw away. He pulled her head upright by both braids and looked into her face. It was her face, he knew that, but he saw an aging which was almost unnatural and a hardness about the eyes which disturbed him.

"Hello, Uncle Walter," she said.

Unexpectedly he was fighting to dam a wall of tears. "I thought this day would never come. Anna, Anna, how good it is to have you back."

She saw the tears and could scarcely hold back her own. "You haven't changed a hair, Uncle Walter, you look the same." Now she did not want to leave his arms; he was clean-shaven and smooth and smelled agreeably of bay rum.

But Katie said, "Look here, will you men please get out of here and let Miss Stillman have a bath and some sleep. Excuse me, Colonel, but I got to insist. You got the rest of your lives to talk."

"Certainly," Degnan said, only slightly surprised. Out of the corner of his eye he noticed Linus was leaning against the wall and that his face looked somehow preresolving and a little cynical and that some of the wall had crumbled and deposited bits of itself on the shoulder of his uniform. "Linus," he said, "Mrs. Callahan's absolutely right."

But Anna was clinging to him.

"You sleep, Anna," he said. "Don't think about anything. Just sleep. You're safe. You're home."

Somehow he disengaged himself. Anna was looking up at him, searching for something more than solicitude, more than love. When Linus came up she did not turn her head, and he bent and kissed her on the forehead.

"Good night, Anna."

"Good night, Linus. Good night, Uncle Walter."

But the door was half closed when she cried out in a low, urgent voice. "Linus."

He came back. "Yes," he said quietly, statement, not question.

And she said, "Nothing. Nothing. Good night."

Anna stood there for a long time, after the door had closed behind him, and was still standing there when an orderly came in with two steaming buckets of water, looked curiously at her, set the buckets down, and went away.

Katie touched her on the arm. "Come on now, let's get out of those clothes. I'm too tall for you, but you can wear one of my nightdresses and Bess Layden's about your size. Well, come on."

Her eyes went appraisingly, intuitively over Anna and noted that she looked neither starved nor mistreated . . . that in point of fact she looked rather comfortably blooming, maybe even smugly so, and she read Anna's resignation as fatigue.

The hot water was not terrible and not wonderful, as Anna had imagined it might be; it was simply the weapon which cracked her last defense. Katie said, "We'll just burn these things. . . ." and Anna stood on the border of hysteria.

"No! Mrs. Callahan, please. Those things are mine and I want them and I do not want. . . ."

Katie shot her a look. "All right. And call me Kate."

"I haven't got lice, if that's what you mean," Anna said rather sullenly. "We do take baths, you know."

We, Katie thought. Dear Lord in heaven. She wanted to put the girl at ease; after all, the lieutenant's bride and everything. . . . She said, "Just take your time. You know, I'm getting real good at this, Miss Stillman. There I was takin' care of the little Mexican girl last spring, the same way."

"Ysabel," Anna said, half to herself. "Ysabel Vasquez."

"That was her, poor little thing." Katie leaned out the window and shook the soft buckskin into the night. What in the world anybody would want to keep this stuff for. . . . "She was the lucky one, wasn't she?"

Anna said slowly, "Yes, I guess she was."

"Pretty as a picture," Katie said. "And all scarred up like that. Those Apaches must be about as bad as anybody can get." She folded Anna's clothes. Her voice was very competent and implied that she was perfectly capable of taking care of any Apache ever born. "Imagine just deliberately doing that to anybody." She looked at Anna. "I bet it could be worse, though." She tossed the buckskin on the bed and came over and began to unbraid Anna's hair. "You have got the prettiest hair. Do you want some curling rags while you sleep?"

"No, thank you," Anna said. "Here, what are you doing with my moccasins?"

"My goodness," Katie said, "I'm just going to beat the dust out of them."

Anna felt her hair as a great weight. The soft flannel of Katie's nightdress was rich as fur against her flesh. Standing, she put her hand out and touched lingeringly Katie's tortoise-shell hairbrush. "This is beautiful," she said.

"You can have it if you like," Katie said impulsively.

"Oh," Anna said, "No, I couldn't do that, really."

"Go on," Katie said. "I'd like for you to. I've got another."

Anna shook her head. "I couldn't. I don't need it. I've a comb."

"Not a tortoise-shell comb," Katie said gently. "And a comb's not a brush. Now please come to bed and sleep as long as you can."

"I'm putting you out of your bed," Anna said suddenly. She sat down in the little wooden chair.

"No, you're not. Rafe can sleep to barracks and I'm going to sit with you so's you don't wake up and want for anything." She squatted down and looked up at Anna. "Look, Miss Stillman, on the outside, just you and me, we got to keep everything sensible as we can. I know you got things to think about, but you should try and not think about 'em right now. A good sleep is going to make the whole world look different. You just got to remember everybody here's been worried to death about you, and now we just want to take care of you and make you forget everything that happened. The only thing you got to think about is that you got a grand young man out there waiting to make you happy. I don't hardly see how a girl would need much else. Now, is there anything you want before I tuck you in?"

The tears were spilling down Anna's face. She drew a wild gasping breath and took Katie by the shoulders so fiercely the girl winced. "I want John Shafter. Now. Please. Get him for me."

"But he'll be here tomorrow. He ain't going any place," Katie said. Then she added, "I hope."

"Now," Anna said. "Now."

Her face scared Katie. Katie got up and bolted for the door and remembered she would have to get back in a hurry so her charge wouldn't be receiving in her nightdress. But Shafter was right outside quarters and, by the time she told him, Anna was out in the hall. The whites of her eyes were clear and bluish in the falling-off light of the lamp and they never left his face. "You won't go away, will you?" she said, on a rising note of apprehension.

He wished Katie would leave, but she seemed to be nailed to the floor, behind him. "I won't go away," he said. "Provided you start bein' a good soldier and doin' what you're told."

"Will you find him?" she said. "I can't sleep unless you tell me you'll find him."

He said, "I'll do my best."

"I believe you," she said. "Just remember that. I believe you."

"Annie," he said, "if it was the good Lord Himself, I give you my word I'd try."

She went into the room and closed the door behind her.

"Well," Katie said. "Very funny she wanted you instead of the lieutenant. Funny indeed. Now what are you up to?"

"Nothin' more'n usual," he said. "I'm just a good-natured help-meet to everybody on this lousy goddamn post. And quit naggin' me, sweetie, or I won't be sorry any more I ain't married to you."

She ran her fingers through the unruly red hair. "There's other things in marriage besides nagging," she said hotly.

"There is?" he said.

"Yes, there is. Oh, you're so smart, ain't you?"

"You're evil-tempered, too," Shafter said and leaned forward and kissed her.

She moaned at him. "Why did you do that?"

"Only way I know to show you how lucky you are just the way things stand," he said.

She backed away from him. "Liar," she said. "You lie. All you do is lie, lie, lie."

She would have slammed the door but Anna was asleep.

When Shafter started up to commandant, he spotted Obre riding the hard earth track along barracks row. "You didn't go into town?" he said.

"The hell I didn't," Obre said. "I figured anybody wanted to know I was back, that was the best way to tell 'em. Willson says he's ready anytime you are."

"Well," Shafter said, "I ain't ready."

"Oh hell," Obre said. "You ain't?"

"There's more cussed unfinished business around here."

"Always has been," Obre said. "Always will be. I wish to the Jesus you would make up your mind."

"What time is it?" Shafter said.

"I dunno. Nearly day after tomorrow."

Shafter ran his hand over his face wearily. "I like to drop in my tracks, Ob."

"Sure," Obre said. "Where's Linus?"

"I don't know," Shafter said. "I don't care. Tomorrow'll roll around I reckon."

"She always has," Obre said.

"We're sleepin' in barracks tonight," Shafter said.

"Sure," Obre said again. "I ain't stupid."

"What's that mean?"

Obre said, "I just as soon sleep in barracks the rest of my days. On account of soon as Elias knows I'm back I'm liable to be sleepin' dead the rest of my days."

"Maybe you'd ought to pull out," Shafter said, worried. "I'll pick you up in Mexico, couple of weeks."

"Elias, he's back and forth from Mexico all the time," Obre said. He shrugged, his shoulders lifting against the faint night light. "He can push, and I can't push no further. No payroll in it, I reckon, but I'd as soon gun that bastard as any other."

Shafter said, "If he shows up with that warrant again, I'll hire you, Ob."

But he only slept a little over an hour. The section of barracks in which he stretched out was noisy with snoring. He hadn't shaved and he was sleeping in his clothes, so when he woke up he got up. Obre was flat on his back on the floor, on a hay mattress; he looked dead to the world. Shafter stepped over him and went out and felt the fresh cold all around him and saw the bright hard stars moving toward the coming day.

He went and got the dun. He told one of the stable guard that if he was Tahzay he would have led a force against the post while they were all partying awhile back, and the guard spat and told him to tell it to the Old Man.

He rode slowly, aware as always of the ring of hills holding up the sky, the extended arms of the saguaro poised for embrace but holding nothing. In the silence he felt the deep friendliness of the land other men thought savage and unforgiving; it burned brightly in him, like a fire in his belly, and he rejoiced in the small sound of his own breathing and the muscular reality of the dun stepping high and a hair mettlesome under him. He had known fear many times in his life, but he did not fear this country, in the dark, or even the myriad forms of death which he knew it cradled and nurtured. He longed to watch the first pearly morning light touch the mountains while he still rode the night. He longed to ride on and on, and perhaps this time he would know what it was drew him out and up. And if he knew, if he found what lay beneath the floating color, spoke in the gilt-showering palo verde, the trembling silver of the aspens, the wind-patterned desert, the wild red stone, the thousand folded hills, the forever sky, the grasslands tapestried with cloud shadow, the immensity of it all, what would he know? Better to search, better to keep it as it was.

Tucson was black under its hills, but he thought men would be awake within those walls, lying drunk or lying thinking, planning tomorrow, nursing grievances, hating, loving. He did not enter the town but rode down the wall to where he remembered the particular rotten break and admitted to himself why he had been unable to sleep. Several feet from the break he stopped and rolled a cigarette and lit it, letting the match flare on his face so long it finally burned down to his fingers. He barely felt the burn for the icy sweat which came out on him, doing such a damn fool thing. It was the only thing he could think to do, even if Joaquin had murder in his heart, and it was the only place he knew Joaquin might be.

Joaquin said, "Shafter."

Shafter felt his shoulders slump, independent of him. He dismounted and went to the wall and Joaquin slipped through and Shafter was glad they could not see each other.

"How did you know?" Joaquin said.

Shafter said, "She knew. She never doubted."

He heard the boy draw a long, broken-sounding breath. "How is she?"

"Mighty unhappy," Shafter said. "What do you reckon to do, Joaquin?"

His voice was mocking. "I came to visit my father's grave. You said you would go with me."

Shafter sighed. "Here," he said, "have a smoke." He waited. When the match exploded, he saw Joaquin looked shaken. "I reckon you want my gizzard," he said.

"Let me tell you a thing, Shafter," Joaquin said. His voice sounded thick, but it was only the smoke in his mouth. "I want no blood. If you want to cause other men grief for money, that is your concern."

"I'm agreeable," Shafter said. "If you want to do it for the hell of it, that's yours."

"For the hell of it?" Joaquin said. He stood close to Shafter. "You talked to me at Ojo Caliente last year and I would not listen to you. What do I have to do to be a white man?"

"What?" Shafter said.

"I need clothes," Joaquin said. "I need to cut off my hair. I need money. I need to remember my name is Mitchell."

"My God," Shafter said, "whoa a minute. Just whoa, now." But he was thinking fast. "You need an awful lot, boy. Where do you think you're gone to get all this?"

Joaquin said, "You are going to lend it to me."

"Lend," Shafter said. "I take it this ain't a permanent arrangement you're talkin' about."

"Enough to get me into the army post," Joaquin said.

Shafter said, "Well now, let's you and me sit down here awhile and talk this over." He felt surprised enough he wanted to sit down, and he did, but Joaquin remained standing. "So you want to go out to the post," he said.

"I have had time to think this out, Shafter," Joaquin said patiently. "I think in fairness to Ana it is the only way to do it."

"Wait now," Shafter said. "I ain't sure I follow you. You don't mean you think you can walk in there and sort of offer the lieutenant a couple of horses for her or anything?"

Joaquin said, "Pay for my own wife?" He leaned forward. "You think now, Shafter. You think. And you tell me that this can be done. Because if it is not done this way, I will tell you the way it can be done."

"Yes," Shafter said.

"It could have been done last night. Tahzay and I could have done it last night while the *baile* was going on. You see how many hours ahead of you I reached Tucson. You see I did not do what I could have done."

"What else?" Shafter said.

"Or else there are going to be some dead men on that post. Your friend the lieutenant and whoever else stands in my way."

After a minute Shafter said, "You sure do need to remember your name. You sure do need to learn clothes and money ain't gone to change you inside." He got up and hunkered against the wall and scratched his back, where it itched, on the rough dobe. "You don't leave me much choice. How much time will you give me?"

"Time for what?" Joaquin said.

"Well, I didn't mean for me, really. I mean for the lieutenant."

"What does he need time for?"

"He ain't hardly had time to say howdy to your wife."

"For this I should make him a gift of time?" Joaquin said.

"What makes you think I ain't just gone to roll right back to the post and tell 'em what's up?"

Joaquin said, "You know we have always trusted you."

God deliver me of brave men, of foolhardy men, of men who love, Shafter thought. He said, "All right, you spread your hand. Anybody can see you got all the aces. The whole deck's stacked against Linus. You know it and I know it. So I'll tell you your Anna says she's gone with you no matter what. Give her the time then. Give her the time to try and make Linus understand. Stay out of sight and don't make any trouble." He stood erect and reached out and took Joaquin by the front of his shirt and held him. "And for that girl's sake, don't you even try bein' Joe Mitchell for the rest of your life, because your guts ain't in the right place to make it go."

Joaquin said, "Be careful, Shafter. One hour over the week I am giving you and you'll find out where my guts are. You might get to look at your own."

But he knew, and Shafter knew, that there was no animosity in either of them. Joaquin said then, "The chameleon changes with the rock and changes with the sand. The Mimbreño does not. You are right. Cochise was right." He held out his hand and Shafter took it. "Will you tell Ana I am waiting for her?"

"No, I don't reckon so," Shafter said.

"What is your reason for this?"

"She doesn't doubt you. Maybe in a week's time she'll have decided she wants to stay where she is."

Joaquin was silent. Then he laughed. "Maybe in a week's time the sun will fall out of the sky."

Shafter mounted up. "How do I find you if I want you?"

"Here," Joaquin said. "But early. Before dawn."

"I ain't promising anything," Shafter said.

"I don't want your promises," Joaquin said. His voice came out quiet, and warm. "I'm grateful to you, Shafter."

"Aw, that's all right," Shafter said with fine light irony. "I'll get my reward when I get to heaven."

Now he rode through the wall and down the deserted street, figuring to rouse Willson and have himself a couple of drinks and, at last, sleep.

Eighteen

The narrow trace crossed the desert plain and curved under the old cottonwoods, the only sign that man had ever been here. When the trees fell away the naked land, studded with greasewood, began again, and the eroded white walls and towers of the mission rose to the sky.

Facing south, old San Francisco Xavier del Bac, Saint Francis of the place of the water, stood raw and beaten by the southern rains and winds. The God of the Jesuits was less real than the Apache and had been driven away by the Apache, and the Papagos who had worshiped here for centuries were dispersed. Behind the sandstone façade the saints stood headless and handless because Apaches had no fear of mutilating the *santos* of the white eyes, the dark nave rang with echo, no foot disturbed the dust. The desolation was enormous, honeyed with the silence and jeweled with sun.

The shade of the walls was thick and soft. The horses stood within it drowsily. Linus jammed the cork back into the neck of the wine bottle with the flat of his palm and sat back and pulled off his right boot.

"What's the matter?" Anna said. She was sitting on a spread blanket, the hot, dragging skirt gathered around her knees.

"A stone or something," he said. He dumped it out and worked to pull the boot on again.

"Where did the Papagos live?" Anna said.

"All around here. They were farmers."

"How long has the mission been closed?"

"Five or six years. Since Cochise went wild. Everything closed down. San Xavier. Tubac. Tucson, almost."

She said, "They'll open it again someday. It almost seems too bad."

"Too bad?" he said.

"It's lovely the way it is. Do you know if you close your eyes you can smell incense."

"I don't smell anything," he said. "Do you want any more wine?"

"No, thank you, Linus."

"That's pretty good wine. Ochea brings it in from . . . oh hell, I can't remember the name of the place."

"Yes, I feel quite civilized."

He looked at her. "I wish you wouldn't say things like that, Anna. It sounds so damned. . . ." He stopped, trying to remember what tolerance was.

She did not seem offended; he had the uneasy feeling that if she had baited him purposely she had, with equal purpose, ignored his reaction. They had spoken, desultorily, always in the presence of others. Now, alone, he knew that perhaps they had nothing to say to one another after all. The surging finality which had swept over him on the night of her return was still sweeping, and receding and returning. He thought that he had searched himself honestly, that there was not a doubt in his mind as to what he wanted or did not want, that he had not changed, even in the face of the fact that she had. He was learning the danger of image bearing; yet what other path was there, who had borne the image with him all his years? He looked over at her. He did not remember her as being so small and light-boned, in spite of which she seemed to him to wear some aura of fullness, almost solidity. Her skin was smooth and, to him, unbecomingly dark, but there was a tautness around the mouth and shadow lay under her eyes like bruises. Things he recalled were gone and things he could not recall had replaced them. This was apparent to his father also: his father fumbled and bumbled and avoided discussion, but Linus knew he was opposed now to any alliance between them. He would not say it, he would not press it, but it was there. And for himself? Out of the search, stubbornly, he maintained that his own heart had not once touched upon rejection, that he was bigger and stronger and better than any aspect of this situation, that there was nothing he could not conquer.

Her head was buried in her arms. She raised it and picked at the stuff of her skirt and then hiked the hem down over her feet, knowing he hated the sight of the moccasins. "We were foolish to come out here alone," she said.

He said, but gently, "You've nothing to fear, have you, Anna?"

She rose and went to him and sat down beside him and put her hand on his updrawn knee. "Linus, I can't decide whether it's lovely or most inconvenient to have so many people fussing over me. We haven't been able to talk and we have to talk."

He said lamely, "I went over yesterday to see you, but Katie said you were with my father."

She was sad. "Your poor father. He doesn't know how to treat me. He acts as if I were six years old and the only child he knew who didn't have any toys to play with. Except yesterday, when he was very much Colonel Walter Degnan."

"What do you mean?" he said.

"Questions he knew I couldn't answer. How many men did Cochise have and where Tahzay's bases were. Things like that. All I could tell him was where Victorio was."

"He already knew that," Linus said. He could feel his throat closing off with disgust. "My troops were out around Santa Rita when he moved out to Ojo Caliente. And the minute we pulled out of Santa Rita the Mimbreños went in and killed all the miners."

She looked down at her hand, resting on him. "What do you want me to say, Linus?"

"I just want you to know," he said.

She raised her eyes to his face. It was the strangest and saddest feeling she had ever known: to love someone, to live for years in the shadow of the knowledge that you would love the same someone always, to have it stripped away with storm force, to know the tragic fact that to be loved is the most difficult facet of human existence. Now all the freedom, all the ease, all the quick laughter and taking for granted were gone. "I don't know where to begin, Linus," she said.

He covered her hand with his own, heavily. "There isn't any place to begin. If you want to know how I feel, there was a time I was about to cut my throat. Now I don't think I'm even curious. You know how it is when you wake up from a nightmare. Everything's all thick and funny and you're depressed and not quite able to make yourself believe it was just a dream and you hate to go back to sleep again." He wouldn't look at her. "I don't want to know anything more than I already know. Not yet, anyway. Someday maybe, when it's got all worn out with time, but not now. The only thing I have to know is how you felt, honestly, about this man."

She said cruelly, as honestly as he had wanted, "Linus, every thought I have is for him."

"And all our lives, you and me, means nothing to you?"

"You know that is not so." She could feel herself beginning to quiver, nervous, hollow, wishing she could find something to say but truth, bald and ugly and agonizing.

"What was it, Anna? What the hell was it, you couldn't hold out? You were pretty much assured they weren't going to kill you. You must have known we were making every possible effort to get you out of there. What was it?"

"I don't know. Maybe it was nineteen years of being pushed around from one army post to another, of living with nothing but polite thoughtless men and a maiden aunt who might as well have been a man. Maybe it was circumstance letting me know in the only way possible that nothing is certain, that all our plans and hopes and dreams come down to dust in the end. Do you really think I can search myself and come up with a reason? Oh Linus, Linus, what can I say to you? Do you think I'm not sorry, that I haven't cried and prayed and begged for some answer?"

He was quiet for a long time. She could see the pattern of his breathing, rather slow and forced. He said, "I suppose you are telling me you don't want to marry me?"

"Linus, I *can't* marry you. I *am* married. Why won't anybody understand that?"

"Nobody will understand it because it isn't true. White women do not marry Indians. Paying out horses and mumbling gibberish, or whatever it is they do, does not make a marriage."

"What does?" she said wildly. "What makes a marriage? Mumbling the Protestant rite or the Catholic mass and exchanging rings? That makes a marriage?"

"You know what I'm talking about," he said.

"But oh God, Linus, of all the bigoted. . . ." She was on her feet. "Joaquin is not an Indian."

He said, "If I could accept that, dear girl, I could accept anything." He held out his hand to her. "I will accept anything. Anna, you know that things have reversed for you just as abruptly as they did last spring. I don't want you to be unhappy."

She sank down beside him again. "I'm bewildered, Linus. And guilty."

"No, don't feel that way. Shafter proved to me there shouldn't be any right or wrong, there should always be what is. God knows I don't want to judge. Not anybody. Not anything. Everybody shirks something in life, I suppose. I don't even want to judge that desert rat scrambling around inside the church." He smiled at her, wanly, but with hope. "So we just make the best of the worst."

"Linus," she said quietly, "you know I can't stay here, with you."

He said, "Father won't have any trouble getting me a post in the East. We'll get out of here while it's good traveling weather. Your aunt Mattie wants you back there." His eyes were haunted. "I'll give you time, Anna. All the time you need." He rose and drew her to her feet. "I think you can forget. I think I can."

She was watching him. "Linus, I can't."

He said, "You must. No matter how much you think you can't, you must. For yourself, for your own good, you've got to begin living in your own world again and forget this. Anna, I won't intrude, I promise you that. I want to help you . . . tell me how to help you." The desperation on her face brought the words out of him in a rush. "Do you think I ever stopped loving you for one moment, even when I knew the truth? Do you know that I could have killed him with my bare hands when he came down to deliver that madman's message of Victorio's? All summer I prayed to find him. When I knew I'd killed I knew I had killed with pleasure. Yes, I liked it, every minute of it, it gave me something I couldn't have got any other way." He was tense, hard-eyed. "Don't tell me you're shocked, Anna. Do you think your Mimbreño friends have some private right to savagery?"

She burst out at him, "No. No, all men have it, all men. Why else do you think women behave as they do?"

She was cornered, he was cut to the quick; she crouched away from him and she was frightened; he was so wild and hurt he was shouting. "You were such a good girl, so good and so nice and so honest, always, all the time, and nothing ruffled you; you could have handled God Almighty and some lousy murdering buck hands you an ultimatum. . . ."

She swung away from him and she was shouting, too. "So now I am not so nice, but I am still honest." She bent to pick up the blanket, holding it before her, letting the dust imprint itself upon her. "Nobody handed me an ultimatum, Linus. Nobody. I did what I did because I wanted to." She wanted to hurt him now. "And I'd do it again. I'd do it over and over and over. . . ." She stopped. His eyes were terrible.

His voice came out slow and uncomprehending. "Forgive me, Anna. It's all very . . . difficult. You do know that I love you? It's important to me that you know it, whether or not it means a damn thing to you."

"Yes," she said.

He came up behind her and put his hands on her shoulders. "I am trying to understand. I'm going to keep trying." But she could feel his hands tightening, pulling her back against him, and she was stiff with resistance. "We are going home. You are not of legal age yet; you are still my father's ward, and he is sending you back to Washington. The Callahans will return with us as chaperones. To all intents and purposes we are returning to be married. You will at least save my face before my troops."

"So it is all arranged, behind my back," she said tightly. "And that *is* an ultimatum?"

"That is. I still want you, Anna. Whatever happened has never happened as far as I'm concerned."

Nervous exhaustion set her shaking. "Do you believe you can live such a lie, Linus? Or that I can? That this wouldn't stand between us?" She turned to face him, escaping his hands so obviously that he was stung. "I am not going East. I'm sorry. I'm going to stay in this country. It suits me. It's young, as I am. It offers me the necessities and the few small creature comforts I require. It offers me beauty, and love. I can't refuse it. I am bound here now. Willingly. And I will tell you what I believe. I believe we will beat Joaquin's people in the end, simply by wearing them out and down. I believe the end will be horrible and that there is no hope for them. Whatever that end is and whenever it comes, I am going to be there and I am going to be there with Joaquin."

His face broke her heart. "You force me to take steps I had wished to avoid."

"You cannot stop me," she said.

"You are quite wrong," he said.

She whispered it. "Linus, let me go."

He said, "I am through talking about it."

She brushed past him, spent, wavering. He helped her to mount. He rolled the blanket and stuck the wine bottle in a saddlebag and mounted and turned the horse. There was no sound; the dreaming silence of the old mission reached her so forcibly that she stopped to look back at it. It wore, as reflection, all the starkness, all the purity, all the nobility of the land around it. She looked back once more before the track wound under the cottonwoods and the spread

of bough and leaf shut it off from her sight. The late afternoon sun
was melting brass, and she pulled off the folded scarf which served
her as sash and tied it over her head. Seeing her perform the simple
act he was both moved and alienated: it was a gesture used as a
matter of course by the people of the sun, Mexican, Indian. It was
beautiful and unnatural to him, and he thought that if she had suddenly produced a hat out of nowhere and donned it, he would
have been less surprised. She rode without speaking, steadily, as
if with some unrevealed determination, and he noticed how often
her face turned to the eastward mountains. He sensed an intent
in her, and he could define it only in the crudest physical terms;
an actual attempt at escape. He did not know that she knew she
could not survive a full day alone in this desert.

She said bluntly, "You thought I was at Santa Rita?"

"Yes," he said, grateful for her silence broken. "Victorio shows a
lot less heart for a fight than Cochise."

"Victorio will want to talk terms, I think," she said.

He came to a dead stop. "Anna, what are you saying? How do
you know this?"

"Even when he was at the Stronghold he believed he would
have to treat," she said. "Cochise also. He is sick, and tired."

"Why in God's name didn't you tell us this?" he said irritably.

"Does it matter now?"

"But our scouts say the Mimbreño war parties are coming out of
Ojo Caliente," he said.

"Then he isn't ready yet," she said composedly.

He moved after her. His face was thoughtful. "Anna, do you
think there is any chance. . . ." He hesitated and then spat the
word in exaggeratedly perfect Spanish, "Joaquin . . . would see
his way to arranging a meeting . . . ?"

She shook her head. "No. He wouldn't interfere; he would do
whatever Victorio decides."

"And he wouldn't dare go back there as the white man you
claim he is."

Again she shook her head, sadly. "You don't understand, Linus.
It's not a question of daring, it's a question of accepting what can't
be changed."

He was annoyed. "That's right, I don't understand. I don't understand these people who would rather die than be anything but

Apache and who call themselves in Spanish. Victorio, Joaquin, Delgadito, Mangas Colorado. Why?"

"Linus, those names are blood-bought."

He cleared his throat, as if something was stuck in it. "I should have known that. I remember the story of Mangas Colorado, washing his hands in Mexican blood, clear up to the elbows."

"That is not true," she said mildly. "He was called Red Sleeves because he wore a red shirt. Mangas Chie has never. . . ." She stopped. He saw her face darken and close against him, shutting him out, breaking off the communication so abruptly that he felt cold in his bones. The familiarity with which she dropped the Apache name, the same ease with which he might have mentioned Sergeant Stern, reminded him of the immensity of the problem which faced him. More than some kind dealing with an orphaned child. More than an appeal to common sense. He saw now that she was hung on an emotional balance which bore nothing of logic or reason and that the slightest weight of word would swing the scales. He looked around him. There was nothing but the desert and the circling hills and the sky, no dust cloud, no movement but the movement of the sun edging west. Yet his horse shied at a lizard and tossed its head, and he felt the coldness in his bones as fear. The silence and emptiness threatened in some way he could not recognize, and he reached out and slapped Anna's horse smartly on the rump. It jumped ahead and began to run, and Anna looked around at him, startled, and saw the grimness in his eyes. He forced her to ride at full gallop until the post swam up out of the shimmering heat waves. Only then did he let himself shiver, and it was more a single tense shudder which ran through his shoulders and which brought him no relief at all. Halfway across the cantonment he came abreast of Stern and issued an order, clearly, deliberately, so that Stern would understand, so that Anna would understand.

"Sergeant, from now on I don't want Miss Stillman allowed off the post unless you have permission directly from me. Inform your guard details."

Her face was white, but she managed the smile, for Stern.

"Why Linus, aren't you going to let me off this dreary old place for some exercise now and then?"

Stern was mad. There were troopers waiting with their tongues hanging out to draw escort detail, in case Miss Stillman wanted to ride out. He gave Linus a murderous look. "Sir," he said, "if you will excuse me, I would like to say. . . ."

Linus said evenly, "That's an order, Sergeant."

"Yes, sir," Stern said as nastily as he could get away with.

Dismounting, Linus stood heavily in one stirrup for a moment. He helped Anna down. A trooper came to take their sweating horses. Walking down the line of dobe buildings, Anna said, "That was clever of you, Linus."

"Not at all," he said with a half smile. "Merely a precaution."

She said then, "If you wish to help me, should we begin with trust?"

He looked at her, still smiling. "In another time, another place," he said.

She, too, was smiling now. She looked around her, at the bleak hard-favored post, wall-less, shadeless, naked, sun-baked. A wind was coming up, and dust was beginning to swirl in long twisting ribbons along the ground. Joaquin said when the dust devils came The People would cover everything and hide their heads, but the children would fling themselves joyously into the midst of the stinging blowing sand, whirling round and round in it. Far off, where the wind was strongest, she could see the funnel of sand leap into the air and blow headlong and drop again. She felt an affection even for that relentless sand which was never still. She reached up and pulled the scarf from her head and turned to Linus.

"Linus, thank you. Will you do one thing for me?"

"Anything," he said.

"Will you not worry about me?"

"That's a great deal to ask," he said. "I'll try."

At the doorway she held out both hands and he took them. "Good-by," she said.

Again he laughed, but he was puzzled. "That's an awfully final word somehow."

"Yes," she said. "Isn't it?"

Shafter hollered, "*Agua caliente*," down the stairwell, and pretty soon fat little Remedia came up balancing a basin on one hip and an *olla* on her shoulder.

"*Desayuno*," Shafter told her. "*Huevos fritos. Frijoles. Carne de vaca fresca. ¿No carne seca, sabe? Y mucho café negro.*"

She agreed indifferently and went out. "My God," Willson said. "You got a hollow leg?"

Shafter didn't bother answering. He could tell by the way the light lay across the thick dobe where the window was cut in that it was the middle of the morning. It looked like some thunderheads piling up over the mountains. He had to borrow a clean shirt from Willson and he figured he'd better get his hair cut since it was falling down inside his collar. He shaved and trimmed his mustache, taking his time. Willson stood at the window, looking out.

Somebody was shooting down at the end of the street, probably at a bottle. A couple of wagons rumbled through and men went back and forth. Willson said, "Here comes Will Oury and Elias. What you reckon they gone to do?"

"Get married, maybe," Shafter said.

Willson looked grave. "Should I ought to have my eats downstairs?"

"Anybody wants to see you, they'll come callin'," Shafter said.

Remedia came up with the tray and the inevitable dried beef. "*No carne de vaca fresca*," she said cheerfully. The eggs were swimming in oil and the frijoles almost tore his throat out. It all tasted wonderful. He left the jerky where it lay. "Go shoot me a cow," he said to Willson.

"We could go out to the post and eat," Willson said around a mouthful of beans. "Obre's prolly had pig for breakfast."

Remedia came bouncing back to the doorway. "*Señor Elias*," she said. "*Bajo, para ti, Señor Shafter.*"

Shafter nodded and finished the frijoles, not hurrying. When he stood up, he picked up his gun belt and buckled it on. "You don't care if I trail you," Willson said.

"Hell no, I don't care," Shafter said.

They went downstairs. Oury was talking to the bartender; Jesús Elias sat at a table alone with a glass of tequila before him. He stood up, smiling, when he saw Shafter. "Ah, gentlemen," he said, "good morning." He had trouble with his *g*s in English. "Will you join me?"

"Sure," Shafter said. They pulled out chairs and sat down.

"What will you drink?" Elias said.

Shafter belted himself in the belly a couple of times. "Nothin' right now, Elias, just finished breakfast."

Elias was in an expansive mood. "Tequila is very good for the full stomach," he said.

Oury came over and pulled out a chair. "Howdy, Shafter. Willson. Mind if I sit down?"

"Help yourself," Shafter said. "You wanted to see me, Elias?"

"Yes," Elias said. He took a small delicate sip from his glass and waved his hand at the bartender for salt. He smiled. "We were happy to hear the news, Shafter. About the lieutenant's lady."

Shafter didn't say anything. Oury said, "You did a good job, Shafter. I can remember when it looked pretty hopeless." He grunted a small laugh. "You want to watch out, they'll end up givin' you a medal. Doesn't seem possible one man could get back two women and all those horses, all in one summer."

Shafter listened politely. "It must've taken some smart negotiating," Oury said.

Shafter looked at him. "All it takes is saddle sores, Oury. If you mean what I think you mean, the Indians these days ain't even interested in negotiatin' with us Indian lovers."

Oury's eyes narrowed; then he laughed. He said, "You knew Dave Mitchell's boy was in town?"

He took Shafter short and Shafter couldn't hide it. He could feel the guilt spread over his face. "No, I didn't know it," he said and knew Oury knew he lied.

"Sure," Oury said. "Walked in bold as brass and went down to the church. Then he and the padre went up to take a look at the deaders."

Shafter could feel not only the guilt now but the clenching of his hands on the arms of the chair. The stupid kid. The stupid damn kid. He said, "I expect he likes to see nobody's tore up his old man's grave."

"I wouldn't have known him," Oury said. "Bill, bring me a whiskey, will you? He's no kid any more."

"Where's he now?" Shafter said.

Oury shrugged. "Came and went, I guess."

"You didn't look for him?" Shafter said, leaning back in his chair.

"You're goddamn right we looked for him," Oury said. "He could tell us plenty. We found where he holed up, in a canyon about eight miles out. He wasn't alone."

Take it easy, Shafter told himself. "Had a war party with him, I suppose."

"One other man. Five or six horses."

After a moment Shafter said, "So what do you think I can tell you?"

Oury said, "You knew he was here. We figure you might know where he is now."

Then Shafter said, "All right, yes, I knew he was here, but I don't know where he is now. Every once in a while he gets a hankerin' to take a look at his pa's grave. Ain't anybody in this town got the right to stop him from it."

Oury said calmly, "I don't know about that. You think it's right he can steal and murder half the year and come in like a white man the other half?"

Shafter pushed his chair back and made to get up. "Oury, what you do is your business and what I do is mine and what the Mitchell kid does is his. That way nobody gets an upset gut and there's fewer buryin's."

"Hell, sit down," Oury said, "I didn't mean to rile you, Shafter. We just wanted to congratulate you, buy you a drink. How about it? Willson?"

"Nope," Willson said. He was looking gravely out the open door.

Elias had a big brown leather wallet out and was poring through it. Shafter had the sudden feeling Elias was about to offer him a reward. But when Elias found what he wanted, it turned out to be a faded peeling photograph, creased down the middle. Elias spread it out on the table, so they could all see it. Shafter counted eight children grouped together, unnaturally rigid, staring directly into his face.

He looked up at Elias. "Yours?" he said.

"No," Elias said. "Kiernan's. These are Kiernan's children."

There was a silence. Willson said, "He was a busy boy."

"His wife is in the East, starving," Elias said.

Willson stood up. "You ain't palmin' these Mex kids off as Kiernan's. Not on me, Elias. Look at 'em, black as a bang-tailed bull. You stickin' here, Shafter?"

"Sure," Shafter said. It was funny as hell and he felt like laughing. Willson went to the bar and ordered and looked morosely into his glass.

Shafter said, "Well, I am sorry for the starving Mrs. Kiernan and her starving kids. What do you want me to do, take up a collection?"

Elias's control was cracking. "You are a just man. I thought you might want to see justice done."

"I think you'd ought to take this out and show it to Obre," Shafter said slowly. "He'd prob'ly contribute something."

Elias was beginning to fidget. "You were present when that gringo colonel ordered me off his miserable little post. You tell Obre to stop hiding behind the U. S. Cavalry and see what he thinks about this."

Shafter stood up. "Tell him yourself, Elias. You know what I think? I think you're scared to tell him, unless you got Oury and Logan and a whole passel of teamsters backin' you. You're scared of Obre."

Elias said, "I am always afraid of insane men. Do you know what I have here? I have a. . . ."

"You have a goddamn warrant," Shafter said. "You ain't never been near a judge nor a marshal nor even the governor. You faked that warrant just like you faked this picture. I'll tell you something else. You don't give a damn about Kiernan and you never did. . . . What the hell was he to you? A teamster you can replace any day of the week. What you want is a little Indian blood. When you get real ready, you better come with every teamster you got."

Oury said, "Because you will be with Obre?"

Willson swung around and said, "Count me in."

Elias's head was lowered; his hands moved nervously but he kept them on the table. Oury said, "You and Willson and Obre? And Joaquin Mitchell?"

Shafter turned his back on them square and walked out. The sky was dark in the west, but the sun was hot overhead. Willson followed him. "You gone to the post?"

"I got to," Shafter said. He was worried. He said, "I figure you got to watch a coward a lot harder than you do a brave man."

"If you tell Obre, he's liable to be right in here," Willson said.

"I got to tell him, Willson." A shot ricocheted across the corner of the building. "Watch it," Shafter said, preoccupied.

They went down to get horses. "What you expect is eatin' that half breed?" Willson said.

Shafter said, "I wish I didn't know."

"Aw," Willson said, "you figure that girl? Hell, kids is always playin' house, ain't they?"

Shafter said, "They ain't playin'." He exploded suddenly. "God-

damn him, if he figured to use the church for a shield he's a bigger
fool than any fool I ever came across." He chewed his lower lip.
Sure. Feeling for the only contact, only association there was: a
flattened-out grave with a leaning rawhide-bound cross stuck in it,
not even any writing, a few stones piled over it, and a bunch of
other crumbled bones to keep company. Like the kid figured that
was all he had, all he had left in the world, and he had to say
good-by to it no matter the cost. . . . Shafter thought, and if it had
been my pa, if my pa had done a thing like that to me, I'd of hated
him, God, how I'd of hated him.

"*Señor Shafter, dinero, por favor. Para el caballo.*"

Shafter looked down at the little Mexican, sitting in the sun under the brush *ramada* by the stable. "I'm gone to pick up my pay
now, *chico*. You tell your old man I'll pay him tonight."

The boy lifted one hand in a fatalistic gesture. He didn't believe
a word the gringos spoke, ever.

Willson didn't have a thing to say, mainly because he knew
Shafter was worried about Obre. Shafter didn't waste any time in
the saddle. The dust had been blowing two days straight, and they
needed the rain in those dark western clouds to lay it again. They
rode with their scarves over their faces. When they hit the post,
Willson pulled his scarf back around his neck and sighed. "I et
those freeholies four times since breakfast," he said. "What I need
is a good cigar to settle 'em."

Shafter kept his eye peeled, but he didn't see Obre and he
didn't see Anna, and he was looking for them both. When they
went into commandant, Degnan had their pay ready but he didn't
look happy about it.

"You know I'll take you permanently," he said.

Shafter shook his head. "I ain't enjoyed it, Walter."

"I know that," Degnan said. He opened a desk drawer. "I've got
something here for you, Shafter." He took out a long heavy white
envelope.

"A letter for me?" Shafter said. Offhand he couldn't think of a
soul would write him, unless it might be Jessie Bell Huggins and
he didn't think she could write.

Degnan said, "I'll tell you before you open it. It's a letter of commendation from the War Department." He sat back in his chair,
savoring the mingled astonishment and dismay on Shafter's face.

Shafter said flatly, "What for?"

Degnan grinned around his cigar. "Well, as I believe Tony Bleeker pointed out, you're the first man to manage a personal communication with the Mimbreños in over a year. You are responsible for obtaining the release of Miss Vasquez. A fairly respectable record, I'd say." Shafter was tapping the end of the envelope against his palm; he made no move to open it. Degnan said, "Of course they've only just found out about your recovery of Miss Stillman, so that doesn't count."

Willson chewed his cigar from one corner of his mouth to the other. "For that they gone to give you the whole C.S.A. back," he said.

Shafter said shortly, "That was a lousy Yankee trick to pull on me, Walter." He rose.

Degnan kept grinning. "Aren't you going to open it?"

Shafter said, "Look, you do me a favor. You keep this here for me till I can come get it someday."

"What?" Degnan said.

"I ain't got any place to put it," Shafter said, kind of desperate now.

"You can frame it and wear it around your neck," Willson said.

"For Chrissake, Willson, shut up, will you? Well, Walter?"

Degnan said, "You're not refusing this, Shafter?"

And Shafter said, "No. I'm proud, and I'm scared of pride. You'd ought to be horsewhipped all the same." He held out the envelope. Degnan took it slowly. For the brief instant their hands held it, it was more than anything either of them might have said.

"Well," Shafter said, "I got to look up Fox P. Canby."

"He's not here," Degnan said. "I had to get off some telegrams and he's gone with the San Simon detail. I'm transferring Linus East, you know."

Shafter looked at him. "Is that right? He wants to go back?"

"We've got to do what's best for Miss Stillman," Degnan said.

Shafter thought viciously, you mean you got to do what's best for you, and Linus, and public opinion. He said, "Well, I'm right sorry. You and Linus come on in and have a drink with me before we pull out, will you?"

"We'll try, John," Degnan said.

They felt better for the vagueness of the invitation and the vagueness of the response.

Outside, Shafter said, "Let's find Ob and get this over with. I got a bad taste in my mouth."

"It's them freeholies," Willson said. He took the cigar out of his mouth, looked at it for a minute, and then dropped it on the ground. "These Yankee cigars ain't no help at all," he said.

Nineteen

Obre was sitting down by the laundry with his hat tipped over his eyes, disinterestedly looking at a six-month-old issue of the Washington *Daily Morning Chronicle*. Shafter said to Willson, "You're kind of flabber-mouthed today; be careful what you say to him."

"You say it," Willson said. "Nobody was talkin' to me."

"I'm liable to lose my temper," Shafter said. He kicked at Obre's outstretched foot. "Howdy, Ob. How's the ladies this morning?" He went on and looked in the laundry, where Katie and Bess Layden were bent over the copper tubs. "Good morning," he said.

Bess Layden's sharp face turned up to him. She was pretty muscular from a lot of years of army laundry. "It's afternoon," she said.

"So it is," he agreed. Katie wouldn't look at him. When he glanced around, he saw Anna was sitting on a wooden cot in the corner. She was sewing something. He took off his hat. "Howdy, Miss Stillman."

"Good afternoon, Shafter," she said. She put the sewing aside and got to her feet. When she did, Katie turned and gave her a look which trailed clear back to the wall, circled around, and settled on Shafter. Anna said clearly, "I have a message for you, from trooper Canby."

He wasn't much of an actor, but he got out a natural-sounding chuckle. "Old Fox P., eh?" he said. "I hear I missed him. What's he got to say?"

Again he was struck by the clarity of her voice. "It is a private message."

Even the back of Katie's head was furious. "You just go right on and talk," she said. "We've got hangin' up to do." She bent to a filled basket. "Where's that lummox Willson?"

"Are you speakin' of me, ma'am?" Willson said, looking in.

"Come and carry these baskets for us," she said. He was obliging. Obre came in and took Bess Layden's basket. The room smelled of harsh soap and lye and the floor was red and muddy where water had spilled on the dobe.

"My God," Anna said. "They are telling me when to draw breath."

"I figured," Shafter said.

"Linus won't let me off the post. You heard . . . Uncle Walter's going to get me out of here within days. Shafter, what am I going to do?"

He stood looking at her. This was no longer any of his business, in consideration of hard cold cash, yet he was now so involved that only a superhuman effort could pull him out of it. His original dislike and distrust of the girl had become pity so powerful that he could feel his heart contract at the very thought of what lay ahead for her, either way. She had been touched by something strange and frightening; he could not fully comprehend it; it was not a total empathy, but he was in sympathy with it, and deeply. He was afraid for her, for he knew that in her misery she could do one of three things: destroy herself in a frenzied attempt to break away, slide without effort into a madness which would set her up to shoot her way out, submit to the machinations of the Degnans. She was tough, yes, but he wondered how much more, or how little, might unbalance her. For himself, if he chose, there was only one course to be taken.

"Did you see Joaquin?" She said it so low and quickly that he had to go over it in his mind to make sure he had heard it at all.

But he wouldn't tell her. "I got to know," he said. "You got to be truthful with me. Ain't there one little doubt in your mind? Just one we could sort of work with?"

She was shaking her head. Very fast, very resolute.

"What about Linus?" he said.

"We are strangers."

"I don't think so," he said. "Maybe for a while, but not forever." He made one final effort. "Annie, you don't belong there."

"But I don't belong here," she cried.

"Maybe not. But you don't belong there."

"Then if we are both right I don't belong anywhere."

"Don't you panic on me," he said, starting toward her.

"But it's true . . . I have no place to go then." Her voice came out flat and hard. "You said you would do anything for Joaquin but that you did not know what you could do. I am Joaquin. I am more Joaquin now than I am myself. This is something you can do. Please. Please."

He said heavily, "There's more than what you are. There's where you are. That kind of life, this country. It's not for a woman like you."

She said passionately, "This country is all over me, Shafter." Her face was beautiful and ugly, all at once.

The rack pulled tighter and he felt himself coming apart. She screamed at him under her breath. "Quickly, they're coming back."

He said, "You be ready tonight. Late. You meet Obre, right here. You do what Obre tells you, understand?"

For a minute he figured she was going to collapse, because she swayed and reached out and steadied herself on a laundry tub. She saw Katie's red head bob by the window and she stood upright and said in a shaken voice, "Mr. Canby also said his enlistment is up in a year and he'll come looking for you then. He said something about sticking the pieces back on, and that you'd understand."

So she hadn't been frauding about Fox P. He said under his breath, "Thanks, Annie," and then Katie came right in and said, "Excuse *me*, but I got work to get finished here."

"That's all right, Katie," he said. "I'm surely powerful grateful to you, Miss Stillman. When you see Fox you tell him I'll be lookin' for him." He ran his hand through his hair and settled the dusty old Kossuth hat. "By the way, Katie. Good-by."

She still wouldn't look at him. "Good-by to you, John Shafter. I don't suppose you heard Rafe and me is goin' East where there's trees growin' and the grass stays green nine months of the year." Two tears fell in the laundry tub. "Good riddance, I say. Anybody would stay in this country is just plumb crazy. . . ." Now she looked up. "You take care, won't you, John?"

"Sure," Shafter said. "Hell, I'm all I got to take care of, and that ain't much of a strain." He went out. Obre was sitting down again, with the newspaper folded over his drawn-up knees and Willson hunched against the wall beside him.

"Say, I'm rich," he said.

"We're all rich," Shafter said.

"This here's the first money I made in a coon's age. It don't feel right."

Shafter looked questioningly at Willson. "I told him," Willson said.

Obre shoved his hat back. His face was leaner and blacker than ever but his voice was contained. "Now, if I go in there again and they lookin' for me, somebody is gone to get laid up, and it might be me. Like I told you, Elias can see me over the border if he's a mind." He dipped into the breast pocket of his shirt and came up with a shin plaster. "Here, would you give him this for Kiernan's starvin' kids."

"I wouldn't do that if I was you, Ob," Shafter said.

Obre laughed. Shafter jerked his head violently at him and finally Obre caught on and stood up and moved off to the corner of the laundry with Shafter. Shafter said conversationally, "Say, sometime after midnight, what would you reckon is the best way for you to get the little girl out of here?"

"Why damn you," Obre said. "You ain't gone to do that, are you? I spent the whole summer gettin' her in here."

"Come on, how you gone to do it?"

Obre folded his arms and thought about it for a spell. Then he said, "If I had me a burro and a *rebozo* and a big straw *sombrero* like the *chicos* wear. You couldn't send some Mexes out here on some errant or other, could you? Or maybe with a wagon."

"Too much commotion, a wagon pullin' out at that hour," Shafter said. He snapped his fingers once. "You know the *chico* at the stable. . . . His pa wants his *dinero* for boardin' our horses, but he don't figure to see it. I'm gone to give that kid more *dinero* than he's seen all year."

"Go on," Obre said.

"I'll send him out before dark with a message for you." Shafter grinned. "I'll write you a letter, Ob. He'll bring out some extra stuff. . . . say you want to buy a *rebozo*. Then you tell him there's Apaches around and he's got to stay the night and go home with you in the morning."

Obre said admiringly, "Would you like for me to shoot the little feller or just slug him in the head?"

"Bed him down for the night. I'll tell his pa he's all right and settle up our debt. If anybody calls you in the dark, it's you and the kid gone into town."

Obre lit a cigarette and closed one eye. "It ain't bad enough I got Elias on me. Now all three of us gone to have Yank cavalry chasin' us from here to next year."

Shafter said, "You're right. This ain't your war, nor Willson's either. I'll do it myself."

"Too late now," Obre said. "What I want to know is how come the little honey wants to go sashayin' off again with that breed *Tá-ashi*? It sure don't make sense to me. They'll turn the whole damn army loose." Then he said, "I always did think the Yankees was a bunch of screwheads."

"You ain't keen on knifin' Linus, is that it?" Shafter said.

Obre poked him in the chest with an emphatic forefinger. "You are doin' Linus one big favor, *amigo*," he said. "And I'll tell you somethin' else. You better do it fast, because if that half breed thinks he's gone to hang around here all white and ten feet tall, he ain't got long to do it. Somebody is gone to lift his hair."

Shafter said shortly, "And it's gone to be a rough run for 'em. If they make it into New Mexico. . . ."

"You ain't figurin' on gone to Mexico by way of Ojo Caliente, are you?" Obre said.

Shafter's laugh was sardonic. "I wouldn't go to Ojo Caliente if they were givin' away beautiful women and solid gold beds," he said. He looked up. "There's Linus. You take your time, Obre. Don't let her get nerved up and give you away. I'll meet you halfway into town." He walked on down the line.

Linus was riding up. "I was afraid you'd gone, John," he said. "I just drew a great one. Bunch of Chiricahua ran off some stock from Pete Kitchen's ranch. Pete gave 'em his usual good fight but I'm taking out a pursuit detail."

Shafter looked up at him and felt as if a sword had been driven through him. He thought he had never seen or known anyone as vulnerable as Linus, and as dogged.

"You wouldn't want to come along, would you?" Linus said.

"Linus, I can't," Shafter said.

"You ought to stay around a few days anyway. Bleeker'll be back. And this will be my last duty in this damn desert."

"I got an awful thirst to go," Shafter said.

Linus said, "What's the matter, John?"

"Matter?" Shafter said. "Ain't anything the matter. I got a sight of money to play with and I'm free as a hawk. I feel good."

Linus was just looking at him. He said, "I never could stand saying *adiós*. Where can I write you?"

"Why, right here, I reckon," Shafter said. "I got to come back someday and pick up that howdy from Washington, D.C. your pa so kindly ordered for me."

Linus saw there was no rancor in him. He said, "You set your mind on coming East."

Shafter laughed. "It seems like every time I try to get east of Texas something always ropes me back." He hesitated. "Linus, about this trouble you got . . . you're gone to be a lot better off, in every way. I know you don't think so, but it's gone to turn out that way."

Linus thought he understood him, "I know, John. It won't be easy. But we're going to start all over again. In a year's time we won't know what trouble is."

Shafter flattened his upper lip. He said, "Thanks for the boots. They sure did raise the best blisters I ever had." They shook hands. Shafter felt the severing of the bond as a nagging pain. How did you say good-by, to a son, to a brother, except to say it. He walked off. Judas, he said inside himself. You dirty Judas. And for free.

All Obre could see of trooper Price was his thick mustache, which bristled warningly out into the night. Once identification had been established, Price didn't want to quit, because he was bored. He said it was past the kid's bedtime and Obre said he aimed to get the kid home. Price said Obre'd ought to wait for daylight and Obre said he had a call from Shafter and wondered if, if Price turned his head just a little more to the right, he could shoot off one side of his mustache, and finally Price retreated into the vacancy of his own mind.

Anna twisted on the pony and saw the looming buildings of the post begin to suck up in the dark. Almost immediately an uncontrollable trembling began in her. And recognition: without compromise, she had cut the last tie.

The pony seemed to lag. Obre said low, impatient, "Keep up with me, can't you?" and she urged the pony, anxious to prove something, she was not certain what, to him because he had been good to her. It had been very simple. She had heard guard change at midnight. An hour later she walked out, wearing only the clothing which belonged to her, leaving Katie Callahan's tortoise-shell brush on the bureau. She stood against the wall of quarters. A moment later Obre came, mounted, leading the pony the *chico* had ridden. They did not speak. He handed her the big woven shawl and the straw *sombrero* and she put them on and mounted. The stirrups were a little short; she let the edge of the *rebozo* hang down to cover her skirt and moccasins. She did not falter during the exchange with trooper Price. Beside Obre, she said, "Shouldn't we hurry?" and he said, "You just stay with me, ma'am."

He was for hurry, but it wasn't unusual for men or wagon teams to be jacking into Tucson at this hour, and he did not want to arouse suspicion. The night was almost clear as day, but there were clouds lying in compact mile-long drifts, and it was still trying to blow up some rain. He heard riders ahead long before he could make contact, and he rode with his hand on the Dance's slick familiar butt.

It was two men and a pack horse coming toward them. "At least it ain't Indians," he said to Anna.

"How can you tell?"

"They always ride file, even if there's just two of 'em. It's only white men ride 'longside of one another. So's they can palaver."

It was Shafter and Willson. Shafter said, "It went all right?"

"Like a greased sidewinder," Obre said.

"Let's go," Shafter said. They started on. He pulled around beside Anna. He tried, but he couldn't do a thing about the tone of his voice. "You made your bed now, Annie. Don't you cry if the slats keep bustin', will you?"

She shook her head. "I can't thank you, Shafter, I haven't any words."

He said, "We ain't in the clear yet."

They went down through the old saguaro forest, with the thick cloud rolling overhead, toward the ragged horizon which lay on the mountains. There was the Old Pueblo in the night light, and Anna said, "Is this Tucson? Are we going into the town?"

"Yes and no," Shafter said. When they reached the walls, Obre stopped. "Wait you here," he said. "Yes, sure," Shafter said. Well, they had everything, they were ready to roll. "Easy now," he said to Anna, but she called across to the two men at the wall. "Good-by," she said, and they called back, "*Adiós*," and Obre tipped his hat although he felt it was a little late for it.

"Stay behind me," Shafter said. He rode down the wall very slowly. At the corner he said, "Stay here," and went on alone, hoping to God they weren't going to have to do any waiting. It took him some time to roll a cigarette, and after he'd got it rolled he lit it, figuring that as better than any other signal. He strained to see through the break in the wall, and he noted that the roof of the old stable had caved in completely and there wasn't anything there now but the rubble of thatching lying over some piles of straw and grama grass within the crumbling stable wall. He said, "Joaquin?" and Joaquin got up from behind the broken dobe wall and came toward him.

"I thought you might not be here," Shafter said.

"I have been here every night," Joaquin said. "You are a long time coming."

"Time to spare," Shafter said. "Where's all your gear and horses? Who you got with you?"

"We had to move," Joaquin said. "There is only Mangas Chie. How did you know?"

They want out through the wall. Shafter said, "I know because you let yourself get seen by the two men in this town you shouldn't of let get to see you. What in the hell did you want to go and do a thing like that for?"

Joaquin said, "Because I am here and my father is there. I knew it was foolish. I had to do it. I knew it was for the last time. Have you seen Ana?"

"She's here," Shafter said. "We brought her out tonight." He didn't want Joaquin to say anything, so he dismounted and went along the wall and took the pony's bridle and led it up. Anna tore off the big concealing hat and slipped off the pony and ran, and Shafter heard Joaquin say, "Ana? Ana?" as if he didn't believe it.

When Shafter turned, he saw that they were only standing, close to one another, but not touching, and it provoked him: if that wasn't as Indian a thing as could be. . . . He said, "Look, Joaquin, you know the odds against you now." He gestured at Anna. "Make sure she knows 'em, too. They're gone to turn out every trooper in the Territory on you and they'll prob'ly go against Ojo Caliente."

He thought Joaquin hesitated. Then Joaquin said, "Victorio is not at Ojo Caliente. We had a runner, yesterday, from the Stronghold."

"He's back up there?" Shafter said.

"No," Joaquin said. "But he is close. In the mountains."

"A war party?" Shafter said.

"No," Joaquin said again. "Delgadito has taken the big war party out of Ojo Caliente."

"Why are you telling me this?" Shafter said.

"Because I want you to know where we will not be," Joaquin said. "And I want you to know where we will not be so that there will be no senseless attacks on my people."

Now he reached out and took Anna around the waist and drew her close to him. "Whatever warning Victorio gave you at Apache Pass is taken back," he said. "The word will go to the rancherías that you are welcome among the Mimbreños."

Shafter pulled the dun's head around. "I may need it," he said, not without humor. "Now boy, you pick up Chie and your stuff and hightail it out of here like you had wings, you hear?" He swung up on the dun.

Anna said, "Shafter," but she had turned to Joaquin again. "My mare? The saddle you made me?"

And he was saying, "All here, Anacita, and the lion skin. I told you it would bring luck."

She came to stand beside the dun. She reached up and touched Shafter's hand. "I will wish for Mexico to be kind to you."

He looked down at her. "I wish for life to be kind to you, Annie. I don't think you're off to much of a start myself." He looked over at Joaquin. "You be good to her. And listen to her. She might be kind of headstrong but she understands a lot of things you don't."

He pulled off down the wall, feeling pretty good and pretty sick. When he got around to the *entrada* he saw a few lights were dim inside, and just beyond the wall somebody was coughing the kind of cough that made his hair stand on end.

"I tell you what we'll do," Willson said. "We'll lay in at Pete Kitchen's and get us some first-rate grub."

"Sounds good to me," Shafter said. "Especially if that rain blows. It's been circlin' us for two days now." He heard, very distinctly, the running of hoofs, away from them. He said, "You all got your *dinero* some place safe?"

"Sure," Obre said. "I belted her right around me."

"I swallered mine," Willson said.

Under the changing sky, blue depth rising, even the smell of the air lighter and colder, Shafter speculated on how much of man's business was conducted at night. All he'd ever heard, the most nefarious transactions took place under cover of dark, an evil time, an evil color, and he thought now this might be true. He knew that the two men who rode with him were as free as mortals could be in this world or any other, and he remembered that he had been with them in this and wondered if he could ever feel that way again. He wanted to, badly, wanted the old ease of nothing much on his mind and the continuation of the long search, of drifting quietly and letting the beauty of the earth imprint itself achingly on the eye, and the heart. It seemed like damn little to ask for. But he didn't feel like one of them again, for a long time. Not until Obre began to sing, sitting rather slackly in the saddle, with both hands resting on his thighs and three stars riding over the wide forward brim of his hat. Like his hands, his voice was very fine and powerful, and when he muted it down it took on some clear blue quality which might have been drawn from the night itself.

> The years go slowly by, Lorena,
> The snow is on the grass again.
> The suns go down the sky, Lorena,
> The frost sleeps where the flowers have lain.

It was a sad song. He'd heard it all through the war, and yet he never tired of hearing it. He guessed there were times a man actually took a kind of pleasure in being sad. So what was he complaining about, that he'd done good deeds and bad, when he was loose on the country again with a friend who could sing and had a good gun and another who could make him smile now and then. He was getting to be a terrible complainer, in his soul.

Then he was lying on the ground on his right side. He wasn't hurt. Even as he made to pull free he realized the dun had hit a hole. But he couldn't move. The dun made a straining sound and rolled heavily on Shafter's leg, struggling to get up again. When he felt the horse gain ground, he yanked his foot out of the stirrup. The dun was standing upright, shaking so hard he could actually see it.

"Check his leg," Shafter yelled and then was standing himself, walking toward the dun. Willson had the front leg up and was running his hand over it with gentleness and skill. "It ain't broke," he said. He dropped the leg and prodded the dun into moving and picked up the leg again. "I don't think he's tore nothing loose either. You all right, Shafter?"

"Sure," Shafter said. He walked to the horse and went to put his hand to the pommel and was lying on the ground again, this time on his back. He looked down and saw something white, like a knob of bleached wood, sticking up, and it seemed good as anything to haul himself up with, so he took hold of it and then the vomit came up in his throat, strangling him, and he thought, but I walked, I walked, and dropped his hand away from his own shattered, thrust-out leg bone.

Twenty

The time of Earth is Red Brown lingered in the mountains, bronze, gold, red, all blues bluer, clear water floating curled leaves, pines singing in the wind. The nights were clean cold. The Mimbreño wickiups were pitched creekside.

Half The People were here; Delgadito still based out of Ojo Caliente. While this was not a war camp, Cuchillo Negro, Black Knife, went out of the ranchería with a small party and joined Tahzay's Chiricahua, running south to Sonora. There was still some harvest to be taken in. The squaws sang but they were restless; they did not wish to be caught here in the high places when Ghost Face came. The men sat around the fires at night and told Coyote stories.

No one knew where the Coyote stories came from. The eyes of the old men gleamed in the light when they told the old fables. The mouths of the old men laughed. They identified with Coyote, who was the greatest trickster of them all, but who was often tricked in turn.

Tonight Coyote was tricked. Cuchillo Amarillo, Yellow Knife, was growing old and had no taste for fighting as he had had when Mangas Colorado ordered out the war parties. He sat at his fire and The People came and he told them how Coyote was tricked by Rabbit. They all knew the story. They never tired of it. Coyote came upon Rabbit and Rabbit was tossing up into the sky two round shiny things. Coyote said, What is that you are playing with, Rabbit? Rabbit said, I am playing with my eyes, Coyote. Coyote said, This seems like a fine plaything and I would like to do it, too. Rabbit said, I would not do it if I were you, Coyote, and he tossed his two eyes into the air and they fell back into place and he looked at Coyote with them. Coyote said, I must try this game, Rabbit, and he, too, took out his eyes and tossed them up and they fell back into place. Rabbit said, I would not do that if I were you, Coyote, but he did it to himself. So Coyote did it, too, for the second time. It was the best game he had ever found. Rabbit said,

I would not do that if I were you, Coyote. But Coyote said, Only one more time, Rabbit, and he took out his eyes again and tossed them up, and this time they fell to the ground and went rolling down the hill and into the valley, and Coyote never found them.

Cuchillo Amarillo's heavy body shook with laughter and The People laughed with him. Tell another, they said, let Coyote win this time. So Cuchillo Amarillo told them the best story of all.

Coyote came upon a *Nakaiyi* herding sheep and offered to help him. But the man said, No, you are not to be trusted, Coyote. Coyote looked past him, into his house, and saw the man had a wife, very slim and fine, and he said, A man should be with his wife. I will herd your sheep. So the man went to his house and lay down with his wife, and Coyote stayed with the sheep. Pretty soon Coyote ate a sheep, all except the head and the tail. Then he ate another sheep. He ate them all, except the heads and the tails, and these he took and placed to stick up out of a mud hole. Then Coyote cried to the man, Help, help, all your sheep are stuck in a mud hole. The man ran out to see. Coyote said, It is all my fault, I will dig them out. Where is your shovel? The man sent him to the house, where the fine wife was lying on her bed. Coyote said, Your husband says you must make love with me, too. The wife said, Only if he tells me so himself. So Coyote went to the door and called to the man, Your wife will not give me what I came for, and the man called back loudly, You must give it to him. So, while the man was waiting to dig out his sheep, Coyote made love to his fine wife.

The women loved this story and laughed hardest of all at it. It was good to think of the *Nakaiyi* woman tricked by Coyote. Victorio rose smiling and looked across the fire at his smiling wife. She had grown heavy, but her face was narrow and placid, and her eyes when she looked up at him were full of laughter and said she would not be tricked, not even by Coyote. Even as he looked at her, her eyes clouded. One son was out with Delgadito, one with Cuchillo Negro; she was still not sure what Victorio did in this mountain camp at this time of the year. For the Chiricahua the heights were home, but the Mimbreños were desert people, and this was an alien place. She had learned not to question, which was often difficult, for she was a woman of strong sensible opinion and was in no way averse to passing it on to her man whether or not he asked it. It chafed her, when she did not know what was in his mind.

She was thankful that he was not waging war on the white eyes on the scale Cochise had undertaken, but she saw that he was often silent and depressed. She, too, worried, for before too many days they would be delving into their reserve food supply. It was all very well to sing and tell of Coyote, but it did not make her forget that her sons were at war and her man engaged in some affair which he had not discussed with her.

It pleased her that Joaquin had returned. In her heart she believed that perhaps, this time, having gone back to the places of the white eyes, the people who were half of him, he would not come again. But he had come, with the big-eyed frightened girl, and he looked the same and was the same. For herself, she set at once to make the girl welcome, for the other women were occupied with their own round of tasks, and distant, and this was a difficult thing and would take time to overcome.

When she was very small, Victorio's wife had been called She Who is Slow to Speak. At puberty, when she took her permanent name, she had become Shastazah, She Who Speaks Quietly. Her father was a war chief. At her first social dance, meaning to tap Victorio so that he must dance with her, she accidentally brushed her fingers across the shoulder of a young brave called Francisco Diablo. At the second dance she touched Victorio. A week later Francisco Diablo brought two horses and tied them before her father's wickiup. Victorio had no horses; he had only a mule and a scrub pony. But he brought them. On the second night Francisco Diablo's horses were nearly crazed with thirst, but Victorio's animals had been fed and watered, and when he came for them it was also to take Shastazah.

He loved her narrow face and eyes which slanted upward a little at the corners, and he learned quickly that while she did speak quietly she was certainly not slow to speak. Not that she intruded, not that she ever concerned herself with things of the councils. Not until he was mature and a chief in his own right and at last father of all the Mimbreños did he see that she was in fact a calm steady loyal woman who spoke wisely in her deep understanding of him. Twice she had knelt at the birthing post, to be delivered of his sons. And even in those days, when they were younger and freer and unharried by the white men who came to despoil their country, he had listened to her.

If she was not so quick to speak, in this older time, she said more with less words than ever before, so that sometimes he was alarmed when he saw she was about to open her mouth. But he had never taken, had never wanted, another wife, who was entitled to more if he chose.

Shastazah went from Cuchillo Amarillo's fire to Joaquin. She had known his mother, had been with his mother when death came, and she remembered with pleasure and pity the white man called Mitch-o who had come and gone among them. She said, "Why is your *niña* frightened, Joaquin?" And Joaquin said, "Give her time; you are strange to her."

Shastazah said, laughing, "But she is strange to us, and we are not frightened of her."

Joaquin called Anna and told her. For the time being she had determined to hold herself as distant as the Mimbreño women promised to do, but the kindness and sympathy on Shastazah's face melted her.

Still, it was a very hard time. She had not, after all, come among people she knew, as she might have done returning to the Chiricahua Stronghold. Nuadin was not here, nor Tayanclee. There was only Joaquin, to hunt and work at his own things as she worked at hers. Sometimes she gritted her teeth, waiting for something to happen, something which would fit her in, totally, without restriction. One day, passing, Victorio said to her in his broken Spanish, "Ai, you cause the Mimbreños much trouble, Ana," and before she could answer, before she could make the attempt to match what she recognized as heavy humor on his part, Shastazah said tranquilly, "You have always made your own trouble, Victorio."

Anna saw the glint go out of his eyes, the slackness come into his stance. He looked at his wife for a long time and she returned his look steadily until he turned away.

That night Anna could not sleep. It was cold, but she sat up and pulled a blanket around herself and went to sit in the open flap of the wickiup. The running water sounded like glass smashing, and she could see the lances of the pines poised at the sky. There was a faint haze of smoke in the wickiup; the draw hole from the center pit fire was not as efficient in practice as in theory. On the other side of the ranchería a dog was barking, an old hoarse dog by the sound of him. Somewhere close an owl voiced a treble lament, and when it began the dog quit. She thought about Shafter, who would be in Mexico now; she was arrested by the belief that Shafter was the only man, the only person she had ever known, who had been intentionally, self-sacrificially, kind to her. Everybody had been kind to her, all her life, because being kind was the manner in which civilized persons behaved, but nobody had ever stepped miles out of their way, beyond the point their own feelings and intentions didn't matter a whit and her own became the prime concern. Except Shafter.

Joaquin said, "What is it, Ana?"

"I am not sleepy," she said.

He got up and came to her. "You will catch cold," she said, turning her head, smiling at him.

"So then you will have to call in the devil dancers for me and what will you pay them with?"

She sensed suddenly a kind of terror in his voice, under the jest. "You were not asleep either," she accused and reached out for him.

"Come back," he said. "Let me hold you. Talk to me."

She was shivering. They lay close, warming one another. He said, "Ana, you are not sorry you came back?"

Her head moved on his shoulder. Out of the certainty of youth she said, "I will never be sorry. Will they make friends with me soon?"

His laugh was relieved. "They are already your friends. You don't believe me. It is their way. Tomorrow you go and ask one or two of the women to help you . . . any small thing."

"But I did not have to ask Shastazah."

"Shastazah is not the same."

She sighed. "That's easy enough to do, ask help, heaven knows."

"Everything will be better when we leave this place," Joaquin said. "I do not like this climate."

"You don't think we will stay here?"

"We cannot stay here," he said without emotion. "We would die here. This is not our country. We would freeze and starve."

"Then why are we here?" she said.

"Victorio is waiting for something."

"For the . . . the war party to get back?"

"No. Don't ask me now." She was silent. He said, "What else, Ana?"

Her arm went out, across his chest. "Joaquin, why couldn't we go somewhere together? Alone."

She felt his breathing stop, for a long, held moment. "Where? To some town where there are beds and tables and chairs?"

"No," she said, trying to shake her head, give the word emphasis. "Don't do that; your hair tickles," he said. "Where?"

"I don't know. Somewhere. We could build a little house and have a garden. What else would we need? Somewhere where it is warm and there is water and we can see the mountains. Joaquin, are you angry?"

He said, "Angry?" as if he had never been angry in his life. Then he said, "It is a very hard thing to break away. I know this." He was rigid, waiting.

She said, "The thing I am afraid of . . . is the fighting."

"The fighting," he said, bewildered. "What fighting?"

"I mean if you should fight. If anything should happen to you. If you should kill someone."

The bewilderment was still in him. Then he laughed. "Do you know what my father used to say? He said, You can't cross a bridge until you come to it. I didn't know what a bridge was. So one time when we were crossing the Colorado he said he meant you couldn't make a ford until you came to it, and we forded and I knew what he meant."

It was not reassuring. She said, "But if we had a small place. A little farm."

"What do you know about farming?"

"Are you laughing? I don't know anything about it. But I would learn."

"To be safe?" he said.

"Yes. So that you would be safe. So that . . . so that if a white man made you his enemy, he would be safe."

He would not answer. He turned her face up and began to kiss her. But she said, "Joaquin, this is not the answer to everything."

"It is the beginning of the answer," he said. "The answer is somewhere along the way. Agree with me and I will make you a promise."

"Agreed," she whispered.

"You don't know what I will promise."

"Promise me anything," she said.

"When we leave here we will talk of this again. I will think about it." He felt that he should be disturbed, but he could sense the happiness that was flooding through her so strongly that it seemed to flow into him also, leaving no room for anything else.

"You see," she said. "Shafter said you must listen to me."

"How can I help listening? You talk all the time," he said.

"He meant listen with your heart."

"Oh, was that it? What have you to say to my heart then?"

"I love you. I love you so hard."

He thought of the night, before she had been taken so unexpectedly away from him. He thought of the time he had been without her; he remembered that he had vowed security for her in a world where there was no security.

"Joaquin, are you asleep?"

"Only my arm. Don't move yet. I was thinking when you are with me, now that I know, I will always listen with my heart."

Her breath was warm on his cheek. When he knew she slept, he moved his arm from under her and covered her tightly and lay looking into the red eye of the fire pit. Before he could make any decision, even for her who had become his first responsibility, he must consider his responsibilities to his people.

In the morning Anna went to two of the women and asked them to help her with some brushwood. They came stolidly, without speaking, although one of them grunted once. She found nothing in their attitudes but a flat acceptance. Then in the early afternoon they both came to her, with Shastazah, and asked her to help them carry wood.

Joaquin was cleaning the Mexican carbine. "Now look what you have got me into," she said to him.

"You are being shown an honor," he said, without looking up. "The wood is for the council fire. Only four are chosen to bring it in."

She found it impossible not to laugh; she could have done with less strenuous honors. But when she laughed she saw that the two squaws were actually smiling at her. There was plenty of wood to be found here. There was a big flat rock near the center of the ranchería, and on this the women first spread small dry sticks. Over it they laid the brush, and near by they stacked wood with which to keep the fire fed. When they were finished, the two squaws burst out volubly at her and so rapidly that she could catch only a word or two. They were thanking her and telling her she worked well. They went home and Shastazah went to Victorio's wickiup, and Anna went for a cold swim and changed her clothing. She was making new moccasins, for hers were worn, and somebody had come in from a raid with some heavy English needles. She was so delighted to see them that she did not even stop to think where they must have come from. Joaquin bought them for her with the promise of a prime skin in exchange.

Late in the afternoon Tahzay came up with a party of eight fighting bucks. With him were Pionsenay, out as war chief, and an old Chiricahua medicine sachem. The Chiricahua washed off their paint, but they were all carrying fresh makings: crushed nut hulls which stained brown, yellow algerita root, boiled red root of mountain mahogany. Tahzay spoke with Victorio and then rode his gray stallion to Joaquin's wickiup. He was heavily equipped; he had a new carbine, a four-foot single curve bow and new arrows, thirty-inch-long carrizo reed fitted with red banded hardwood shafts and hawk-wing feathers. He was carrying his medicine shield, which had been freshly decorated, and he had tied up his stallion's tail with strips of red flannel. He looked prosperous, purposeful, unutterably weary, and his face was the eagle face of Cochise.

He and Joaquin embraced briefly. Half in his own tongue, half in Spanish, Tahzay thanked Anna for the spotted deerhide. It was rolled behind him, and she knew that in it would be his fire drill, jerked meat, hoddentin bag, paints, and perhaps the magnificent scarlet antelope-horned medicine hat which he never wore, but which he would not part with because it helped to insure his invulnerability. Anna fed them, and Mangas Chie. The sun was nearly down when three strange Indians rode out of the grassy meadow at the fringe of the pine forest, splashed through the creek, and came into the rancheria, riding down the uneven row of wicki-ups.

Two of the bucks were young, carrying carbines. The man between them was not quite middle-aged, squat, heavy-set, with a broad expressionless face. He wore a white man's shirt and coat.

"Who is it?" Joaquin said.

Tahzay drew himself up to his near six feet. He licked his lips and then spat casually. "Eskiminzin of the Arivaipa."

"Only two men with him?" Joaquin said. "What escort is that for a chief?"

"He is a fool," Tahzay said. "In his heart he is all fool. All soft, like a woman."

The Arivaipa Apaches had stopped before Victorio's wickiup. Anna saw Shastazah come out with a covered clay bowl. Then Victorio came out. The Arivaipa dismounted, and Victorio and the squat chief touched one another's shoulders, but did not embrace. You could tell by their stances, the slowness of their movements, that they were speaking to one another in the high formal idiom. A boy came up and took the Arivaipa horses, and the men sat to eat.

"Who are the young chiefs?" Joaquin said.

Tahzay shrugged. "Nodakin and Klinnyti. These chiefs know nothing of the making of war."

Joaquin said, "The Arivaipa can fight, Tahzay."

Tahzay squatted down and began to roll himself a cigarette. "They do not like it. They are better at growing corn."

"The Mimbreños grow corn," Joaquin said matter-of-factly.

Tahzay looked up quickly; then he grinned. "Only at Ojo Caliente, where *Ysen* makes the good corn weather. At the other rancherías I have seen the Mimbreños grow good fighting men."

Joaquin looked at Anna. "Do you follow this?"

"A little." She said to Tahzay, "Is this man a great chief?"

"The greatest chief of all, so say the Arivaipa," Tahzay said and laughed a long time at his own joke.

"And what do the Chiricahua say?"

Tahzay stopped laughing and looked at Joaquin. "Your *niña* has a sharp tongue, Joaquin." He said to Anna, "The Chiricahua say the Arivaipa fight if they must. They would rather live in one place and grow gardens."

"Where do they live?" Anna said.

"Here in the mountains," Tahzay said. "For four harvests now. It is very bad for them. Their lands in the Gila Valley have been taken away from them. When your soldiers are all dead, the Arivaipa will go back to the Gila and hoe their gardens and not have to fight any more."

Anna looked him right in the eye. She wished to say, Perhaps the Chiricahua could learn from them, but she did not quite dare.

Instead she said, "They are not my soldiers." She kept her voice quiet but it was barbed.

Again Tahzay laughed. "Joaquin, you must make a hackamore for her . . . the kind with knots at the mouth to pinch off any sound she might make."

Joaquin smiled but said nothing. It was not the first time he had seen men who hoed gardens. He thought there must be something in the Arivaipa heads different from the things in the heads of their brother tribes and bands, and, unlike Tahzay, he did not feel capable of judging which things were good and which bad.

Before dark was complete, Victorio, Cuchillo Amarillo, Mangas Chie, Tahzay, Pionsenay, Eskiminzin, and the two young Arivaipa chiefs went into a newly erected steam wickiup. The doorkeeper sang one song and began to dip water on the red-hot stones. The naked men sweated and grew weak. They sang the four ceremonial songs and came out and plunged into the icy water. When they had dressed they were strong and clearheaded.

The chiefs sat in a circle with Victorio at its heart. Behind him were the men and behind them the women and children. Some dogs also sat down here and there in the circle, begging human warmth. Anna sat beside Shastazah, behind Joaquin. Over his shoulder she could see Victorio, cross-legged, and beside him, on his left, the heavy-set Arivaipa chief. His broad face was not expressionless after all: the black eyes were very shrewd, slightly squinted, and he had a kind-cut mouth. There was plenty of tobacco and corn-husk wrapping, and they smoked, and each man had a *tus* of *tulepah* beside him. The first flare of the fire had died, and now it burned comfortably, neither too big nor too hot.

Eskiminzin, as guest, spoke first. He had a slight but pronounced stutter. There were polite inquiries as to the health of the great chief Cochise, who had sent as his representative his loyal son the great chief Tahzay. There were inquiries as to the health and whereabouts of those great Mimbreño chiefs Delgadito, Ponce, and Cuchillo Negro. Also the great chief of his people, Victorio, and his great warrior sons. The talk was very slow, almost deliberate, and some of it was done with the hand sign every Indian from the eastern shores through the Plains Tribes to the northern peoples understood, and which gave them a universal language in which any Indian, anywhere, could speak always with any other Indian.

Victorio said, "How does my brother Eskiminzin winter in the mountains?" He knew the answer but he held to decorum.

And Eskiminzin said, "We fare badly here. We are not people of the heights. We cannot grow our crops here; the time is too short for our corn and melons and squash." He looked into the fire. "Last time of Ghost Face, my people ate of hide." A glint of humor came into his eyes, in no way sardonic. "It is well known to the Arivaipa there is no nourishment in hide." And the memory flooded back upon him, sad and terrible: the children crying with hunger, the old people dying, the women with their arms clasped across their aching bellies, the men too weak to hunt. He shook his head. He said, "This is between us, Victorio, let us stand upon no ceremony. You know what hunger is, as well as I. Why have you called me here?"

Victorio relaxed visibly. He picked up his *tus* and took a long drink and wiped his mouth on his wrist. He said, "Will the Arivaipa wait out Ghost Face as they waited it last season? Or will the Arivaipa stand with us?"

Eskiminzin was silent for a long time, for as long a time as it took him to roll a cigarette. He did not once drink. Finally he said, "Do you think I have not thought of this? Do you think the Arivaipa have not fought, when it was possible to fight?"

Victorio said, "It is easier to starve than to fight. What do the Arivaipa want?"

"We want back our lands along the Gila," Eskiminzin said.

"Number your people for us," Victorio said.

Eskiminzin stuttered and then began again, heavily. "With me, three hundred, many women. Scattered, another two hundred." He looked across Victorio, at Tahzay. "The Chiricahua know what it is to starve."

Tahzay stared at Eskiminzin. He recalled the winter the eighteen war parties had all gone out, and the second wife of his father had walked many miles through the snow to the mail agency in Apache Pass for a bag of corn. When the thought was through, he said, "We will never stop fighting for our land. This is my father's message, that no white eyes or *Nakaiyes* will cross our lands if we can stop them."

Victorio waited until he was certain Tahzay was finished. Then he said, "If the Arivaipa will fight they will have back their lands."

Eskiminzin said, "What about you, Victorio? You were slow to fight when the white eyes soldiers came out in the summer. The day is not so long gone when Cochise himself refused to carry on the fight. Now he fights harder than ever, and you with him. And the white eyes come on and come on. For every one you kill, twenty spring to take his place. Is this the way you will keep your lands?"

The words brought to Victorio that same dark depression which Cochise sometimes managed to waken in him, so that he would have believed the horse sickness had taken him again had not Nockahoto vanquished it. "You speak as Mangas spoke," he said suddenly.

Eskiminzin looked at him. "And is this a bad thing?" he asked quietly.

Victorio's mouth hardened. "Your head is not in the city of the white eyes," he said. "Speak on, and it may come to pass."

"What comes, comes," Eskiminzin said.

Victorio felt the anger begin to grip him. "What do your people want?" he said.

"My people want their lands back. They do not want to fight."

Victorio thought to mock, but then he rid himself of his anger. "And if the white eyes press you?" he said. "If they hunt you out?"

Eskiminzin said simply, "Then I will fight, if I can." He held out his wide, stubby-fingered hand. "This hand has killed. It will kill again if it must."

Victorio took another long drink. The whites of his eyes were beginning to vein red. "Why do you not take the Arivaipa into the caged earth for the winter? Eat the agency beef and go out again when the weather turns. They cannot hold you."

Eskiminzin shook his head. "Do not say this, Victorio, for the time will come. The time will come for you."

Victorio turned and met his eyes. There was a flashing light in his head, and he remembered the rock paintings of his dream. Into the caged earth, out again, a pattern to break the heart and the spirit. Eskiminzin's words turned him cold. Dreams were not dreams, but the doorway to what was to be. He took another drink and felt his courage return. He said, "We are a people. All our people together would make clear to the white eyes that our nation faces them as one man."

Eskiminzin said again, stuttering, stubborn, "I will fight if I must."

"Then you will ask help of the Chiricahua," Tahzay said.

Eskiminzin thought about this. He said, "Yes, if I need the help of the Chiricahua, I will ask it."

Victorio saw now that Eskiminzin was not to be swayed. Well, who would wish to sway a man who would rather starve in the mountains than go down and fight? He said, "There is a post of the soldiers on your land, Eskiminzin. Which is it called?"

"The post they call Grant," Eskiminzin said.

"That is the post with very few soldiers," Victorio said. "Some mounted, some *infantería*." His head was lowered now, eyes narrowed. "It would not be a hard thing to do, to take it. I will help you take it." He looked up at Eskiminzin.

Eskiminzin held his eyes, levelly. "I cannot accept this gift. Of what use would it be for me to own this post, and how long would we be allowed to remain? With every fight more of my men would die and more of my women mourn and more of my children be cast upon the kindness of others. Soon there will be no more Arivaipa. Soon there will be no more Mimbreños."

An old squaw threw more brush upon the fire. It flamed high, the brush crackling. A fountain of sparks showered up. A scarred yellow dog sat down in front of Eskiminzin and scratched itself.

Victorio said, "You are welcome to my home." He rose.

"*Enju,*" Eskiminzin said. "We go in the morning."

Victorio started to leave the circle. But he was caught by the unmoving squaws. He cast his eye over their firelit faces and was again angered and depressed. He read them, absorbed their message. Eskiminzin had impressed them. A leaner time, a thinner life, without war, without death. They seemed not to breathe, or to see, looking dead ahead.

He held out his empty *tus* and Shastazah came and took it and he followed her to the wickiup. Her face wore no sign. She handed him the filled *tus.* The words burst out of him.

"Well, who am I to listen to, woman?"

"Listen only to yourself, as always," she said quietly.

He raised his hand and struck her across the mouth. She rocked back, but her narrow face did not change; her eyes did not waver on his. He poured the *tulepah* out upon the ground and watched it puddle and sink. He walked into the wickiup and went down upon his knees, pretending to search for something under the piled hides of his bed. Shastazah came and rested her hands on his shoulders, and after a time he put his arms up, around her broad, sturdy hips.

He said to her, "I will go against my dream. I will not go on the caged earth."

She did not say anything.

"Do you hear me?" he said.

"I hear you."

"And where do you wish to go?"

She closed her eyes. "What does it matter? Wherever you go I will go with you."

He said, "Break this ranchería in the morning. We will go to Santa Rita."

"You will not wait for Cuchillo Negro?"

"He knows where the Mimbreño rancherías are."

She said, "Sleep."

He said, "Sleep is for children and dogs."

He sat down before the wickiup. He watched his people disperse and the big fire die. He saw the stars go down the sky. Sleep did not come near him, but at dawn Shastazah found him slumped over, conquered at last, uncovered, and his flesh cold. She saw for the first time the coarse gray strands in his hair and the fingers of age brushing his face. She covered him, but while she was building up the fire, he wakened.

He watched his people break the camp, the women salvaging their hides and skins from the wickiups, the horses and mules being loaded. Eskiminzin had ridden out on the first floating light of day. He watched Tahzay's fighting bucks strip down and begin to paint again. They would ride out ahead. Then would come half his own bucks, under him; then the women and children and old people, then the other half of his force under Mangas Chie, all strung out in separate units of travel. He watched the women arrange their food caches and saw some of them arm themselves, mainly with knives. He watched Joaquin's *niña* go down to the creek for water. Then he saw Joaquin come out. He wore only a clout and a dark blue shirt and carried his carbine. He stopped and dropped some things, cigarette makings, signal mirror, deer-gut water tube, into the turned-down cuff of his right moccasin. Joaquin came toward Victorio and sat down, not speaking.

The sound of the grinding stones in the doorway of his wickiup annoyed Victorio. He turned his head; his face was gaunt, puffy under the eyes. "What is it?" he said.

Then he smelled it, the fine dark rich smell of ground coffee beans. Like a small miracle. He said, "There was no coffee last night for the *yoshte*." But Shastazah said nothing until she had made the brew and cooled it properly by dipping the *tus* in and out of a bowl of cold water. Then she said, "When there is enough coffee there is enough. When there is not enough coffee there is only enough for you."

A long look passed between them. Then she went to her packing. Victorio finished the coffee and said to Joaquin, "You listened well?"

"I listened well," Joaquin said.

"I watch well," Victorio said. "You put tobacco into your cuff." Joaquin took out some leaf and paper and handed it to him. "The women believe I do the wrong thing," Victorio said, rolling himself a cigarette.

"This is not for me to speak of," Joaquin said.

"What does your woman think?"

"She does not want there to be fighting," Joaquin said. "But it is different with her."

"It is not different," Victorio said. "All women are the same. Never living the day that is here, always trying to live the days which are coming." He blew smoke out his nostrils. "So, Joaquin, do you stay with us now? Do you fight with us?"

Joaquin looked down at the ground, between his moccasins. "I do not know," he said. His voice was so miserable that Victorio knew and could have answered for him.

Victorio felt the loss already and protested in himself the unreasonableness of this. Had Joaquin married into the Coyoteros or the Mescaleros or the Chiricahua, he would have gone with his wife's people. He said, "You are coming to Santa Rita with us?"

Joaquin nodded. He felt better for having made Victorio no offer, no covenant.

Victorio gave a single laugh and pointed. Joaquin saw Anna fighting with the lead pack horse. She had not figured the intricacies of Mimbreño lashing, but she knew to the last knot the army's old diamond hitch. It took two people to execute it, and Joaquin got to his feet.

When he did, Victorio said, "Joaquin. You owe us nothing."

"Only my life," Joaquin said. "Only the air I breathe."

"Listen," Victorio said. "I tell you this. I tell myself this. I tell my people this. We come naked into this world. But we have one thing. One thing is given to us. Every man has his time in the sun, and that is all he has." He looked straight before him, and his voice was pitched flat. "What he does in this time is all he does. What he is in this time is all he is."

Joaquin stood looking down at him. He saw with fear how brief this time was, how precious. When he walked away, dread walked with him.

Shastazah had begun to take the hides down from the frame of the wickiup, but Victorio still sat, watching the morning mist begin to burn off and the first glint of sun in the wet golden grasses along the creek.

Twenty-one

They were breaking horses in the sand along the San Pedro. Some of the good Mex riders were passing, and there was a fresh bunch of gelded broncs in. Shafter stood with the stout crutch head jammed into his armpit, watching.

For all-round riding, he thought you couldn't beat the Mex. There were few white men could break like the Mex, and he'd never seen a cavalryman sit a sunfisher more than five seconds, although a lot of them tried and kept trying. There were two corrals down along the sand flats, one with a big cavvy answering to a bell mare and one to break the mustangs. There was a flat-faced little Mex working this morning, and a few more yelling, "Bronco, bronco," whenever the wild one made a good pass at shaking its rider. The army didn't like roughing up, but they needed horses broke to the saddle.

The Mexicans were hazing six or eight thick-coated broncs in the corral, and after a while they picked out a bunch-muscled ratchet head and roped him while the rider got a plain roping saddle on him and a hackamore with blinders and *fiador* knotted under the protesting jaw, throat-latcheted, running clean around the neck.

Shafter watched them turn him loose and the blinders go up. For a minute he just stood there, looking dazed so nobody would guess he was thinking, and then he shot straight up in the air and came down with a crash that must've jarred the little Mex's kidneys loose. He bucked a few times, while the Mex cut off his wind with the throat latchet, but he didn't have as much fight as he looked like he had. Next time he'd submit to the saddle without blinders, and if he felt like renewing the fight he'd have a big Spanish spade bit in his mouth. If he really wanted to push it, he'd get his mouth cut to hell, but if he decided to go along with it, he would eventually discover that the thing that could make his mouth a bloody mess worked two ways. Exploring the iron torment, he'd find there was an intriguing little wheel right in the middle of it. For some reason it was very comforting for a horse, to stand turning that little wheel with his tongue.

The second wild one dumped the little Mex but made no effort to stomp him as a killer horse would do, and they roped him and started all over again. A breaker seldom got killed by a horse. What killed him was the bone-splintering gut-tearing time in the saddle. The good breakers were all young, and if they made it to middle age there wasn't a thing inside them was in its rightful place any more.

While Shafter stood there, Lieutenant Royal Whitman came up, and Marijildo Grijalba, the Spanish-Mexican interpreter, riding short stirrup, *a la jinete*, with his feet cocked way up and his knees clenched, so that he appeared to crouch in the saddle. Whitman was no kid; privately Shafter thought he was pretty old to be sitting around a cavalry lieutenant, even though he had risen from ranks to colonel during the war and had taken the break to lieutenant in order to stay in the army. Or maybe his kind tired resigned face just made him look older than he was, and his eyes, which seldom sparked over anything. Grijalba wore the faint tracing of a mustache and looked like he had to shave his handsome face now and then. He was probably the best interpreter the U. S. Army ever had in the Southwest, speaking Spanish, English, all the Apache dialects, the similar Navajo, and nearly all the far-western tongues, and what he couldn't do with speech he could do with his hands, fast as a snake, having evidently been born with it all as some men are born with a head full of mathematical equations.

"Good morning," Whitman said in his soft middle-pitched voice. He was looking off toward the corral. "Paco's got his work cut out for him, I see."

"I wonder Paco's ribs ain't comin' out his ears," Shafter said.

"Not a very likely-looking cavvy," Whitman said. "Pack stock."

Marijildo Grijalba laughed. "Very necessary, the pack horse. Carries well. No spirit. Apache steals him easily. Rides him to death. Eats him for breakfast."

Shafter didn't feel like laughing. He hadn't felt like laughing in quite a while. The February sun was getting hot and high and he wanted to get in out of it. Camp Grant, near the junction of the San Pedro and the Gila, might be run-down, as Walter Degnan proclaimed, but there were advantages. There were trees and water and pretty country and a seemingly unlimited supply of whiskey. All of a sudden the horse breaking ceased to interest him, and he wanted to sit down so badly he broke out in a sweat. He realized he had been standing motionless a long time. Now, when he took a step, pain went crashing through him and he gritted his teeth. Royal Whitman apparently wasn't even looking at him, but he dismounted, took his mount's bridle, and began to walk along with Shafter. Marijildo turned down to the corral.

"You figure to hold me up?" Shafter said shortly. Somehow he didn't like the gesture, Whitman walking along with him. He didn't like being short either, but it came easier than anything else.

Whitman smiled quietly. He did not know this man Shafter, knew even less about him, but he understood how he might feel in the same circumstance. "I don't expect so," he said, "unless you ask me."

Shafter looked straight ahead, swinging the crutch but putting the foot down in-between as hard as he could, taking a kind of vicious satisfaction in the act. His face felt stiff as a sun-dried hide. Pain had etched short sharp lines around his eyes, totally unlike the lines of squint and weather, and there was a single hard line at the corner of his mouth. One lock of hair, above the left eye, looked strange as the devil because it was coming in white, very odd in the blondness. He felt roughed up as the broncs: the leg hadn't healed properly, mainly because Willson and Obre had been brow-beaten into treating Shafter Shafter's way. Gribbons had had to break it again.

Four months was a long time. He could remember the day four months was nothing, a drop in the bucket of eternity.

Whitman matched his slow progress into the unstockaded post, not a lot different from the Tucson post and fifty-five miles north-east of it, but smaller, with all of fifty troopers and some infantry redlegs in garrison. Shipshape and top-notch it might not be, but there was a roofed porch on Whitman's office and a rocking chair on the porch. The rocking chair had sort of become Shafter's property. He never rocked in it, but he sat in it.

He humped up the single step, slammed the crutch down, and lowered himself into the chair. Whitman pulled the water *olla* off its rawhide sling and offered it. Shafter shook his head. "It's got two vinegarroons and a tarantula in it," he said.

Whitman shuddered and hung it up again. He made a slight bow, as if to an audience. "In that event I repair to my bottle, which, being corked, is safe from the infiltration of all the assorted hairy thousand-legged beasts this country breeds so freely." He straightened. "Join me."

Again Shafter shook his head. "I reckon I'll just sit a while, Royal."

Whitman went on into his small office. Shafter sat with his leg stiff before him, looking off at the green rim of trees in the distance, along the water. The sun was bright and fine; it was hard to believe it was winter, real snow winter, anywhere in this country, but it was. He knew for himself how it would be in the high mountains, and he'd heard from men who had seen it, how the snow lay in the red ledges of the big canyon to the north, how you could stand on the rim and look down the layered snow to where the narrow Colorado raced its churning brown length between the miles-high walls. From southern Texas to the coast of California it was still summer. Like Mexico, but it wasn't Mexico, and the thought of Mexico made him sore with disappointment.

The saving grace about a nightmare was that as a rule you forgot it in short order. But every detail of that nightmare on the desert, while he had been conscious, was clear as glass in his mind. Whenever he thought about it, it was with an almost childlike wonder.

Because even in the moment when he knew he had touched the bone of his own body, knew with certainty what had happened to him, he saw everything he had planned and waited for go glimmering like a firefly, lighting its own way through the sage twilight. So the leg was busted. Or maybe just cracked, but when he walked on it, it had snapped. He could remember hoisting himself on his elbows and looking down impersonally at where his thigh lay stretched out flat. Then there was a funny demarcation, like maybe the laying on of a place of light, or shadow, he wasn't sure which, and then the rest of his leg twisted so that what should have been his kneecap appeared to be the back of his leg, bone protruding right through his breeches, with the ankle lying flat on the ground and the whole leg looking about half a mile shorter than it should have looked.

He heard Willson say, "Jeeeezus Christ."

He heard himself say quietly, with what he did not know was shock, "The damn thing's busted."

Willson was hunched alongside him. "It sure as hell is." There was a kind of awe in his voice.

Nothing hurt, anywhere. He knew he should just twist the leg back where it should be, but as he was thinking very rationally, very coolly, he also knew that this would be impossible. He just lay there, thinking and listening.

Obre said, "What the hell do we do now? He can't make a saddle."

Willson said, "Dunno." Shafter saw him take off his hat and scratch the back of his head. "If we could rig a travois we could make it back."

"So you got a blanket, where you gonna get poles? Rig it without poles, he's gonna get scraped to hell. Or the horse'll kick his brains out."

The shock was coming on now, icy and rather pleasant. He felt like a big slab of felled wood with a thinkpiece in it. Thinking clearer than maybe he'd ever thought in his whole life. While he was congratulating himself on how clear thinking he was, he saw Willson had pulled a knife and was hunkered down by him again. "Don't touch that boot," he said.

"I got to get 'er off, hang it," Willson said. "I sure can't pull 'er off."

"You ain't gone to cut that boot," he said. "Linus gave me these boots and you ain't gone to touch 'em." He hoisted up a little higher.

"Shafter, don't you give me no argyments," Willson said.

"You do what I tell you," Shafter said, numb as a hibernating bear, straining to breathe now. "Split that pants leg."

Willson split it.

"Now you stomp that bone back where it belongs."

Willson got up and turned away.

"Listen," Shafter said, real quiet and steady. "You do what I tell you. If you don't do what I tell you, when I get back on my feet I am gone to bust your leg. I am gone to bust every bone in your body."

They were talking together, apparently not listening. But maybe they did listen, because after a minute Obre said, "Hang on, horse," and he lay back and gripped his own belt and felt one or the other of them take his foot by the heel and jerk the leg out straight again. A hideous weakness flushed him black and empty as a mine shaft, but he still didn't feel anything and he thought that might be a good sign. He said, "Get the Henry."

Obre pulled the Henry out of the saddle scabbard and came over with it.

"Splint it," Shafter said.

Obre laid the Henry along the outer leg, but it didn't seem to conform there, so he laid it along the inner leg. "Unload it, you damn fool," Willson yelled, "you want him to blow off his. . . ." Obre unloaded it and tried again. Willson was ripping up blanketing and talking to himself while he did it. When he had three or four strips he came over and bound the Henry tight to Shafter's leg, and for the first time Shafter noted there was feeling somewhere in him, when the cold metal lay hard against his flesh. When Willson finished he said, "Now you get me on that horse."

"Nope," Willson said. "Ain't gone to do no such thing. Ob, he's runnin' gun now, so he stays with you. I'm gone back to the post and rout out that ambulance wagon."

Shafter said evenly, "And leave me here to get greenflesh? You get me on my feet, Willson."

Between them, they got him up. The minute they did he passed out cold.

"There, by God, providence's on our side," Willson said. "I was tryin' to figure how to do that without usin' a gun butt and addin' to his misery." He was in the saddle fast as Obre had ever seen him move. "I don't need to tell you I aim to get through and I aim to get back. Keep him down, Ob, even if you got to tie him there."

After he couldn't hear horses any more, Obre grabbed his own horse and the dun and the pack horse and ground picketed them. Then he sat down to wait, with near ten miles between him and the post, and as soon as he did it started to rain. It wasn't a hard rain, but it was no mist either. Almost immediately it took away the smell of the dust, or anyway changed the smell of the dust. Now it smelled like wet dust. Obre broke out the 'paulins. He knew if he had some sticks he could tent up the 'paulins, but as he didn't have any sticks he had to settle for laying one over Shafter and wrapping himself up in the other. He thought it was hellish bitter cold as it had ever been, and he felt it badly, but he figured Shafter wouldn't feel it at all. He wasn't about to scout up any wood for a fire that might bring Apaches down on them. Shafter lay like he was dead, with the rain on his face.

With not even a star to tell the time by, Obre calculated it was maybe over an hour before Shafter woke up and wanted some water. Obre gave it to him, and after that Shafter asked him how come it was so wet, and Obre said it was just the boat had sprung a leak but not to worry, he was bailing, and Shafter went back into whatever time and place it was he had disappeared into earlier.

Obre slept in fits and starts. Usually it was his head falling on his chest that woke him up. Half of him was riding with Willson and half of him was just plain mad. It galled him that there wouldn't even be any dawn showing, weather like this.

Shafter started talking and Obre said, "Huh?" before he realized Shafter wasn't talking to him; not talking to anybody, in fact, unless it was to himself. Obre tried not to listen, knowing Shafter was out of his head now, but there wasn't anything else to listen to, except the rain making small noises on the canvas. Obre wished he would shut up, but he just kept talking, and repeating himself, too, which wasn't like Shafter.

Just alike. No place. Nobody. You and me. All the ones dead up above and all the rest walkin' here, and you and me with no place, floatin' four feet off the ground, in-between the dead and the walkin'. Don't ask anything but to be let alone, you and me. And all the time knowin' nothin' good can come of it, all the time knowin' there ain't nothin' ahead but darkness and no hope. No hope. You'd of stayed with me, little girl, we'd of at least been together in the dark, not askin' a thing of each other. We'd of let each other be, but at least we wouldn't of needed bein' alone.

Obre thought he must figure he was talking to his dead girl, but then again it didn't sound like anything anybody might say to their wife. It didn't sound like anything anybody might say to anybody anyway, and it made Obre nervous.

He was dead asleep when the shots sounded. Still pretty far off: a series of three and then two, the whole thing done twice, the signal the three of them had agreed upon a long time ago and never had a chance to use. Or had to use. Then he heard the clicking of the ivory harness rings, and the six-mule team which drew the post ambulance appeared. Willson was riding a fresh horse out of the post remuda; his own horse had been ridden so hard it would never be good for anything again, as long as it lived.

For the first few days nobody bothered him, except Gribbons, who had a lot more in his head than all the bone that showed so plain, and a good pair of hands, although Obre called him a horse doctor. Gribbons right off made sure, as much as was in his power, there wasn't any likelihood of greenflesh, and Shafter lay on his back in the post hospital in company with three ambulatory wounded who hadn't been quick enough to get out of Tahzay's way and stared at the wall and cursed Gribbons and his morphine needle.

Willson hung around but after a while he didn't see Obre and asked, and Willson said Ob was running some duty or other for the colonel and would be back. Shafter didn't push it. After Degnan (and that meeting was a blur to him) the first person came by to see him was Katie, who stood in the doorway and said with satisfaction, "Well, didn't get far, did you?" And he thought back to her pronouncement about the green grass and trees and said, "You either." Then she came and put her hand on his and said, "John, if you want me to, I can nurse you all you need," and he only said, "Katie, just go away, just go away, will you please?" Meaning to say he was sorry, he didn't mean it, meaning to say it sometime when he was responsible for what he was saying. But he was responsible: he threw Bleeker out, too, and just lay waiting for the day Linus would walk through that door.

Willson finally told him the truth, a week later. Somebody had taken a shot at Obre, practically on the post environs, so Obre'd had about all he figured he could stomach. There had been another Chiricahua raid at Pete Kitchen's, down on the Potrero, and Pete told the military if they'd guard while he got his harvest in it would be the last time he'd ever ask their help again, and the military had said yes. So Pete said bluntly, I hear you got a gunslinger around. I need a gunslinger. And that was how come Obre was hired down to Pete Kitchen's, walking around looking for Apaches to shoot.

Then Shafter said, "Why don't you go south, Willson? I'll pick you up wherever you say."

"I was kind of figurin' San Lorenzo," Willson said gravely. He looked down at his hat, which he was holding. "You really mean that?"

"Sure I mean it," Shafter said. His eyes were closed.

"'Twon't be long," Willson said.

"Hell no, it'll be no time."

They didn't look at one another. Willson said, "Well, I'll be seein' you then."

Some days later Gribbons rebroke the leg.

One afternoon when the three ambulatory were all out in the sun playing cooncan with a couple of the Tenth, Shafter looked up and saw Linus was standing in the doorway and didn't feel surprised, didn't feel anything, knowing it was going to come to pass. Linus looked just like he always looked, a little stern-lipped maybe, but self-contained. He didn't smile, but he said, "You always were an awkward fool."

"Me?" Shafter said. "I was just sittin' there mindin' my own business."

Then Linus said, "The day you decide to mind your own business will be the day the world comes to an end." There wasn't any anger in him. Shafter thought again that one of the first things that had drawn him to this boy was his ability to get up after he'd got knocked down. Linus pulled a straight-backed chair away from the wall and up to the bed and sat down in it. He looked at Shafter very directly.

"You look like hell. How do you feel?"

"I feel like hell," Shafter said.

"Your own fault. If you'd stayed where you were, the way you were, till Willson got back with the ambulance. . . ."

Shafter said, "I wasn't aimin' to come back."

Then Linus said, "John, why did you do it?"

Shafter lay there and thought for a long time. He lay perfectly still, with his eyes narrowed and his upper lip flattened out in that way he had. He said, "I did it because it was what she wanted, Linus."

Linus was sitting forward, on the edge of the chair. His voice and his eyes were probing, relentless, not sparing Shafter, but more, much more, not sparing himself. "I've had a long time to think, John. I think to myself, God in heaven, am I ever going to see the end of all this? Is this the end, what's happened now? What you made happen."

He was silent. Shafter said, "Is that all you think?"

"No. I'll tell you what I think. I think, do you still love that girl? Do you still want any part of her, knowing she's been with that half breed? What would you do tomorrow if she came back and said she'd marry you? How would it affect your life, the career you're so set on, your rise in the army? Are you rather . . . what? . . . vicariously excited by what she has done, or is the whole thing so repugnant to you you couldn't ever face her again? In short, are you really the noble little Jesus you pretend to be? That's what I think."

Shafter said, "Well, that all makes sense, I reckon. The only thing you left out was how wronged you feel. That always kind of itches a man where he can't scratch. Before you add that one to your thoughts, you ponder on the old saw you can't live anyone else's life for 'em." He made a move to push the rough cotton sheet off his half-naked body. "If you had kept that girl here against her will, that would of been the great wrong."

Linus' voice was harsh now. "I want to feel the inevitability of this, and I can't. My pride is involved . . . to be hamstrung with the fact that after all this time she preferred someone else over me. All the way over me, and not even a white man at that." His hands made a meaningless jerking motion, almost independent of him. "No, I didn't mean that, about being white, it doesn't matter any more."

Shafter said, "I reckoned you could stand on your own feet, Linus. I saw that in you the night Cec Horne got killed. I'm sorry, about how it is for you. But I'm sorrier about Joaquin. I got a sadness, a great sadness."

Linus moved restlessly; then he laughed. "Save your sadness for the helpless and the hopeless. Your friend and Anna are well matched. Any two people so set in their own way that they'll lie and cheat and maybe even kill, they belong together."

"I look at that another way," Shafter said. "It's a kind of courage, maybe."

"Courage?" Linus said.

"The guts to beat down every obstacle in the way, not ever counting the cost, so's to have some of the damn little happiness and peace granted to man in the span of his days. You think that doesn't take courage? Most of us drift because that's easiest. . . . If a little of what's happy comes our way we'll take it, but we won't work for it. Most of us don't know what we want to make us happy; that's part of the reason we sit tight, hoping whatever it is will show. And selfish. Strange partners, maybe, but there they are, courage and selfishness. I like people who know what they want, right off. I like you, but you don't know what you want any more, do you?"

Linus said, "I thought I did. Now I'm frightened of how I feel, and I keep telling myself it doesn't matter, because there is little possibility I will ever see Anna again. And yet I think that even with that knowledge I should keep feeling the way I felt all these years. What is wrong? What's wrong with love itself, that it can't be sustained on the highest plane at all times?"

"Love?" Shafter said. "How about pain? How about fear? Or grief?" He was very tired now, and yet he felt closer to Linus than he had ever felt before, even on that night he had gone down to run out the Apache herds. He no longer felt that he had betrayed or that he had executed a major kindness, so that there was nothing further for him to be condemned for or absolved from, that he had only done what had to be done. He said, "I don't know, Linus, I never gave much thought on it, but I expect that people who love are hung together by the simple thing of bein' together, day in, day out. You can't spend every hour thinkin' about loving, most of the time you're just together and the good thing is when you don't have to think about it, it's there and granted and you feel it and know it. Two people always got to keep their separate ways, be themselves, and there's a part of everybody, even the loved, you can't ever reach. That's part of the sadness of loving. You don't think loving is a sad thing?" He looked up at the ceiling, not wanting to watch the opposition to this idea spread on the boy's face. "You can believe me, loving is the saddest thing in the world, sadder even than dyin'." Now he looked back, and Linus was clear-eyed, responsive. "So you don't know how you feel?"

Linus shook his head.

Shafter said, "Why don't you go on back East, like your pa figured for you?"

"And run out on her? Leave her here, when sometime she might need me?"

A corner of Shafter's mouth dragged down, wry, a little sardonic. He said, "For a man doesn't know how he feels, you sure know how you feel."

Linus sat there for a while. It was quiet in the big dobe room, and sunlight shafted in and they could hear laughter and exaggerated groaning and hissed importuning of the dice, where the men rattled and threw them, outside the door. The soft, slurry Negro voices. Looky them sevens, three in a row. Don' you touch a finger on them dice, you'll colden 'em on me. Shafter said, "Could you turn me some, Linus? My back sure feels like it's cracked in half."

Linus shifted him, deftly, efficiently. Shafter winced. "Is there anything you want?" Linus said.

Shafter said, "I want to get out of here."

Linus smiled a little.

"I'm not foolin', Linus. I don't want to stay here. I get my mind set on gone someplace, I want to go."

Linus said coolly, "You don't want to have to call Linus Degnan every time you want to turn over in bed."

"That's about it," Shafter said levelly.

"All right. As soon as Gribbons says you can be moved. You want to go into Tucson?"

"I ain't thought about it."

"Think about it," Linus said. He was standing now, looking down at Shafter. "I never did know why it was I liked you, Shafter."

"Do you know now?" Shafter said, bitter, intractable, wishing he'd broken his neck instead of his leg.

"Yes," Linus said. He went away.

A month later they moved Shafter over to Camp Grant. It was Bleeker gave him the idea, one red evening when they were sitting outside hospital watching the sun set and the flag come down and feeling taps in the marrow of their bones. Bleeker said, "Talk about nothing happening anywhere in the world. I don't know what there is about Grant. A feeling there's not a soul around for four hundred miles. Not that I was bored there; Royal Whitman's an educated man. We talked a lot and drank a lot, but if that isn't the post God forgot. He's a lonely man, too, Whitman, for some reason or other. Something lacking. I don't mean in him, but something he needs to do to make up for the lack. And what can he do, him and his half a hundred, wandering off now and then on scout, but mainly stagnating. Just stagnating. General Stoneman was so quick to close down posts he felt were useless out here, it's a wonder he overlooked Grant. Well, it's too late now."

"How's that?" Shafter said.

"Haven't you heard? They're pressuring Stoneman out of command. He killed too many Indians."

"He what?" Shafter said.

"He did. Two hundred accounted for last summer. The Indian Department's up in arms."

"I thought that was what they sent him out here for," Shafter said, amused but a little riled, too.

"No, no, not at all," Bleeker said. He took out an immaculate handkerchief and wiped his eyes with it, as though he were laughing, or crying. "That was what the *War* Department sent him out here for. The *Indian* Department gave its blessing because they thought he was going to save every red soul in the Territory. They have pressured him badly. Tremendous editorials in the eastern papers."

"You ain't tellin' me a newspaper editorial can put a man off his horse, are you?" Shafter said.

"Shafter, my friend, you would break out in a rash if I told you what my profession can accomplish."

"So your profession has stretched Stoneman's neck for the ax?"

"Totally," Bleeker said. "When the Indian Department pushed him, Stoneman eased off. Of course they didn't take too good a look at the record."

"What record's that?" Shafter said.

"Don't misunderstand me, Shafter, I hardly ever read newspapers. I merely write them. I recall writing, just recently, the record. The record reads, in part, in the last two months: a successful series of raids on the stage stations at San Pedro, Cienega Springs, and Picacho. Stock stolen from Kitchen's. Dead, one army paymaster and escort near Fort McDowell, two Mexicans near Fort Wallen, and six on the Potrero, one mail carrier at San Xavier, big cattle raid on the Gardner ranch, with one Mexican boy captured, three men of a supply train near Fort Crittenden killed . . . not to mention goods worth six thousand dollars captured, twenty-some mules taken from Fort McDowell." He paused thoughtfully. "Let's see, then there was that big killing that made all the papers: Kennedy and Israel, prominent citizens in these parts. Oh, and the girl . . . another Ysabel, returning home to Sonora with a big escort. Only they didn't take her home to wash the pots and sweep out the wickiups for them. They killed her."

Shafter said, "You think Ob and me were kind of lucky to get in off the desert that night?"

"You know Apaches never attack at night. Or in the rain." He smiled briefly. "And you know that Apaches, when the going is as fine as they're having it right now, will perhaps change their minds and attack when and where they can."

"And how does the Indian Department feel about this, they got tears in their eyes?" Shafter said.

"Wedded to their theory. Unfortunately Stoneman backed off when the shot was thickest. You should see what the Arizona *Miner* and the Tucson *Citizen* are doing to him. They're making it plain that far from killing enough Apaches he's barely tapped the source. The verdict seems to be, don't kill them or quit, or kill them all or quit."

"That does seem to be kind of a predicament to be in," Shafter said slowly. "I think Stoneman's done a lot of good, but of course the Indian Department don't listen to me or none like me. By God, every poor officer got stuck with a command out here was gone to wipe out the Indian trouble, wasn't he? You reckon there's one made could do it?"

"There might be," Bleeker said. "There's talk they're turning the command over to Crook."

Shafter said, "I hear tell he's an Indian fighter for sure."

"Crook," Bleeker said, "is *the* Indian fighter, gunpowder for blood and cold steel for guts."

"Quit talkin' like you were writin' for one of your damn newspapers," Shafter said. "Well, I think I'll hang around and watch 'em pressure Crook, too."

"I think not," Bleeker said. "There's nothing in his record says he's ever been pressured before. He's stern, but he's got a reputation for justice. Do you know he doesn't even wear a uniform half the time? . . . White duck suit and a sun helmet, like he'd just come out of Africa."

"My, my," Shafter murmured. "What are the Yankees comin' to?"

Bleeker didn't seem to hear him. "After Crook, I should think Howard would be the choice. A more temperate man could perhaps accomplish. . . ."

Shafter said, "Old one-arm O. O. Howard. He's the one they call the Christian general, ain't he? Just what Victorio needs, a little Jesus-ing. Of course, you could all just go home and forget about this country and leave it for us that can get along with the Apache without the army."

Bleeker looked at him. "You are a very peculiar man, Shafter, if you'll forgive my saying so."

Shafter laughed. "This Texican does his mourning for the underdog. Be he Confederate Texican or be he Apache."

"Who ever heard of a Texican wasn't the biggest, smartest, strongest, most successful braggart that ever lived?"

Shafter looked up. Degnan was coming across the compound toward them, and Shafter spoke quickly. "I don't feel too strong right now, even for a Texican. About Grant. You think this Lieutenant Whitman might like some Texican company?"

"I think the poor man would welcome it," Bleeker said. "Are you restless?"

"I was born restless."

Walter Degnan had a bottle of brandy with him. It was queer, almost exasperating, how grateful Walter Degnan was to Shafter, as if Shafter had removed from his life an obstacle he felt completely unable to overcome. His entire comment had been a brief reference to the fact that he believed the girl irrevocably gone, that he was saddened beyond measure, and that he knew her incurably insane. He would see to it that the troops believed she had been stolen again, offer a reward for the capture of the half breed, and that was an end to it. Over Shafter's mild protest at his judgment on Anna's mental state and a defense of Joaquin's natural rights, Degnan remarked shortly that it was a known ethnological fact that Apaches did not know romantic love in the sense white men knew it, and that therefore Anna could not be in her right mind when she chose to lead a barbaric existence with a barbarian. Then the only thing Shafter said was, "But Walter, you keep forgetting, barbarian or whatever, he ain't but half Indian." Degnan looked at him sharply, half-formed reprimand in the look, and then dropped it.

While they drank the brandy, Shafter said as soon as Gribbons gave him a pardon for all his crimes he thought he would maybe go over to Camp Grant and recuperate there for a while. Degnan agreed a change of scene was perhaps what he needed, among other unexpressed needs, and Shafter wrote a letter to Obre, telling him where he was, and went out in the ambulance again over Gribbons's protest.

The winter at Grant had been bearable. Whitman was unobtrusive and had some books, Fox P. Canby came over to see him, the weather held pure as crystal, and he was relieved to hear that a big party of Chiricahua had considerately waited until he left the post to stage a big raid on the very walls of Tucson, driving off a large herd of cows and oxen. On Christmas Day the cook came up with a brace of quail for officers' mess, a couple of wild turkeys, and a somewhat soggy plum pudding crowned with blazing brandy.

Leaning back in the rocking chair, Shafter let his hand hang over enough to rub the flank of Whitman's Dalmatian pup, who was trying to sleep and keep his tail out from under a rocker at the same time. While he half dozed himself, Marijildo came up and reached for the *olla* and tilted it up.

"I wouldn't," Shafter said.

Marijildo dumped the water out, along with the two centipedes and the tarantula. "All drowned," he said.

"Hard luck," Shafter said.

A lanky infantryman was running up from the corral, not just hurrying but at a dead run. "Paco has broken his head," Marijildo said. "That third one did all things but lie down and roll upon him."

The redlegs jumped the porch step without speaking and ran into Whitman's office. They could hear him, excited and without much coherence. They heard Whitman say, "Where?" and then he came out and said, "Come on, Marijildo."

"Where do we go?" Marijildo said.

"This boy says there's five Indian women down along the Gila. On this side. He couldn't understand a word they said, and they're so weak they can hardly walk."

They went off, down toward the river. Shafter sat up straighter in his chair, and the dog got up and loped off after Whitman. After a while Shafter saw them coming back, four or five redlegs, with the squaws bunched between them and hanging back, walking very slowly. Whitman brought them up on the porch, into the shade.

It was quite a spell before the women would talk. They were scared and sick, but they wouldn't sit down. Then one of them opened up, taken with Marijildo's perfect palaver and simple exhaustion. She talked quietly enough, but her flat, flesh-hanging face was twisted, either with emotion or hunger, Shafter thought.

"They're Arivaipa, sir," Marijildo said. "They came down to try and find something to eat. They say the Arivaipa are starving. As bad a winter as they've ever put in."

The woman spoke again, and when Marijildo listened now his face seemed to twist in sympathy with hers. "She says they wanted to see their own lands again, and if there was anything growing here they could take back for the children." Again the woman spoke, and this time she put her hand on Marijildo's arm. "The old people are dying quickly. She says for the old people death is

never far off, at any time, but the children die, too, and the whole
ranchería is one place of mourning."

Royal Whitman was standing with the dog at his heels. When he
spoke, Shafter sensed absolutely no hesitation in him, saw that he
was in complete command of the situation, saw that nothing would
sway him. He said, "Feed these women. I want provisions loaded
immediately and taken into that camp."

Shafter said, "You mean you gone to go in there, just cold, Royal?"

"What have we to fear from a starving ranchería?" Whitman
said. When he turned away, his eyes had gone dark, morose. "Merciful God," he said, almost to himself. "What are we doing to these
people?"

Half an hour later the wagons, two of them, and the five squaws,
and a detail of ten men, were on their way into the winter reaches
of the mountains.

Whitman was preoccupied and withdrawn for some days after
this. Whatever his starvation detail, as Shafter called it, had reported to him had pulled him into some shell in which he en-
couraged his already taciturn nature and his addiction to whiskey.
He was quietly drunk a lot of the time, and Shafter didn't bother
him about it.

It was a week later, without being spotted by a soul, guard or
chance observer or anybody else, mute testimony to the already
legendary unmarked appearance of the Indian, that the man suddenly stood before the porch of Whitman's office. They were all
sitting there, Whitman, Shafter, Marijildo, and the little breaker,
Paco, and the man came around the corner and halted before them,
very straight, almost proud, stocky, but with weariness carved all
over him like knife carvings in rock.

Royal Whitman got to his feet calmly, instantly sober, without
surprise. Shafter thought he looked, in that moment, as if this were
something he had expected, something he had been waiting for.
There was a spark in his eyes now.

Marijildo listened. When he turned to Whitman he said, "He
says he has come to thank you for the gift of food to his people. He
says he comes in peace and that he wants to place himself in the
hands of the military. He says his name is Eskiminzin, and that he
wants only to return to his lands here on the Gila and grow his
gardens again."

Twenty-two

The little Mexican village outside the Santa Rita copper mines had been deserted from the time Mangas Colorado had settled on Santa Rita as one of the principal Mimbreño rancherías. White men still came occasionally to work the mines, tough, experienced, well-armed men who knew what they were up against and were willing to take the risk. Depending on the presence or absence of the Mimbreños in or from the ranchería and the vagaries of the Indian mind, the miners were let alone or fought off. The Mexicans, many of whom had died of a plague, or simple terror, had not returned.

This was a good desert place, but Victorio had always been partial to Ojo Caliente and thought of it as the Mimbreño home. Out of their great emotional feeling for their land, the nomadic People, following not only the paths of war but the seasons of harvest, were prone to return to the place of the warm springs, where the great willows grew and the pleasant weather stayed the year round. But with his decision to remain at Santa Rita, and the journey safely accomplished from the mountain camp where Eskiminzin had refused his counsel, Victorio now oversaw the temporary dispersing of a portion of his people. Groups of them would come and go, women and children, too, establishing camps where the hunting or raiding were good, moving all they owned, erecting new wickiups, and, if the troops came near on their relentless pursuit and scout details, they would find only burned rancherías, women and children fleeing, men fighting rear-guard action, running even into the cold high places if they had to, long enough to hold off their pursuers.

Joaquin had in his mind several places where it might be possible for him to move with Anna, places where there would be water and fertile earth. Yet always he found some reason for rejecting the places he considered. He wished to be near enough to Victorio to maintain contact, and he felt that any proximity to white men might prove an insurmountable problem. The only solution to this problem would be Anna herself. She was white and would remain white. For him, even if he attempted the transformation from Mimbreño to white rancher, he had been thrown enough upon the world to fear bitterly the day of identification. He did not believe Anna was unhappy with his people, but he knew from experience the terrible need to belong. He admitted within himself that she no more belonged here than he belonged with her people, so that he was willing to accept, even to share, her longing that they live apart, build another life, forget many things, discover many things. Sometimes, watching her, he felt humble in the face of the gift which had been bestowed upon him.

To Anna, a new world opened at Santa Rita. For the first time she saw the wonderful mountain spirit dancers in their masks and headdresses, watched a few skilled Mimbreño women fashion clay pottery decorated with grotesque and amusing insects and animals, unique among the tribes of Apachería, who did little such craft work. And for a whole afternoon she sat fascinated while two men made a medicine disk, a sand painting for a boy who was ill. When it was finished, and the prayers sung, and at sundown the great wheel of red and black and blue sand destroyed, she was shocked at what seemed a desecration and not at all surprised that the boy's fever broke almost the moment the final grain had been brushed away.

There was talk that Cuchillo Negro was returning, and this was a time she dreaded, hoping there would not be prisoners. She thought she would speak to Joaquin now, quickly, suggest that they go out with one of the hunting groups, search for the place green and sheltered she was certain only awaited their finding.

She lost the opportunity. She was unsure of the month, but the spring rains were already threatening, promising benediction, and some of the chiefs had been in council with Victorio for nearly three days and late into the nights. On the second day, when Anna had gathered all her arguments, in the event they might be needed, Victorio sent for Joaquin and she did not see him to speak to until the decision had been made for them. It was some time before she connected this council with the two runners who had come into Santa Rita the day Victorio called the *yoshte*.

The council had demanded the erecting of a big new wickiup some distance out of the main ranchería, and of the ever-necessary steam house. Victorio had used the steam house only once. To

Cuchillo Amarillo he said, "I will go into this *yoshte* with a clear head, and I will keep my clear head until it is finished."

The second day the runners went away again, and Ponce came to tell Joaquin he was wanted. Joaquin was puzzled: both Victorio and Shastazah treated him more and more as a son. But he was not a chief, and he had never sat at chiefs' council. When he entered the wickiup, there were only Victorio, Cuchillo Amarillo, Ponce, Mangas Chie, and the old chief Nané, with loops of Mexican silver in his ears. Joaquin sat down on a horsehide directly opposite Victorio.

Victorio said without preliminary, "Joaquin, my sons are out upon the war trail. For a long time you have been a son to me. When you have a good hunt you give the best of it to my wickiup. When your *niña* has made special food she brings it to my woman. When my woman needs two more hands at any task your *niña* comes without the asking. Now I ask you a thing. Do you wish to go out as a war chief?"

Joaquin felt the blood rise in him, muscle jumped in the plane of his jaw.

Victorio said, "No man here is your enemy. All men here are your brothers and fathers. Answer."

"No," Joaquin said. He looked a long time straight into Victorio's steady black eyes.

"*Enju,*" Victorio said, almost casually. He began to roll himself a cigarette. He said, "You answer honestly. Had you said yes, we would know you say yes because you wish to please us. Your brothers and fathers gathered here know that you are honest and brave. They know your reason for refusing this thing. A small reason, some men might say, but when was a woman ever a thing but a man's whole reason for being here upon this earth at all." He half smiled, watching Joaquin. "And there is another reason. I remember Mitch-o. You remember him, and that he came among us, and that a woman of our people was his reason for many things."

"Yes," Joaquin said in a low voice. He was aware of the unwavering eyes upon him, and he sensed in their regard a greater thing than sympathy, an understanding, and he knew the wild questioning in himself that these people could understand and the white eyes could not. He said, "You show me great honor, my father."

"I only tell you my feeling in this," Victorio said. He drew on the cigarette, letting the smoke out his nostrils. He said, "The runners come to us with the news that the Arivaipa have returned to their own lands."

"They fought the soldiers at Camp Grant?" Joaquin said.

Victorio shook his head. "No, the soldier who commands this Grant sent food to them when they starved. Eskiminzin himself went down to the camp and talked with this soldier. There are now five hundred Arivaipa on their own land. They begin to hoe their gardens again, the soldier protects them, and they are eating good beef. They have also the promise of work at the *ranchos* when the harvests are ready." Again he smiled, but faintly. "Eskiminzin is on the caged earth, but it is his own earth. He will be rich and contented. Perhaps he shows us the way."

Joaquin said, "This is a good thing, I think."

The faint smile lingered on Victorio's mouth. He said, "I wish to see if this is a good thing. I wish to see if this is a good soldier. I wish to see how the Arivaipa fare with this soldier. I wish you to go as my *mensajero* and observe how go all things for Eskiminzin."

"Go to Camp Grant?" Joaquin said. "What is in my father's mind?"

Victorio crushed out his cigarette. His back straightened, and he was taller than the men who sat around him, and there were little glints like diamond, hard and bright, in the black pupils. He spoke harshly. "What is in my mind? What was in the mind of Mangas Colorado? What is in the mind of my brother Cochise, what is eating his heart, no matter how hard he drives his fighting parties? What is in the mind of Eskiminzin? Peace, Joaquin, peace."

"What is it you would do?" Joaquin said. A new hope was in him, and yet he felt also a heavy sadness come to do battle with it.

Victorio raised his hand and let it lie upon the arm of the old chief, Nané. "Of all my chiefs," he said, "Delgadito, Ponce, Chie, those who went with me to the Stronghold of my brother Cochise, these knew that I was at war within myself. But these are young chiefs, and their blood is restless. Delgadito says he would rather know a lean belly than beg beef of the white eyes. I cast back in my mind to think when Delgadito knew a lean belly, and I could find no time of my knowing. Yet I know this: Cochise knows it: more and more soldiers come, more and more *rancheros*, more and more miners. They come with their women and children, and this is a sign to me that they are certain they will win their war against us." He leaned forward. "All my chiefs here believe that there is only one way to tell whether or not we can live on the caged earth, and that is to go upon the caged earth. All but Nané." He regarded the old man beside him tolerantly, almost with affection. "He has seen nearly seventy harvests, but the old fires still burn in him."

"I will stand with you in this only to see you wrong," Nané said glumly. The silver in his ears glittered when he shook his head.

Joaquin said, "Surely you will not go to stay with the Arivaipa, even if they would have you there. They are not our people."

Again Victorio smiled, and now Joaquin could see that despite the attitude he assumed he was despondent. He did not answer Joaquin's question. He said, "Take your *niña* and go. Speak with Eskiminzin and see if he is satisfied." He saw Joaquin's hesitation. "There is no reason for any man to know your *niña.* . . . She looks more Mimbreño than you!"

This was a joke, and they laughed, but Joaquin was very grave. He said slowly, "I still believe this is a good thing. We will go at once."

"Chie goes to the Stronghold to tell my brother Cochise of this," Victorio said. "Take what men you will."

"Let us go alone, my father. We will travel swiftly and take the higher trails where the troops do not come."

"As you wish," Victorio said. He raised his head when Joaquin stood up. "For your people, look only for the true things. For yourself, look along the way for the place you and your *niña* will be content."

Joaquin felt a wetness behind his eyes. As he turned he caught Mangas Chie's glance and was torn, as if they had said good-by to one another.

Outside the wickiup he stopped, looking off to where the copper-veined hills rose. He sensed Victorio at his side and turned to him, meaning to speak his gratitude, but Victorio spoke first, quietly, firmly.

"Joaquin, make no promises in my name. You know me, and I trust you. But the white eyes can choose in this matter: they can have me at war now with every fighting man of the Mimbreños. Or they can grant us, for all time, our lands at Ojo Caliente."

Near the end of March two things happened to John Shafter. He mounted the dun for the first time since it fell on his leg, and he got a letter from Willson. The former was accomplished with grit and cussing, the latter through teamsters and riders, Mexican and American, coming in from the upper reaches of Sonora.

> *Dere horse,* Willson wrote. *I got here to San Lorenzo and there wasnt nothing here. There is considerable Mexicans in Mexico. I got the promise of a job with a man owns a big ranch over to Assenshun so when you come down I will be in Chewawa. The eats here is good if you flush with tekeela of which you can drink a lot and feel midling till dawn. At which time you think a fresh shod mule has tromped your hed. Ha ha. How is the leg coming I hope you will get fine soon. How is Ob doin making a onest living for a change. Well I will see you when you get here and Ob too I hope. Well I will close for now.*
> *Your frend G. T. Willson. In Chewawa.*

Shafter was aggravated. All he'd heard, San Lorenzo was quiet and peaceful as a man could want, and here Willson had to go and take him a job he didn't need. Plus Shafter would now have to ride into Sonora and then east, or else head up into New Mexico Territory and cut down over the border into Chihuahua, and Ascensión, he supposed Willson meant. When Fox P. Canby came loping in that afternoon with a small detail out of the Tucson post, Shafter wasn't in as good humor as he might have been considering he'd managed to get on the dun a few hours before. He read Fox P. the letter and remarked a trifle sourly that if Fox P. had any notion about trailing with Texicans once his time was up, he'd better keep track of where in hell they were. Fox P. said he would get word to Obre, down to Pete Kitchen's, where they were standing off Apache nuisance raids about once a week, and cautioned Shafter about setting off on a long hike south just because he'd managed to amble around the compound on the dun.

They sat on Whitman's porch, where, it felt now to Shafter, he'd spent the entire winter. The pup kept him company unless it was at Whitman's heels, well trained, handsome, and brainless as dogs went, but he nevertheless had spent a good part of his time in its company, or it in his. He had exhausted Whitman's small library: a lot of army manuals, some kind of peculiar French novels, a novel by an American lady writer in which the hero quite often had the swoons, and some English poets, all of whom made him nervous and some of whom he would have enjoyed throttling. He told Whitman he had never known there were so many versifiers versifying about nature who appeared to know so little about it. Take this Shelley, for instance; there wasn't anything he had found there a man could get his teeth in. All those clouds and blue skies and birds twittering. He wondered what Shelley would of written if he had seen, say, a road runner noiselessly build a barricade of thorns clean around a sleeping sidewinder and then go in and peck him to death. Whitman's laughter was helpless if not hopeless.

He said now to Fox P., "Do you know who Percy Bysshe Shelley was?"

"I hopes to tell you," Fox P. said. "He run the ordinary down to Bolt's Ford, along about '48, when I was a little shaver."

"By God, so he did," Shafter said. "I wondered where I recollected that name from."

They sat looking out at the spring-coming land. Already there were flowers in the sand, so fragile you marveled how they would last their season. The hills looked bluer and softer, and the sky, too, and there was softness in a sunlight which had been tempered by warm winds. Water glinted high through the feathering willows, and the shadows of the towering cloud rushed over the desert. Here and there, outside the post, Eskiminzin's Arivaipa moved at their chores, squaws bringing in bundled hay, men leading horses or mules. Their wickiups were set up half a mile from the post, but Whitman had given them permission to cultivate their gardens five miles farther on, in the rich soil of the canyon on Arivaipa Creek.

Shafter had taken more than a mere break-in-the-boredom pleasure in the changes at Camp Grant. And the change in Royal Whitman. The evening of Eskiminzin's arrival, he recalled Bleeker's words, the filling of the lack, and thought Bleeker had chosen the word badly. He had meant need, not lack. Yet there was no assertion of false authority, no grasping for authority, in this man. When Eskiminzin had finished speaking, through Marijildo, Whitman had stood there with the pup at his feet and said, "I am glad you have come, Eskiminzin. But I am only a subchief. My big chief is at Tucson, and the great chief of us all at Washington. I will tell them what you wish. In the meantime, you and your people come back here. I will feed you and care for you as well as I can." His

voice was easy, but there was a warning in it. "As long as you are
good Indians, I am sure my chiefs will let you remain here."

The first party of Arivaipa to come in numbered two hundred.
Then, over the month, in ones and twos, in parties of twenty, thirty,
forty, they came down out of the mountains. They were destitute,
in rags, without blankets, carrying their sick in litters. Near the end
of the month, according to the every-other-day count Whitman in-
stituted, there were five hundred and ten of them, and within a
few days they were no longer the ragged lot they had been. Whitman provided them with government beef and blankets, the protection of the post, and, although he did not immediately know it,
with spirit and hope. He was rewarded by their industry, their
cheerfulness, their desire to help themselves. He went among them
as easily as he went among his own kind, did the count himself,
dispensed rations himself, took the most personal interest in their
rehabilitation. By the time April had spread its time of green and
color and sunlight and warm passing rains, there was more at
Camp Grant than a contented people on their own land, in their
own gardens again; there was a man among them who had not
touched a whiskey bottle in days, who smiled often, who wore ac-
complishment in his eyes.

This very morning he had given Eskiminzin permission to set up
his main camp in the canyon, where the gardens were. When he
returned, Shafter said to him, "You got quite some project gone
here, Royal. You ain't heard from the big nantans about it yet,
either, have you?"

Whitman smiled and put his pipe in his mouth, speaking around
it. "You can't discourage me, Shafter. No, I haven't heard, but I
will, and what can they say but carry on?" He took the pipe out of
his mouth and looked off at the hills. "Shafter, I have a wonderful
family out here in the desert. These people are winning me completely. They're far removed from anything we were taught to
expect from the Apache. I feel that all the tribes can be won. After
all, what do they want? Their own lands, enough to eat, to clothe
themselves, to be treated fairly, honestly. Is that unreasonable of
them?" He pointed the stem of his pipe at Shafter. "I know what
you're thinking: that they've got to be left their pride, too. Well,
why not? Eskiminzin keeps his pride, and so do his people. They
need help, to show them the way to a higher civilization, and I'm

going to give them this help as long as they're permitted to stay with me."

Shafter only looked at him. He had a mind full of doubts and reservations, but it was lower than a snake's belly to bring them out in the open to a man in the throes of the kind of dedication had laid Whitman by the heels. Everybody, especially the Apache, knew how the army operated, and after a while it was just too much trouble even to summon the thought, well, maybe this time. . . .

Fox P.'s detail had brought the answer from Division Headquarters. It wasn't until Fox P. had gone down to take a look at what these tame Apaches were up to that Royal Whitman came out of his office and sat down on the step with his back to Shafter and a letter in his hand.

Shafter could read the back of his head, just like it was his face, and when Whitman finally turned around he saw he had read it correctly. He said, "If you tell me they said send 'em back to the mountains, or kill 'em all, I ain't gone to say I told you so because I didn't tell you so, but I ain't gone to be dumbstruck with wonder either."

Whitman was shaking his head. "It's incredible, it's absolutely incredible."

"You'd ought to be able to finish 'em off like sittin' ducks, the way they are now," Shafter said. "Get 'em while they're hoein', with their backs to you."

Whitman kept shaking his head. "It's not that." His hand, holding the papers, was trembling, and Shafter had the feeling that it was half rage and half laughter that had upset his control. "Shafter, I have here five hundred and ten Arivaipa Apaches. I trust them implicitly and I know they trust me. I will go further. I am learning to love these people. They are obedient, industrious, they don't make *tulepah*, they have all the potential of becoming good citizens." He looked up at Shafter, almost wildly. "And their fate, their future, is in my hands. I advise Division HQ of what is going on out here, of what we are doing so well, and listen to what I receive in return. Lieutenant Royal Whitman, Camp Grant, Arizona Territory. Sir: your communication has not been endorsed in accordance with official etiquette and is therefore returned to you. End of communication. Period. All."

Shafter laughed. "Well, that ain't so bad as I reckoned it to be.

You oughtn't to be so sensitive, Royal, just because your military manners need polishin'."

Whitman managed a smile, but it was rueful. "By the time I get another letter off, worded by the book, anything can happen. My God, all I want is permission from Division to continue as I am, for Eskiminzin to continue as he is."

"Continue," Shafter said. "If they crave to investigate, I reckon they'll get around to it."

"But I've got to have some authority for requisitions, for beef, for blankets, for medical supplies . . . for most anything you can name."

"Keep on requisitionin'," Shafter said. "They ain't stopped you yet." But he knew what Whitman had finally come to fear: they could stop him.

Whitman got up and went into his office and threw the letter and his own returned letter down on the desk and stood scratching his head. After a time he went to a file cabinet and took out a bottle and removed the cork and looked down into it and then put both cork and bottle back where he had found them.

The following day a noncommittal captain named Stanwood arrived from Division with half a cavalry company. He had written instructions for Whitman to hold and feed the Arivaipa. He personally inspected the ranchería in Arivaipa Canyon, five miles on, greeted Eskiminzin with neither friendliness nor hostility, and went off the same day on a scout south.

The spark came back in Royal Whitman's eyes. Day after day he went into the ranchería, helping, making suggestions, lifted out of himself by the gratitude of the Arivaipa, growing closer and closer to Eskiminzin. If he walked in a rosy cloud, Shafter was still not the man to point it out to him.

Mangas Chie rode with Joaquin and Anna as far as Fort Bowie, which they gave a wide berth. The trip had been uneventful and, despite the steady pace of it, more than pleasant, for the spring glory was on the land, and there was no place the eye fell that all was not color and beauty.

Still, Joaquin seemed unreasonably moody when the time came to part with Chie. They were in the foothills of the Dragoons in the early morning, and Anna did not understand his despondence at the parting, particularly when Chie said he would come on to join them later if he felt it advantageous to do so. He went on, to take the Apache corridor to the Stronghold, and Joaquin turned northwest, meaning to strike and follow the water courses. The pattern of their travel changed now; as they came into more populated areas Joaquin insisted on riding at night, hiding by day. Hiding, yes. She hated the word, told him she hated the word, and he only said, a little tightly, "It is what we have to do. I hope it is not what we will always have to do."

She preferred to camp at night, to see the stars come, to sleep when it was dark, when men should sleep, with the comfort of fire, seeing the looming shapes of the tethered Appaloosa and the paint mare with its silver trappings and the shaggy-coated pack horse. She did not miss Chie and when she was finally allowed a night camp under the cut banks of a canyon she thought to tease Joaquin out of his depression.

"How can you be unhappy, Joaquin? It's Chie has left you, not I. Suppose it was I had to go up there, and you and Chie to go on alone? Or is that what you wanted?"

He was in better spirits, but he was very watchful, and it seemed to her he was not fully at ease. "No, I would not want such a thing. Why are you so happy, Ana?"

"Why not?" she said. "We are free, we are having a wonderful journey. You are here." She came and sat beside him, leaning against his shoulder. "And we are on a hopeful mission, you know that, Joaquin."

"Yes," he said. "I know." Then he said, "You should have gone with Chie."

"With Chie? How can you say that?"

"There will be white soldiers at the post," Joaquin said matter-of-factly. "We will be accounted for. Suppose they are looking for you?"

Then she said hesitatingly, almost perfectly, in Apache, "I am Mimbreño, from the ranchería of Victorio at Santa Rita del Cobre."

He stared at her. Then he began to smile, and then to laugh, and he put his arms around her and they laughed together. She said, "So, you believe in signs, isn't that a good sign? I am trying."

And he said, "You will learn . . . always you win what you have your mind set upon, don't you? And don't speak so lightly of signs. When did you set your mind upon me, Ana?"

"I?" she cried. "I? I had not one thing to say about it," and was laughing again, but he was now frowning, serious.

"Have you thought, it is just one harvest, one year, since you came to us."

She shook her head. "It amazes me how you twist words to suit your purpose. First I set my mind upon you, and now I came to you." She made a wry face. "I recall quite clearly what a kind invitation to the Stronghold I was given."

He said, "But it was planned that way, you see . . . even the cruelties we had for one another, even that was planned for us."

"You believe that," she said. "You believe that it was something we could do nothing about?"

"Yes," he said. "I believe it. What is the word for feeling this way?"

She thought. She said, "Fatalistic. I think your people are fatalistic."

"White men never are?"

"Oh yes, sometimes, very religious people are, I guess. But not by nature, by learning more than they can understand and needing an excuse for believing in things they can't understand."

He said, "Then there is a sameness between our people in this. I wish there were more samenesses. This fatalistic is not much of a thing to build on."

"Fatalism," she corrected. "No, it's not very practical. There will have to be something besides practicality; there will have to be an emotion, something in the heart besides something in the head."

He stretched out, pulling her down with him. A little offering of sparks shot up and was snuffed by the overhanging edge of the bank. He said, "It is too bad you are not many people, my Ana, for then you could be all the army nantans and all the reservation agents and even the great nantan in Washington, and the Apache would have no more worries as long as his kind remained."

"I should hate to be a soldier, or a nantan either. Then I would not be with you. Can you smell the flowers?"

He murmured affirmatively. His eyes were closed, and she could not see the anxiety which was still reflected on his face.

In the morning she found the place she had known she would find. Coming out upon a slope covered with new grass and flowers, she looked down and saw the clear running creek, and across it more grass and flowers and beyond that the desert with the stark saguaro rising, the mountains lifting gray, rosy, gilded with sun. Joaquin had pulled in the Appaloosa. She rode to his side. He did not look at her; his eyes were sweeping the place, noting its sheltering side hills, how thick the grass grew, the slope of the hill they rode, with trees on its shoulders.

When he spoke he said, "Is this the place, Ana?"

"What do you think?" she said, delighted but unable to read his face.

"I think it is good. I see no sign men come here. The earth is good or the grass would not be good. The hills protect; there are fine trees." He looked at her now. "I would build back into this slope, so that the hill is always behind us for strength." Before she could speak he said, "We will return this way and decide if this is the place."

She had already made the decision by the time they forded, and she turned and looked back at the hill and could see the house, whitewashed dobe with orange tiles for its roof, built as he had said, into the green slope.

They kept close to the water now whenever Joaquin felt it was safe. He was guided by an instinct she did not have, and by sign she did not see. He knew by the age of horse droppings how long since men had been here, appraised old campsites, read the bending grass, the tracks of animals and men, smoke in the spring sky. They stayed well east of Tucson, following the San Pedro north and coming down on the Gila on a warm glistening morning. She waited while he went ahead and, having dismounted to adjust one of the packs on the pack horse, felt suddenly empty and dizzy and very tired and sat down on a rock beside a small lizard which accepted her presence philosophically. They had ridden half the night and had not eaten, so that there was excuse enough for the spell which came upon her, and when she felt better she banished it entirely by eating a potato-flour biscuit.

Joaquin came back and they went on, passing out of sight of the post. Then she saw the wickiups and the people working in the sunlight. Joaquin said, "Now you must be very quiet and say nothing, Ana." He smiled, reassuring her. "You can't go around repeating that you are a Mimbreño of Victorio's ranchería. There are times it might not be the answer."

The People came to meet them. When Eskiminzin came, Joaquin spoke to him and the stocky Apache listened without interruption.

When he was finished, Eskiminzin first held out his hand, to be shaken, and then threw both arms about Joaquin's shoulders.

Eskiminzin had three wives. Anna was taken in tow by the youngest, who had two small children, a boy and a girl. She let them ride the mare, and then it seemed to her that every child in the camp came for its turn. She finally had to call a halt, in order to spare the mare, and she was bringing it back across the ranchería when the soldiers rode in, four of them on horseback and two in an army buckboard. Then she went to stand silently near the wickiup of Eskiminzin's third wife. While she stood there, Eskiminzin and Joaquin and a chief named Munaclee got up from the ground where they were sitting and went to meet the soldiers. She was near enough to hear, and she understood it all, for Eskiminzin got out more than a word of stuttered strangled-sounding English for Royal Whitman.

Eskiminzin said the time was here for a council with his friend Whitman. These people, the man and his squaw, were Mimbreños, sent by the great chief Victorio.

Royal Whitman dismounted with open excitement. He shook hands with Joaquin, but Joaquin uttered no word of English, speaking rapidly in Apache. Marijildo came to the rescue, while he went on with the pretense. The Mimbreños had heard of the great thing which had happened at Camp Grant, that the Arivaipa were on their own lands. The Mimbreños said that if such a thing could be arranged for them, then there would be a council to discuss it. In the meantime, Victorio himself sends a representative to see if the truce is kept faithfully. A pause, and the slow amendment: by the soldiers.

Royal Whitman felt he was standing not upon his beloved desert, among his beloved people, but somewhere slightly off the ground. He shook Joaquin's hand again, and Joaquin was struck by the warmth of his face, voice, bearing. He thought, this is a good man. Victorio would know this man for a good man. The gnawing worry he could not attribute to anything in particular, but which had come upon him with Mangas Chie's departure, was gone, and again a deep and flaming hope rose in him.

When Whitman went back, after his count of the ranchería, he met Shafter riding slowly toward the camp. Shafter knew instantly that something was up; Whitman's face gave him away, and it was more than pleasure; it was downright elation. Shafter turned the dun and fell in with him.

"You couldn't guess," Whitman said. "You couldn't guess in a thousand years. We've got two Mimbreños in camp."

Shafter said, "Mimbreños? Somebody's pullin' your leg, Royal."

"No, sir, they are not," Whitman said. "A buck and a squaw. From Santa Rita. Whether you know it or not, the word is reaching the tribes."

"From Santa Rita? From Victorio? Aw hell, Royal."

"They couldn't fool Marijildo. Eskiminzin knows them. What more do you want?"

Shafter said thoughtfully, "Well, I'm damned. I wonder what's got into Victorio, he wants to see the lay of the land."

"I don't know yet," Whitman said, "but we'll know tonight. Got to get plenty of cigarette makings and some meat over there for a celebration. Let the women and kiddies have themselves a good time while we grownups talk." He laughed. "Well, what do you think of this, doubting Thomas? What would you think if Royal Whitman was responsible for bringing about the surrender of the Mimbreños?"

"I ain't told anybody this," Shafter said, "but I got a howdy from Washington for gone to see Victorio last spring. When I talked with him he seemed about as set on surrenderin' as a loafer wolf when you're layin' down and he's got his paws on your gizzard."

Royal Whitman knew his Indian background. "Any chief who learned under Mangas Colorado is a chief of intelligence and honor. Does it occur to you that he sees the handwriting on the wall?"

"Maybe," Shafter admitted. "But he's a good game player. At most any game you can call. Who are these Mimbreños?"

"I didn't catch the names. Nice-looking people; the woman's quite pretty, what I could see of her. A young chief. Oh, an odd thing about him, he has blue eyes."

Shafter sat the dun, looking at him. After a time he said, "Royal, I offer you my congratulations. Honest to God. I think I will keep on where I was aimin' to go; I want to see how things are comin' up in the corn patch."

Twenty-three

It was Shafter's first trip into the Arivaipa ranchería, and he did not go directly into it, but rode along under some trees, where horses were bunched into a timber-fenced corral. He saw the black Appaloosa with its fat white-spotted rump right off, and he knew whom it belonged to. There were precious few of the breed around; they came in from the far Nez Percé country, either by trade or steal, and Shafter could recall seeing one or two others in his entire life.

He wished for Obre's gift of palaver but did his halting best, a lot of it with his hands. The boy with the horses thought he wanted to buy the Appaloosa, and it was with main strength and awkwardness Shafter finally got it across he wanted to find the man owned the horse. Then the boy said the man was not there, but that his woman had started up the canyon to the *campos*.

Shafter had no intention of riding five miles up the canyon but he went off in that direction, passing some women going along chattering, with hoes over their shoulders. They smiled at him, and he saw neither fear nor hesitation in their eyes. Farther on, where the walls of the canyon began, he saw some more women, and children, one of them riding a high-stepping walking paint. He didn't hurry; he didn't have to, because before he reached it the group ahead split up after a brief conference, and the woman riding dismounted and sat down under a small willow tree.

She was sitting with her head in her hands, the sick emptiness she had felt earlier in the morning having come on her again. Something warned her: she looked up and saw him walking, limping on the shortened leg, leading the dun, and it was all she could do not to run to him. When he reached her she said half unbelieving and very glad, "Is it you?"

"Nobody else," Shafter said, looking down at her. "I reckoned Royal Whitman had come down with a fit of the imaginaries." He threw the dun's reins over a limb of the willow and said, "Mind if I sit down?"

She made room for him, but he did not immediately join her. "You look a little peaked, Annie. How's everything?"

Her smile took away any doubt that might have been getting ready to stir itself up in his mind; it was full and genuine and not one curve of it forced. But she said, "Shafter, you didn't go to Mexico. Every time I thought of you, I thought of you in Mexico. Lying in the sun and watching the days go by."

Now he sat down. "You thought of me, with all you had to think on. I take that kindlier than I can say."

She looked at him fully. "I think of you a great deal. What happened to your leg; did you break it?"

"I didn't." He jerked his thumb at the dun. "He did it for me."

"And you've been here all winter." She kept watching him, and he saw that his initial judgment had been too quick, that she looked well and contented and more vivacious than he remembered her. "I'm so happy to see you, Shafter. Joaquin will be glad. You know why we are here?"

"Something about Victorio getting a burr in his tail," Shafter said. "I ain't certain I can figure why he didn't send Chie or Ponce, or maybe come himself."

She said with ill-concealed distaste, even with a trace of anger, "Come himself? I expect he knows too much about chiefs who come in for councils and end up in irons. Chie has gone to the Stronghold. Anyway, we wished to come, Joaquin and I; we had a reason." She looked up and said, "Joaquin is coming now," and again Shafter noted the lighting of her face.

Joaquin was on foot. When he saw Shafter he said, "The Appaloosa is not for sale," and held out his hand and Shafter thought that his face mirrored the girl's, open, natural, with more of ease on it than Shafter had ever before noticed. And even while Joaquin shook hands, his eyes were on Anna. "What are you doing here, Ana? I thought you were going up to the gardens."

She said rather crossly, "I felt a little lightheaded. I hope I'm not coming down with something." Then her voice was teasing. "Look, Shafter broke his poor leg and had to sit in a chair all winter, instead of a saddle."

Joaquin sat down facing them. Shafter said, "You both look fine, but I reckon some big wind blew your heads clean empty. Don't you think it's kind of risky, bringin' Annie in here?"

"I thought so at first," Joaquin said. "But no more. Every time I think of some time or place where there might be trouble for Ana, I think further and remember that she faces all things calmly and takes care of me in the bargain."

"You took my advice and listen to her then, eh?"

"Yes," Joaquin said. His eyes flickered to Anna's and they laughed, at some private joke, Shafter knew. It made him feel pretty good. Then Joaquin said, "Are you coming for the council tonight? When I must guard my tongue and speak only through the Spaniard."

"So it's true," Shafter said. "Victorio wants to negotiate. What's he askin', Joaquin?"

Joaquin leaned forward. "He wants his lands at Ojo Caliente."

Shafter pushed his hat back. "Well, that doesn't seem like much of a price. By damn, you never know which of the big nantans in Washington might think it's too high though." He looked at Joaquin, flattening his upper lip. "I reckon Victorio's holdin' out a choice."

Joaquin said, "I think you know it, Shafter."

"Yes," Shafter said. "I reckon I do. Blood from here to hell and gone." He shifted, suddenly restless, and his voice was hard. "What do you think of all this, Annie? If Victorio ain't happy with what he finds out about life on the reservation, if he keeps to the warpath, where are you gone to stand?"

"That's what I was going to tell you when Joaquin came." She looked at Joaquin and then at Shafter. "We found a place. A little valley. We are going to stay there."

"We are?" Joaquin said.

She nodded at him, her head on one side.

"I said we would decide this when we returned."

"But it wasn't a place we had to think about, either of us, so I think it is settled. It was in your mind the moment you saw it. You can't deny it."

Shafter made to whistle, almost self-defensively. "I don't aim to arbitrate in any family hassles here. Offhand I would say don't fight her, Joaquin, her mind's made up. Women got a special way of makin' up their minds, and if you fight it it's something like when you try to knock over a brick wall with your bare hands."

Joaquin laughed. "Come and see this place with us, Shafter." His face for the first time was boyish again, for Shafter had marked the settling in him, the hard-cut cast of his features. "Tell us how we will look a year from now, with our house built into the hill and

Ana worn to a shadow with hoeing and I with my shorn hair and my white man's boots."

Anna said, "Joaquin, are you going to cut your hair?"

"I think it necessary."

Shafter said, "We covered this ground before, didn't we, boy?" His voice held a small warning.

"You and I," Joaquin agreed. "You said it would not change me inside, but I say it is a beginning and I will change inside."

"Oh no," Anna said with childlike concern. "I shouldn't like you to change, not at all, Joaquin."

"*Amigo,*" Shafter said, "you don't know how lucky you are. I never did hear tell before of a woman didn't want to change a man. Spend their whole lives tryin' to make you over into what they think you'd ought to be, so persistent you wonder what came over 'em to marry you the way you were." He reached over and took Anna's hand. "No, I ain't comin' to council. I'll tell you something, though, and you tell Victorio for me. If there's one man in the length and breadth of this land he can trust, it's Royal Whitman. What's too bad is that Whitman's got no authority for anything, except to keep the Arivaipa here. He's near as low in the military order as you can get, a lieutenant, and no kid at that. Maybe something will come out of all this, but if it does, Victorio's gone to maybe have to carry more than his share of the load."

Anna said, "I have only just noticed that there is a 'but' in nearly every sentence you speak, Shafter. Are you a pessimist?"

Shafter thought about it. "I reckon you might call me that." He looked at her. "I got to admit, though, that the last couple of times I been lucky enough to run into you, little girl, you make me think life's a pretty fair proposition after all." His eyes were searching; she saw something pensive in them. "You make me recollect somebody I knew a long time ago, and I ain't sure whether that's good or bad." He stood up. "You got it planned right, both of you, a good future if you keep workin' at it. I don't reckon there's anything two people like you hold back from one another, so I think I'll say before I go back, is there anything you'd like to ask me about anything, Annie?"

He thought she flushed slightly, and he was half sorry he had put Linus in her mind. But she said, "Nothing."

"Fair enough. How long you gone to stay around here?"

Joaquin said, "Until we are certain everything is as it appears to be. I think Mangas Chie will come on and return to Santa Rita with the word. Ana and I will go to find our valley, if the post will give us tools and supplies when we leave."

Shafter said, "If it goes to his liking, Royal Whitman will supply you with the shirt off his back." He was a long time getting into the saddle. "You and me are just speakin' acquaintances now. I'll come over to see you when the soldiers ain't around."

They watched him set off slowly toward the post, and to Joaquin it felt now that they were doubly safe, that this, too, had been planned, as surely as two stars crossing one another in the April sky.

When Fox P. Canby got word to Obre that Shafter was in the saddle again, and Willson in Chihuahua, Obre gave Pete Kitchen his time, collected his pay, and headed for Camp Grant. He was sorry in a lot of ways to leave the ranch, the best big ranch ever was, raising up corn, potatoes, cabbage, oats, barley, and fine fat pigs, and with the only waterfall in the area. Kitchen farmed rich black reclaimed bottom land; harvesting seventy bushels of barley to the acre as against the average thirty bushels, plus drawing thirty-five cents a pound for top-grade ham and bacon, he could afford good wages. Obre was taken with the tough little rancher who wouldn't give up his land to Apaches, who stuck it out through thick and thin, and he gave him his money's worth to the tune of three Apache scouts who tried over the winter to get inside the house. He couldn't rightly tell how many he had killed off during the several raids the ranch suffered, but even though he was back in business again it wasn't long before he was bored. He'd never been as keen on or as trusting of Apaches as Shafter, and it was a strain keeping yourself keyed up enough to know whether every blasted shadow was an empty one, or every ball of brush unoccupied by anything but its own twigs and foliage.

Kitchen was sorry to let him go, but Kitchen's middle name should have been luck if it wasn't already; he would hold out and he knew there was no sense trying to keep a man didn't intend to be kept.

Obre took his time going to Grant. He stopped at the Tucson post and said howdy to Linus and picked up some dispatches to carry to Royal Whitman. On the way out he passed the Californian Logan coming in with a wagon train. Logan, either taken by surprise or bearing no ill will, spoke to him, but he looked after he'd done it as if he wished he hadn't. Obre went on, looking behind him a few times, like a man did on trail turns to make certain he wasn't followed. He was just as glad, at the moment, that he was going to join Willson in Chihuahua, instead of Sonora where Elias's trains ran.

It seemed to him, after he'd got into Grant and took stock of Whitman and practiced palavering with Marijildo one hour after another, that he had barely got his head down before the arrows started to fly. There were Chiricahua all over the place, and some Tontos, too, another raid on the walls of Tucson, some pack trains ambushed. And as far as the Mimbreños were concerned, Cuchillo Negro and Delgadito, coming home with their war parties, were raising hell along the way. They wouldn't know about Victorio's decision, and even if they did, nobody had shown them a white flag or mentioned the word treaty. Obre hoped Pete and the men who manned his stockade were making out all right.

He recognized Joaquin right away, but when Shafter said to clamp his chops he did so with no questions asked. He mostly did whatever Shafter said as a matter of course, and it was no skin off his teeth if Shafter wanted to pretend he didn't know a living soul up in that ranchería. But he felt rotten, real rotten, when the news came to Grant the middle of the month that Pete Kitchen's eleven-year-old kid had been killed by an Apache, practically in the front yard. Obre gloomed and said maybe if he'd of been there . . . and it didn't even help when Shafter said, yes, if Sam Houston had been to the Alamo in '36 maybe your pa wouldn't of got his either.

A young trooper from Tucson rode in one afternoon, preceding Lieutenant Degnan with a small detail, carrying dispatches. Shafter sat up in the rocking chair, but he didn't have to say a word, because Obre rose casually, called up his horse, and went off at a deliberate gait for the Arivaipa camp. Just in case Linus Degnan was on an inspection tour he wouldn't find a thing around but what he came to observe. Shafter was glad to see Linus and thought he looked pretty fair, only tired and thin, like he kept long hours and wasn't eating on schedule.

Linus wasn't carrying any good news. There was trouble in Tucson like never before. Or hardly ever before.

"What kind of trouble?" Whitman said. The porch was getting worn shiny, and the step saggy, from all the sitting they were doing.

Linus said, "If we could put a finger on the exact kind, we might be able to do something about it. What it amounts to so far is rumbling. I'm afraid the military's in complete disrepute." He looked at Shafter. "Guess who's got him a pulpit to shout from, right in the middle of it all?"

"Shucks, ask me a hard one, Linus," Shafter said. "Will Oury."

"He's got the Mexicans all stirred up. He's got the Papagos all stirred up. The ranch owners are up in arms. The army is a sniveling bunch of incompetents. And the only good Indian is a dead Indian."

"Men have been talking that way ever since I came out here," Whitman said. "If they feel that way, let 'em go on out and kill off a few Indians. The more they get, the easier it's going to be to negotiate with what's left."

Shafter grimaced. Whitman was more realistic than he'd thought. "By God, Royal, that don't sound like you." He turned to Linus. "Is Oury just makin' noises, or do you figure he's loaded for some real huntin'?"

"Personally, from what I've seen of Will Oury, I don't think he ever just makes noises. You've got to give the devil his due. But last week Elias came out to the post."

"After what your pa told him?"

"He reminded Father of that. Very proper and correct, stiff as a corpse. Said he recalled that Father'd warned him not to come there unless he was asking military assistance, and he was now asking it. Something had to be done to stop this raiding, and if the military wouldn't finish it once and for all there was going to be more trouble than even Washington, D.C. could handle in a year of Sundays."

Whitman was apprehensive. "What in the nation did he mean . . . that they're going to organize and go Apache hunting on their own? I can't say I object to that; we've had little enough help from hollering civilians."

Linus said, "Yes, but Oury is a very smart gentleman. Once he found out my father would only act on orders from Stoneman, he went to Stoneman."

"Cornered the bear in his den, eh?" Shafter said.

"The way I hear it Stoneman spent most of the interview trying to back out of the room."

"Did he say something or did he just wring his hands?"

"Oh he said something. He said his troops were limited, but that what troops he had were in the field. He also said that as Tucson has the biggest population in the Territory, it would just have to do the best it could."

"Great galloping gander," Whitman said. "What kind of answer is that for a general to make? And they complain about *my* military manners. I suppose Oury was fit to be tied."

Linus said, "There was a public meeting in Tucson Friday night. Must have been close to three hundred all standing around, torches burning, guns going off, drunks. And Oury. Not yelling either. Hard as hell, and getting cheered every word of the way." Linus picked up his hat and began to brush dust off the brim with the sleeve of his shirt. "I hate to pass along the word, Royal, but Oury started off by saying he knew there wasn't a man in town ever approved the Arivaipa settlement at Camp Grant. He says now he's got proof they're just using this for a base and striking out of it. As a matter of fact, he says it's the Arivaipa have been responsible for all the raids in the last two months."

Astonishment and anger flared in Royal Whitman's face. He half rose from his chair and then sat down again, making a sound such as a deflated balloon might make. "The Arivaipa. *My* Arivaipa. The man is stark raving mad. Eskiminzin hasn't been out of this reservation, except for his hunting parties, and his hunting parties are the only armed Apaches on this post. They've accounted for every hour they're out. . . . A man doesn't go on a raid and return with fresh deer meat." Agony was in his eyes. "My God, Degnan, this is an outright lie. The man has no more proof of such a thing than I have proof the Holy Ghost made wine out of water."

Linus nodded, but he did not look up. He said, "That's what I told them. Have you ever seen a cavalry officer damn near forcibly put in his saddle and driven out of town?"

Whitman's clenched fist drummed on the arm of his chair. "From what you say, my Arivaipa can thank their most benevolent spirits they're camped on a military establishment. You can tell the colonel there won't be one civilian allowed on Camp Grant on any pretext." He was thinking quickly. "And I'll be obliged if he'll issue passes over his own signature for every wagoner and supply outfit coming in here from Tucson." He looked over at Shafter, but Shafter was only slumped on his spine in the rocking chair, his hanging hand just touching the sleeping dog's head. "Shafter. . . ."

"Please," Shafter said. "The milk of human kindness is all curdled in me right now. I don't trust myself to speak when I get to feelin' in this manner."

Whitman relaxed quickly. He had a great capacity not only for rising to a situation but for rising above it. He was still angry but he would never be guided by anger. Already, in his mind, the great embracing protective arm of the army, of Royal Whitman, had been thrown about Eskiminzin and his Arivaipa. And what, after all, was talk? Men talked and talked and talked all their lives. Talking was not acting. These might be influential men who incited in the streets of Tucson, but they were civilians after all, and if they were of the stature they professed to be, they would not allow themselves to be branded renegade or outlaw. He thought pragmatically that he could not depend on Stoneman in any way now, but that Walter Degnan and Camp Grant itself were better in any foreseeable emergency than the piddling interference, sanction or lack of it, of a man broken clean through by his own authority, hoist with his own petard, damned if he did and damned if he didn't.

Then Shafter said, "If I were you, Royal, or Linus, or somebody, I would hire my friend Obre, very fast and very quiet, and point out Will Oury for him."

Whitman half smiled. "You sometimes manage to lighten my darker moments, Shafter, but this is hardly a time for joking."

Shafter said, "I ain't joking."

Whitman looked at him. "You actually mean that is what you would do?"

"Yes," Shafter said quietly. "That's what I'd do."

Linus' eyebrows rose, but he understood Shafter. He stood up. "Royal, I'd like to stay, but I can't. I'm going to catch a couple of hours sleep, if you'll give me a bed, but I've got to get back to Tucson. You want to write my father an affidavit?"

"I certainly do," Whitman said. "To the effect that my Arivaipa have not been off this post. Shafter can vouch for it."

"Put that in," Linus said. "My father's come to the conclusion the only men he can trust any more are graybacks."

Shafter only made a pretense at grinning. After they had gone he continued to rub the pup's ear. He could feel, fully for the first time, the lines of wind, squint, years, pain tighten in his face, the slow dull ache of aging, of the body yielding to the persuasive stresses and tensions of decline, the muscles playing out like uncoiled rope, the heart asserting its increasing unwillingness to play the game. No sir, by God, he'd had enough, and it was time he thought of pushing on to where he could age a little slower, carry less in his mind, and unlearn himself how to meddle.

But when Whitman came out of his office he had to get it off his chest. "Say, Royal, if I was you I'd quit callin' them your Apaches."

"Do I?" Whitman said, not knowing he did.

"Just habit," Shafter said offhandedly. "It might come off a harmful habit, though, a man goes around braggin' what's his."

Whitman objected. "Have to feed your soul on something, don't you? Do you want to go around discouraging all the braggarts in this country, just because they cultivate a bad habit?"

"Couldn't do it," Shafter said mildly. "You could kill 'em all, far as that goes, and they'd just keep comin' up from Texas."

Mangas Chie arrived the last week in April. He carried a lance fluttering with fresh dyed feathers, but when he came into Grant the first thing he did was hand his carbine to Royal Whitman.

Whitman was his usual firm warm self. He thought this Apache's face was uniquely impassive, but he saw a flicker of emotion in the eyes when Marijildo repeated his words.

"The nantan says it is a great honor for him to meet the son of Mangas Colorado. He says he wishes that you will be friends, and that he is happy the Mimbreños have come to see how the Arivaipa are living under military protection."

Chie said, "Is my brother Joaquin among them?"

"He tells us he is glad to see how well the Apaches live when they are treated fairly," Marijildo said.

Chie said, "If my brother Joaquin is satisfied, I will be satisfied."

Whitman's face was flushed with pleasure. Marijildo told Chie, "The lieutenant says there has been a successful council, and that the wishes of the chief Victorio have been made known. Many letters have gone out, to the city of the great nantan and to the nantans of the army, asking them for council with the great chief of the Mimbreños."

Chie lowered his head gravely. He said, "And will the great nantan give my people what they ask?"

They were standing in the sun, and there was a morning sound of birds, a stirring of warm wind. For the first time Whitman's face clouded a little. "We cannot tell this until our letters are answered by all the nantans. But there is reason to hope, because they are allowing the Arivaipa to remain on their own lands."

Chie nodded, but only once, with dignity. He looked up and saw Shafter limp down off the step, and his dignity dissolved. "*Buenos,* Shafter."

"Howdy, Chie," Shafter said. "How's everything up to the Stronghold?"

Chie's eyes went over Whitman briefly. He said, in English, surprising Whitman who had not thought he knew any, "Bad with Cochise. Much sick. In here." Chie struck himself over the heart. "No treat. Victorio treat, but no Cochise."

"No?" Shafter said. "Why not?"

"Say fight now. Treat some day, but not now. Say good for Arivaipa, maybe good for Mimbreño, no good for Chiricahua. Say peace come, peace go. Someday maybe peace stay. But not now."

Whitman was not ruffled. He took his pipe out of his pocket. "You speak English very well," he said pleasantly. Again Chie's eyes went over him, expressionless. Whitman motioned to the sergeant holding Chie's carbine. "Give this chief his arms," he said. He looked at Chie. "You understand that you are on your honor, and that you must not use this carbine. For any purpose."

"Understand," Chie said, with faint contempt. He mounted and rode off toward the canyon. "Sergeant," said Whitman, well satisfied, "add another single to rations count."

"You're cheerful, seeing Cochise don't want to play your way," Shafter said, falling in with him.

"How far is Victorio influenced by Cochise?"

"I wouldn't know."

"I still think the right man could do the trick with Cochise. It was done before. Maybe if the Mimbreños come in, it will swing him."

"Maybe," Shafter said. "You might have to look a long time for the right man, though. Ain't that gone to be Crook's problem?"

"Who told you about Crook?" Whitman said, taking his pipe out of his mouth.

"Bleeker. What's it, some secret or something?"

"No, just not official. Not even certain, actually."

"I figured so. Stoneman's still in command, ain't he?"

"Ha," said Royal Whitman.

The six mounted men rode out of Tucson about dawn, taking the road east. They carried side arms, but there was nothing unusual about them, three Mexicans, three Americans, except that they did not continue on the road farther than a wash a few miles out of Tucson. By full light they had staked to camp. They stayed there all day, lying around in the wash, keeping an eye on the road.

Linus had gone out to San Xavier, trying to pick up the trail of a raiding party which had driven off some cows near the mission. He had been in and out of Tucson an almighty amount of late, according to the lights of Corporal Rafe Callahan, and because Callahan, like every other man in the army, was receptive to any sliver and paring of rumor which came his way, he figured to take up where the lieutenant left off and keep his ears open. He had always felt bad about the lieutenant's trouble, and now he felt extra bad because the trip East and reassignment to another post had come to nothing, for Katie and for him, and for the lieutenant. He drew a good spell of off-duty, mainly by shining up to hog-jowl Stern, and he spent most of it hanging around the Old Pueblo trying to look innocent. He was so innocent he even quit drinking, although he frequented the bars a lot and even got friendly with a Mexican girl who had taken a shine to him, not getting himself involved, but thinking you never knew who was going to be able to do you a good turn or pass along a good word.

When he came into the post just before noon mess, Stern met him grinning. "I got you nailed now," he said, sidling up to the sweating horse like a fat crab. "Wondered how come you spent so much time in that town, but I never took you for a lady-killer. And you speak mealymouthed to me so you can get off duty, you lousy tail-chasing. . . ."

Rafe Callahan said, "Get the hell out of my way, you lard-butted trap jaw," and brushed past him on a run for commandant.

Stern plowed right in behind him, but by then Callahan was talking his head off and the Old Man was sitting like an icicle behind his desk, listening. When Stern stomped to the door the Old Man said, "What in the devil do you want, Sergeant?" and all he could think to splutter was, "Sir, this trooper is insubordinate. . . ." and didn't get a word further. The Old Man got up, said, "Don't bother me with your problems, Sergeant," and shut the door in his face.

When he sat down again he said, "All right, Callahan, start over again, and take your time. Here, no sense your standing, sit down, sit down."

Callahan sat down uneasily, balancing his hat on his knees.

"Now," Degnan said. "You counted how many of these groups going out of town?"

"It ain't an exact count, sir," Callahan said anxiously. "Around ten or eleven. Mostly Mexicans and Papagos."

Degnan reached for a cigar. "And what exactly did the girl say?"

"I was scared to question her, sir, for fear she'd get suspicious, but she said it was all right for me to come over to her house because her father and brother were goin' away for a spell. Then she said her older brother had got killed, put in a anthill by the Apaches, and now her father was goin' to get even."

"My God," Degnan said. "How many men would you estimate went out?"

"Sir, I couldn't count." He lowered his eyes, feeling he had failed miserably. "Around a hundred. Maybe more than a hundred."

"A lot of men," Degnan said grimly. "Moving out in small parties because they think they'll be less noticeable that way. Any men you knew?"

"Yes, sir," Callahan said. "Some of the greasers . . . excuse me, sir, Mexicans. A few Papagos I know by sight. And some of them teamsters of Elias's."

Degnan was calm; his very presence gave Callahan a new sense of security. "You didn't see Elias?"

"No, sir, but I saw the other one. Mr. Oury."

"Will Oury?"

"Yes, sir, he went out with the teamsters. The two men Logan and Auden and three others I didn't know."

Walter Degnan stood up. "Thank you, Callahan, good work. You'll have another stripe in the morning."

The Old Man was just standing there, so Callahan saluted and went out, taking the silence as dismissal, and ran nose-on into Stern, still fuming and waiting.

Callahan didn't touch him, except with his voice. He said, "Listen, Stern, you can make it as rough for me as you want to, but I'm telling you now that I just got me another stripe. You know what that's goin' to make me? That's goin' to make me Sergeant Callahan, and when it does I'm goin' to remember every little thing you said to me and every little thing you done to me, so bear it in mind."

Stern fell back, staring at him, and didn't even open his mouth until Degnan came out and snapped at him. "Sergeant, I don't know what in the devil's going on around here, but I want to get word to Lieutenant Whitman. Well, double, damn it!"

Stern doubled. Twenty minutes later a fuzz-cheeked trooper, carrying Walter Degnan's warning to Whitman, rode out of the post and set off for Camp Grant.

Twenty-four

After some studying on it, Shafter decided that the main thing about Royal Whitman which made him pretty singular as army, as administrator, as reservation agent, as whatever you wanted to consider him under the press of his present duty, was so simple it was funny it wasn't the most part of a government training course for West-bound officers. He was unerringly fair. He was disarmingly honest. He was always courteous.

(When Shafter found out, a long time after, that Whitman had been kind of vaguely shifty with some army contracts in which he stood to make some money by being vaguely shifty, he refused to be impressed. Cavalry lieutenants were poor folk; he didn't care if Royal Whitman had done the U. S. Government out of a few shin plasters; the way the U. S. Government was providing, or not providing these days, it might turn out to be every citizen's bounden duty to cheat a little. Because he had seen Royal Whitman with the Arivaipa, and he knew Royal Whitman had what counted where it counted.)

The core of his conduct appeared to be that he let Eskiminzin know right off that he was the boss, without once having to say it. Any baby kissing he indulged in wasn't politically motivated. He just happened to like the Arivaipa kids. Maybe a lot of people thought all he had to do was sit back, count noses, dispense rations, and smile, but Shafter knew different. Apaches had problems, just like anybody else: personal problems, tribal problems, and Whitman sat as judge and jury and somehow managed to please everybody. There wasn't a soppy bone in his body either, Shafter thought; he was logical but kind, sympathetic but not sentimental. When he came into the ranchería he was surrounded on the instant by women and kids, and the men coming more slowly, as befitted their station in life, but coming, like they were drawn to a magnet. It was in Shafter's mind, God help the Arivaipa if he gets pulled out of here, and it was also in his mind, God help Royal Whitman if that day comes.

He was about to head over to the ranchería, it not being count day, so that there was less likelihood of soldiers around. He noted by the calendar in Whitman's office that it was the twenty-eighth of April already and reminded himself to speak to Obre about packing up their gear and getting on the trail. There was a lady with a bustle and a head of hair like a mission tower on the calendar, which advertised tea. She was drinking a cup of the tea, with her little finger stuck straight out. Somebody with a not inconsiderable talent had thoughtfully provided her with a mustache, burnsides, and a full beard.

Shafter was riding out past dispensary when he spotted the sub-chief Nodakin humping in. There was an enlisted man on duty, post surgeon Briesly's regular assistant, and he couldn't do a thing but look helpless until Marijildo got there. Shafter sat grinning and listening. When the boy had diagnosed Nodakin's complaint, he rummaged around through his battery of bottles and handed one over to Nodakin. But Nodakin was insistent. A lot of the Arivaipa men had this complaint. He went away with three bottles.

"My word," said the young enlisted man professionally. "I wonder what they've been eating over there. I hope we don't have a run of the scours."

Shafter was still grinning. "There ain't nothing wrong with Nodakin or anybody else in camp. You're just out three bottles of castor-bean oil."

"But his symptoms," said the boy.

"They ain't gone to drink it because they got any symptoms," Shafter said. "They're gone to drink it because they consider it's powerful tasty."

"My word," said the boy again, with profound awe.

Shafter rode on, passing Obre down at the corral, where he was fooling around with Paco and the bronc crew. Shafter didn't stop, and after he'd got out of sight he pressured the dun, testing out how he could take the saddle. He gaited him, paced him, loped him, cantered him, galloped him, and in-between he cussed some but decided he was going to make it or bust. Right now the only thing on his mind was he intended to get *adiós* over and done.

Being a guest, Anna was not expected to work, so that she spent most of her time observing. Growing a garden didn't look to be so difficult; the very idea of it filled her with impatience to be riding back to the little valley. She was on her knees in the doorway of

Eskiminzin's third wife's wickiup when Shafter rode up, and her face brightened like it always did when she saw him coming. For himself, he got that awful squeeze in his chest he always got now when he saw her.

"Anybody around?" he said in a low voice.

"No, the men are up the trail talking, as usual. Stay and talk to me." She turned, and Shafter saw Eskiminzin's *niña* Chita, a little bitty kid, about two or so. The child regarded him, sober and unblinking, clutching a doll made of old corn husks. "It's all right," Anna said. "She doesn't talk much yet." She gave the child a little push and told her to go find her mother.

Shafter dismounted. "What are you doin' there anyway?" he said, seeing she appeared to be sorting things into hollow gourds.

"Seeds," she said. "Look, squash, melon, bean, corn, and pumpkin. Joaquin says we have to get them in the ground before we do anything else because it's getting late."

He stood watching her. He wasn't puzzled any more, only glad for her in a strange way which didn't contain even a shadow of gladness for himself. He knew in that instant that he couldn't say good-by to her, and that when he rode out it was going to be quiet and cowardly. He hunkered down as best he could, the best being mighty uncomfortable, and helped her to pour the seeds into the gourds, where they rattled with a pleasant little rhythm.

Joaquin found them so. Shafter straightened up and said howdy and when Joaquin went into the wickiup he noted for the first time the heavy ridge of muscle had settled in the boy's shoulders and remembered somebody had remarked he wasn't a kid any more. Who was it? Hell, yes. Oury, would you believe it? Joaquin came out with his carbine. He had, by this time, found it advisable to inform Anna of his plans, but she had, by this time, learned to anticipate him. "Are you going to hunt?" she said, disappointed.

"Only a few of us, Ana," he said. "Five or six. We will be gone two days at most. Chie said he would go, and I must, too. There is a party out for mescal also." He looked at Shafter. "The Arivaipa have been good to us; we can at least thank them with meat. And we will need meat when we leave."

"When you leavin'?" Shafter said.

"As soon as we return from the hunt. Chie is anxious to speak to Victorio. Are you coming out with us, Shafter, to see our land?"

"I'm studyin' on it," Shafter lied.

"Good. Come when we return. Ana, where is my fire drill?"

"My goodness, I don't know. When did you have it last? With all I have to keep together."

She went into the wickiup and he followed her, and Shafter smiled to himself not only at the prosaic interchange but because he knew they wanted a moment alone. He walked off aways so he didn't have to listen.

"I will miss you," Anna said wistfully.

He put the carbine down and his arms around her. "Only a little time. You have Shafter to talk with."

"Come back quickly." She put up her fingers and touched the side of his face and then his mouth. "And we will go home. Do you remember we have a home now?"

"I remember. I think of little else. One reason. . . ." He stopped.

"What reason?" she said.

"I think I will not have to look over my shoulder any more to see if there is anybody else in the wickiup, or outside it, before I make love to you."

"A sensible thought," she said. "Even noble."

She followed him out. Shafter wandered back. "Talk to my Ana while I am gone," Joaquin said.

Shafter said, "Good hunting. And keep your feet turned in."

Joaquin looked uncertain for a moment; then he laughed. Apaches had a conscious habit of treading slightly pigeon-toed whenever they were walking attendance on anything they considered of great importance. It was the best Shafter could get out for *adiós*.

Joaquin swung up on the Appaloosa. Chie and the chosen Arivaipa hunters were already gathered. He did not say good-by, but rode to join them and, when he had reached them, turned and lifted his hand and set the carbine stock down on his thigh and rode off.

Anna went back to her seed sorting, but now Shafter didn't bend to help her. He all of a sudden felt so restless he thought if he had a couple of horsehide balls he would try juggling them, just to have something to do with his hands, and he knew now it would have been good to go off on the hunting trip with the men. While he was thinking it, she looked up and said, "You would have liked to go with them."

"How do you know?" he said.

She lifted her shoulders, smiling. "I don't know. I suppose I sensed it. I suppose men who live with guns all the time need to use them, even if it's only on defenseless animals."

"Don't cry," he said.

She caught the note of bitterness in his voice. "Don't concern yourself, Shafter. I don't like seeing animals shot, but I don't like being hungry either. Is that practical enough for you?"

"Sure," he said. "You're lucky you got a good hunter in the family."

"I pray never to take my blessings for granted. By the way," she said, "thank you for sending Mr. Obre the other day."

"He came on his own," Shafter said. "Just didn't want to have Lin. . . ."

"Yes," she interrupted hastily, stonily.

There was a silence. Then he said, "Well, I'm no account here, so I expect I will go back to the post and climb into my rockin' chair."

She shook her head at him, half admonishing. "Shafter, sometimes I still do hate you, do you know it?"

"I reckon I do," he said. "You want to be careful. I recollect I read somewhere hate and love are kissin' cousins." He hadn't meant to say that. . . . Goddamit, what was the matter with him anyway, he was getting as flabber-mouthed as Willson. But she only laughed; she stood up and walked to the dun with him. When he said good-by he kind of croaked it.

Whitman looked up from a stack of reports when he got back to the office. "Been over to the ranchería quite a bit lately, haven't you?" he said, stopping to light his pipe.

"It's the only place I can study on to go around here," Shafter said.

Whitman said pleasantly, "You know those Mimbreños, don't you?"

Shafter didn't flick an eyelid. "Never saw 'em before in my life," he said.

Corporal Herbert went out of the Tucson post not too concerned about being unescorted; in fact, he was feeling a little heroic, but that was superficial, as he was naturally, honestly, youthfully eager. He was slightly surprised but not daunted when three men came up out of the wash and blocked the road by stringing clean out across it, right in his path.

"Howdy," said the man in the middle.

Herbert pulled up short. "Anything the matter here?" he said, hesitant at their appearance. They were Americans, but they were the kind of rough-cut Americans always gave him a pause.

The man in the middle didn't answer. He said, "Where you bound, trooper?"

For a moment Herbert considered telling him it wasn't any of his business, but something in the set of the man's eye changed his mind. "I'm on my way to Camp Grant with a message from Colonel Degnan, and I'll thank you to let me pass."

The man laughed. "Well, well, from Colonel Degnan. What do you think of that, boys? From Colonel Degnan."

They all laughed. Herbert eyed them uneasily. While he was trying to figure how to handle this unexpected turn of events, the man got down from his horse and walked over to him.

"You ain't in no hurry," he said.

"I am too in a hurry," Herbert said defensively. "I'm in a terrible hurry."

The man said, "He's in a hurry, boys. Maybe we oughtn't to hold him up."

They laughed again. Herbert began to sweat. Hold him up? My God, they were road agents. He said, "I ain't got any money, if that's what you're after."

The man looked hurt. "Money. That's a unkind thing to face a honest man like me with. Naw, we don't want no money. We're just lonesome, out here all alone, and we would like for you to keep us comp'ny."

Herbert got mad. "What is this, some kind of a joke? I ain't got time for any such foolishness. I told you I'm in a hurry."

The man said, "Trooper, you know what we got down in the wash?"

"I don't know nor care," Herbert blustered.

Then the man said, "Sonny, you get on your lip with me you goin' to come up short and sorry. You get off that horse and come down in the wash with me and have some nice whiskey and keep us comp'ny."

"Damn you," said Herbert, the sweat pouring down his face, "I don't *drink* whiskey."

The man made a solicitous clucking sound with his tongue. "You don't drink whiskey? By damn, sonny, I am about to interduce you to some good fun like you ain't never dreamed of." His hand moved to the butt of the waist-high pistol. "Now you get the hell off that horse."

Herbert dismounted. They escorted him into the wash. When they told him to sit down, he sat down. They took his .44 and his boots and destroyed Degnan's dispatch. He looked at the men, and the three Mexicans who had joined them, and he gagged down the whiskey they held out to him, and the tears came clear and innocent in his eyes and ran down his cheeks.

Trooper Price, walking the forward outer boundary of the post, hallooed loud enough to finally reach Stern, and Stern came out and peered under the flat of his hand.

"What the hell is it?" Price said, mystified.

Whatever it was was coming in out of its own dust, and from here it looked like a riderless horse.

Stern had a sense of foreboding, but it didn't really reach up and grab him until the horse ran in, in a lather to get back to its stable. It wasn't going to stop, so Stern grabbed its bridle and Herbert wobbled bonelessly and fell off on the ground.

"Get the colonel," Stern said. There was such a stink of whiskey on Herbert that Stern recoiled, and the boy had vomited all over himself, evidently not once but several times. Stern knew he wasn't just dead drunk; he was actually damn near dead.

Degnan came up. He stood there looking at the inert slow-breathing body in the dust at his feet and calculating. Herbert had left the post over three hours ago. . . . He looked at Stern.

Stern said, "Sir, I never knew Herbert to take a drink in his whole enlisted time."

Degnan stood with his eyes closed, pounding his fist into the palm of his other hand. When he spoke, his voice was controlled but at the breaking point. "How long has Lieutenant Degnan been out, Stern?" A time like this, and Linus was off chasing cows.

"Lieutenant Degnan come in a little over an hour ago, sir," Stern said. "He's down catchin' a little cat nap."

"Get him," Degnan said. "And get this man into hospital and let him die in bed."

Linus reached commandant in nothing flat. His father was sitting behind his desk, staring at the wall, with his hands crossed on his breast. It struck Linus as an old man's gesture and alarmed him. His father said, "I'm sorry. I know how tired you are."

"That's all right," Linus said. Now his father looked at him and a small ray of cheer lightened him. Well, here was one steady hand, one steady eye, in the wreckage. He saw the exhaustion on his son's face, but he saw that steadiness and the steel where a normal man's backbone hinged. He said, "Shoot the first man that puts out a hand to stop you."

"Don't worry," Linus said. "I will." He went to the rack on the far wall and said, "I'm borrowing your Sharps if you don't mind."

Degnan watched him take out the heavy .50–700 carbine, along with its band of cartridges. "I just gave it to you," he said wearily.

"Thanks," Linus said. "I never wanted it less." He went out, gave his orders about water and a spare horse, mounted the roan. For the first time in his life he put spurs so deep in a horse it groaned, but it knew and dragged out as it was, laid heavily into the bit.

A strange thing came upon Anna in the evening. She spoke when she was required to, using her growing store of Apache and Spanish and, seeing no questioning eye upon her, informed herself that she was doing very well and had barely done so when Eskiminzin came up to the wickiup. His young wife and the two children were inside, and Anna was brushing up around the fire area. When she saw Eskiminzin, she straightened and inclined her head a little toward him. He stood, looking back at her, his face set in that peculiar stoic cast which seemed almost a deliberate affectation to the Apache, but unable to conceal his geniality and good-humored shrewdness. Quite before she was prepared for it, he said somewhat hoarsely and gutturally in English, "Good day."

Seeing her startled face, he went on, stuttering a little. "Arivaipa *sabe americano*. Mimbreño brave have *americano* blood. Eskiminzin say it not bad, is welcome."

And she could only say, "Thank you, Señor."

He swept his arm out, indicating the ranchería in the dying sunlight. He said, "*Americano sabe* much good here. *Americano* soldier much good. For Victorio, much good."

Then she said, "Yes, much good for all Apache, I think."

There was something close to a twinkle in his eyes. "Woman no think. You woman think."

"All women want peace," she said.

"You stay with Mimbreños?" His eyes were searching now.

She shook her head. "Mimbreños friends, always," she said. She hoped this was so, knowing the unconditional and often irrational behavior of these people. Eskiminzin nodded and passed on up the canyon where the yellow light lay on the garden plots.

Anna had thought with luck that Joaquin might return this day, but it was now drawing so late she knew that the men would already be camped for the night, somewhere in the mountains. If the hunting had been good, perhaps they would not linger, but return in the early morning. Two days at most, Joaquin had said; surely he would be no later than tomorrow night.

She felt no desire for sleep. The wickiup seemed stuffy and the clear cold air infinitely preferable. She still had the heavy Mexican *rebozo* Obre had brought her, and with a hole worked in it for her head it made an admirable and quite handsome poncho, being so heavy-woven it was fairly water resistant except in a cloudburst, and of such fine-quality wool that it was warmer than an army blanket. The children slept noiselessly, the little girl on her knees, with her small rounded behind straight up in the air. Anna got up and slipped the *rebozo* over her head, belted it with a ring of *conchas*, and went out into the night.

All over, the fires had died to red points of light, glowing up the canyon. The camp was silent, and the clear stars were big and warming. The rounded bulks of the wickiups rose under the canyon walls, and the creek shone, night-lighted, between the trees. She walked down to it, disturbing a dog which came out to sniff at her heels. She sat on the bank for a time and thought Joaquin would be sleeping now, in some cave or canyon in the high places, with the fire burning for warmth, and the men taking turn at vedette duty. She thought of him sleeping, with his face relaxed and dreamless and his heart beating evenly, steadily, and his small-boned flexible hands half reached out to her even when she was not there. Longing swept over her; she put her head in her arms and when she raised it felt the dizziness which had plagued her these four weeks flood on her with a force which nearly made her fall over and blurred her vision until the water seemed to float miles off in the distance, milky and wavering.

When she had recovered she walked back to the wickiup, meaning to sleep now by concentrating on sleep itself, but could not bring herself to enter the door. Some distance off, between the last cluster of wickiups and the horse corral, there was a big mound of hay the women had brought in from the foothills grasslands, and which they would bundle and take into the post in the morning. It was fresh, fragrant, and she sat down on the edge of it and leaned back into its receptive softness and looked up at the stars and without any concentration at all fell into a sound and heavy sleep.

Sound woke her. For a thick and chilling time she could not remember where she was. It was not night any more, but it was not day either; the stars were paling but still bright in the west. In the east, a dawn showing gray before the upward rushing of the sun had begun to streak the sky. The grass pricked the nape of her neck and she recalled where she was and went to sit up when the sound came again. She could not identify it: it was a dull, plunking sound, quite hollow, the sound a pumpkin might make if you cracked it with a slat. She heard it twice more, and at the end there was a scream that brought her bolt upright, with her heart in her throat. Under the washing gray of dawn she saw that the whole ranchería was filled with moving shapes and for a time, suspended, detached, wondered who had screamed and why they were all rising so early. Swift, unreal on the surface of the eye, she saw a man standing halfway across the ranchería, saw him lift his arm, saw the shape in his hand, saw him lower it with brute force. And she cried out. It had been a club he swung. *A club.* Then there was not a single scream but a lifting wail which began and was joined a hundred times over, expanding until it seemed that sound itself was a shaped and finite thing which would burst its own confines. Feet ran, men ran, the hollow thudding went on and on, and far up at the very end of the camp she saw a wickiup burst into flame.

She was stone. She did not know what was happening. There were no soldiers. She saw no women. Only men, running and running and crying and striking and falling, under the dawn. The men had clubs, knives. It was a long time, with the clubs and the knives.

Movement at her side drew her up in terror. It was the little girl Chita, standing soberly beside her, holding the bundled cornhusk doll. In her first sane moment, Anna reached for the child, clamped a hand over her mouth, pulled her down. Then she was

burrowing, fighting the grass which had seemed so loosely piled
a few hours ago and now seemed to possess the substance and solidity of adobe. Someone was moaning. She was moaning. She
fought desperately, tearing at the grass with her hands, bucking it
with her shoulders. She thrust the child inside, squirmed in with her,
scattering grass in all directions, certain they were still exposed,
dragging the piled stuff down over them. She lay there panting;
the child made no sound. Anna was flat on her belly, her arms
thrown over the child's legs. The sound was muffled, but even here
the screaming came, and that other terrible sound, and then, at last,
the guns. She turned her head, gasping in the smothering grass.
A sickness which was more than knowledge began somewhere in
her thighs and crept up the walls of her belly and lodged like a
lance head under her heart. She began to retch uncontrollably, feeling she would die without air, without water, so sick that she did
not hear the silence when it came. The last thing she heard was
horses moving and shrilling, and when the stillness laid its cold
hands on her senses at last she was too spent to move. The child
did not move either; she thought it might be dead.

After a long time she clawed the grass away with a hand so
weak that it was limp at the wrist. Air rushed at her, reviving
her, but it was not clear air; it was thick and heavy with smoke.
She half turned and her eyes came to rest on daylight.

Most of the wickiups were burning, had already burned, dry and
incendiary as they were, and where they had stood were only black
charred smoking heaps of ash. The burned hides stunk in the air.
Nothing moved. Not even the smoke, standing straight up the canyon walls. No, the creek was moving, as always. It was the same.
Sprawled bodies were strung up the canyon. When she turned her
head she saw that the horses were still in the corral, standing
quietly and switching their tails.

She pushed grass away. Then she saw a man was walking toward
the hayshock, coming with preciseness and care, as if he were just
learning to walk. She drew back.

The sun showed a thin rounded lip of light. The man was
Eskiminzin. He was the only man standing. Blood was pouring
down his head and neck. She crouched in the grass, staring at him.
The blood made its way over his shoulder and breast. She thrust
her hand into the grass and found the child's feet and pulled it to
her.

Eskiminzin came up. He was blind with the blood running in
his eyes. He put up his hand as if it were some separate thing
which did not belong to him and tried to brush away the blood.
He saw the child. His face was the face of a dead man. He took
the child in both hands. He went down on his knees in the scattered grass. The child watched him with trust, still holding the doll.
He could not weep, for the water could not reach through the
blood which ran again in his eyes. He rocked back and forth on
his knees, holding the child. A cry of anguish broke in his throat.

The roan smashed the last of its second wind trying to get up
the wall of a wash. The foam that blew back in Linus' mouth
tasted of blood, and when the roan made the top of the wash it
stumbled and made to go spraddle-legged, with its head hanging.
It had too many miles under it, what with the cow chase, and
Linus knew another one would break its heart. He threw himself
off and unsaddled, holding the spare horse in, and shot the roan
through the ear. The spare jumped off nervously and Linus fought
him back and got him saddled.

The road was clear all the way, but he hadn't stuck to the road,
taking crosscuts he figured would be shorter, like the wash which
had finished the roan. The sun was spattering the first clouds with
tints light and delicate as water color when he raised the post and
nearly rode down the forward sentry. Whitman was at his desk;
the sentry's yell brought him out.

Linus didn't dismount. "Royal, for God's sake get up the canyon
and get the Arivaipa in."

Whitman's questioning face infuriated him. "Don't ask questions;
there's over a hundred Tucson men laying around here somewhere
with nothing good in mind. Get 'em in."

Whitman was calm and authoritative. He sent Jerry, his orderly,
for Marijildo and when Marijildo got there detailed ten men and
sent him off to the ranchería. "Tell Eskiminzin not to be troubled;
this is for his own protection. I don't want any panic. Just get them
in here quietly and in order. On the double now, Marijildo."

He turned to Jerry. "I want every man on this post at station.
Forty rounds of ammunition per man, and on the alert in twenty
minutes."

Jerry ran off. Marijildo and the detail were making time; even
their dust had dispersed. The sun kept climbing and bird song was

pure and clear. A morning breeze stirred fresh and light. Linus sat down on the step, hollow-eyed, gray with dust, and felt the fingers of weariness work along his spine and grab at the small of his back. There wasn't much he could tell Whitman. There wasn't much he knew to tell.

Marijildo came back alone. Not at the speed he'd gone out, but not lagging. He sat his horse before the porch and the pattern of beard shadow was steely blue in the pallor which had come upon his dark Spanish face. He looked at Linus. "You are too late." He looked up at Whitman. "You are too late also." He looked down at his own hands, where they clasped the saddle horn. "It is all too late, Lieutenant. The thing has been done."

Twenty-five

Limping around the side of the office with the dun's bridle over his arm, Shafter heard Marijildo and stopped, his hand flat out on the wall. The fingers bent, clawed, as if they would force themselves into the flaking building. The leg was shaking so bad he wasn't sure it would hold him up. He went on around, dropping the reins on the ground, and he and Linus saw one another but did not speak. He had the feeling they were all of them frozen there, Marijildo still mounted, Linus on the step, Whitman standing, himself looking up, none of them moving, three-dimensional but free of any dimension of reality, carved out and propped upright, never to move again.

Then Linus got up and went into Whitman's office. Whitman said in a cracked voice, "Top file drawer." Shafter took the step and seized Whitman's arm in a grip that should have caused the man to cry out, but Whitman didn't seem to feel it. Shafter shot a glance into the office: Linus was taking a long pull at the whiskey bottle, and it seemed to Shafter that his face, what he could see of it, looked blank and thoughtless. He dragged Whitman off the porch.

"Keep Linus out of that camp . . . got to, understand?"

Whitman did not understand at all, but he was under the impression that he understood everything, and he felt that for some reason it had become imperative that he be agreeable in all things; he was like a man hanging on the point of a fever break. Shafter kept dragging at him and he kept submitting. But after a moment he protested; shock crested over him and he looked up at Marijildo. All he said was "What," without any question mark after it.

Marijildo said, "They are dead. Some have gone; we saw their tracks."

Whitman said, "Did they fight?"

Marijildo's voice was steady now. "I do not think they had a chance to fight, Lieutenant. This thing was done quickly with knives and clubs."

Shafter thought he was going to have to sit down because the fear in him was more terrible than any fear he had ever known. He didn't even see Obre when Obre came up wondering what was going on. His leg gave out and he leaned against Marijildo's horse.

Whitman said, "Eskiminzin."

"I did not see his body, but I did not look too far." Marijildo lowered his head. "Lieutenant, I saw no bodies but those of women and children."

Shafter made himself stand up and walk to the dun. Inside the office Linus was slumped at Whitman's desk with his head in his arms. Shafter mounted and turned the dun upstream and Obre followed him.

He rode into the ranchería. He did not know any way to stand up to what he knew was coming. He saw the horses still in the corral. He saw the bodies, making bright spots of color, blue and red, and russet of deerskin, and the charred places the wickiups had stood. The stink in the air made his throat close. Whitman's troopers were walking in the carnage, subdued, communicating in low voices, as if they did not want to disturb the dead. The dun walked through a circle of warm ash, picking up its feet, and around the body of a woman, flung upon her back, head smashed in. Flies swarmed thickly. The black birds had come to hover. The humped pile of grass looked in its form like a wickiup. The dun walked through its scattered edges and Shafter saw her sitting, looking up at him with eyes which held the flat apathy of madness.

It was he who was saved, after all. He dismounted and went to her and lifted her, feeling the rough scarlet wool, feeling the grass which had caught in her hair. He held her head in both hands and then he was holding her so closely it seemed to him that they supported one another.

"It's all right, little girl. It's all right."

It was not all right, but that was what was left to say. Behind him, Obre shifted in the saddle, closed his single blue eye, and pushed off. He had heard Shafter mention ladies by various names in his time, but never as little girls, and he remembered the only time he had heard that was the rainy night Shafter had been off his *cabeza*, waiting for Willson to get back from Tucson.

Shafter was still holding Anna when Whitman rode in with Marijildo, an infantry detail, and the surgeon Briesly. Calm had returned to him but his face betrayed him; at one moment it screwed up as though he would burst into tears; at the next it was blank with acceptance. He was unsurprised to find Shafter standing with his arms around a squaw and went on.

It was easy to see what had happened. No alarm, the silent entering of the camp, the smashing clubs, the sure arc of the knife. In the throes of his particular personal paralysis he looked down incuriously at a small child whose hacked-off leg lay at its side. The bodies he passed were those of women, and children.

He dismounted near a knot of troopers. He said wearily, "Is there anyone alive in this camp?"

A steady voice came out of a steady old Indian fighter. "Sir, there's a young woman just up the pass there ain't hurt. She says they all gone into the hills. That was all we could get out of her; she won't say a word."

When Whitman sent Marijildo to find the woman, she was gone. Whitman said, "Ten men, detail. Get dead together. Get count." He walked back to where he had seen Shafter with the woman, and they were standing exactly as they had been when he passed them. The woman's head was turned on Shafter's chest; her eyes touched Whitman without interest or comprehension. He knew then it was the Mimbreño woman. He knew then Shafter had lied to him.

"Ask her where Eskiminzin is."

Anna said, "He has gone into the hills. They are all gone."

Only the words registered, not the tongue. "Then he is alive. Where is your husband, Señora, he did not leave you here alone?"

An elusive, almost halting sign of life came into her face. "He is with the hunting party. There is a mescal party out. I do not know where they are. Eskiminzin will not come back now."

He started to turn away. Then he swung back, staring at her. "You are not a Mimbreño."

Shafter said, "It's no matter, Royal."

Whitman knew. The half breed. Walter Degnan's ward. The least of his troubles. He went up to where Briesly was scribbling on his report board, where the bodies were being collected. "These two women have been raped," Briesly said. Whitman's glance passed over them, spread-eagled naked, dead in the dust. He said, "I do not need proof white men were in this camp. Or Mexicans." He watched his men coming in, carrying their burdens in blankets. "You had best look," said Briesly grimly. "I'm not the only one with reports to make."

Whitman looked. He knew all about death, as much as any soldier who may legitimately call it his profession. Death was always for somebody else. He had never seen such deliberate mutilation, or perhaps it was only the quantity of the senseless destruction, so much of it to look at that it no longer made him sick or stunned him, any more than a week in a stockyard might have done. He wanted a drink so badly he half thought to go for it, wanted not just the drink, but to be stone blind drunk. Forever more. An infantry corporal came up to him.

"Sir, there's two women behind some bushes, just up the trail."

"Dead or alive?" Whitman said.

"Alive, sir. There's an old one, I think her arm's broke. And a young one, she's coughing blood."

"I'll go," Briesly said. "There's nothing I can do here."

Whitman went up with him, and Obre. The women shrank and tried to hide when they saw the men. The young one had been shot through the lungs. The old one spoke at last to Obre, hard-mouthed, taut with hate. Obre hunkered at her side, glanced up at Whitman.

"Lieutenant, they think you done it. They think the soldiers done it."

"Yes," Whitman said calmly. He looked back down the long narrow corridor of the years of betrayal. He said, "What did you expect them to think?"

When he came down again to the main camp a sick-faced sergeant met him with the only thing he waited for. "Lieutenant, sir, I am sorry to say. . . ." He stopped and drew in his breath. "Sir, we have a count of one hundred and eight dead. Eight of 'em's men."

Whitman rode out of the ranchería. He felt the silence and peace of the spring morning like a blow. His shoulders bent under it.

Shafter watched him go. He and Anna were sitting in the grass. She tried to tell Shafter, but it didn't make much sense, to either of them. She was close now to hysteria. Any misspoken word would send her over the brink. She asked Shafter three or four times why anybody would do it, and Shafter said, each time, he didn't know.

A long while afterward she drank some water from his canteen and was instantly sick in the grass.

Shafter gave her plenty of time. When he felt she was ready he told her she'd better come on in to the post with him, but she was determined to wait where she was for Joaquin. He was gentle but insistent. She couldn't stay here, in the midst of this. He wouldn't permit that. It wasn't until he promised he or Obre would be here to meet Joaquin when he came in that she agreed. He found Obre and Obre said he was staying anyway, to lend Marijildo a hand. Because unless the hunting party ran into the fugitive Arivaipa in the hills, they were going to be coming cold to a thing which would either turn their spirit to fire or their blood to tears or maybe both.

Everything was burned. He went to put the McClellan on the paint mare for her but she wouldn't hear of him riding saddleless with his leg like that. He put his blanket on the mare. It reminded him of something, but he couldn't for the life of him think what it was.

He waited until they were well on the way before he told her. He said, "Annie, it wouldn't be fair not to let you know Linus is at the post."

Her face turned to him, grave, without reproval.

"He did his best," Shafter said. "He tried to get here. In time to stop it."

It was merely something else to be absorbed and accepted. What could she not accept now? She said, "How did he know? They were Indians. I know they were Indians. I saw them."

He nodded. "I reckon so. Mexicans, too. And white men."

"White men?" She whispered it.

"I reckon so," he said again. "The big man from Tucson. He was the one wanted it."

She did not speak again. When they rode into Grant he lifted her from the mare. He knew she was going to be all right. He knew she was no problem to anybody but himself and that didn't count. He said, "Come on, Annie, you got to eat something and get some sleep." He had in mind he could get the boy in dispensary to maybe give him a sleeping draught for her. But the mention of food made her nauseous, so that it was all she could do not to be sick again. When she raised her head, some soldiers had gathered, curious, on the compound and Linus was coming off the porch with the same kind of look on him that she had seen on Shafter when he found her, a few hours back.

Her eyes went through and past him, as if she did not know him. She flung the words out, voice pitched low and vicious.

"And you call Victorio a savage."

A big pinwheel-shaped object whirled in her head, going off in a long funneling cone. She started to follow it. Shafter caught her before she hit the ground.

All morning Eskiminzin lay in the hills watching the ranchería. Munaclee pleaded with him, but he only raised a weary hand and said nothing, motioning Munaclee away. He no longer bled, but he was covered nearly to the waist, all down his right side, with the thick crusting stuff of his own veins. He did not remember a great deal, except that he knew on the instant he had been wakened what was taking place, and that he had meant to call his men to stand and fight. His men, who had no arms but knives. The soldiers had always been clever at the game of taking their weapons as a safety measure. Whatever had been in his throat, waiting to be called out, had emerged a broken grunt when the war club crashed into his head.

But he was tough. Even in his pain he knew he was tougher than any white eyes soldiers who ever came on his land. His eyes were narrowed in contemplation. He had gone out of the ruined camp swiftly, carrying Chita in his arms. When he reached the hills he gave his child to a squaw and settled to wait, although he did not know what he was waiting for. His people went past him, living, wounded, dying. He, having brought them to this, had no word for them. They, knowing he had lost three wives and all his children but the smallest *niña*, had no word for him.

He lay in his own congealing blood, and after a time no longer had strength enough to brush away the sucking flies. They covered the side of his head and fought at his eyes. He saw the soldiers come into the ranchería. He saw his dead collected. He saw the gringo *vaquero* go out with the white eyes woman. Still he would not leave. Something was in him, something which made him refuse to believe what his people believed, even in this time of the worst thing of all, worse than war, which was at least proud, worse than starving, which was at least honest.

In the early afternoon he saw twenty soldiers ride into the camp, and at their head the lieutenant who had been his friend, his adviser, his last hope on earth. When he saw what they were about, he rose to his feet and walked steadily down again, between the canyon walls.

He did not pause until there was only the length of a man between himself and Royal Whitman. Then he said, "You bury our dead."

Their eyes reflected one another. Pain beyond bearing, grief beyond grieving.

Marijildo came up and Whitman made a gesture of dismissal. There was no longer any barrier here. They understood one another. He said, "Yes, we bury your dead, Eskiminzin. You know we did not do this thing. You know that we love the Arivaipa and that we wish only to help and protect them." He lowered his head, unable to meet Eskiminzin's sympathetic regard. "We have failed," he said.

After a time Eskiminzin moved, shaking his head slowly from side to side. "Friend no fail. Soldiers come too late." He raised his hand and looked at his blunt fingers, almost in wonderment. "See Papago. See *Nakaiyes*. See white eyes. Arivaipa say soldiers do this."

"What do you say?" Whitman said miserably.

"Eskiminzin say soldiers friends. No do this thing."

Whitman took a deep breath and looked up again. "Will the Arivaipa return? We bury your dead. We will care for your hurt and sick. We will put soldiers on your land so that this will never happen again."

Eskiminzin said haltingly, "My friend Whitman tells me this thing. It is true. Arivaipa no want come back. Eskiminzin bring them back."

Whitman put his hands out on Eskiminzin's shoulders. "I repeat. This will never happen again."

Eskiminzin's mouth twisted. Dried blood flaked away and settled on his chin. He said, "No happen with friend Whitman. If friend Whitman go, happen many time. All time." He turned away.

"Wait," Whitman said. "Your head. . . ."

He came back. "No hurt. Hurt all inside. I take horse, friend Whitman." He held Whitman's eye and he did not stutter. "Give me gun."

Whitman turned to Marijildo. "Saddle up for him. Give him my carbine."

Eskiminzin took the gift of speed and the gift of war and went away with them.

In the afternoon the Arivaipa came back. There was a monotonous and terrible silence in their movements, filtering in from the hills as they did, because Eskiminzin asked them. There was a great proportion of men. They had gathered and spoken together and knew their wives and children were dead. A runner had found the mescal party. It was not an easy thing to spread word among nearly four hundred fleeing, stricken people. Somehow Eskiminzin did it, sitting the borrowed horse stolidly and holding the carbine across his chest, where it could be readily seen. Nodakin carried the message for him, and Munaclee and other trusted men, and the return hinged not only upon his appeal but on the word that the soldiers were burying the dead.

When the first of them reached the fringe of the camp, with others coming behind them, the wailing began. It took a long time for twenty men to dig one hundred and eight graves, and the detail was a sweating exhausted one which must soon be relieved. To Whitman, standing bareheaded in the sun, came the wish that the job had been finished before the people came back to look, to identify their own. It was the women who wailed, down on their knees in the dust. He saw men beating their fists on the ground. He saw the frantic searching. He stood there, unable to do more, in the midst of the digging and the wailing and the searching.

At last Eskiminzin came to him and dismounted. He handed over the carbine. He said, "Friend Whitman. The children."

"I know," Whitman said. "I know." He was so tired his shoulders slumped.

Eskiminzin was shaking his head. "Children gone. Many gone." But he did not know how to say it and lapsed into Spanish. "*Viente y siete. Todos niños.*"

Whitman stared at him. "Twenty-seven children. Not dead? Where, Eskiminzin?"

"With *Nakaiyes*," Eskiminzin said. "Apache steal *Nakaiyi niño* all time. *Nakaiyes* steal Apache *niño*." Then he said simply, "Friend Whitman get back Arivaipa *niños*."

They looked at one another. Whitman knew how easy it would

be to lie. Eskiminzin said, "*Niños* better dead. Boy work and starve. Girl use for men, die of bad sickness."

Whitman already knew this. He said, "I will do everything I can to get them back, Eskiminzin." And could no longer face the man, the people, and for the second time that day took the longest five miles of his knowing back to Camp Grant.

Shafter was having a little drink in the office when he came in. He looked up and said, "I'm sorry, Royal, but you ain't got any bed for the moment." He nodded toward the closed door of Whitman's room, off the office. "We gave . . . uh . . . Miz Mitchell a little unconscious powder."

Whitman didn't want to talk about that, didn't care. His mind was on his one small triumph, or Eskiminzin's. He said, "They're coming back. They're going to try again, and this time, God willing, we're going to make it work."

Shafter's upper lip flattened. "That so? Well, some folks ain't happy unless they're bein' shot at or gettin' their skulls smashed or. . . ." He saw Whitman's face. "Hell, Royal, forget it. I wasn't aimin' to talk down to you."

Whitman didn't want a drink now. He stood leaning on the top of the file cabinet, on his crossed arms. "I thought burying their dead would show them how we felt. My God, Shafter, how could I show them how I feel? Those women who've lost their children are crushed with grief. And the children . . . those same kids who were laughing and sliding down the slope on a horsehide yesterday. Yesterday. And I have got to promise them more than the return of the stolen, more than material restitution, more than the protection of the army."

"What else is there?" Shafter said.

"There is the justice of the United States Government."

Shafter laughed and poured himself another drink.

Whitman's eyes were red-rimmed from dust and weariness. "I will not rest until I see justice. I will work day and night. Shafter, I'd rather be drummed out of the army than leave these people. Or see them leave here. Listen, if we can grant justice now, if we can show them the impartiality and honor and integrity of the United States it will be the means of making good citizens of them and their children. If we fail again, we can drive them to a hopeless war of extermination."

Shafter raised his glass. "*Buena suerte.*" He finished the whiskey and got up. He said, "About the worst thing I can think of, for any man, is to be right all by himself." He limped out on the porch and sat down in the rocking chair and pulled the dog's ears. After a while he heard something and twisted around so he could see inside and figured Whitman must've thought he had pushed off, because while he was still leaning on the file cabinet his head was down on his folded arms. He was weeping.

Joaquin shot a heavy doe with a spring fawn in her. He did not want to run her, because even mortally wounded she could go a long distance. But she only went a little way and lay down. When he came up, keeping out of range of her hoofs, she was already dead. Chie rode in and bled the doe, but they did not gut her because of the fawn. Among them, the men had taken ten deer, most of them does with fawn, which was very good because unborn fawn was the finest meat of all. The horses were used to carrying dead animals, but they did not like it. The pack horse shied from its burden.

"How much longer?" Joaquin said. "They say two days, and it is the second day."

"They do not know how good the hunting is when they say two days," Chie said. "There should have been a larger party."

"Then let us go in and tell them. They can send out more men."

"I am ready," Chie said. "I wish to return home."

Joaquin sat down where the needles of a pine made comfort on the ground. "Have you thought what you will tell Victorio?"

Chie looked at him. "A man does not need to think when he tells another man the truth."

Joaquin said, "Can you live like this, Chie?"

"My father would have lived like this, if they had let him. He knew it was the only way. And you, Joaquin?"

Joaquin said, "We have found our place."

"*Enju*," Chie said. Then he said suddenly, "For myself, I would rather fight. Victorio says this is because I am young. Do you know, when a thing is in us which is not the same thing as in other men, it is because we are too young. Or too old."

Joaquin laughed and got to his feet. It was half in his mind to chide Chie, and he would have done so had Chie spoken more gravely, with less humor. Chie had ever been a bit too open and frank for the taste of his elders, and Joaquin knew this talk of the reservation was difficult for men of Chie's, and Tahzay's, tastes, years, knowledges. He let it pass.

At the main camp they learned that a subchief named Santo had found the sign of antelope in large numbers on high ground to the north. When Joaquin suggested he and Chie return to the ranchería with the meat to be butchered and send out a larger party with fresh pack horses, Santo nodded in approval, for he had his eye and appetite set upon the antelope. Joaquin and Chie were a long time packing the carcasses and preparing the pack horses. The men decided to keep two horses beside their own, intending to hang what further meat they procured until the horses returned. Klinnyti said he would stay in this camp and continue to hunt the deer while the rest of the party went on to the north in pursuit of the antelope; that way he would be here to guide the coming hunters.

Riding down out of the high places when the sun was near its meridian, Joaquin stiffened, bracing in the stirrups and lifting his hand flatly to Chie, who rode the end of the bunched horses. Chie came to him. Joaquin said, "What is that, off there, Chie?"

Chie looked but saw nothing, even though he shielded his eyes with his hand. "Where do you look, Joaquin?"

Joaquin pointed. "Do you see where the two hills come against one another? A little to the right."

Chie made a circle of thumb and forefinger and looked through this circle, directing his sight upon the V of the hills. Nothing. A black buzzard going around on still wings, dropping lower and lower. Then a whitish, misting wash, almost vaporous, hanging for a moment, in the cleft.

"The sun comes through there," Chie said.

"The sun is not striking from that direction," Joaquin said patiently. His eyes were narrowed against the light.

"It is mist rising," Chie said. "Perhaps there is water lying in that canyon."

"Mist, in this sun?" Joaquin said. "I think it is a mirror."

Chie sat watching. The horses stirred restlessly behind him. He could hear Joaquin breathing, even over a coming of soft wind which stirred the leaves of trees and pushed the tops of the lush grass patches. The vague light hung again, but only for a second. The wind passed, the grass stood upright, the leaves settled. He said, "It does not flash like a mirror; it is not bright or hard enough."

"I think it is something which picks up light," Joaquin said. "The light has no place to go and spreads out in the wash. Watch that bird."

The buzzard had ascended, very high, but it did not go away. It went up the wall of the sky, gliding, began to circle widely, slowly. "A rabbit has died," Chie said with mock sorrow.

"The fur of a rabbit does not reflect," Joaquin said briefly. "That is not a signal to our party; it is not directed at us."

"It is not a signal at all," Chie argued. "Some bit of metal in the arroyo picks up the flash, as you say. Now let us be about our journey."

But Joaquin still sat. He said, "I do not like this, Chie."

"Ai," Chie said, "the land is free for those who wish to signal upon it."

"That may be," Joaquin said. "But the land is not safe unless all men can read the signal." He dismounted and began to pull the rolled deerhide off the Appaloosa.

"What are you about?" Chie said.

He was throwing the roll on the near pack horse, behind the hanging body of the doe. When he came back he shortened the stirrups and checked the single Mexican-style cinch. Chie shook his head. "Wherever you ride, you ride in a hurry. That is a long way off, Joaquin, and does not lie in our path."

"Go on to the ranchería," Joaquin said.

"No, I will not do that," Chie said. "We will tie the horses here and return for them."

"And when we return they will be gone perhaps. Other men like deer meat and horse meat. Animals like it. Go on, I tell you."

He mounted. Chie said, "Ride ahead. I will follow you with the pack. When you have picked up your empty *americano* food tin or broken whiskey bottle, I will meet you."

Joaquin kicked the Appaloosa and cut off toward the draw. Chie was wrong. It was not such a long way; that had merely been an attempt to deter him, although he knew Chie would come grumbling along. The reflection, if that was what it was, no longer lay in the hollow, and when he drew nearer, the hills appeared to grow and fall away from one another, separated by the canyon. The sky was so blue, the air so clear, that even the massed flowers of the sand seemed reflective, even the clouds rushing across the flatlands.

He was not incautious, who had been overcautious all his life. The Appaloosa was very fast and, when he felt it had gone fast enough, far enough, he pulled in and sat watching the silent and somehow desolate slash of the wash. From this end, looking down it, he could see the deep curve of the arroyo to the extreme left. The curve was clean and, where it began, boulders began also, all sizes, worn round by some long-ago time of running water between these banks. Where water had once run, rocks would be, not only in the bottoms but in the earth wall which had once held and framed them. There was earth on these banks now only because there was no longer any water to wash it away.

Nothing stirred. He felt that he had been hasty if not actually foolish, but he could not shake off the compulsion which had come over him when his eye fell on the cleft in the hills. A small reddish bird came up cheerfully, unalarmed, out of the wash. He rode out into the open and up the lightly sloping bank.

The shot was badly placed, grazing the Appaloosa's neck. Joaquin flung himself clear of the saddle and struck the ground rolling. There was no other sound. No birds sang. He lay motionless. The Appaloosa shied off, its nerves jerky from the sting and whine of the shot. It ran awhile, rather dispiritedly; he saw it stop and stand, with its head down.

It was odd the birds did not begin again. After a moment he rolled over and let himself fall off the lip of the wash, bringing a shower of small stone and earth with him. He worked himself flat, listening, but nothing moved, nothing spoke. He was near the bend of the wash, where the boulders began. He did not understand any of this, but he knew the shot had not been a wild one coming in of its own accord from nowhere; it had been at close range.

He thought of Chie. When he did he was violently angry at himself for the first time. He sat up behind the jumble of boulders, knowing anger would only distort and confuse him. He had to warn Chie off. He fired the carbine into the air three times and looked over the lip of the wash. The Appaloosa was nowhere in sight.

He crouched under the bank, feeling the warm red dirt filter along his backbone. It seemed to him a long time before he heard three shots, and even then he did not know whether Chie had answered or whether it was the delayed echo of his own carbine. The only thing he knew was that he was trapped, until darkness came.

Somewhere down the wash there was a clanging sound, metal on rock. He pulled in behind the natural fortification of the boulders, digging his back into the bank. The sound came again, closer, and he knew now that whoever, whatever, was in this wash with him crouched also, around the turn, ahead of him. And the waiting was nothing, who had been trained to lie and wait.

Pretty soon a voice said, very low and soft, "Howdy, down there."

That was all. He went slack, but sweat was running in his eyes. He said, "Who is it?"

It was quiet again. Then he heard other voices. They were muffled, not directed at him, and he could not distinguish the words or how many men spoke to one another. He waited for the one voice. When it came it was still soft and quiet.

"Hey, who's down there? Call yourself out, pardner."

Joaquin bit his lip, angry again, stubborn against his own reason. "Who are you and where are you from? I don't trust any man who puts a shot at me without warning."

The voice was disgruntled now. "Thought you was a goddam Indian. Come on down, Jack, we're Yanks."

Joaquin swung the carbine up, over the top of the boulder. "Show," he said.

There was another muffled conference. A new voice took over, a firmer, more insistent voice lacking the easy idiom of the first.

"Sorry Logan was so quick on the trigger. We mistook you. We're just laying up here for some grub. You've got a rifle, hold it on us if you want to. Come on up and have some coffee."

Joaquin hesitated. If he took the corner slowly he'd have them under cover until he could see if he wanted to join them or wait them out. There had been no smoke before, but now he could smell it and he could smell the coffee, too.

The same voice said, "You out of Tucson?"

He said, "Camp Grant." A strong and racking emotion came up in him without any warning, a thing newly rich with warmth and pride. "I have a small place in the valley, east of here. The name is Mitchell." He thought a moment. Then he said, "Joe Mitchell."

They were talking together again. The man called down the wash. He sounded friendly, eager. "I bet I knew your father, Mitchell. . . . We were good friends." Silence. "Coffee's about done."

Maybe it was a good thing. He had identified himself not only for other men but to himself, and this had been the block, the thing he continually stumbled over. Now he had stopped stumbling and taken the step which brought him over the block, cleanly. He stood up and walked down the wash. When he took the angled cut of the bank, the first things he saw were the heavy silver-mounted pistols he had seen once before, outside the walls of Tucson.

Twenty-six

Night had fallen by the time the detail, with Colonel Walter Degnan at its head, reached Tucson. Degnan was a fine horseman and there was about him such an air of control, command, that men moved out of his path with deference and largely with respect, inclining their heads, touching the brims of their hats. Yet he acknowledged no man; his jaw was up sharp, and his eyes were cold.

There was about the town now not the feeling that something had occurred but that something was about to occur. The tension was thick, muddy, stifling. A few fires burned in the street, a few wagons turned aside, out of the way of the detail. Men went in and out of the saloons; now and then a Mexican woman scurried by, eyes averted, head shawled. Papagos sat as they always sat, smoking, flat against the walls of buildings or cross-legged in the dirt. The church door was open and spilling light. The word preceded the detail, not obvious, but with its passage suddenly nobody knew the military; nobody recognized Walter Degnan.

The word reached Oury. He came out the bat-wing doors of a saloon and stood on the sloping porch with his hands in the side pockets of his buckskin coat. He looked directly into Walter Degnan's face, shoulders bent forward a little. "Good evening, Colonel," he said.

Degnan held up his hand. The detail came to a halt.

"I am looking for you, Will."

"I expect so," Oury said.

"Where is Jesús Elias?"

Oury turned and called inside the saloon. Elias came out, alone. He appeared calm, but his hand was already on the butt of the whip.

Degnan said, "You are free in your own recognizance, until you are tried for murder."

"Colonel," Oury said, "we haven't been arrested. You can't free us without arresting us first. Where's your warrant?"

There was laughter in the street. Degnan said, "My warrant comes by telegraph from the President of the United States. It will be posted, in Tucson. Arizona is to be placed under martial law unless the men responsible for what happened at Camp Grant are brought to trial."

Elias had the whip out, hanging at his side. His mouth twitched. "It is not a wise thing to ride into this town, Colonel, and accuse us. You are accusing us?"

Degnan was blunt as ever. "You are accused, on an overwhelming evidence. If you care to deny it, you may do so to a federal judge."

Will Oury leaned over the edge of the porch and spat. "Deny it. Hell, Colonel, it would take a bigger man than me to deny the few decent things he gets a chance to do in his lifetime. I won't deny it. Elias won't deny it. Every man in Tucson knew what was happening. Every man went into that filthy Apache camp with us was a volunteer." He looked squarely at Degnan. "I'd like to see the day the military asked for volunteers and got 'em like that. One hundred and forty-six men, Colonel. You think you can fit 'em all in a courtroom?"

The laughter was derisive, ugly, around them. The crowd was swelling.

"No courtroom will hold that many murderers," Degnan said. "No place on earth will hold that many murderers. But it will hold you and Elias, and the United States citizens who went with you."

"We'll wait," Oury said. His voice was almost pleasant.

Degnan snapped it at Elias. "Where are the twenty-seven Arivaipa children who were taken?"

Elias spread his hands. "I do not know what you are talking about, Colonel."

Logan had come out of the saloon. He was drunk, carrying a bottle by the neck. He said, "Them lousy little bastards'll be so deep in Sonora by the time. . . ."

"Shut up, Logan," Oury said.

Degnan said grimly, "I trust you will all be as co-operative when court sits."

"Why not?" Oury said. "For myself, I hope court will sit long enough to see it takes a posse of volunteer civilians to do what the military has never been able to do here. You've never been able to even dull an Indian's appetite for raiding, Colonel, whereas we are making certain he's never hungry again."

He had a responsive audience and it was pressing nearer the detail. A few troopers were moving their hands nervously, closer to their belts, closer to the .44s. But Walter Degnan was stone, jaw as set as if it had been lined out with a square. He said, "Don't leave Tucson."

"Set your mind at rest," Oury said. "We'll be here." He smiled, but only slightly. "We'll all be here. Not a single man of our command has been hurt to mar our success, Colonel. We came back with the satisfaction of work well done. There's nothing going to take away from that satisfaction."

Degnan went to turn his horse and then checked. He was sicker in his soul than he had ever been, even in the years he had killed his countrymen. "Since you are so co-operative, Will, perhaps you'll satisfy my curiosity on one point."

"Anything I can do to oblige," Oury said.

"You had a wagonload of arms and ammunition. Where did you get it?"

Oury's smile was full now. "Why, as you know, Colonel, we found General Stoneman as unwilling to give us a hand as the rest of the military around here. We had to go a little further, seeing as how we wanted to forestall any chance of one of us maybe getting killed. We got the whole match, wagon and all, from Sam Hughes."

This time Degnan turned the detail, but he hardly knew he gave the routine hand signal. In the flaring light, his face had taken on the white crumbling look of chalk.

Samuel Hughes was the adjutant general of Arizona.

The little orderly, Jerry, came up on the porch where Shafter was sitting reading the kind of editorial Tony Bleeker had indicated as capable of producing rash. It was a local editorial, commending the recent destruction of the illegal reservation at Camp Grant. Jerry said, "Did the lieutenant go already?"

"Yes," Shafter said. "What's the matter now?"

"I don't know as anything's the matter," Jerry said. "There's an Indian down by the creek says he wants to see the young lady. He's got a white flag."

Shafter folded the newspaper. "He must be touchy. Can't blame him, I reckon." It would be Joaquin, he knew, but he wondered why Obre wasn't with him, and why he would come under flag. Unless he'd returned and got only a glance at what had happened at the ranchería. But, even so, the wickiups were already starting to go up again. That shouldn't have scared him off. He stood up.

"He didn't say he wanted you," Jerry said. "He said he wanted the young lady. The *niña,* he called her."

"In English?"

"Kind of broke-up English . . . you know how they talk it," Jerry said.

Shafter frowned. Then it couldn't be Joaquin. He turned around and Anna was standing in the doorway. She looked better rested, but her eyes were shadowed.

"What is it?" she said.

He held out his hand to her. "Come on, little girl, let's you and me go for a walk. You feel up to it?"

Jerry said, "But Shafter, he didn't say. . . ."

"Go write a report or something, will you?" Shafter said. Anna came out and he took her arm and led her off toward the creek.

"Shafter, something's wrong?"

"Lord, what a gloom-and-doom lot we all are. I don't know anything's wrong, or right either, until it comes and tells me so, and I expect the same of you, Annie."

They went under the trees and she saw Mangas Chie and stopped. The recognition flashed over her. Chie. Herself. But it was not here. Where was it? The Stronghold. She stood upon the trail and he came to meet her, as he came now. The bend of his knee was the same. Smoke rose behind him, from a small fire on the opposite bank. She thought, now a bird will sing. The bird sang. When she stopped, Shafter looked down at her. Her face was shattering, like a cracked mirror.

"It's only Chie," he said, and wondered why he had said only.

She tried to say something, but it was a funny sound in her throat. She pushed his hand away and began to run and then stopped again.

Chie had thrown away the stick he carried, with a tatter of white cloth bound on it. He came up slowly. He looked as he had always looked, but when he faced her she saw that his eyes were full of tears. He said, "Joaquin is dead."

Shafter wanted to move, wanted to go to her, but he couldn't make his feet work. The shock washed over him so thickly he forgot for a moment that she was there. She was standing flatly, hands at her sides, with her head thrown up at a peculiar twisted angle. The funny sound came out of her again, but it was words.

"Where? Chie, how?"

Chie was trembling, legs, hands, all of him. "In arroyo, in mountains. With guns. Not think he knew. . . ."

Shafter came up. Chie did not look at him.

"Who?" Anna whispered again. "Who? Mexicans?"

Shafter shook his head warningly at Chie, but Chie did not notice, and Shafter knew this was out of his depth, that he was being deliberately excluded.

"I think white eyes. Find tinned food, *americano* cigarette papers."

Anna said, "Get my mare."

"No," Chie said. "Not go. I do everything. Nothing to go for."

She turned and began to walk steadily back to the post. Shafter wondered what she was walking on, or with. He looked at Chie for a moment and then began to limp after her. When she reached the porch she took hold of the pillar and hung onto it and finally put her head down against it.

"John."

"Yes," Shafter said.

"Why can't I kill the whole world? Why can't I reach out and destroy everything?"

Shafter came around and looked her in the eye. He said, "I reckon you can, if you want to. Shuffle and deal and try for it."

She went up the step and crossed the porch and went through the office and into Whitman's room. Shafter stood there, trying to think, banging his fist into the porch post in futility and anguish. He had a hole in him like a mortar shell might have made. By God, he was never again in what life was left to him going to mix or meddle in the affairs of anybody. Red. White. Or black. He pushed Whitman's dog away from an investigation of his boots and went into the office and closed the outer door and thought if anybody, man, woman, or child, came through it, he would strangle them with his bare hands.

She was crying wildly, hysterically; he could hear her through the closed door. Well, if that was what she wanted to do, he was Jesus-well going to see she got to do it. The sound she was making didn't bother him much, even though it appeared she wasn't ever going to quit. She did though, after what seemed hours; he heard her retching violently, and then it was very quiet.

Somebody knocked on the door. He got up. It was Jerry. He wouldn't let him in.

"I'm going to tell Lieutenant Whitman," Jerry said.

"You do that," Shafter said, closing the door in his face.

The next time he went, it was Linus. He didn't know any way to keep him out and wasn't certain he wanted to.

Linus said, "Is it true?"

Shafter nodded, once.

"Where is she?"

Shafter jerked his head toward the door of Whitman's room.

Linus was gnawing at his lower lip. "I'm pulling out in an hour. If she wants to come to Tucson, bring her in when you come."

"She don't know what she wants right now," Shafter said. "Any more'n you do."

Linus flushed. Shafter went around and sat down in Whitman's chair. "Want a drink?"

"No, thanks," Linus said stiffly.

"Well," Shafter said. "Hard times kind of comes down on all of us. Makes you wonder why it is a man fights so hard to stay on his feet. Knock him down and all he can think of is gettin' up again. It's more comfortable layin' down."

Linus said in a low voice, "What's the text of your sermon today?"

Shafter swung around in the chair, stretching out the stiff leg. "Linus, from now on the only thing I can say for sure is what I am gone to do. I can't speak for anybody else in this world. So I will tell you what I am gone to do." He shoved his hat back, looking up at Linus from under lowered brows. "I don't know what use I am on this earth . . . if a man's got to be useful for anything more'n breathin'. I ain't gettin' any younger and I'm puttin' on some flesh around the middle. Got a bum leg, too; it ain't ever gone to be much good to me again." He spread out his hands on the desk. "Always been able to make a livin' with these hands, though. Never been real hungry in all my days. With a little extra pushin' now and then, I'm more'n a fair provider."

He picked up his hands and set them on his thighs. "When the little girl feels like talkin' again . . . or maybe I should say like livin' . . . I'm gone to tell her she can come with me."

"You bastard," Linus said quietly.

"She deserves better, no question about that. She had what she deserved, and now she ain't got it any more and got to take second choice. You understand me. I would never aim to lay a hand on that little girl, not ever, not unless she said that is what she would like. But if she is willing, then I am willing. Sometime, no matter how comfortable you are layin' down you got to raise yourself off the ground and act like a human bein'." He resettled his hat. "I reckoned I should tell you, in case you want to hit me or shoot me or anything. Because that's the way it stands with me, and it's gone to take a sight more'n a Yank cavalry lieutenant that's still got a big empty space where his head ought to be to tell me otherwise." He got up and stretched and looked at Linus. "You want to say anything?"

When Linus didn't answer, just stood there watching him with his face gone white and haggard, Shafter walked out. The dog followed him off the porch, going along slow with its nose to the ground.

Linus opened the door carefully, in case she might be asleep, but she wasn't asleep. She was lying on Whitman's cot, flat on her back, with the blanket drawn up around her, staring at the ceiling. He guessed she didn't know it was him, but after a while she said in a tired voice, "Hello, Linus."

"Hello, Anna." He shut the door and came into the room, but she never took her eyes off whatever it was she was looking at, straight up over her head. Whitman's single chair had books and papers piled on it, so he sat down gingerly on the edge of the bed. When he did she took her hands out from under the gray army blanket and locked them across her belly, they were shaking so badly.

The edge of the cot creaked. "Anna, I'm sorry. I wish I could find some way to tell you how sorry I am."

She didn't move her head, on the pillow, but her eyes found his face. She said, "Poor Linus."

It astonished him that she should say this, that she could find room for pity, particularly as he had been certain he was the strong one now. A fly went around in circles on the wall. Out the single narrow window he could see that the sun had disappeared and a massive low-hanging cloud was pushing in under the hills. The trees bent over and the dust got up and went somewhere else in a gust of wind. Rain came in a burst, and some of it blew in. He saw Whitman had an oiled paper to tack over the window, but he didn't move to put it up.

There were a lot of things you were supposed to say, he knew, about helping any way you could, or getting her anything she needed, the nice, kind, polite things people said by rote, but not meaning them any the less because they were said by rote. They didn't seem appropriate. He looked at her hands, clasped outside the blanket. The nails were worn down short. They were the hands he had seen on the wives of enlisted men, on Mexicans, on Indian women. When his eyes went to her face he saw she was staring at the ceiling again.

"Linus, I'm going to have a child."

He didn't feel any particular reaction to this for a moment; then the hollow drum beat of his own inadequacy sounded in him. He said, "Then there's a great deal to live for, isn't there?"

"Is there?" Her voice was dead. "Another man in this world not privileged to carry the pure and faultless blood of the white race? Maybe to live as his father lived, because he will be a quarter Mimbreño?"

He was shaking his head, slowly. "Is that what you're going to tell him? Is that what you'll burden him with? Anna, didn't Joaquin live as he chose? Won't your child live as he chooses? If you don't believe this, then you are right; there isn't anything to live for. Hope for. There will never be anything to hope for."

She turned her head for the first time and looked fully at him.

He said, "You will be very foolish, very mistaken, if you don't tell him the truth: that his father's people are neither right nor wrong. That they are simply people, human beings, subject to all the ills and goodnesses of human beings, and that somehow they manage to rise above everything. You will be denying him something that might be the whole purpose in life to him if you don't tell him who his father was, what he was, that he was no different from any other man, in that all he asked was his own place in this world and the freedom to live it as he saw it."

She was crying again, her eyes closed. He said, "Would you like me to leave, Anna?"

She shook her head. She did not open her eyes. Her hands fell apart on the blanket, without strength, and he reached out and touched the overturned fingers nearest him but did not take them into his hand. The rain blew in strongly for a little, spending itself, then tapered off to mist, passing on. She made no move to draw away from him; neither did he sense any response in her. She said finally, faintly, "Is it raining?"

"It's stopped now."

In a moment she said, "I can't believe it, Linus."

He said impotently, "I know."

"Tell me it isn't true."

"It's not as if he went away and left you nothing, Anna."

"No. But it seems such a burden to have to . . . to have to live at all." She could not stop crying; the absoluteness of the sound brought up the short hair on his neck. "Linus, I can't stand it, I can't, I can't."

He looked down at her, saw her totally exposed, defenseless, could not speak, continued to sit quietly on the edge of the army cot, years older than she, years wiser, reaching out now with certainty toward the only things which mattered. He knew there was no way to take upon himself the burden of her grief, her readjustment, her loneliness; he, who had declared to make up to her every moment of her life away from him. He would have laid down his life to give her back the gift of that time. He had got up off the ground. He knew that everything rushed to the finality of ending and that nothing, in itself, ever came to an end. No way, but he chose the agony of the course.

Shafter went into Tucson. He rode out of Grant early in the morning, figuring to see Whitman when he got to town, but not saying anything to him or anybody else. The last living soul he saw was Tony Bleeker, rotund as ever, neat as ever, whacking with his hat at the settled dust of his ride, the tools of his trade firmly under his arm. Even then Shafter didn't offer hello or good-by, and Bleeker merely looked up at him in passing and said, as he had said once before, "This will arouse the populace."

He had some gladnesses in him: glad to pull out of this place a suspicious man might look on as cursed, glad he'd got a lot of things off his mind that had been bothering him, glad he'd made the kind of break with Linus he knew would have to come sooner or later. Not that he had pressured Linus; he had meant to do what he said he meant to do. He could count his gladnesses on the fingers of one hand, but he couldn't have counted his sorrows if he had twenty hands, all with six fingers.

There might be a federal judge larruping around town, but it wasn't bothering anybody in the Old Pueblo much. Things were as noisy and potholed and stinking as they ever were, maybe even a little worse, what with ranchers and their families and near everybody wasn't blind or laid up crippled come to get in on the excitement. A few left town, though, those with a price on their head, those who had known somebody with a price on his head, none of them eager to be recognized, all of them believing that federal judges were appointed by God and bore with them at all times, if only in their recollection, full descriptions of anybody who had done even some little thing, like maybe shoot a bank teller. Remedia didn't want to give Shafter back his old room, over the saloon. She appeared to be mad at him for some reason, and it cost him double. He was lying on the bed with his boots on, and even his hat, in the middle of the afternoon, listening to the noise in the street, which had diminished because about three quarters of the population was sleeping, when Obre came in without raising his eyes from the newspaper he was looking at. Shafter thought he was about to walk right through the room and out the window and half raised up to remind him they were on the second story.

"Listen to this here," Obre said. "It is a well-known fact that Lieutenant Whitman is a drunkard and a . . . a *con*sorter of Indian women." He looked up. "What the hell is that?"

"What is what?" Shafter said.

"That thing about the Indian women."

Shafter said, disinterested, "Like you and Little Fire."

Obre thought it over. "I figured it was something dirty the way they got it wrote here. You ever see Lieutenant Whitman doin' that with any squaws?"

Shafter shook his head.

"If he did, if he was in the wet goods ninety-eight hours of the day, what's that got to do with it?"

"I wouldn't know," Shafter said.

"Ain't you gone to the trial and find out?"

Shafter shook his head again. "Not if I can help it."

"I am," Obre said. "I by Christ am. I hope to see Jesús Elias and

Will Oury hung by the neck until dead. I would almost hang with 'em just to see 'em in hell."

"And whistle 'Dixie' on the way down."

"Say, what's makin' you so screwheaded anyway?" Obre said.

"I just want to get the hell out of here," Shafter said.

Obre threw the newspaper on the floor. "Then saddle up. I'd a hoot rather be blisterin' my butt between here'n Chihuahua than listen to you take the cork out."

"Can't," Shafter said. "Might have to testify."

"Have to what?"

"Testify. I was there. Anyway, they ain't gone to try Oury, or Elias either."

Obre looked at him, hard. "Shafter, I rather swallow a fly right now than hear any funny stories. It hurts me to say I got to short-rein myself with you, but facts is facts. If I had a bit in my mouth I'd sure warped my jaw some by now. This here trial is ready to go. They are gone to try somebody. Now you gone to tell me they maybe gone to try Eskiminzin? I don't reckon I would drop down in a fit if they was."

"They're gone to try Sidney R. DeLong," Shafter said.

"Who in the crossfire is Sidney R. DeLong?"

"Sidney R. DeLong is the kindly soul who damn near killed trooper Herbert with redeye in Pantano Wash," Shafter said, eying the ceiling blankly. "He is standing proxy for one hundred and forty-six men, and if the jury says Sidney R. DeLong is guilty of murder, it means one hundred and forty-six men are guilty of murder."

Obre's hand went slowly, almost thoughtfully, to the butt of the right Dance. Then he tilted the flat-crowned black hat down over his eyes. His lean, angular face was morose. "That so? Well, I tell you something. I wish to the hell I was with Willson."

Shafter turned over, with his face to the wall. "I wish to the hell you were, too," he said.

He waited all the next afternoon but they didn't call him. He thought Obre shouldn't be walking around so free and easy, but Obre grinned and said with all this U.S. justice being brought down on the heads of the guilty, nobody was going to look sidewise at a two-bit gunslinger.

Shafter figured, with all he'd heard and seen of court trials, which wasn't much, that the thing might drag on for two or three days. From the saloon door, downstairs, he crossed glances briefly with Linus, saw Walter Degnan come in, drew a weary greeting from Royal Whitman. The town was full of military. In the middle of the afternoon all hell broke loose down on the street, and when he went to the window and looked out there were men running every which way and the walls of the saloons began to look as if they were going to bust right out. There was a lot of whooping and singing down at the end of the street, and a big gang of men came marching down it with Oury and Elias in the middle front. Shafter leaned against the dobe, watching, knowing. They came pounding in downstairs. That was when he went over and started to get his gear together and roll it up in his blankets. He did it methodically, automatically, and was standing with the Henry in both hands when he heard the measured tread of hoofs and went to the window again, thinking it might be Whitman's men, but it was Linus with his father's detail.

He looked up and saw Shafter and signaled to Stern and pulled out of line. Shafter had to yell, because of the noise.

"I reckon they're all free to start again."

Linus was grim, incredulous. "You heard?"

"Not guilty," Shafter said.

Linus only looked at him. A Mexican kid ran in front of his horse and the horse backed off.

Shafter yelled again. "Took that jury a sight of time to call the shot, didn't it?"

"Yes," Linus said. "Twenty minutes by the clock."

Shafter was still holding the Henry. He was going to say something else, something which had nothing to do with the trial. He didn't. He said, "See you around, Linus," and Linus didn't answer this time, just gave him a kind of cocky half salute and went off to catch up with the detail. Shafter stood there and watched him go.

Obre came in a while later. He was going to let off steam until he saw Shafter was ready to pull out; then he started to pack his own gear. While he was rolling his blankets, the shouting began downstairs, and the pounding, loud, rhythmic, with a real beat to it. Obre looked up from roping the roll. "What the. . . ."

Shafter held up his hand. In a moment they could make it out.

Oury for sheriff. Oury for sheriff. Oury for sheriff.

They stood staring at one another. Obre said, "I bet you by God he's good as elected."

Eskiminzin was riding out when Whitman came into the ranchería. When he saw Whitman he came over slowly, and, for the first time since he had known Eskiminzin, Whitman thought there was no expression at all in his face, or his eyes.

The new wickiups had been erected; the people were working in the neat thriving gardens. The two men sat their horses in the center of the camp. Marijildo told Eskiminzin the news, but Whitman saw that somehow Eskiminzin had already known.

When Marijildo finished, Eskiminzin nodded. He understood: the men were free; he could count his twenty-seven children dead. He had tried to believe otherwise; now he would accept that this was the way it would be. The soldiers were on his land, to protect the Arivaipa. He was not disappointed, expecting nothing more, but he knew that there were men of his people who would carry this thing with them and wait, and in this he could do nothing but hope that time would heal them.

He said, "You are here, friend Whitman."

"Yes," Whitman said heavily. "I will be here. Where are you going now, Eskiminzin?"

Eskiminzin told Marijildo. "There is a family, with three children. They will not return. Munaclee and I go to the hills, to tell them to come." He looked at Whitman. "To tell them all is as it was before."

He and Whitman shook hands. "I will see you tomorrow," Whitman said. It was the emptiest triumph he had ever known, but he pulled himself together. If Eskiminzin was willing to make this sacrifice, he must double his effort to encourage and support him.

But he saw Eskiminzin again before the afternoon was out. Eskiminzin came down slowly, out of the hills, down the canyon, and his people, working in their gardens, straightened and were motionless, staring, frozen were they stood. Eskiminzin carried Munaclee before him on his saddle. Munaclee was dead.

Whitman, running, knew with despairing certainty that he, that no man, that not God Himself could speak another word which would mean more than dust to Eskiminzin. The stocky Arivaipa

chief sat looking down at him. The women were coming, beginning
the mourning wail.

"Soldiers," Eskiminzin said. "In the hills."

Whitman was beaten at last. "Not my soldiers."

Eskiminzin shook his head. "No. Know soldiers. From White
Mountains. Hunting. Hunt Apache, good sport. Now Munaclee
dead."

"Not my soldiers," Whitman said again, dully, stupidly.

Eskiminzin's head went up. He motioned to Marijildo. He said,
"I should cut my throat, as a warning to my people. Here, on this
horse, I should cut my throat, to show them." He twisted and began
to shout in a high hoarse voice which set Whitman's teeth on edge.
Men were running, too, now, but not toward them, away from them.
Eskiminzin turned again; all his movements were stolid, heavy.
"The peace we are promised has been broken twice, both times
by Americans. He who breaks the peace takes on his shoulders
the guilt. Cochise has said a man carries his life on his fingernails.
I say that a man carries his life on the word of other men. The
word of Americans is the word of the lie; it is nothing. We will not
come here again, on this land which was our fathers', and which belongs to us. We will avenge our dead."

Whitman was standing with his head bowed.

Eskiminzin said very quietly, in English, "Good-by, friend Whitman."

By nightfall the wickiups had been burned. Not a living thing,
not a scavenging dog, remained in Arivaipa Canyon. Already the
dust had begun to sift lightly in. Within days, hours, the gardens
would be desert again.

The weather was holding fine and fair. You had to say about this
piece of country that it warmed a man's bones all year long; you
had to say that in the event you couldn't find anything else to say
about it, as some could not. Shafter had never been much for following roads, although it was easier. Not that he looked for it to
be easy. Obre knew Shafter often had fits of the wanders: it
didn't matter to him, having hoped aloud to God he had seen the
last of Tucson and being in no hurry.

They were traveling east. It seemed to Shafter there was a
sight more folks around than he could recall when he first came,
continually on the move, drifting in, and with their families, too.

He did his best to avoid them, but when this was not possible he told them howdy and how many miles to wherever they were going and to watch out for Apaches even if they didn't cut sign for days at a stretch. Wagon trains, singles, coaches, soldiers, civilians. All bent West. At this rate there wouldn't be one lonely soul left in the East. All coming to spoil the country, the last good country left.

Obre listened but wouldn't say much, except that Shafter didn't own the country. But Shafter knew he did. Not that he could explain it. He knew how an Apache looked at it. There weren't any words, in English or Apache either, maybe not in any language, to say in what way he owned the land. And if there were, how could he say them out?

This wasn't any hard push to get some place, and they kept to whatever pace Shafter set, depending on the weather, his leg, his mood. The sun went the circle of the days; the season was going the span of its allotment; everything changed and moved but the mountains. They ran into some Gileños, a split-off band not over-friendly. Nobody in it knew the woman Obre inquired for, but they knew the *rubio* who had been granted safe conduct by the Mimbreños. If Joaquin had been as good as his word, Shafter hadn't expected anything less and didn't even have to turn it over in his mind.

They heard the sound of passage long before the sight of it came on them. You could put your ear to the ground and hear it, a long way off, vibrating in over the taut drumhide of earth. It was late in the afternoon when they saw it, a slow passage and a big one.

From a thin grassed slope they watched the columns come down the desert, mounted men heavily armed, women with pack horses, children, old people, mules, a few sheep, dogs, more men flank and rear. There would be a heavy phalanx of scouts out, way out, with a camp this big on the move. It looked to Shafter as if every Indian in Southeast Arizona was down there, but, counting light, he saw there were three or four hundred.

They were seen, studied. No hostile move was made toward them, no cadre broke off to raise lances in the thick westering sunlight. They rode down without haste, flanking for the point of the column, where the spearhead of bucks rode single file. When they approached, the file slowed, not stopping, cutting the gait of

its ponies and horses to a walk. Shafter did the same, edging up
the file to the man who led it.

He leaned on the saddle horn. "Howdy, Victorio. Kind of figured
it might be you."

The march was flowing on, around them, still at the same un-
hurried pace. Victorio reined in, the carbine set lightly on his
naked thigh and angled up at the sky. Shafter thought, he remembers. I remember. And then we both forget. Apache Pass never
happened. It's all sanded clean. "Ask him where he's gone, Ob."

Victorio said, "We go to Ojo Caliente."

"Movin' a big camp," Shafter said. "I reckon you know how much
army is layin' around this country these days."

Victorio inclined his head in an affirmative gesture. Shafter noted
the aging in his face, bringing the aquiline features into sharper
focus, the graying hair. The eyes were as steady and penetrating
as ever, but there was something in them, an underlying purpose
maybe, he couldn't rightly read it. Whatever it was, the presence of
soldiers didn't appear to be needling under his hide. And he still
had to move this camp three hundred, maybe three hundred and
fifty miles, Shafter figured.

He offered his own destination, like they were trading favors.
"We're trailin' south. I reckon Mangas Chie got back all right."

The eyes upon him were different now: darker, maybe, and som-
ber. Victorio said abruptly, "My sons are dead."

Shafter didn't say anything. Your sons go out with war parties,
you got to expect they might get killed. Then he knew Victorio
meant something more than he had said, and he could feel the
same dull ache that showed in Victorio's eyes flatten and spread in
his own chest. Victorio said, "Grieving is not a single thing but
divides itself among all men." He cut Shafter off, harshly. "Hold your
tongue. With us a name is buried with our dead."

Shafter nodded. He didn't aim to stir up anything he couldn't
get out of; he wished he could think of some way to let Victorio
know he knew a lot of things he didn't figure to try and build
words around. He said, "You aim to summer in at Ojo Caliente?"

"We will stay at Ojo Caliente for as long as this is possible,"
Victorio said.

"And if they run you out?" Shafter said.

Victorio shook his head. The long graying hair moved on his
shoulders. "We go to Ojo Caliente under flag."

"Under flag?" Shafter said. "You're quittin'? You're givin' up?"

Victorio breathed it. "We want our land at Ojo Caliente."

"I reckon you do," Shafter said. "But that ain't sayin' you're gone to get it."

Victorio said, "The white eyes come to Ojo Caliente. A new nantan comes. I go to talk with him."

Crook, Shafter thought. He tried to read Victorio's face and saw in it only stern inflexibility. He said, "You know what happened to Eskiminzin. He couldn't make it work, and he wanted it bad. What makes you think you can make it work?"

Victorio said calmly, "Eskiminzin could have done this thing. I can do this thing. The white eyes cannot do it. They do not know how. It is not a hard thing to do. The white eyes make it a hard thing to do." He was faintly mocking. "Perhaps in time they will learn."

The corner of Shafter's mouth drew down, reflecting Victorio's scorn. "Maybe they'll learn when it's too late for the *cihéné*, eh? Maybe they'll wait till there's no Mimbreños left before they learn."

Victorio considered a long time. Finally he said, "A treaty will work only when it is to the good of both men who sign it. When it is no longer to the good of one man, then that man must break it. The People have done this when they must. But The People speak the terms of the treaty with a straight tongue. It is not often the white eyes speak these terms with other than a split tongue, like the snake. They know what they offer. They know where the lie is written. They know at which time to strike out all words but the lie." He raised his head suddenly, watching Shafter. "Still, we are all men," he said.

Shafter was thinking. Crook was coming and Crook wasted no time, setting up a council for the Mimbreños right out of the hopper. Shafter went back a little and heard the echo of the rumbling: not just Crook; General Howard, General Miles, the good old soldiers of the good old war, the President's new Peace Commission, all the churches rushing to protect and lift up, and maybe ruin, like they did so well with those hadn't been hung head down in a baptismal font or led into the nearest river of salvation. He thought how much Victorio couldn't understand, could never understand, maybe not even if he was physically confronted with it: not just the mass of the war machine, not only steam and railroad and cities building a mile high, something more. A concept maybe, not fully developed yet, but pulsing and growing, with the power to change the face of the world. The old chivalric day was dead in its own ash, and out of the ash rose the word, out of that war he had outlived sprang the theory. Unconditional surrender. You could explain that, to Victorio, only in terms of annihilation. He would know, he would understand that. Men would say if to Victorio; men would say maybe; but what they would mean was, it is, it will be, unconditionally. Fact makes a hard bed for the harassed, the outnumbered, the weary.

What he said was, "We're all men, like you say, but that don't take away that some men are better men than other men."

Obre palavered and then said, a little grimly for him, "And that lost a war for this white eyes. For myself, I like to see you get the good men."

Victorio looked at him. He said, "Look only for a beginning, Comanche. That is where my eyes are. What is in the head of this nantan, what is in the heart of this nantan, that is where I look."

"Look close," Shafter said.

Victorio nodded. The big black horse he rode threw up its head, as if its rider had tightened his grip on the hackamore. "This may be a nantan who does not say here are the stars and hold out a handful of air. I will listen to him." The horse settled and stood. "But he must listen to me."

"That's fair as you can get," Shafter said. He held out his hand, across the little space between them. "You and me, we had the word said for us, Victorio. Even without the flag, no more massacre for us."

Victorio took his hand. He said with humor, "If my men come and kill you, Shafter, it is a massacre. If your men come and kill me, it is a great victory." He took his hand away and lowered the carbine. "Ride with us."

"Thanks," Shafter said. "But I reckon we got to make time now."

Victorio pointed suddenly, with a swift, stabbing, single motion. "This man remembers. You still wear the gray hat."

Obre grinned when he switched this, but Shafter said, "Sure. Why not? You gone to take off your sweatband if you win Ojo?"

Victorio said, "A man must do what he must do."

Shafter's face had gone dark. "Good luck, Victorio."

The last of the column was passing. Shafter raised his hand briefly to Mangas Chie. Victorio said, "In the days to come, if you hear my name, remember I do only what the lie frees me to do, what the truth binds me to." He kicked the black horse, driving it off-side, setting the carbine up again and putting the horse into a run, up the column.

The dust lay in the stillness. Shafter sat watching. Then he turned the dun and put him southeastward, where the land stretched out and rose to a saddle through the mountains.

"Now where the hell you gone?" Obre said.

"I am gone to Mexico," Shafter said.

"I aim to see that when I get there," Obre said.

"My mind's set on it." He took off the Kossuth hat and looked at it for a minute and then settled it again. "Ain't anything gone to fetch me short," he said.

When they reached the pass the light came in on them flat and waning from the west, but the far mountains standing across the desert had fallen off dark where the light slipped away. The sky made to burn itself out. The dust of the Mimbreño passage still hung, hazing up across the red edge of sundown.